Dragon Queen
An Ancient Mirrors Tale

Jayel Gibson

DRAGON QUEEN: AN ANCIENT MIRRORS TALE
PUBLISHED BY SYNERGY BOOKS
2100 Kramer Lane, Suite 300
Austin, Texas 78758

For more information about our books, please write to us, call 512.478.2028, or visit our website at www.bookpros.com.

ISBN-10: 1-933538-46-5
ISBN-13: 978-1-933538-46-4

Publisher's Cataloging-in-Publication available upon request.

Library of Congress Control Number: 2006923644

Cover art, maps and internal illustrations © 2005
Michele-lee Phelan, Art of the Empath
Cranebrook, N.S.W., Australia
www.artoftheempath.com

Praise for Dragon Queen

". . . set in a wonderful and magical world. Yávië is the perfect heroine . . . smart and honest."

Writer's Digest commentary

". . . powerful storytelling. The characters leap from the page, grab you and don't let go. Finally, a new writer has come, one who tells an original tale and revives your desire to read fantasy."

In The New York Times Sunday Book Review

". . . will transport you to the world of Ancients, Guardians and Men; a world where you will savor the thoughts, feelings and adventures of many magical beings, totally forgetting everything else around you. Jayel Gibson weaves magic with words."

In The Bloomsbury Review

". . . all the elements that make a great fantasy – a quest, life and death stakes, romantic tensions, magic, suspect loyalties, and an overwhelmingly powerful villain."

Andrew Eather, Editor

"Legends of magic, adventure, and courage set in a mythical world of Ædracmoræ."

In Realms of Fantasy magazine

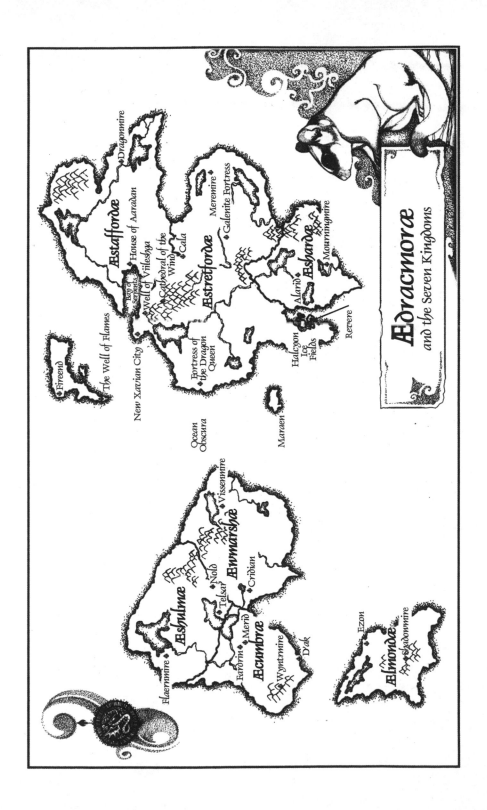

Ædracmoræ
and the Seven Kingdoms

Æstretforðæ

Lake of Lost Memories

Merewire

Sea of Sorrow

Plains of Crimson Grass

Galenite Fortress

Verdant Forest

Northern Mountains

Malochian City

Xavian City

Ebony Plains

Trembling Sea

Maelstrom's Lair

The Wasteland

Fortress of the Dragon Queen

Azure Sea

Dobbinwort's Furnace

Ruby Sea

Halcyon Ice Fields

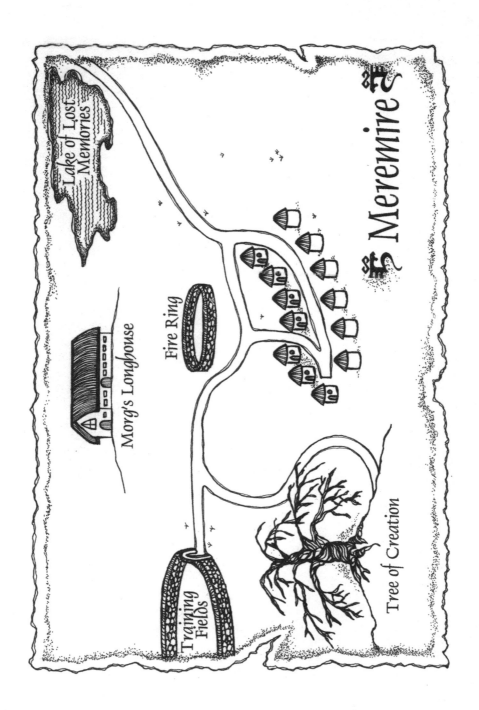

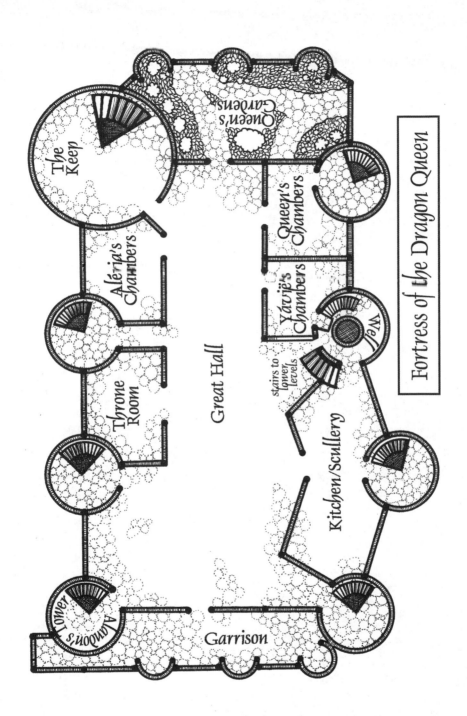

Fortress of the Dragon Queen

The Keep

Queen's Gardens

Aléria's Chambers

Queen's Chambers

Yârije's Chambers

Throne Room

Great Hall

Well

stairs to lower levels

Kitchen/Scullery

Aldnon's Tower

Garrison

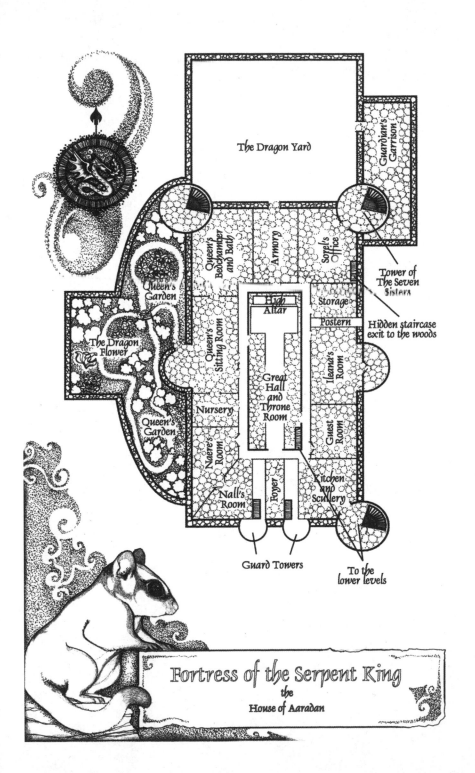

The Dragon Yard

Guardian's Garrison

Queen's Garden

Queen's Bedchamber and Bath

Armory

Sorel's Office

Tower of The Seven Sisters

The Dragon Flower

Queen's Garden

Queen's Sitting Room

High Altar

Storage

Postern

Hidden staircase exit to the woods

Ileana's Room

Nursery

Great Hall and Throne Room

Guest Room

Naere's Room

Nall's Room

Foyer

Kitchen and Scullery

Guard Towers

To the lower levels

Fortress of the Serpent King
the
House of Aaradan

Dedication

In loving memory of Joni Anderson

And to:
Ken Gibson
Sarah Gibson
Peggy Brewer
GliderCentral
Jeff Shockey
Dan Bargess
Chris Overcash

For their friendship, support and encouragement

Acknowledgements

Any work of fantasy is a union of magic and madness that includes golden grains of potent sorcery from those who are sometimes totally unaware that their enchantment has rubbed off on the author. My gratitude to these and all my friends for their encouragement and touches of thaumaturgy:

Michele-lee Phelan, my artist and friend, for the inspiration of her artworks. They grace my books, website and walls and continue to fill my mind with magic.

The city of Port Orford, Oregon, my home, for her beauty, tranquility and people – truly a writer's paradise.

Gold Beach Books (the coffeehouse bookstore) in Gold Beach, Oregon for the wonderful inspiration of the rare book room, a quiet table and lots of café brevés.

The South Coast Writers Conference for the encouragement they provide all writers and Southwestern Oregon Community College for their sponsorship of this annual event.

Josephine Ballantyne of Wordwing Editors, a true member of the Errant Comma Enclave. It is with tongue in cheek that I assure you any errors you may find belong to her.

Collaboration

Sean W. Anderson has collaborated with Ms. Gibson in the development of ideas and storyline, as well as created a number of characters used in the Ancient Mirrors novels. The characters Nall and Talin are based on role-play characters originally created by Mr. Anderson for online gaming.

Mr. Anderson lives with his family in southern California.

Illustration

Fantasy artist Michele-Lee Phelan is the official illustrator for the Ancient Mirrors series. Her artwork appears on the covers, as internal illustrations and website graphics for this series. Works are created using traditional and digital media. Ms. Phelan is featured as one of Epilogue's New Masters of Fantasy 2005.

The artist lives with her family in New South Wales, Australia.

Table of Contents

Prologue

Red-gold fingers of lightning snaked across the eastern sky to fuse with their blue-white counterparts, culminating in a booming voice of united condemnation. With heavy heart and furrowed brow, the Sojourner Alandon watched his offspring vie for control of the dying world below. It was his fault. A ripple of guilt raced up his spine and twisted painfully in his gut. Fear had led him to attempt the destruction of the House of Aaradan. It was fear that had directed his call on Abaddon's armies, setting in motion the final destruction now taking place at the fortress below, and it was fear that had caused him to steal the birthright from one daughter and give it to the other.

Abaddon, thief of souls, now held Alandon's wife captive and was lurking within the gathering gloom in the hope of adding the souls of his daughters to the collection gathering in his abyss.

"Abaddon!" He cursed his brother. He should have known; he should have seen Aléria's weakness, her jealousy and her desire for absolute power. Too late he had discovered his child's wickedness and Abaddon's growing control. It had already cost him the soul of his wife and, should he do nothing, would cost the soul of another daughter.

Howling in rage and frustration, the Sojourner whirled and flung out his hands. A flaming golden orb formed in his palms. Each potent globe surged forward from his fingertips into the seething caldron of storm clouds below. The fiery spheres detonated, releasing their cataclysmic strikes to extinguish the seven kingdoms of Ædracmoræ, leaving their shattered fragments to drift as dark flotsam under the final brilliance of the life-giving topaz star.

Screaming curses and promised resurrection, Alandon swept the soul of his betrayed daughter into the heavens as an ominous and silent darkness cloaked the former realm of the Dragon Queen.

Until the willow weeps and the Age of the Ancients is upon you, you will sleep. When at last you awake, seek your forgotten truth. I shall leave the keys of restoration within your reach.

As Alandon swung toward the cavern where he would await the call of his daughter, a movement caught his attention. Guardians—led by a tattered remnant of the hated House of Aaradan—who had sworn their service and pledged their protection, but who had failed, leaving his daughter alone to face her enemies.

Snarling with long-festering rage, Alandon flung them away, but not before he wrenched the soul from the one they called Captain and swept it into the abyss.

"You, Sōrél, will remember! You will suffer the endless memory of your failure throughout the eternity of darkness with no hope of her forgiveness. Without her your House of Aaradan is dead."

And for a man's eternity, the world was to remain lost in silence and shadows . . .

PART I

Chapter 1: The Ancients

The Prophecy

"Dust of the earth, ash of the fire, whisper of the wind, tears of the tree."

It had been foretold in the last days of Men on the dying world known as Ædracmoræ that a tree would bring forth a new age, the Age of the Ancients.

The earth lay ashen after the fire of the wars, barren except for one willow tree. Its stout trunk was twisted and gnarled, and pendulous boughs stooped as if to drink. A multitude of braided strands wandered from the crown. Slender branches that had once held tender leaves trailed to the ground, no longer moist and green. Now they were bare, dry and lifeless. Just below the lowest branch of the Tree of Creation, a wort extruded from the bark, scabrous and foul. From the wort fell a teardrop, clear and pure. It traveled down the trunk, in and out among the twisted strands until it reached the base of the tree. As the tear neared the parched soil, a small puff of wind lifted dust and ash, and mingled them with the teardrop of life.

The wind, ash, earth and teardrops formed the body of the first Ancient, and from the first came the six in fulfillment of the Sojourner Alandon's Prophecy of the New Creators.

Broad and stout, born old with the wisdom of the ages, no Ancient was over six hands tall. Weathered and wizened, their leathery skin was the color of poorly tanned hides. It was as dry and cracked as a muddy riverbed too long in the sun. Eyes of brightest obsidian peered

31

out from beneath drooping lids overhung with bushy brows. Wild hair as white as the first fallen snow formed a halo around each face. Their waistcoats and trousers were created from the leaf litter that lay below the tree, and from the roots of the same tree came the staff carried by each Ancient.

They came, seven of them; each created from the other, save the first who was named Willowort. To each one the Tree of Creation breathed a name: Rosewort, Morgwort, Dobbinwort, Brundlewort, Mallowort and Weezelwort.

Head bowed, Willowort waited patiently beside the Tree of Creation. Slowly, over the past ages of sleep time, the Tree had filled her head with prophecies. As the first Ancient, she was the keeper of the Seven Prophecies destined to create the new world under the guidance of the Tree. While the others slept the waiting sleep, wrapped in their gauzy cocoons, Willowort would prepare for their final awakening.

"A place of warmth and beauty, Willow;" called the Tree to Willowort, "with crimson fields and ebony plains, and waterfalls so high; with seas of azure waters, mountains to the north, an icy realm far to the south, and caverns all beneath. Create this place for me. When you have finished, release the beasts to graze and swim and fly. An Ancient will then summon the Guardians to protect the lands and bring about the new Age of Men.

As Willowort listened, she spoke magick to the barren earth, covering it with fields and plains, water and ice, and mountains and caverns. With her final incantations, she set free the beasts to swim and graze and fly before going to the others to lift them from sleep.

They constructed a cluster of small bothies at Meremire at the southeastern edge of the Lake of Lost Memories, and the Ancients then set about preparing for the calling of the Guardians.

The Appointment of the Summoner

Each Ancient carefully cut a branch from the Tree of Creation and carried it to the edge of the Lake of Lost Memories. In a row the seven stood, each placing his chosen branch on the ground. The Lake would confirm which of them would be the first summoner of the Guardians. It was a grave responsibility, and not one any would choose. As foretold in the Prophecy, only one would become the summoner. With solemn incantations, each called the Lake to take his branch. One by one, the branches were swept away until only one was left. Rosewort's branch still rested at her feet. Clutching her tiny hands together, she smiled a lonely smile and hugged each in turn, knowing that although she would do the summoning, each would henceforth be forever bound to the Guardians.

"Rosie, what shoulds we do?" asked Weezelwort.

"Each one needs to bring a gift," Rosie replied. "It is prophesied that each Ancient gives the Guardians a gift."

One by one, the others left. Rosewort began the preparation for the calling of the Guardians. She knew that she must choose each element wisely in order to summon Guardians of strength, wisdom, kindness and truth, hoping that if she were very careful they might never see the betrayal that haunted her dreams. The sorrow of past betrayal was an ever-present, deep and hungry wound, eating at the soul for aeons beyond the deed itself.

While each Guardian would work independently of the others, she knew that they would also be bound to one another in thought and deed. Not only must she call the best and strongest, but three who could work together as well.

Taking the summoning elements from her satchel, Rosie began to whisper the first of many incantations. With her first finger, she drew a circle in the earth, blessing it with the herbs of truth and the oils of wisdom. Inside the circle she drew three smaller, interconnected circles, one for each of those she was about to call.

Within the top circle, she placed a deathawk's feather to give far sight and swiftness. Next, she placed two stone daggers forged by magick—these would bring the strength of a warrior to the Guardian. She gently placed the violet gemstone of an ice beast and the flame of a fire dragon beside them—gifts of fierceness and determination far beyond that of mortal men. Finally, she added petals from the mountain blackthorn flower to give beauty and the ability to heal, and a lock of Willowort's hair to add wisdom and the knowledge of true justice.

"I gives to you two extra gifts," Rosewort whispered, "one to catch a maelstrom wind and one to plant the seed of your truth." And with that, she placed a tiny crystal in the center of the circle whence all three came together whispering the name Sōrél.

In the circle on the bottom right, she placed a tiny sliver from an accordant dragon's heart shard, a gift from Adra, Matriarch of the Emeraldflyte. This would implant the gift of empathy in the Guardian receiving it. Then an amber arrow from Brundlewort's quiver to give the gift of marksmanship, a piece of spider web for strength, and two blades of crimson grass to bind this one to Æstretfordæ. Last of all, she added the heart of a deathawk for honor and wisdom.

Reaching into the circle at the lower left, she first placed the brilliant emerald flower of the Crimson Grasslands to give radiant youth and beauty and the wisdom of the fields. Then a clutch of oyster eggs to give dominance over the seas and the dragons therein, and a stag's heart turned to stone for difficult tasks. To these she added the beauty of a wind song and a blade from Dobbinwort's furnace for a true eye in the hunt. Finally, she sprinkled the dried tears of the lonely lark, for empathy with sorrow.

Hearing a cry overhead, Rosewort looked up and saw a klenzingkyte flying far above. A sudden chill gripped her heart as she quickly looked down again, but she had not seen over which circle the bird's shadow had passed. She cast a spell against shadow bane and hoped that it would help, but in her heart, she knew that one of these would indeed betray the others. Shaking her head sadly, she continued her work.

"Child of mine, Guardian of Æstretfordæ, seeker of the Truth, I calls you forth from sleep within the stars. Come, child, come quick to me," called Rosewort, swiftly passing her hand over the first circle, "and let no shadow cover you." A sudden pulse of violet light emanated from the first circle leaving the Guardian standing before her. "I calls you, Yávië, for the warm season of the star." Rosewort quickly wrapped the tall, raven-haired beauty in a spider web of gauze. "Rest now, sweet Yávië, for the rediscovery of your life begins with tomorrow's dawn.

"Child of Adra, Guardian of Æstretfordæ, brother of Rydén, protector of a future queen, I calls you forth from sleep within the stars. Come child. Come quick to me." Rosewort's hand moved again, summoning the second Guardian, "Let no shadow cover you." A second pulse, this one of amber, flashed blindingly over the circle. There stood a broad-shouldered youth, his face as handsome as the moonrise over Meremire.

"I calls you Nall, the dragon rider," she spoke as she covered him for the night ahead.

One circle remained. Rosewort took a deep breath, and felt a flutter in her chest, as if a small trapped bird was trying to break free.

She raised her voice one last time to call the third and final Guardian, "Child of the Sea and Crimson Fields, Guardian of Æstretfordæ, sister of Nall, I calls you forth from sleep within the stars. Come child. Come quick to me. Let no shadow cover you." This time the pulse showed the deepest green, and left in its wake a fair-skinned girl with auburn hair and startling emerald eyes. Covering her in spider webs, Rosewort said, "I calls you Rydén, for the land of deep red twilight."

Rosewort smiled at her accomplishment. Then, quickly concealing her satisfaction behind a solemn face, turned to face the six Ancients now moving into the fading green light.

"Is they here?" asked Morgwort. "Was there a signs of betrayal?"

Lowering her eyes to cover the lie, Rosewort responded, "Nay, nary a one. Summoned smooth as spider's silk they did; strong, brave, wise and good, each one of them. And aren't they beauties?"

"How do you 'spects us to see them when you covers 'em up like a pot waiting to boil?" Brundlewort complained.

"Leave them to sleep now, Brundle. Tomorrow they begins their studies," Rosie chastened.

"We'll sleeps here beside them and keeps them safe," she said, drawing her own spider's silk around her and closing her weary eyes as she whispered silent dragon thoughts.

From within the depths of sea and earth, the great dragons crept into the world. Matriarchs called out to waking blood clans, flytes of wind, fire, water, and earth-born dragons. As Ancients and Guardians slept a dreamless sleep, those dragons who had been bound, before the shattering of the world, to serve all past and future Dragon Queens sought out their long ago abandoned homes.

Morning arrived with a sudden crash. Sleep-laden eyes flew open, darting around to locate the source of the noise. As they realized what had caused the commotion, they began to laugh. In an attempt to get up while still secured within his silken blanket, Nall had tripped and fallen over Rydén, who was kicking and screaming at him in a very unladylike fashion.

"I know you," Yávië said to Rosewort in a soft, halting voice as if she were using it for the first time. "You called me from my slumber and spoke to me of the Truth."

Nall and Rydén managed to untangle themselves, looking curiously at Yávië.

"I don't remember you," Nall's statement was really more of a question.

"Nor I you," replied Yávië, looking at Nall and then Rydén.

"You are all Yávië, Nall and Rydén," said Willowort, pointing at each in turn, "and we are Morgwort, Rosewort, Dobbinwort, Brundlewort, Mallowort, Weezelwort, and I'm Willowort. Now you knows."

Rosewort smiled and handed each a morning bun with prickleberry juice running over the top of it and a cup of spidergrass tea, cold from the falls. "I am the one who called you," she said. "We needs you Guardians here to keep Æstretfordæ safe and fulfill the prophecies of the Sojourner."

They examined one another closely as they ate, eyes averted so as not to seem too obvious. Each measured the others for strengths and weaknesses. Rosie looked carefully at each one, knowing that they would soon reach adulthood and set off to call forth all manner of men. She also knew that Yávië would eventually set off to discover the Truth of her past. She gave a sigh, and determined to do her very best for each of them, to be sure they were prepared for their part in the Prophecies.

Willowort went off to her bothie, returning shortly with the clothing she had prepared for each Guardian. For Nall there were leggings of soft hide, a tunic that reached just below his waist, and soft boots sewn with such precision that no seams were visible.

For Rydén and Yávië there were soft riding leathers and blouses of the finest spiders' silk, feminine yet practical, as Willow knew that their lessons would be demanding, and would require great freedom of movement. Their clothing came in shades of green for Rydén, and violet and lavender for Yávië, to compliment their eyes Willow told them. She directed each to a bothie where they might dress in privacy.

When they returned, looking a little self-conscious in their new finery, Willowort proclaimed it to be the time for gift-giving.

Standing shyly before Rydén, Morgwort slowly extended his cupped hands. Rydén smiled at him from where she sat and placed her hand, open and palm up, beneath his.

"I give you the gift of the grass cat," Morg said. "She will bring you stealth and vision for dark nights and in the depths of the seas."

He slowly opened his hands and placed the tiny kit in Rydén's open hand. She lifted it and looked into its eyes, then kissed it on the tip of its nose. It stood staring back at her, then hissed and slapped Rydén's face.

"Already I love her dearly," she laughed. "I will call her Valia, for her bravery.

"Yávië, I gives you this stone," Mallowort said, causing Yávië's eyes to grow wide as she accepted the small gray stone graciously.

"This stone's from the Caverns of the Wind, and it'll give you the 'bility to take the shape of stone. Might be important someday," he nodded.

"Thank you, Mallo. I will practice turning into stone so that I will be prepared should the need arise," she responded, hiding a smile, which did not go unnoticed by Nall, who smiled back at her.

Brundlewort now stood before Nall who, even seated, was the taller. Pointing upwards and giving a shrill whistle, Brundle reached up and handed Nall a small piece of raw stag meat. Just as Nall took it in his hand, he heard the beating of wings as a large deathawk descended. At the last moment, its talons swept forward landing on Nall's outstretched arm. With a wag of its tail, the great bird gently took the meat and swallowed it in one gulp. Nall could not help but smile and he looked down at Brundle proudly.

"He's green still," Brundle said, "but he'll be a good hunter and shows you the way. With his eyes you'll have the far sight. I'll shows you how to command him with the beast speak."

"He is wonderful, Brundlewort. I thank you for this gift. Does he have a name?"

"I calls him 'Hawk,'" Brundle confessed grudgingly.

"Then Hawk he will be!" Nall proclaimed.

Weezelwort now came before the three new Guardians.

"I gives my gift to all of you: 'tis the veil of mist. It gives you the gift of stealth. When you moves there'll be no sound and none will sees you."

He threw up his hands and a gentle mist floated over Yávië, Rydén and Nall. It was suddenly as if they no longer existed; it enveloped them so completely.

Rosie clapped her hands and laughed aloud, "I just called 'em, and already they've gone!"

With a wave of his hand, the mist rose and hovered above the three Guardians. "It'll be there when you needs it," Weezel said.

Rosie went to each of them in turn, cupping their faces in her hands and looking deep into their souls.

"I knows you best of all. I've seen what you are made of and I'll watch over you as long as you are here, but I can't always follow you when you leaves. So, I gives you great healing power to brings you home again. But don't be deceived: you aren't invincible! You can get you bones broke, and bleed out on the ground, but you won't be dead lest some poison draws the spell out of you, or an arrow from the Bow of Ages strikes your heart. You'll heal and comes home to me again," Rosewort said.

She smiled at them as a single tear rolled down the crevices of her cheek.

Dobbinwort jumped up and tossed a piece of bark to each of them. Each picked it up and looked at it, puzzled.

Winking at Rydén he said, "Since Rosie won't makes you invincible, I gives you all the bark from the Tree of Creation. When your bones are broke and you is bleedin', like she said, just use the bark to heals yourself."

"You can use it to heal each other—or a stranger too," Morgwort interceded, receiving a frown from Dobbinwort.

"I was goin' to tell 'em that part too! It's *my* gift!" Dobbin stomped as the others laughed.

Willow spoke softly, "Now 'tis time for me to give these last gifts. The days will be hard now. The trainin' is not easy. I gives to each a Staff of Souls to shares your pain and sorrows, your disappointments and dreams. Each staff will gives you the power to summon the others long as you haves their talismans. The staffs bind the three of you together, and to Æstretfordæ, as they were cuts from the Tree of Creation. The staffs will also lets you travel without walkin'; takes you where you wants to go in the blinking of an eye. Blessings of the Ancients on you now and always, Guardians."

Her smile made them feel warm, as they knew they had been summoned there for some great purpose, even though they knew not what it was.

"Today you trains with Morgwort," Willow said. "He will teach you the beast speech; and since two of you has a beast, it shouldn't be too hard. Now goes and meets him in the field."

They sat, uncertain, until Willow pointed toward the field fenced with a rocky wall. Nall and Rydén stood and then moved off towards the area, with Yávië rising to follow.

As Yávië turned to go, Dobbinwort stayed her with his hand and pulled from his pocket a furry creature. It was small—no longer than

Dobbin's forearm—and its body was covered with the softest gray fur. A black stripe ran from its head to the base of its bushy tail, but it was its face that captured Yávië's attention, for the little beast had the most enchantingly mystical face. The nose was narrow and ended in a pair of small pink nostrils framed with wispy whiskers. The tips of two tiny teeth were just visible as the face looked up at Yávië. The creature's ears were gently rounded with white bars at their base, and the eyes were so black there were no visible pupils. "Just like mine," Dobbin chirped.

"'Tis, for you, Yávië. A wee downy flier. He is small, but he is wise and will helps you on a day of need. I see it in the Prophecy of Time to Come."

Leaning down, Yávië gathered the small pile of fur in her cupped hands and gently exhaled her scent onto him before tucking him inside her tunic. "Thank you, Dobbin," she whispered, kissing the top of his head, causing his leathery skin to turn a rosier shade of tan.

Chapter 2: Training

In the Still Air of Wisdom

The three Guardians sat on the floor of Willowort's bothie, listening to her tales of prophecy. They were each expected to recite them around the evening fire, but Yávië's mind kept wandering to far off fields and she felt the call of Mallowort's magick lessons. She had become very good at spells and incantations and could create a Man merely by thinking him into being. She had only done this out of sight of the others because she knew that Men belonged to a future part of the prophecies, but she saw no harm in practicing.

Yávië had never breathed the breath of life into her creations, merely conjured up the shell and immediately sent it back to the depths of her consciousness. She wished to bring one to life for it seemed to her that Æstretfordæ needed Men to populate it and mates to bring children and joy to the empty space.

She looked up, suddenly aware that three pairs of eyes were examining her closely.

"Forgive me; I was lost for a moment."

"Perhaps you would likes to show us the magick of your mind, Yávië," Willow suggested.

Nall and Rydén chuckled, causing Yávië to flush with embarrassment.

"I don't know what . . ."

The stick struck her swiftly, without warning. She felt a knot rise on her shoulder and a bruise began to spread.

"Yávië," Willow whispered, "it's bad to break the Prophecy, but its worse to lies about it."

"It wasn't a lie. I haven't broken the Prophecy, only practiced for the time to come."

"Show them," Willow instructed her.

Yávië bowed her head and let the image settle beneath her closed eyes. A tall man with thick, dark hair, chiseled features, eyes of darkest brown and a smiling mouth stood before them. His shoulders were broad above strong arms and hands and tapered to a narrow waist above well-muscled thighs and calves. His clothing was made of hides, tanned to a soft suppleness.

As Yávië opened her eyes, she saw him standing there, an empty shell waiting to live; there was nothing in his lifeless eyes save her own reflection. How she wished to give him life but it was not the time and she pulled him back inside herself, looking quickly at the others and waiting for the stick to fall.

Willow smiled and said in a hushed voice, "By the whisper of your name, Men will call on you. You have shown great wisdom in upholding the Prophecy. Let your name be Man's reward."

An Oath in Blood

Before the daystar broke the horizon, Weezel rousted Nall and Yávië from the warmth of their beds, "to hunt the boars."

As short as he was, Weezelwort could still set a grueling pace. He seemed to glide just above the ground as quickly as Nall and Yávië could run. Their hunting lessons had been interesting, introducing them to the beasts and fowl of Æstretfordæ. Most were edible, but the inedible ones were quite fierce, providing the challenge of a good fight.

Today they were hunting bane boar, one of the inedible but fierce beasts found in the Northern Mountains. Both Yávië and Nall were armed with daggers they had forged with Dobbinwort, and each had a bow and quiver filled with arrows blessed with Rosewort's hunt spells. The day was bound to be a success.

As they approached a heavily wooded area, Weezelwort signaled for them to stop. Nall and Yávië obeyed. The penalty for failing to obey was a swift crack with a stick. Both carried bruises from previous attempts to "think for themselves."

"I smells something," Weezel said. "Something very bad."

Suddenly the "bad smell" sprang from a nearby prickleberry thicket, knocking Weezel to the ground, unconscious, before turning on Nall and Yávië. Quickly backpedaling, both drew and nocked arrows, each circling the beast in opposite directions. It was indeed a bane boar, a large and angry female. The beast stood nearly nine hands at the shoulder and carried the scars of many previous battles.

The quills on her back stood erect in alarm and her lips drew back in a snarl, green saliva stringing from her lower jaw. The boar's eyes were small and glittered with hatred. Her enormous snout and six long tusks were caked with dried blood. She spun in circles trying to keep both hunters in sight. Giving a loud bawl, she charged at Nall. In an attempt to leap over the bane boar, he grabbed the two fore tusks but his timing and balance were off. The weight of the bane boar threw him to the ground, where she gored him repeatedly before Yávië could take a clean shot and bring the beast to her knees. As she fell forward, the tusks pushed even further into Nall's midsection, causing a great tear from his abdomen to his chest.

"Ah, Nall," Yávië whispered as she attempted to pull the heavy beast from him.

"Wait!" Weezelwort stumbled forward in a daze. "We'll cuts the tusks and leaves 'em in him. We needs to get him back to Willow and Rosie mighty quick."

With the large serrated blade they generally used to butcher their catch, Weezelwort quickly sawed through each of the tusks. Together, he and Yávië managed to pull the heavy boar away from Nall and roll it onto its side.

"Weezel, why are you so worried? Nall will heal. Rosie gave us the gift . . ." Weezel's worried look stopped her in her tracks. "What is it, Weezel?" Yávië whispered.

"This boar has the slitherwort poison. See her droolin'? It drains the spell from you when you gets it in your blood. If we don't finds help for it soon, Nall . . ." Weezel hung his head as though their predicament were his fault.

"What is it Rosie and Willow will do?" asked Yávië.

"They're goin' to cleans his blood. Takes it out and gives him new."

Yávië looked down at Nall. He was struggling to draw breath and his face was deathly pale. "We can't wait, Weezel. We have to do it now. Can you help me give him my blood?"

"I can binds him up, and we can try."

Weezel began to pull strands of spider cloth out of his pack and bind them around Nall's body, carefully removing the tusks. Blood had pooled on the ground around Nall, and his skin was taking on a greenish cast.

"Is it the poison causing that terrible color?"

"Aye. Comes here, girl. Kneels down and take his arm in yours."

Weezel made a swift cut in Yávië's arm and the same in Nall's. Pressing their arms together, he bound them tightly with leather strapping.

"Now we just waits a bit," he said, looking quite uncertain. "I have to tells you, Yávië, when you gives another one your blood, you takes an oath; it binds you two for always." He was shaking his head.

"Why does it matter, Weezel? We just won't tell him, and he will never know he owes his life to me," she said with a twitch of her lips.

"Not so much owing life, as the lives become the same. Anything you does is just like Nall did it, and anything he does is just like you did it. Do you sees? Blood oath is so serious that dragons will consider you two to be one person." Weezel shook his head again. "Willow's goin' to be mad. Rosie too."

Yávië looked down at Nall again, relieved to see his color turning from a sickly green to a rather grayish hue. His eyelids fluttered and she became aware of how long his eyelashes were as they brushed his cheeks. Yávië could think of worse things than swearing a blood oath to Nall, but wondered if he would feel the same.

Weezel made a litter out of waffle roots and branches from the prickleberry bushes. Together Weezelwort and Yávië lifted Nall onto it and bound him tightly so he wouldn't be jarred as they dragged it to Meremire. While Nall remained unconscious, his color was much improved and his breathing seemed normal. Yávië placed a wet cloth on his forehead and brushed back his hair. This time, his eyelids fluttered and remained open. Nall gazed at Yávië with a faraway look in his eye.

Their arrival at Meremire quickly descended into a chaotic shouting match. Willowort and Rosewort *were* mad. Rydén seemed amused. Morgwort started mumbling to himself about how this would affect the dragon flytes and for some reason Weezel went off to start a fire.

"Yávië, do you understands what's done?" Rosie asked.

"Yes, Weezel explained it in great detail on the way back. Do you think Nall will be angry?"

"It doesn't matter if he is, what's done is done. Most folks that takes a blood oath are kin to one another, and doin' it for battle. Not sure what to do with the two of you."

There was more shaking of heads. Yávië thought to herself that she had seen more head shaking since joining blood with Nall than in her entire previous existence.

"Nall is like a brother to me, if that helps any," she told Rosie.

Rosie gave her a sharp look that pierced her heart. Looking away, Yávië felt her face grow warm and knew her cheeks were flushed.

"Well, he *is*!" she shouted, embarrassed by her own behavior.

Why was she shouting at Rosie? None of this was Rosie's fault. She turned away toward the bothie where Nall lay sleeping. The least she could do was check on him.

Yávië stooped to enter the hut. Nall lay on a pallet of spider cloth as Willow tended to him with herbs and broth. Rydén sat in the corner with her arms around her drawn up knees.

"I guess this makes us family," Rydén smiled up at Yávië. "You liked us anyway, right?"

Yávië felt tears welling in her eyes. "Oh, Rydén, I more than like you. I love you like a sister," she said, "and Nall like a brother," she added, trying to convince herself that things would work out for the best.

Rydén rose and gave her a hard hug. "I'll leave you to explain it to him," she shrugged.

Willow nodded to her and left the bothie carrying the soiled bandages. Yávië sat down cross-legged next to Nall, who smiled and reached for her hand.

"I heard you were a hero," he whispered in a rough voice.

"I've made you take a blood oath . . . while you were unconscious," Yávië began.

Nall raised his fingers to her lips. "I know, Willow told me. The way I understand it, you had best not be making any promises I can't keep," allowing his eyes to close in the safety of her presence.

Chapter 3: Independence

Within a Crystal Cavern

When winter's cold heart began to thaw, the Ancients intensified the Guardians' training, encouraging the three young warriors to wander independently and familiarize themselves with the new world. For the time had come for the Guardians to seek their talismans.

Hawk soared far above Nall so that the rocky terrain ahead could be viewed. The sun was warm on Nall's back, giving him a feeling of peace as he reviewed the past weeks of training. He had particularly enjoyed learning to communicate with Hawk and the forging of metals with Dobbinwort, though Morgwort drove him crazy with his nonsense.

He allowed himself to think of Yávië, so very beautiful and so very serious. She rarely smiled, and he did not think he had ever heard her laugh. In wondering why that might be so, he missed a narrow crevice in the rocks and went tumbling down into a small cavern.

"Teach me to think about women!" he chastised himself, looking around for hand and footholds to help him climb out.

Silently communicating with Hawk, he waited until the large bird landed on a rocky ledge above him. "Well, as you can see, I am stuck!" he told the deathawk. "Go on ahead; I will meet you at the encampment."

Hawk eyed him steadily, then seeing that Nall did not appear to be in any danger, he launched himself into the air and headed for the valley floor where Nall had left his provisions and bedroll.

Nall looked around again and noticed a small passage leading deeper into the cavern.

"*Can't climb out—guess I will have to go around,*" he thought to himself.

The passage was narrow, pressing against his back and chest as he squeezed through and stepped out into a larger chamber. He realized there was a light source ahead.

"Daylight, I hope."

It was not daylight but an immense cavern of luminous Gaianite crystals. Golden light played among the crystals, creating a multihued dappling on the walls and floor. Stepping up to the wall nearest him, Nall peered closely at its flat surface. Within the crystal was a small object that radiated a flickering crimson light. Taking his dagger, Nall began to chip away at the surrounding crystal, trying to expose the object inside.

Unexpectedly, the crystal split and a multitude of shards crashed to the cavern floor. Looking down, Nall saw the small pulsing light and reached forward to pick it up from the fragments now littering the floor. He gazed into its center—no larger than a grain of sand—so bright and pulsing with deepest scarlet. Looking deeper, Nall saw his face reflected. "*The first of many mirrors,*" whispered a small voice within his mind, "*a talisman for your soul.*"

He placed the tiny scarlet gem inside the small pouch he carried around his neck and turned to renew his search for an exit. To his surprise, there before him was an opening, just above their camp for the evening.

A Warrior's Heart

Of all of their lessons, Yávië enjoyed dragon diplomacy most. Like the ancient game of chess, it was all show, strength against strength, threat for threat. In the final moments, one would seize the upper hand and a dragon or Guardian would win the game.

Brundlewort called on dragons from differing flytes: wind dragons, ice dragons and accordant dragons. Yávië had even gone to the sea to practice with the emerald, sea dragon flyte but loved the wind dragons best of all. Their ethereal beauty enchanted her, and their elegant posturing and windy bellows caused her heart to feel full.

Brundle had said that the Guardians would each command a dragon flyte sometime in the future, and Yávië could not help but hope for a flyte of wind dragons.

Her challenge for the day was to meet a trio of wind dragons and perfect her skills of arbitration. Each of the dragons would provide a different perspective on the same problem. Using her gift of wisdom, it would be Yávië's task to choose the correct perspective.

As Yávië approached the appointed gathering place, she sensed the dragons before they came into sight. The air around her grew colder and moved in unusual patterns, lifting her hair away from her face and causing her clothing to billow about her. It was an electrifying feeling. As she saw them, her breath caught as it always did and she felt her heart swell. They landed in nearly silent splendor; only the faintest whisper of a breeze accompanied their settling.

"Blessing of the Ancients on you, Guardian," spoke the largest of the three in a rumbling, thunderous voice.

"Honor and glory of the Ancients upon you and the Suunflyte, Aerodorn," Yávië replied, her voice strong and steady, as dragon etiquette required.

"We come seeking counsel, Guardian. In today's challenge, a breach has formed between the Suunflyte and Sailflyte regarding the air above the Trembling Sea. Alangor will represent the Sailflyte in this exercise and Valcort the Suunflyte. I will provide the Matriarch's thoughts," Aerodorn explained.

As Alangor began to present his side of the argument, a loud rushing of air caused him to pause while they searched for its source.

An enormous dark cloud had formed above them. Dust and debris whirled and rushed in all directions below it and blue-green flashes of light struck the ground around them, causing the wind dragons to spin uncertainly, their eyes wide. Yávië quickly sought cover behind a pile of stones, watching as the intense wind eddied then surged in every direction.

From the chaotic mass of air and debris flashed a broad head with trailing beards of wind—a mistral dragon! Without hesitation, he threw himself into a dive, extending his neck toward the closest of the wind dragons. His talons swept forward, gripping the dragon's neck and swiftly pulling him into the cloud mass. The wind dragon lashed back and forth in an attempt to free himself, but his efforts were unsuccessful. A second mistral dragon swept in from beneath the wounded wind dragon, raising its talons to slash the captive dragon's underbelly.

As quickly as they had come, they departed, dropping the doomed wind dragon to the ground below, still struggling feebly.

Yávië sprang from her hiding place and rushed to Aerodorn, mate to the Matriarch of the Suunflyte. His legs were twisted beneath him and his breaths came in short gasps.

The other two wind dragons flanked him, lying down against him with their necks across his broad back.

"Lord Aerodorn, what is your wish for your heart shard?" Valcort asked, well aware that his leader was dying. "Shall we return it to Azaeria?

"Nay, give it to the Guardian. She will take it to Azaeria at the gathering ground. Fly ahead and tell Azaeria that it was my wish," Aerodorn spoke.

"Guardian, do you understand my request?"

Yávië swallowed hard and nodded, not trusting her voice. A tear betrayed her heart as she placed a hand upon the giant neck.

Valcort and Alangor pierced Yávië with their stares, but were quietly chastised by Aerodorn. They rose to the sky, circling once before they headed for the lair of the Suunflyte.

"By trusting you with my heart shard, I am binding you to my flyte for all eternity. It is my wish that you become the Huntress of the Suunflyte, accepting my son as your pledge, binding him to you for the honor and glory of Æstretfordæ. Do you accept this pledge, Guardian?"

"I do, Aerodorn. But what will become of you?" she whispered.

She could no longer stay the flood of tears, but her sobs brought hope to Aerodorn, the hope of a union between this Guardian and the wind dragons and hope for the future of Æstretfordæ. With his soft breath, he dried her tears. This Guardian was undeniably the Huntress foretold in the lore of his flyte, a great huntress to lead the Suunflyte to honor and glory, a woman of valor, the seeker of Truth.

"Weep not for me; I only go to hold a place in the night sky for Azaeria. As long as my shard is kept safe I will be with you. Speak the magick you have learned to release my shard. When my body fades from this place, my shard will remain. Take it and gaze into it for it is one of many mirrors on your soul. Your reflection will please you, I think. Carry it to the Suunflyte—Azaeria will await you there."

Yávië had no concept of time as she spoke the words that would release Aerodorn's shard. She sat stroking the dragon's airy scales until she realized at last that she was stroking the earth. Aerodorn had gone.

Looking down, she saw the heart shard glittering upon the grass. She lifted it gently, holding it before her. Deep inside she saw a woman warrior dressed in battle raiment, a fierce look on her face. Her hair was cropped close to her head, and was as white as the southern ice fields. She tucked the shard inside her tunic beside the sleeping Xander.

"Keep this safe, sweet Xander," she told the downy flier.

Emerald Reflections

Rydén did not like dragons. Those she had met during her training had done nothing to change her mind. Attempting diplomacy with dragons seemed a foolish thing and in her opinion, slaying them would be more appropriate. As far as she could tell they were obstinate and untrustworthy. Even the gentle accordant and wind dragons, summoned by Brundlewort for Rydén's practice, had scowled and exhaled great clouds of steamy breath when they thought no one was looking.

Being sent alone on an errand of "dragon diplomacy" caused Rydén some anxiety. She always felt uncomfortable in their presence, no matter how "tame" they appeared. Why Brundle felt she was the right choice for this task was beyond her.

As she crossed the vast plain of glossy ebony, she considered turning around and returning to Meremire and telling the others that she had completed the task. Surely, no one else would come all this way to find out?

The sound of leathery wings caused her stomach to tighten, and the realization that it was too late to turn back without encountering the dragon made her hands slick with sweat. Looking up, she braced herself for the giant beast's landing. The ground shook and boulders rolled as the animal came to a stop in front of her.

Its head snaked forward and its teeth clashed together. "I see you fear me, Guardian," the dragon remarked with distaste.

"It is only your foul breath I detest," Rydén replied, fully expecting to be crushed in its jaws any second.

Drawing closer, the dragon sniffed Rydén and then drew back, shaking its massive head as it exhaled.

"You say my breath is foul? You should smell the stench of your fear! How do you expect to appear before my Matriarch reeking of terror?"

"I don't intend to meet your Matriarch, your brothers, or your sisters. I intend to return to Meremire and tell the Ancients that you refused my counsel."

The dragon roared, shaking with laughter, causing further damage to the rocks around them.

"And who would believe you?"

"I am a Guardian, who would *not* believe me?

"I have seen a Guardian, one of jet-black hair and violet eyes! You are *no* Guardian. You are merely a whelp, cared for by the Ancients. They will soon realize you are never going to be worthy, and will send you back to the ageless sleep. Æstretfordæ will be better for it. Your heart is clouded; you are no Guardian."

He turned his back on her and, with a downward sweep of raised wings, lifted himself into the sky.

"You have made an enemy, Guardian," a voice hissed from behind Rydén.

She whirled around and was dismayed to see another dragon. However, this one was not an earth dragon, with which she had become familiar. This dragon was transparent and its scales seemed to be in constant motion, shimmering and pulsing. She could see a faint white light coming from within the beast's chest. As it scowled and stretched its neck toward her, its scales lifted threateningly.

"Have you learned nothing from Brundlewort?" The dragon cocked its head and peered at her. "Come with me, young Guardian," the dragon said, lowering its head and neck before her, "I will show you something."

Trembling, Rydén backed away.

"I have no desire to go with you," she said, attempting to appear brave.

"Mount *now!*" the dragon bellowed.

Without further thought, Rydén complied, leaping nimbly up onto the dragon's withers and clutching its scales.

The ethereal dragon lifted soundlessly into the sky, leaving a long misty trail in its wake.

"You will grow strong, and become a great huntress one day," its voice trailed back to her. "In the time of Men, you will become a savior. Do not let the words of Dielmor cause darkness to settle in your heart. He is a poor example of his kind."

"Dielmor? That is the dragon I was speaking to?"

"Yes, mate to Dahrea, Matriarch of the Direflyte. They deal in death and cannot be trusted."

Suddenly they were over the Trembling Sea, far from Meremire and the safety of the Ancients. Rydén's heart pounded at the thought of abandonment here by this windy beast.

"There, look there!" the dragon roared. "Soon those dragons will be yours to command!"

Below, Rydén saw a flyte of dragons skimming just beneath the surface of the water. They speared through the water as easily as this dragon did through the air.

"What are they?" she shouted.

"Sea dragons. Emerald sea dragons," her mount bellowed, as it brought itself around to land on the tip of a sea mountain. "I will introduce you!"

With the elegant posturing that Brundlewort had described in such detail, the airy dragon hailed the sea dragons.

Raising its scales in a show of strength, her mount spoke in a thunderous voice, "Honor of the Ancients to you, Sybeth, and to the Sailflyte."

"Honor to you, Azaeria, and to the Suunflyte," replied the Matriarch. "What business brings you here?"

"I bring to you the young Guardian from Meremire, the one who was prophesied." Azaeria lowered her neck allowing Rydén to dismount.

Sybeth approached, raising her scales and drawing back her head in a display of dominance.

"Young Guardian, I bear a gift." She plucked a shiny stone from between her eyes and held it out in her great claw.

Leaning forward, Rydén accepted the stone and examined it closely. It was a beautifully carved emerald dragon.

"In the future we will meet again, Guardian. Until that time, this emerald, symbol of the Sailflyte, will serve as a talisman and I as your mirror. You have been taught of the talismans?"

"Yes, Sybeth, Matriarch of the Sailflyte, Brundlewort has taught me well. I will thank him when I return to Meremire. Honor to you and the Sailflyte, Sybeth."

Rydén realized that what she said was true. Brundle had taught her dragon diplomacy very well–she need only choose to use it.

"Until next we meet, Guardian!" roared Sybeth as she led her flyte beneath the sea.

Azaeria approached Rydén, neck extended, head lowered.

"Why did you help me, Dragon?" Rydén asked.

"My flyte is pledged to Yávië. She is our huntress by the words of our promise. I helped you because she would expect it of me. And now she would expect me to return you to Meremire, young Guardian, and so I will."

Awaking much later, Rydén shook off her sleepiness. "*What a strange dream I had*," she thought to herself, "*very strange indeed*."

Feeling a pebble rubbing against her toe, she removed the boot to turn it out. There on the ground lay a small, perfectly carved emerald dragon.

By the Breath of the Beast

Yávië discovered that she liked hunting alone, without the Ancients, Nall or Rydén, for although she enjoyed their company, she found they distracted her on a hunt. But she was not completely alone. Xander, the downy flier, accompanied Yávië at all times. Since learning beast speech from Morgwort, she enjoyed frequent conversations with the tiny flier. His eyes were quick to see things hidden in the night, and he quickly passed knowledge of a threat to her with a slight shiver of his body against hers.

Yávië had no particular prey in mind this day, and was moving through the woods at a brisk and steady pace, headed for the crimson fields where bane boar and stag abounded. Wouldn't the rest of them be surprised when she brought home the meal without the task having been assigned to her?

Slowing as she broke the cover of the trees and reached the waist-high grass, Yávië cast the veil of mist and moved forward at a stealthier pace. A sudden shiver from Xander put her on her guard, and she heard the death rattle of a creature off to her left. The kill of another hunter, perhaps? She crept forward, wary of surprising a beast with its prey.

Suddenly, Yávië was thrown backward, landing flat on her back, unprepared, with no weapon drawn. As she struggled to draw her dagger, an immense beast lumbered toward her and stopped in a crouch above her. Stooped, knees bent, arms hanging loosely at its sides, with its upper lip jutting forward over protruding teeth, it glared at her with one slightly swollen red eye. The other appeared to have been gouged out, leaving only a bleeding socket. Its pointed ears were set high on either side of its head and pulsing blisters of yellow pus covered its face, chest and forearms. A cloth hung loosely around its hips, sagging to cover bulging male organs. It was the ugliest creature she had ever seen.

Glimpsing the dagger in Yávië's hand, the beast let out a grunt and moved back a few steps so that it no longer presented a direct threat.

As she realized that the beast had seen her even through the veil of mist, Yávië raised herself up and looked at the creature with a new respect.

"You could see me," she stated, "even though I was veiled."

"Yes, Guardian," the beast replied in a voice that sounded like Willowort's stag stew boiling in a pot. "You cannot veil yourself from me, for I am one of many mirrors, one reflection of your soul."

"But you are. . .."

"Ugly?" the beast finished for her with a gruff laugh. "And so is one residing in your center. Be cautious of that one, for there is danger there."

The beast struck quickly, grabbing her arm and pulling her toward him, causing Xander to burst from her tunic with tiny teeth bared.

The beast gave a deep chuckle. "I see they have given you a tiny guardian," he grumbled, staring intently until Xander returned inside. Then, with a large claw covered in coarse black hair, he turned over Yávië's small, fine hand and placed a tiny crystal in her palm, his fetid breath blowing across it.

"A talisman to bind us," he proclaimed, before turning and disappearing into the dense underbrush at the edge of the field.

Yávië tucked the crystal in the pouch she carried around her neck, wondering what darkness she bore within her heart. With a sigh, she turned away and raced back toward Meremire where Weezelwort and Nall awaited her.

Out of the Sacred Sea

Rydén followed the dry stream bed toward the Sacred Sea. Weezel-wort had assigned Rydén huntress duty for the evening meal, but she had not yet come across game large enough to feed the ten of them. Valia accompanied her, and she loved to watch the young grass cat as it loped alongside, fluid and graceful.

As they approached the grassy area adjacent to the sea, Rydén heard the sound of weeping. Slowing to a walk, she employed the veil of mist to create a shield of invisibility around her. She crept forward, then dropped to her belly and proceeded at a crawl as the crying became louder and more insistent. It was clearly a woman, and one in great distress judging by the sound of the wailing. Through the tall grass, Rydén could see a red-haired woman doubled over, clutching her midsection and rocking back and forth. The wailing intensified to a howl and the woman fell forward to her knees, still rocking and clutching herself.

"Woman," Rydén said, "What is it that causes you such pain?"

As the stranger turned toward her, Rydén saw that the woman's face was unlined and without features—no eyes for tears to spring from, no nose to run in sorrow, and no mouth from which to utter the horrible sounds of sadness that Rydén had heard. Puzzled but unafraid, Rydén stepped forward, dropping the veil of mist from around her body.

"What affliction is this?"

As the woman turned directly toward Rydén, features began to form on the empty face: emerald eyes, a turned up nose, and a full mouth with rosy lips. With a sharp intake of breath, Rydén stepped back. She was looking at a mirror image of herself.

"What magick is this?" she asked, drawing her blade and preparing to defend herself against whatever manner of sorcery this proved to be. "I can cast spells, too!"

By way of evidence, she threw a bolt of white and scarlet lightning into the grass at the woman's feet to set a small fire there.

Using a copy of Rydén's mouth, the woman smiled, blowing gently and putting out the flames.

"Do not fear me. I am simply a mirror in which you will see your innermost soul."

"Why were you weeping?" Rydén asked.

"I see your future and all your suffering," the woman replied. "I see darkness in your soul. In the future, the salt of my mourning will serve as your talisman. Until you need me, I will be waiting near the Sea of Sorrow."

As the woman faded, a large simplestag appeared in her place. Rydén quickly nocked an arrow and fell him where he stood. As she bled the buck, she pondered the woman's words. They weighed heavily upon her as she made her way slowly back to Meremire, carrying the evening's meal.

The Earthen Empath

The many voices in his mind drew Nall to the mound of earth in the midst of the crimson field. He had been coming to sit near the mound for several days in an attempt to understand what the voices were trying to tell him. The language of the voices was unknown to him, which was odd since he spoke most of those of Man, as well as the language of the Ancients and the Guardians.

It was nearly starset. He had come to stay the night, hoping his thoughts would be less cluttered without the sounds of the day. He sat and closed his eyes, arms folded across a chest that now bore the scars of a bane boar attack. Save for the constant voices, he allowed his mind to empty and grow calm.

"Nall."

He heard his name quite clearly.

"I am here," he replied.

Within Nall's mind, a mist began to lift allowing him to see those who called. A group of Men seemed trapped beneath the ground. They were clearly Men, though their skin was extremely pale—as if they had not seen the daystar for generations. Their eyes and hair were also a pale blue. What clothing they wore was soiled and torn, and their feet and arms were bare. They cried out for help, and some appeared ill or injured. Nall wondered where this place might be, since he knew that no races of Men inhabited Æstretfordæ. The Ancients had made this very clear—the realm of Men had ended long ago in the time beyond remembering. The

Guardians would populate Æstretfordæ with new races of Men when the Prophecy dictated it.

"Where are you?" Nall asked. No answer came, only their continued calling and moaning for help.

Rising, he walked to the mound of earth, continued around it, and then climbed to its summit where he sat, seeking out these Men with his compassion.

A sudden pain struck the side of his head, as if he had been hit with a forge hammer, leaving him reeling and his mind fogged. Breathing deeply, he opened his mind further and saw a scene of carnage in the still unknown location. A second race had appeared, with skin a deep bronze, and hair and eyes dark as well. They seemed wealthy, their clothing woven with strands of gold and silver. Bracelets of gold and precious gems adorned their wrists and upper arms. They carried forged weapons with which they were systematically butchering the lighter-skinned race.

"Stay your arms!" shouted Nall. There was no reaction among those he watched within his mind. Grabbing his temples, he began to rock to and fro, suffering the pain of the victims, feeling each wound and dying breath. As the last man fell, his pain subsided and he opened his eyes to see a pale man standing before him.

"I am Xavier, the third of your soul's mirrors. I give to you this golden feather as a talisman. You would have helped us if you could. Do not feel sorrow at our passing, for it is just one small part of the journey of life. We will meet again in the future, Nall, Guardian of Æstretfordæ." The man began to crumble into rich brown earth, then to a graying ash, which was carried on the light winds to the four corners of the world.

From the Anger of the Sea

S orrow covered Rydén like the angry, iron gray sea she watched from the sand. Her heart felt leaden, as if it were some giant stone inside her chest. Her eyes glistened with tears she would never let Nall or Yávië see, tears of loneliness that would make her seem weak to them.

She wondered what suffering her future truly held. Was it real or just something imagined by the woman who called herself a talisman? Rydén wished she knew. She had been happy in Meremire, happy with Nall and Yávië. She had learned to trust and admire them both, although she occasionally felt jealousy's ugly head rear when she was around Yávië. She knew Yávië sensed it but felt none in return.

Hearing the sound of water dripping, Rydén stood and turned to see a great wave rising up from the ocean. It towered above her, then raced toward her at an astonishing speed. As the wave reached the sand, it seemed to become denser as it finally formed the shape of a man. It separated itself from the rest of the sea and sprinted up the sand on liquid legs.

As Rydén swung to flee, a watery voice reached her.

"Stay, Rydén. I bring a gift."

Turning to face the gelatinous form, she asked, "How do you know my name? What are you?"

A hand reached out, seawater flowing from its half-formed fingers. "Take the gift and look inside."

Reaching out, Rydén took the silver sword offered to her. It was lustrous, the late afternoon light creating rainbows around it. As she peered into the blade, Rydén saw only her reflection.

Looking toward the watery figure, Rydén whispered, "I see only myself."

"It is your soul's third talisman, Rydén. Keep it close. Keep it safe." Even as it spoke, the watery being began to lose its shape and slip back into the sea.

"A great weapon," Rydén said. "I will indeed keep it close and safe."

Chapter 4: Dragon Quests

As the daystar moved further from the world and a new winter knelt at the horizon, the Guardians' training came to its end. They had grown tall and strong, wise and just. It would not be long before they were called to create the races of Men as foretold in the Prophecy. The Ancients met and spoke of the future of the Guardians, of the joys and sorrows they would bring to Æstretfordæ. They expressed their concern that one might betray them, but the name of the betrayer was kept in shadow, even from the Ancients. They spoke of the time Yávië would rise to seek the Truth and bring about the rebirth of the world called Ædracmoræ.

At last, the time came for the three young Guardians to receive the pledges of the dragons. While the Ancients had decreed that all dragons were bound to the Guardians, only those flytes that chose to pledge themselves would hear a Guardian's call.

Five flytes had requested pledges. The Suunflyte and Kilstoneflyte had called for a pledge to Yávië, the Sailflyte swore allegiance to Rydén, and the IIzenflyte and the Emeraldflyte had appealed for a pledge to Nall. Each of the flytes required that their chosen Guardian complete an arduous quest before the Ceremony of the Pledges.

On the eve before the dragon quests were to begin, the ten sat in council around the fire outside Willow's bothie—seven small and wizened Ancients and three tall and stately Guardians.

"Each one will seeks something lost to the dragons. When all lost haves been found the ceremony will take place. Each will haves a starting place: Yávië, beyond the Northern Mountains above the Azure Sea; Nall to the Well of Viileshga and Rydén goes to the Trembling Sea. All must travels only by foot or dragon, and you must listen for the dragons' calls. Blessings of the Ancients upon each of you. We will not meet again until your quests is complete."

Willow got to her feet and retreated into her bothie. Following her lead, each of the Ancients left the fire and disappeared into his bothie for the night. The Guardians would leave before first light, long before the Ancients had arisen from their night's rest.

They stood within the darkness of the night, visible only by their auras. Their eyes were sad—they realized there would be many days to come before they were together again.

Nall hugged Rydén. "Be safe, my first life sibling. Blessings of the Ancients on you and your quest."

"Yávië," Nall said in a hoarse whisper. "You are the life and breath of me now; be safe, and avoid the slitherwort while we are apart." He smiled as he gave the warning.

He glanced self-consciously at Rydén before holding Yávië in his embrace just a moment too long, eliciting a knowing smile from his sister.

"Safe journey to both of you," Yávië replied, hugging each tightly. "Last one back brings a stag for the spit!" she added to lighten the increasingly awkward moment.

Without a backward glance, she set off toward the Northern Mountains and her first quest.

By the Clutch of the Wind

Six days northwest of Meremire, Yávië saw the first of the Giant Stones, an indication that she was approaching the Northern Mountains. She knew that her first quest was for the wind dragons, even though no one had told her. She still carried Aerodorn's heart shard next to her own heart. This quest would return that precious shard to Azaeria, Matriarch of the Suunflyte.

"*Guardian,*" spoke a tiny voice within her head. "*Do you seek the wind dragons?*"

"Aye, I am traveling to the Suunflyte to speak with their Matriarch, Azaeria." Hearing a rustle behind her, she turned to see a small being slip into a prickleberry thicket.

"*You have the ability to mind speak. What sort of being are you?*" Yávië questioned silently.

"We are stone sprites. We live within the Giant Stones," the small voice replied.

"We? But I saw only you."

"Nay, we are many, set free by your passing. You are the Guardian Yávië, are you not?"

"I am Yávië. Should I be concerned that I have freed you from the stones?"

"Oh, nay, Mistress. We have waited for you since the time before the Ancients. We hid within the Stones during the last days of Ædracmoræ. At the world's death we became trapped. Your coming was foretold in the Prophecies of the Tree of Creation."

Several small sparkles of light drifted from beneath the bush. Each held a tiny being no more than four thumbs in height, perfectly formed in the image of male or female. Each was dressed in trousers or skirt of darkest grey with a matching waistcoat. Upon their heads, a crown of delicate sylverbell blossoms was worn over golden curls. They formed a circle around Yávië and, taking hands, began to dance about her feet. Watching them made her quite dizzy, and she dropped where she stood, fast asleep. The tiny sprites laughed and danced long after the daystar had set.

When Yávië awoke, the shimmer of the night stars had lit up the small meadow. Three sprites stood close by watching her.

"We did not mean to make you sleep, Mistress. We were joyous in our freedom and we forgot the effect our dance would have on you. Please forgive us."

Yawning and rubbing her eyes, Yávië sat up and smiled at the little sprites.

"No harm has been done, and I am rested, so perhaps it was for the best. I must go now. I still have far to travel before I reach my destination. Will we meet again, little sprites?"

"Aye, Mistress. We will follow as far as the Giant Stones go, for we can go no further. We will see you on your return from the dragons' lair."

"Set the pace then, wee ones, and I will follow you to the end of the Stones."

The sprites raced ahead, hovering just above the ground, as they wove in and out among the stones. Yávië followed at a gentle jog, stopping briefly to say good-bye at the last of the standing stones.

By the following day, Yávië had reached the summit of the Northern Mountains. The grueling pace she had set for herself had paid off as she gazed, exhausted, upon the Azure Sea. Along the eastern margin of the sea ran a rugged cliff face. It was within these cliffs the flyte of the wind dragons would be found. Three days more and she would reach the foot of the cliffs. Then one more day of climbing should bring her face to face with the flyte's Matriarch. Her heart felt heavy at the thought of Azaeria's sorrow at the loss of Aerodorn, and the knowledge that she would soon be parting with Aerodorn's heart shard. Being in possession of a dragon's heart is a powerful thing—calming and soothing the carrier. Yávië permitted herself a moment of self-pity before reproving herself for such a selfish thought.

As she rested, she allowed her mind to call to Nall. Within moments, she felt his presence.

"Are you well, my heart?"

A shadow drifted through her mind and she felt a chill. The one who answered was not Nall.

"Yávië, Nall, this will only lead to your destruction. You share a blood oath: your love is forbidden by the law. You are not mere mortal man and woman, you are the Guardians of Æstrctfordæ, and the price you often pay is solitude and sometimes loneliness. Your hearts break now, but I will show you great happiness in your dreams. You will not remain alone forever; the right one waits for each of you. Heed my warning, Yávië, Nall, that you do not bring ruin upon the great quest for the Truth," whispered the soft voice of the Tree of Creation.

"I will heed you, Giver of All Prophecy, but I will also weep for my loss. Nall is good and kind, and his heart pumps my blood through his veins. His wisdom gives me strength. I will *never* not love Nall, but I will keep my love hidden deep inside my soul until my return to Meremire. Then I will make journey to the Lake of Lost Memories so that the lake can take it from me. Until then, I will sorrow with it. Your gift of dreams is kind, but I do not believe I will ever love another."

Yávië closed her mind and wept as her heart shattered beneath the weight of the Creator's words. The heart shard she carried began to pulse, pulling the pain away from her and easing her to sleep.

"Yávië? You are Yávië, aren't you? I have been looking for you," said a pleasantly deep male voice from behind her.

Spinning around, Yávië looked into what seemed like the depths of the sea, eyes of the deepest sapphire, so dark she could not see the soul.

As she took in the rest of the face, she saw a smiling mouth and a sudden flash of spirit in the depths of those eyes that blinded her with its beauty. Velvet lashes framed the sapphire pools below dark brows, one raised in curiosity. The nose was perfect, straight and true. Dark hair hung down to his shoulders, framing that amazing face. His aura radiated brightly, proclaiming his status as a Guardian.

Unable to stop herself from smiling, she said, "Do I know you?"

She felt foolish at the words for she knew quite well that somewhere she had met this man, this Guardian.

"You probably know quite well you do, but, to answer politely, yes, we met long ago in another lifetime. I am Sōrél, Guardian of Æshardæ. I have come to help you seek the Truth. This," he gestured towards the woman beside him, "is Näeré, my sibling and fellow Guardian."

Yávië turned to stare in amazement at the woman beside Sōrél. Näeré was almost identical to her brother. Except for smaller, softer, more feminine features her face was cast from the same striking model, beautiful and bold. Her hair was longer, falling heavily to the small of her back. She smiled at Yávië with the same warm smile her brother had given. "*She is so beautiful*," Yávië thought.

"*But not as beautiful as you*," she heard Sōrél's deep voice in her mind.

Waking with a start, Yávië realized that Xander had returned from his nightly hunt and was trying to slip inside her shirt. Lifting him up, she held his downy fur against her face.

"Xander, I met the most incredible Guardians in a dream. Do you think they are real? Remind me to ask Morg about a place called Æshardæ. If it exists, then perhaps, so do they."

Xander snuggled with his mistress a moment longer. With a sneeze, and sitting in the palm of her hand, he began his daily grooming ritual. He paused, looked up at her, and said, "*Not a dream, a vision from your past truth.*" His tiny voice entered her mind. "*Vision from the mother of Æstretfordæ.*" Then, with a flick of his tail, he slipped inside her tunic to sleep for the day.

Without his distraction, her mind turned to Nall and the words from the Mother of All Prophecy. She let out a deep sigh and shook her head. It was hard to imagine any pain greater than that her heart was giving her. She closed her eyes for a moment before, with another deep sigh, resuming her journey to the Suunflyte's lair.

As Yávië reached a flat ledge, she stood and surveyed the surrounding area. She had assumed she would have been able to hear dragon sounds by now, but the cliffs were silent.

Yávië found a small niche among the sharp rocks, just large enough to slip through. On the far side, a long narrow crevice ran downward into the face of the cliff. Veiling herself against exposure, she slid forward along the narrow passage, pausing at the point where it entered a large chamber.

"Come, Guardian!" A loud roar filled her head. "You are the Guardian who carries the heart shard of Aerodorn. I am Azaeria, Matriarch of the Suunflyte. Blessings of the Ancients upon you."

Unveiling herself and stepping into the chamber, Yávië got her first glimpse of the dead Aerodorn's mate. She was large, her girth broader than that of Aerodorn. Her shimmering scales flashed blinding light that played around the chamber, shooting from one crystal structure to the next before returning to be refracted off the scales once again in an endless dance of light. In contrast to the deep scowl etched on her brow, the dragon's eyes were moist and sorrowful.

"Aerodorn held much faith in you, Guardian. He left his heart shard in your keeping, and by doing so has bound this flyte to you for all eternity. Do you know how long that is, Guardian?"

"Aye, Matriarch. I feel as if I have already lived and died an eternity on my journey to this flyte," Yávië responded.

"Your heart is broken, much as mine. However, yours will heal with the telling of the tale to the Lake of Lost Memories. Mine can only heal with the passing of Aerodorn's heart shard."

Yávië stepped forward and drew the shard from within her clothing. It pulsed in a slow and regular rhythm, an audible throb in the quiet of the cavern.

Holding out her great claw, Azaeria received Aerodorn's heart shard. As it touched her scaly palm, its light grew in intensity. The throbbing strengthened and the pounding pulse became deafening.

"Aerodorn, you are home," Azaeria said as she placed the shard among the scales on her massive chest. Its light moved, penetrating her breast to rest next to her own.

She looked up at Yávië. "Now it is time for you to meet your new bond, Huntress. He is called Aero, in honor of his father. Follow, Guardian."

Azaeria led the way from the crystal chamber and through a broad expanse of caverns void of any sign of life. When she finally paused, it was in a room filled with heat and steam, the deep humidity of the clutch.

"He is there, awaiting your voice." Azaeria pointed to a large leathery egg, set slightly apart from the others. "You will be the first to speak to him and in doing so create a life bond. In every generation, a son of Aero will be your bond for as long as the stars remain to light the night skies. You are pledged to the honor and glory of the Suunflyte, as is the one with whom you share a blood oath. What one does is done by both; what is done by the Huntress is done by the Suunflyte. Do not betray our trust, Guardian."

"I will leave you now. Fill Aero's mind with your voice by the telling of the Prophecies. He will come to you on the eve of his first flight. Seek him in the setting of the daystar, on the eve of Æstretfordæ's birth." With great dignity, Azaeria turned and left the room.

Yávië moved to Aero's side, seeing movement within the supple skin of his leathery cradle. She stroked it gently.

"I knew your father," she began.

The Well of Viileshga

Hawk had flown to his evening perch and Nall had just finished a meal of ground hare and boiled willow bark when a sweet voice spoke in his mind, within his very soul. A vision of Yávië's violet eyes brought a quick smile to his lips.

"Are you well, my heart?"

Yávië's question came, but his reply was stayed by the most ancient voice of wisdom. The calm, breathy voice of the One, who prophesied all knowledge, was telling them they must take care, must not listen to their hearts, but follow the path of the Guardian, alone and lonely. He heard Yávië respond with great hurt and passion, saying she would take the memory of their silent promise to the Lake of Lost Memories and forget her feelings for him.

The very thought brought a great weight to bear on him. His breath became ragged and his mind fogged, as if he were suffocating. Slowly Nall let himself lie down. He pulled the heavy coat over his shoulders, surrendering himself to what he hoped would be a dreamless sleep.

"Perhaps, I too will journey to the Lake of Lost Memories," he offered to himself as solace.

As he slept, a Willow-wisp appeared near his head. With her hands, she stroked his brow, smoothing its lines.

"Sleep," was her incantation, "sleep free from pain."

With her hands held wide, palms up to call the rain, the incantation continued. "Rain, come take his pain. Cry for him and take his tears. Rain, take away his pain. Cry for him and take his fears."

As the rain began to fall, Nall relaxed within his dreamless slumber.

Nall awoke with the realization that his sleep had indeed been dreamless. It was a gift from the Tree of Creation, a few hours peace before his soul was again shaken by the memory of her warning.

As he prepared for the day's travels, Nall attacked the warning with his mind. What he would give to return to his days as a mortal, amid the smoke-filled cities, now merely dying recollections in the past prophecies of this world. Then he realized such foolishness came from his sudden heartache. The needs of Æstretfordæ far outweighed the desires of two Guardians. He had been called as a protector for this new world, and the pain of losing Yávië would only make him stronger, as pain had always done. Unconsciously, he placed his hand over his heart, where Yávië's blood pulsed through his veins.

"Come, Hawk!" Nall called, and greeted the morning of the seventh day of his quest.

In puzzlement, Nall scanned the area above the great forests where the Well of Viileshga lay. The deep green forests far below him should have been covered in mist at this time of the day, but they lay dry and dusty. The outlying edges of the dense tangle of trees and vines appeared brown and dead. Concern drove him forward at an increased pace.

On reaching the fringe of the great forest, he saw that more than just the vegetation was dying. Scarlet lizards, downy fliers and many small birds lay dead among the decaying plant matter.

"What could have caused such destruction?" Nall asked himself.

"The Well is tainted, Guardian, by a veneficia, a haruspex, a diviner by entrails. Her filthy practice has infected the Well of Life," bellowed a voice followed by the sound of leathery wing beats and trees toppling behind him as a great dragon landed.

"From within the depths of the Well of Viileshga comes the life force of Æstretfordæ. If the Well is not cleansed, then every living mortal will soon be dead. Dragons will return to the depths to await the next calling; your precious Ancients will crumble to dust, and the very Tree of Creation will become dormant for another age.

You, Guardian, will have no reason to exist and will be returned to the star fields of your slumber. The fate of Æstretfordæ is in your hands this day."

Suddenly, the dragon leaned closer towards Nall, coming within a hand's width of his chest.

"Your soul is cracked, Guardian, be careful that the witch does not drive a stake into it, breaking it apart." And so saying, the great beast took flight on its leathery wings and was soon lost from sight.

"Thanks for the help," Nall mumbled.

"You do not care for my mate?" a second dragon's voice called.

From the forest an even larger dragon approached—a female, judging by her girth. She carried herself with an air of expectancy.

"I think he did not care for me," Nall laughed.

"Perhaps not. He does not like those who have merely been 'given' power. He will respect you when he feels you have earned the right to your authority over dragons."

"My mate's words were true. The Well is poisoned by the witch, and you are in grave danger from her if your soul is not healed before your meeting."

"What can I do? I do not control the pain of my soul," Nall said with a shrug.

The dragon stepped closer. "I am Adra, Matriarch of the Emeraldflyte. You are pledged to me even now by the calling of the Ancients. You carry at your center a small piece of my heart shard. Because of this I have the power to end your sorrow and heal your soul if you wish it."

"And what will be left of Yávië if you do?" Nall asked.

"Do not fear the loss of the blood oath, Guardian. You will never lose her, but you will not hunger for her as you do now. This is a dangerous thing you feel for one with a blood oath. Have the Ancients not spoken to you of this?"

"Yes," Nall sighed, "and the teller of prophecy as well, but it has done nothing to dampen the passion."

"You would endanger Æstretfordæ?" Adra looked at him intently, and then shook her head. "No, I do not believe you would. Your sorrow is pointless if you do not intend to act on the passion. Give it to me, Guardian; let me heal your soul."

Not trusting himself to speak, Nall merely nodded, noticing that the great dragon had drawn her tail around behind him and was pulling him closer. Adra closed a great claw around Nall and gazed deeply into his soul, pulling the pain from him as the Willow-wisp had done when he slept. But while the wisp could only ease the pain temporarily, Adra would remove it altogether, leaving only peace and a deep feeling of friendship for a forgotten love.

Nall stood at the Well, wondering when he had arrived, as he had no recollection of the journey from the forest's dying edge to its verdant heart. Calling Hawk, Nall stationed him at the top of the Well and, through the deathawk's piercing eyes, looked down into its depths.

The stench of rotting flesh rose from the Well. At the bottom, far below, Nall saw a haggard old woman, naked to the waist with filthy rags tied about her hips, her teats exposed to suckle the evil imps she raised. Beneath the Well she had constructed a rotten hovel, made from the bones and decaying flesh of her victims. Nall watched as the veneficia spun in circles, surrounded by fire imps screeching for her putrid milk. About her lay the rotten entrails of those forest creatures she had slain. He recognized simplestag and bane boar and could hear the cries of terror from captive beasts awaiting their slaughter.

Nall sensed the witch's power, and knew that he would need strong spells and incantations blessed by the Ancients to overcome her evil. He withdrew the stone dagger given to him by Dobbinwort—said to be a match to the one in Yávië's possession and therefore given the strength of both Guardians. Nall cringed, wishing he had a weapon that allowed him to keep a greater distance. He shrugged off the thought, knowing that the dagger held a power far stronger than that of any arrow. It contained the strength of a blood oath between Guardians. There was no greater power.

Believing the haruspex would have designed her den with an entrance somewhere within the forest, Nall sent Hawk on a search.

"Return with the morning light, Hawk. I will begin the descent to end that hag's filthy contamination then."

Nall slept a dreamless sleep once more, his soul relieved of yearning for anything other than the death of the witch.

Deep within the earth, at the heart of the Emraldflyte, the Matriarch

Adra chastened her mate, "You judge Nall too harshly, Ardane."

"Nay, he is weak; you will see. He will betray us, as his kind always does."

"He already carries a piece of my heart shard, Ardane; one day he will carry it all. Do not encumber Nall with your hatred. It will only serve to weaken you both."

"We will see, my Queen, we will see." Ardane said with a shake of his great head.

With the morning light, Hawk led Nall to the entrance of the witch's lair. Deep within the tangled vines, beneath the rotting roots of an ancient chale tree, a tunnel began that descended to the den below the Well.

"Wait at the Well, Hawk!" Nall commanded, "I will seek you there on the morrow."

Nall ducked into the tunnel where the stench from the gore of a thousand denizens coating the walls caused his stomach to churn. What manner of being lived with such filth?

"A rich and powerful one, Guardian," cackled an evil voice. "Hurry! Come that I might kill you and use your entrails to foretell the future of this failing world."

The silence grew thick and palpable. It was clear that Nall's enemy intended to be elusive. Lights began to play on the walls of the passageway ahead and grew ever closer. As he rounded a tight corner, a blaze of fire imps attacked his head and arms, leaving burning sores wherever they touched, then fleeing amid a frenzied wailing of success. At every turn the imps flew at Nall, raging and burning, then screaming and keening to their Mistress. He covered his eyes to avoid being blinded.

Recovering, Nall drew the stone dagger and crept forward. He considered using the veil of mist, but decided it would not hide him from this veneficia. As the stench grew stronger, Nall began to recite the incantations taught him by the Ancients. Holding the stone dagger before him, he entered the lair of the witch and confronted her amidst the detritus and filth of the dead.

The haruspex smiled, showing her decaying teeth and swollen gums. She spat thick, foul-smelling saliva at him, missing by no more than two hands' breadth. Hooting and shrieking, she whirled and danced around him. Her imps raced in to add to the confusion, but the incantations of the Ancients held them from him. Screaming in rage and frustration, they spun around the haruspex.

Grabbing a flaming branch from her fire, the witch rushed at Nall, striking a glancing blow to his shoulder. His dagger swept out, slashing the back of her arm as she spun away.

Nall watched her warily as he continued to recite the incantations of the Ancients. Each word seemed only to enrage her more and she rose from the ground to fly about, and then above him, sent a hot, reeking stream of urine over his head and shoulders.

Holding his breath Nall wiped his face with his sleeve, but the noxious stream had blinded him, leaving him open to her blows. Repeatedly the witch struck him with her flaming stick, vile vomit streaming from her mouth, covering Nall's face and chest and driving him into a ball on the ground.

Laughing manically, the veneficia dropped to the floor beside Nall, seizing a long-bladed knife from the wall above his motionless body.

"Now we will see what future is held within your steaming bowels, Guardian," the witch cackled, stooping to push against his shoulder and drive him back to expose his abdomen.

As the haruspex was about to strike, Nall blocked the blow with his forearm, then drove the stone dagger up and into the witch's throat.

For a moment time seemed to freeze, making each detail strikingly clear. The dagger protruded from the witch's flesh as gangrenous blood flowed from the great wound. Each of the veneficia's fire imps flashed brightly as they too, were extinguished, leaving only acrid smoke behind. Nall watched as the hideous hag fell forward, retching and gagging before writhing in agony and emitting an ear-piercing wail as she expelled streams of evil gray vomit.

Gasping, the witch cursed Nall and all his kind, promising the wrath of Abaddon and swearing they would meet a fate that would make even an eternity of damnation and hellfire seem like paradise. With a final keening wail, she burst into flames, her black ash carried aloft by the heat, up through the opening of the Well of Viileshga and thence to be lost in the darkening sky.

Alone in the empty lair, Nall took a final look around. Against the wall, he found a shimmering shield of dragon scales, large enough to cover his entire body. As he lifted it, the deep, familiar voice of Ardane reached him from above.

"You will probably want to cover yourself with that, Guardian, for I am about to send down a cleansing fire ripe with Guardian-eating acid."

"Ignore my mate's rudeness," thundered Adra with a voice of authority, "he has much to learn of diplomacy and the art of thanking a hero for his work. Move into the tunnel and hold the shield before you. We will cleanse the Well of the witch's remaining taint."

Nall did as Adra instructed, backing into the narrow passage and using the shield as a barrier against the fiery, acidic dragons' breath. He wondered at the shield's ability to protect him from such a conflagration. It appeared so fragile, the scales so glasslike in their transparency that he could see the flames rushing down from above. When it was safe, Nall continued out of the tunnel the way he had entered, running directly into Ardane as he exited beneath the chale tree.

Ardane's scales rose in threat before lowering in submission. "It is only my mate's desire to keep you as a pet that protects you, Guardian. Without that, you would already have disappeared."

Ardane tossed Nall out of the way with a turn of his head and exhaled his fiery breath into the vacant tunnel.

Nall brushed himself off and returned to the wall of the Well, where he found Hawk waiting as instructed, though his tail feathers were slightly singed and his composure obviously ruffled.

Adra, too, waited near the wall, examining Nall carefully for any damage caused by her obstinate mate or the haruspex. Satisfied that Nall was whole, save for the burns of the imps, Adra offered her gratitude.

"You have shown great strength of will, Guardian. I give you the shield of Viileshga as a symbol of our pledge. Keep it safe, for there is no other like it in all the worlds."

Joining Ardane at the edge of the clearing, Adra called back to Nall, "We will meet again at Meremire for the Ceremony of the Pledges."

"I hope when she says 'we', she means to bring someone else besides Ardane with her," Nall told Hawk.

The Pearl of Perception

Rydén shuddered as she reached the sand at the edge of the Trembling Sea. She hated being alone. The Sailflyte of sea dragons made their home in the ancient caverns of the Sirens, deep below the water's black surface. Just when she thought she had overcome her discomfort in the presence of dragons, the Ancients expected her to find her way to a dragon lair at the bottom of the sea.

"Why couldn't I be pledged to dragons that live on dry land?" Rydén asked.

"Because they don't like you," replied a voice from the water.

A scaly, battle-scarred head surfaced, its remaining eye focused on the waiting Guardian, "I am Eonis, and I am to take you to the caverns where we make our home. Come, Guardian, for I do not wish to leave the sea."

"It just gets better and better," Rydén complained. "Now you expect me to get wet!"

Extending himself to his full height, the sea dragon towered above the water. Rydén was relieved to think that he would at least allow her to mount from the shore but instead of placing his head on the sand, he allowed it to crash back into the sea, drenching her in a wave of cold, salty water.

"Come, Guardian, I do not have time for your whining. Why it is my mother chooses to pledge to *you* I cannot begin to understand." With that, he extended his tail to within a few body lengths of the sand. "Swim!" he shouted over his shoulder, giving off the heavy "shuff, shuff" that was a dragon's laugh.

Wading out, Rydén climbed up onto the tail of Eonis and walked unsteadily along to his shoulders, grasping his streaming sea-green scales.

"You really are beautiful," she found herself saying without thinking.

"Sorry I cannot say the same for you, Guardian, for your naked skin is rather repulsive. It is good you choose to cover most of it. Lean forward and I will cover you with my scales and keep you safe and dry as we descend."

Leaning forward, Rydén watched as the dragon lifted his scales and crossed them over her small form, creating a cocoon of air and dryness for the journey to the depths, for which she was grateful.

As they surfaced within the flyte's great hall, Eonis lowered his scales, freeing Rydén. He lifted his bulk out of the water and onto the soft sand floor of the expansive chamber.

The earth began to tremble violently. A wall came crashing down as two large male dragons rolled in, twisted into a tangle of necks, legs and tails. Jaws snapped and scales rained from their bodies. Rolling into the far wall, they broke apart and stood a few paces from one another, breathing heavily. The weightier of the two then rushed forward, throwing his huge mass against his opponent.

"Boys!" A roll of thunder hit Rydén's ears as Sybeth entered the chamber.

"My apologies, Guardian. They have been told to play outside the lair, but they never seem to remember." Sybeth looked fondly at the two young dragons now hanging their heads sheepishly, glancing sideways at their Matriarch and Mother.

"Go now," she instructed. "Eonis, take them out for a hunt—put some of this energy to good use!"

Eonis turned. "But I had hoped to . . ."

"Not this time, Eonis. Go."

Eonis followed the other two as they dropped into the sea, throwing an angry glance back over his shoulder at his mother and the Guardian.

"You have the talisman I gave you, Guardian?" Sybeth asked.

"Yes, I keep it with me always."

"Eonis says he does not know why you have pledged your flyte to me," Rydén continued.

"Eonis is young and foolish. I pledge you because it is demanded by the Ancient laws, not because I choose it. Do not ever believe I would have chosen you," Sybeth spat. "I would break the law if I could do so without the destruction of my flyte. Unlike the weak wind dragons, or the warm and kind accordants, sea dragons do not wish to be managed by Guardians and Ancients, but it is the law, and breaking the law would only bring doom to my flyte."

"It is required that I give you a quest, thereby binding you to this flyte. Perhaps, if I am lucky, you will perish attempting to accomplish this quest," said Sybeth, glancing slyly at Rydén.

Rydén felt a cold hatred in the pit of her stomach. She would not fail in this quest, no matter how difficult, no matter how long it took. She would return to this beast and make it cower.

"Honor of the Ancients to you and the Sailflyte," Rydén spoke calmly and sweetly, all the while seething. "What is the nature of my quest, Dragon?"

Sybeth lashed her tail, lifting her scales to a position of full threat. She raised her head and glared at Rydén.

"You will recover the Pearl of Perception held in the caverns beneath this flyte. It is guarded by a trybrac, a nasty beast armed with the spell of invisibility and a quiver of arrows tipped in slitherwort poison that he will use to defeat you." Sybeth touched Rydén's chest with a long, sharp talon, pricking her to leave a drop of blood.

Standing her ground, Rydén eyed the drop of blood. "One day, dragon, it is your blood that will be spilt, but today, I will do your bidding. I will return within a fortnight. Do not wait up for me."

She brushed past Sybeth and headed to the rear of the cavern in search of a way to the trybrac below. In her mind, Rydén recited a mantra:

"*I hate dragons. I hate dragons. I really hate dragons.*"

As Rydén entered the passage leading to the trybrac's den, she recalled the lessons she had been taught about the creature. She recalled the words of Weezelwort about its ability to veil, and she vaguely recalled words like hideous, ugly and three-headed, but nothing that was very useful now. Yávië would say Rydén had been brushing her hair during that lesson. Rydén smiled. She had spent much of their lesson time trying to increase her beauty, using the dye from red berries on her lips or the blue of sky flowers on her eyelids. Her smile turned into a frown—she did not like Yávië's teasing, even if it wasn't meant to be cruel. Were she as beautiful as Yávië, she would not have to spend time working at it, Rydén thought peevishly.

The passage split in front of her, one branching to the left and the other going straight ahead.

"If I choose wrong, I will waste a great deal of time," Rydén whispered aloud. "But how can I know?"

"I can tell you," a voice drifted from above her head.

Rydén looked up with a start, but saw nothing.

"Then tell me," demanded Rydén.

"If you want to be more beautiful, I can tell you how." The voice came again.

"Beautiful? Why would you . . .? Oh, you heard my thoughts. Who *are* you?" Rydén insisted. "Right now there are more important things than being beautiful," she continued.

"Are there, Rydén? Are there really?" The voice coaxed.

"Of course there are. I have to go to smite a trybrac. Dragon's orders," Rydén snapped.

"If I help you kill the trybrac and make you more beautiful, will you then help me?" asked the voice of the invisible one.

"How can I help one I cannot see?" Rydén asked, her irritation rising.

"Do you see me now?" said the coy voice behind her.

Rydén whirled, dagger ready, but there was no one there except an ugly old woman.

Laughing, Rydén asked, "How can you help me kill a trybrac? Or be more beautiful? Look at yourself!"

Rydén handed the old woman her polished bronze mirror. The woman held it up and gazed into it. As she did, the lines of age began to disappear, her thin gray hair became lustrous blonde, her slumped shoulders and curved back straightened, and her heavy body thinned and grew firm.

"Looks can be deceiving, Rydén," spoke the beautiful, young woman who now stood before her. "I can teach you to do what I have done. You will be more beautiful each time you seek your reflection in the mirror."

"And what about the trybrac? How will you help me destroy it?"

"Why, I will simply put it to sleep with my beautiful song, for I am Syria, one of the Sirens. Then you may kill it by whatever means you choose. You are seeking the pearl it guards, I imagine."

"Yes, I must return it to the Sailflyte as instructed by the Matriarch, Sybeth." Rydén answered.

"Do not be vexed, young Guardian, for one day you will have your revenge on the old dragon. Are you willing to pledge that you owe me your goodwill in return for the death of the trybrac and ever-growing beauty? Do you promise to help me when I call on you?"

"Just what help will you require when you call on me?"

"I will not know until the time for your help is here. But do not concern yourself; it will not be anything too difficult for a Guardian." The Siren answered in a soothing voice.

Rydén looked very hard at the beautiful woman, recalling the transformation from hag to winsome youth she had effected just by looking into a mirror. Although Rydén knew she was already beautiful and would never grow as old and ugly as this woman, the thought of her beauty becoming greater every time she looked in the mirror was overwhelming. She might eventually become more beautiful than Yávië—the mere thought made her light-headed.

"I will promise you my help. Now let us kill the trybrac."

"A drop of your blood to seal the promise," replied the woman. Quickly grabbing Rydén's hand, she pricked a finger with a thorn. She then placed Rydén's finger in the palm of her hand and, as if it were water being absorbed into a cloth, drew the blood into her skin.

"Now," Syria smiled, "we can kill the trybrac."

Together they moved down the left path, stepping carefully to make no sound. As they reached the trybrac's den, the young woman held up a hand, signaling Rydén to wait.

As Syria entered the den, her voice lifted in a song so pure and passionate that it did indeed lull the trybrac to sleep. Beckoning to Rydén, the Siren stepped aside. Rydén nocked an arrow and let it fly, hitting the sleeping trybrac squarely in the heart. The trybrac gave a low moan, twitched, and lay still.

"It keeps the pearl behind those stones." Syria told Rydén, indicating a group of stones above a high ledge.

Rydén climbed up on the ledge next to the tumble of stones. There indeed lay the precious Pearl of Perception. When her fingers touched it, she realized what she had done, and a look of terror crossed her face.

"I do not want your gift of growing beauty!"

"It is too late for your remorse, Rydén. I have helped you slay the beast and you have sealed the promise with your blood. The gift of growing beauty is yours. If you do not wish it, do not look in the mirror again." As she spoke, her voice began to fade, as would Rydén's memory of the promise. "I will call you when the time has come."

Rydén sat down on the rocky ledge, holding the perfect pearl. "What have I done? By the Ancients, what have I done?"

She rose slowly and climbed down the rocks. There was no sign of the Siren. As Rydén made her way back toward the flyte's lair, she began to believe that the Siren would never call on her.

Rydén marched up to Sybeth with the Pearl of Perception held out before her.

"Is this what you wanted, dragon?"

Sybeth pulled back her head and bared her teeth. "How is it that you live, Guardian?"

"I had the good fortune to catch the beast asleep. It was an easy kill requiring only one arrow to the heart."

"I will keep the pledge. My flyte is yours to command. Place the pearl on that pedestal. Did you learn something useful about yourself when you touched it?" Sybeth asked knowingly.

The memories had faded from Rydén's mind, just as the Siren had intended, and she merely shrugged.

"Go now, Guardian. Eonis will carry you to the surface. Return to Meremire. We will meet there for the Ceremony of the Pledges."

As Rydén reached the beach and turned away from Eonis, she whispered one last time, "I really do hate dragons."

The Heart of Æstretfordæ

As Rydén made her agreement with the Siren, Yávïe wandered the lava flows of a long dead volcano. Her thoughts lingered over her dream about Sōrél and Näeré. Could they truly exist? Or were they just a dream? And what of another world, one never mentioned in their lessons by any of the Ancients?

"I will ask Morg when I return to Meremire. Morgwort will know if there is any truth in it," Yávïe promised herself.

From the top of the hollow mountain, Yávïe began her descent to the realm of the war dragons. She could not imagine what quest they would give her because she had never met a war dragon. She knew that the Matriarch was called Faera, and that her mate was Forebodon. Beyond that she knew nothing aside from the fact that they, like death dragons, were evolved from the fire dragons.

With star set, the long shadows within the caldera grew deep, and with the darkness came Xander, bright-eyed and ready for the night's work. He moved across Yávïe's arm and up to her shoulder for a better view of the surrounding area. Yávïe handed him a prickleberry, which he took gently and began to eat, sitting on his tiny haunches, his fluffy, black-tipped tail wrapped around him against the cool air.

"What shall I do, Mistress?" his small voice asked.

"Just be alert while searching for your dinner," Yávïe suggested. "I will spend the night in the cavern below us. Meet me there when the daystar rises."

Xander gave his Mistress a rub beneath her chin before scampering off in search of sweet-sap and butterpillars around the rim of the caldera.

Yávië made her way down to the small cavern. It was littered with the bones and teeth of some beast's prey, but they were old and she sensed no threat in the vicinity. The hike through the volcanic ash and along the sharp rocks on the steep sides of the mountain had taken their toll. She was exhausted and quickly fell into a deep and dreamless sleep.

The sound of a furious downy flier jolted Yávië awake. Opening her eyes, she saw Xander suspended between two large talons attached to a very large dragon covered in black and scarlet scales.

"Does this belong to you?" the unperturbed dragon asked, blowing a small puff of breath at Xander, causing him to swing. The small flier howled and chattered his anger and dismay.

"He belongs only to himself, but he does travel with me. His name is Xander."

The dragon peered closely at the downy flier, causing another bout of fussing and yowling.

"I found it in the litter of my last meal, scooping up butterpillars and eating every one."

"Ah, yes, he really does like butterpillars," Yávië laughed, receiving a scowl from the still captive Xander.

"Not funny," Xander hissed, "not funny at all!"

"I believe he would like to be released now," Yávië explained. "He does not like being confined."

The dragon placed Xander on the floor then opened her other claw and deposited a number of butterpillars next to him.

Xander grabbed a 'pillar and ran to sit on Yávië's knee, looking over his shoulder and barking at the dragon.

"Very brave for such a small creature," the dragon complimented before continuing in her matter-of-fact manner. "You are Yávië, Guardian of Æstretfordæ. You have come to complete a quest for the Kilstoneflyte. It is a difficult one, I fear, but we have been told that you will accomplish it."

"Beneath us lie this dormant mountain's magma chambers. The flyte lives in those abandoned by the molten rock. Long ago, when we first arrived here, we found an ancient mold. It is for a magma sword. Your quest will take you deep into the core of Æstretfordæ. You must fill this cold stone with magma to recreate the sword. The cold stone will open when you reach the magma, drawing in the amount required. Will you accept this quest, Guardian?" the dragon asked.

"I accept," Yávië nodded. "Honor and glory of the Ancients to you and your flyte, Faera."

"You know me, Guardian?"

"I do. Brundlewort described your beauty well."

Faera threw back her head and roared a dragon's laugh. "Did he now?" she asked. "I will have to thank him when I next visit Meremire.

"In the cavern to our right you will find the path to the magma. Return to the flyte chambers when you have filled the cold stone."

Yávië watched as the magnificent Matriarch slipped away, and then examined the cold stone. It was oval and rough, almost icy to the touch. There was no break in its surface, nor any lock or key: a very magick stone for a very special sword. Yávië wondered what need dragons would have for such a weapon. She slipped the cold stone into her satchel for safekeeping. As she gathered her belongings, she found that Faera had left a gift. It was a cloak of dragon scales, hooded and long enough to touch the floor of the cavern when she put it on. The intricately woven pattern mimicked Faera's scales.

She smiled at Xander. "I think you had best stay here with the butterpillars."

Yávië headed out of the cavern down the path to the magma. The circular passageway was low, making it difficult to walk and causing her to stoop as she tried to keep her footing. For many millenniums, molten rock had flowed through these tubes, lifting the earth here and dropping it there. As Yávië moved closer to the magma, the heat became intense, leaving her covered in a sweaty sheen. Finally, she drew out the cloak and placed it around her shoulders, covering her hair with the scaly hood. It was as if she had stepped into a cool pool. The scales created a protective layer of cool air between Yávië and the outside temperature, making her even more grateful for Faera's beautiful gift.

A slow, grinding noise was coming from within her satchel. The cold stone had opened, leaving a long hollow groove along its length.

"I must be getting close," Yávië whispered. "Or at least the stone believes I am."

The grade had become much steeper and, as Yávië looked ahead, she could see molten stone lapping against the far end of the tunnel. Approaching as close as she dared, Yávië removed the cold stone from her pouch and placed it on the floor with the groove pointing toward the chamber now flooded with magma. She watched in wonder as the stone pulled the magma forward and into its hollow core. Once full, the stone closed around the magma with the same grinding sound she had heard before. Reaching out, she touched the stone with the tips of her fingers. Its surface was still as cool to the touch as it had been when it was empty. Yávië picked it up and placed it back in her satchel.

The uphill return climb was more difficult and by the time she reached the cavern where Xander waited, she was flushed with exhaustion.

"We will rest here tonight and make our way to the Kilstoneflyte at first light. Try not to get into trouble tonight, little one," Yávië chided Xander.

"I stay tonight. Plenty butterpillars left. Her dragoness brought more," Xander said, showing his delight with a chirp and a bark.

"Very well, but wake me early," Yávië yawned and her weary eyes fluttered before closing.

Xander woke his Mistress early as requested, his tiny tongue washing the sleep from her eyes and the dust from her cheeks. As Yávië raised her head, he tried to squeeze inside her tunic, ready for his daydreams.

"Nay, little butterpillar eater, since you have already visited the dragon flyte, you can lead me there before you take your sleep." Yávië scratched him fondly beneath his chin.

Xander closed one eye and looked at her with his ears pricked and his head cocked. "Maybe I forgot," he teased.

"Forget the location of those tasty butterpillars? I don't think that is very likely. Come on, lead off. The sooner we arrive, the sooner you will be sleeping."

Deciding Yávië spoke the truth, Xander raced off ahead of her, looking back occasionally to make sure she wasn't lost.

As they entered the first of the flyte's chambers, Xander jumped onto her arm and ducked into his daytime bed next to her heart.

"Sleep well," Yávië whispered to his disappearing tail.

"Guardian!" boomed a dragon's voice. "Do you bring the melted stone for the magma sword's mold?"

"I do, Faera," Yávië replied, carefully unfolding the dragon-scale cape from around the cold stone. "Thank you for the use of your beautiful cape. It kept me comfortable in the deep heat of Æstretfordæ's center."

"Come, bring the stone, Yávië," growled Faera, "you have earned the right to watch the magick."

Yávië followed Faera deep into the lair to a chamber containing an altar. On the altar, the long mold lay open, awaiting the contents of the cold stone.

"Pour the stone into the mold. Forebodon will place the cover on the mold when you are ready." Faera instructed.

Yávië stepped forward and the cold stone slid open, exposing the red-hot stone. With great care, she poured the fiery contents. As she stepped back, Forebodon lifted the heavy lid and placed it over the magma-filled mold. A flash of light erupted from above the altar, followed by a deep, rolling thunder. The mold shattered, leaving only small particles of dust and rock. Upon the altar lay a sword, its blade a deep flaming red, and its hilt as black as ash. The hilt pulsed and bubbled for a moment before settling into the shape of an elegant dragon, the very image of Faera.

"Behold the Sacred Sword of Domesius!" Faera bellowed. "Hidden from the world for ten thousand lifetimes, it lives again."

Instinctively, Yávië moved toward the sword. Her hand reached forward but was stayed by Forebodon's voice.

"Nay, Guardian, the time has not come. By the Prophecy, the sword must remain upon the altar until its calling. Besides, it is hot and will burn your hand," he added, coughing back a laugh.

"Do not let the Ancients hear your disrespect, Mate. They will take the sword's renewal very seriously." Faera cautioned Forebodon.

Faera turned to Yávië. "Take the butterpillar eater and return to Meremire. Your quests are done, and our son, Norgol, waits to carry you home. Blessings of the Ancients on you and the small one until we meet again."

Smiling down at her sleeping downy flier, Yávië accepted the butterpillars Faera offered for the long journey home.

"Thank you, Matriarch. Honor and glory of the Ancients to you and the Kilstoneflyte. We will meet soon at Meremire."

Norgol extended his neck, allowing the Guardian to mount, then, with a single stroke of his giant wings they were airborne, turning toward Meremire and the Lake of Lost Memories. Yávië hoped she would arrive in time to cleanse her memories before seeing Nall again.

Beneath the Frozen Throne

Nall was grateful for the warm coat Morgwort had given him. At the time, he had thought the coat foolish, but that reaction had been in Meremire when it was warm and humid. Here on the Halcyon Ice Fields, in the midst of glaciers and snow-covered mountains, it was welcome indeed.

Hawk flew far afield, searching for some indication of a dragon flyte or clue as to the nature of the quest for the ice dragons. So far, the only visible living things were a small flyte of death dragons and some klenzingkytes circling in the distance over the carcass of some unfortunate. Nall had no desire to attract the attention of either.

"Listen for the dragons' call, Hawk; that is what Willowort said. If they are calling, I have not heard them."

Directly ahead lay a massive expanse of ice, one of many glaciers slowly sliding toward Æstretfordæ's distant ocean. Great caution was required to navigate the ice. It was littered with deep melt pools of turquoise water and hidden fissures that could swallow a Guardian, leaving him trapped and helpless. As Nall advanced across the glacier, he heard its creaks and groans, and the sharp reports of splinters and sudden fractures. It was disconcerting to be walking on something that seemed so alive with sound and motion.

Hawk's alarm caught Nall's attention and he quickly scanned the horizon for a sign of the bird. He saw a flicker of movement on a distant icy escarpment, a shimmering, as though heat were rising from the ice. Nall decided this was highly unlikely, and that the moving air ahead was probably some being with the ability to veil itself. He remembered warnings of ice beasts that, due to the crystal structure of the white hairs covering their bodies, could remain invisible. In truth, however, not many creatures lived in the frozen south.

Arming himself with his dragon scale shield and dagger, Nall continued across the icy expanse, testing each step before committing his weight. As he drew closer, he realized that the heat of a small campfire caused the shimmering, though there did not seem to be anyone nearby.

Hawk dove in, landing on a small hillock of snow, and peered watchfully in all directions.

"I see no danger, Hawk, nor do I sense any, but the fire could not have maintained itself. There must be someone about."

Hoping to warm his freezing hands, Nall stepped toward the fire. As he neared where its light played upon the snow, he heard the sound of ice splintering—the instant before plunging through the melted snow into a deep chasm. Tumbling through the darkness, Nall clutched his shield to his chest to avoid losing it in the headlong drop. Finally, he came to a bone-jarring halt on a narrow ledge far below the surface. The shield had absorbed most of the shock, leaving him bruised and aching, but without the handicap of broken bones.

Across the abyss, Nall saw a dark opening against the whiteness of the ice. Gingerly, he worked his way along the ledge toward an area narrow enough to make a crossing. Tossing the shield ahead of him, he leapt the short distance, landing several body lengths from the low opening. Nall collected the shield and placed the heavy dragon skin strap over his head and across his chest, allowing the shield to rest against his back. He could hear Hawk's cries far above, seeking some sign from his Master. Closing his eyes, Nall sent Hawk a comforting thought and an instruction to wait on the ice cliffs overlooking the hole.

Nall dropped to his belly and peered into the darkness beyond the small opening, but could see only blackness. He reached into his satchel and withdrew a short torch of tarred grass, lighting it with his striking stone. Once the small blaze caught and steadied, he pushed the torch ahead of him through the narrow channel in the ice. Nall began to hear the sound of dripping water as he crawled along. He thought it seemed odd that ice would be melting so deep within the glacier.

At the end of the tunnel, the ice opened up into a small cavity, providing him with sufficient space to stand up. Nall passed his torch over the walls looking for another exit, but could see none. However, there did appear to be something sealed within one of the icy walls. Holding the torch nearer, he gazed at the apparition. It seemed to be a chair of some sort, and it contained an occupant.

Nall began to chip away at the wall with his dagger, using the torch to melt away sections as he broke through the slab of ice. With a final tap of the blade, he entered the chamber. It was a dragon, seated on a throne, but it was not like any of the dragons he had seen dwelling on the surface of Æstretfordæ. Though it was definitely a dragon, it was much smaller than those he had encountered. Upright it would not have stood much above Nall's own height. The elongated head ended in twin horns at the tip near the nostrils, and leant against the side of the throne as if merely resting there, eyes closed as though slumbering. There was no condensation in the air, indicating that it was long dead. The skin was fine, covered in tight scales, and the small wings were folded neatly against its back. In life, with warm blood flowing through its veins, it had probably been blue but here, upon this frozen throne, it appeared washed out and almost white.

Nall saw no injury. There were no weapons in this chamber, merely an ancient dragon ancestor in its final sleep. Nall could see the dragon's heart shard still within its chest. No one had come to claim it, the Guardian thought sadly.

As Nall moved the torch nearer the dragon, a light flashed between its eyes. A gemstone rested there, just visible through a light frosting of ice crystal. The stone was clear, like a perfect piece of lightning glass cut by an expert gem cutter in the distant past. Nall reached forward and touched the dazzling jewel. It caught the torchlight and sent it dancing over the ice.

A tremor ran through the ice cave causing small shards to fall from the ceiling and walls. Nall watched as the dragon's heart shard began to cast a warm glow. It swelled with light and began to pulse its slow rhythm. The ancient dragon opened its eyes and stared knowingly at Nall.

"You have come to end my captivity," spoke a soft voice to his soul. "I have lain here for an eternity awaiting you, Guardian. Will you take my heart shard and keep it safe until the time you return it to the Tree of Creation? My kind moved on long ago, leaving me alone."

"But my quest is for the ice dragons." Nall was confused.

"Aye, Guardian, I am an ice dragon from the time most ancient, a time before the Prophecy was written, a time before your beginning. What you do for me you also do for those who follow, for the IIzenflyte, rulers of this day's ice."

"Dragon, I will keep your shard safe, and return it to the ground beneath the Tree of Creation." Nall promised.

As Nall cast the spell to release the shard, the icy dragon had begun to melt, the warmth of his heart shard liquefying the frozen flesh. The chamber filled with the icy mist of ancient breath as the melting dragon formed a small pool in the corner of the cavern. Flowing upward through a small crevice, the dragon headed skyward, leaving a pulsing crystal heart shard on the ice below the throne.

Nall lifted the crystal, and silently wished the ancient traveler safe journey before heading up the stairway and toward his home in Meremire.

Chapter 5: Ceremony of the Pledges

Upon her arrival at Meremire, Yávië went directly to the Lake of Lost Memories. She was sure that Nall and Rydén had arrived earlier for she felt their pull, and she knew that she must not see Nall again until she had given her desires to the lake for safekeeping.

Yávië knelt on the sandy bank and dug a hole with her fingertips, stopping when it was just slightly larger than her hand. She then placed her hand within the hole, palm up and fingers extended toward the lake, allowing the warmth she felt for Nall to fill her heart one last time.

The lake sent small fingers of its magick water toward Yávië's fingertips and she felt an overwhelming urge to jerk her hand away, but she left it there for the water to claim. She closed her eyes and listened to the whispered secrets of the lake as the memory of her intense feelings was shed.

Yávië stood, wiping her hand dry on the soft fabric of her riding skirt and wondered why she had been weeping. Turning, she headed toward Meremire and her friends.

It was in a field of crimson grass and vivid summer flowers adjacent to the Trembling Sea that Rydén, Nall, Yávië and the Ancients met with the dragons that had come to pledge the Guardians. The noise was thunderous as the dragons arrived and settled themselves at the edge of the field and along the seashore. Only those of the Sailflyte remained within the water. It was thrilling to see them arrive, wind, water, earth and fire dragons side by side, jostling almost good-naturedly for the position they considered most advantageous.

The Ancients were scrubbed and clean and wore their finest clothing, sewn by Willowort for the occasion. Willow and Rosewort wore wreaths of summer flowers on their heads. Looking solemn and a bit nervous, each Guardian wore a scarlet robe and carried a Staff of Souls.

While Yávië wondered whom Azaeria would bring in the place of her slain mate, Rydén silently hoped Sybeth would not simply step forward and tear her to ribbons. For Nall, the ancient ice dragon's heart shard weighed heavily and he wished there had been time to take it to the Tree of Creation before the ceremony.

Silence fell as Willowort stood, and all eyes turned to her for guidance.

"I bears a heavy burden: the burden of all the Prophecies of Æstretfordæ and the ages before. I bears the Prophecies of the Sojourner Alandon, the Ancients, of Guardians and Men, and the Prophecies of the dragons. While every prophecy comes to pass, no ends is ever written. Each plays a part and each has choices they make. Remember this when you is called.

"Dragon flytes is come today to acknowledge pledges to the Guardians they've chose. The bonds made on this field today is eternal. Not only is the Matriarch bonded, but the whole flyte from this day forward is pledged to the Guardian they choose.

"Guardians is bonded to the honor and glory of the flyte. A betrayal by one is a betrayal by all; to betray one flyte is to betray all flytes. Do not let a seed of betrayal grow.

"The blood you sheds today won't never dry and blow away as dust. It will remains here on this field, fresh and wet, as a reminder of the dragon pledges to any who may sees it."

At the word 'blood', Rydén paled; they were going to let Sybeth shed her blood?

"Kilstoneflyte, Emeraldflyte, Sailflyte, IIzenflyte, Suunflyte—send forth your Matriarchs." Willowort's voice rang out clear and true.

Wings opened and closed, the earth shook, and the dragons came forward, forming a circle around the Guardians. Sybeth, on the seaside, remained within the surf.

"Azaeria, Queen of all Æstretfordæ's wind dragons, name your pledge."

Her deep voice boomed across the field. "I, as leader of the Suunflyte, pledge my oath and the oath of my flyte to the Guardian Yávië. She has fulfilled our quest by returning to safety within the flyte's chambers the heart shard of Aerodorn, my mate. She gives her blood freely to the Suunflyte by her acceptance of the quest, and by her blood oath gives the blood of the one called Nall as well."

Taking a deep breath, Yávië stepped forward and allowed the stately Matriarch to pierce her wrist with a razor sharp talon, letting the blood flow freely into the Urn of Pledges.

"IIvaria, Queen of all Æstretfordæ's ice dragons, name your pledge."

"I, as leader of the IIzenflyte, pledge my oath and the oath of my flyte to the Guardian Nall. He has fulfilled our quest by the release of the ancient ice dragon trapped beneath the Halcyon Ice Fields. He has promised to return the ancient dragon's heart shard to the Tree of Creation following this ceremony. He gives his blood freely to the IIzenflyte by his acceptance of the quest, and by his blood oath gives the blood of the one called Yávië as well."

Standing tall, Nall strode to IIvaria, offering her his arm. She speared his wrist, allowing blood to flow into the Urn of Pledges.

"Sybeth, Queen of all Æstretfordæ's sea dragons, name your pledge."

"I, as leader of the Sailflyte, as required by the law, pledge my oath and the oath of my flyte to the Guardian Rydén. She has fulfilled our quest by returning the Pearl of Perception to its resting place within my chambers. She gives her blood freely by her acceptance of the quest."

Grimacing, Rydén stepped toward Sybeth. Sybeth grasped Rydén's arm, causing her to cry out, piercing it and allowing the blood to pour into the Urn of Pledges. Under her breath Sybeth whispered, "You are ours, traitor."

"No, dragon, you and your flyte are *mine!*" Jerking her arm back, Rydén turned her back on Sybeth, causing a collective intake of breath from dragons and Ancients alike.

Morgwort mumbled under his breath, "No good can comes of this, no good at all."

Willowort quickly regained her composure and announced the next pledge.

"Adra, Queen of all Æstretfordæ's accordant dragons, name your pledge."

Staring scornfully at the sea dragon Sybeth before stepping forward, Adra proclaimed, "I, as leader of the Emeraldflyte, pledge my oath and the oath of my flyte to the Guardian Nall. He has fulfilled our quest by the killing of the witch who tainted the Well of Viileshga, allowing Ardane and I to cleanse it, restoring the flow of Æstretfordæ's life-force. He gives his blood freely by his acceptance of the quest, and by his blood oath gives the blood of the one called Yávië as well."

Once again, Nall stepped forward, allowing his blood to be spilled into the Urn of Pledges.

"Faera, Queen of all Æstretfordæ's war dragons, name your pledge."

Faera, the most beautiful of all flyte Matriarchs, stepped into the center of the circle and approached Yávië.

"I, as leader of the Kilstoneflyte, pledge my oath and the oath of my flyte to the Guardian Yávië. She has fulfilled our quest by bringing forth the molten stone from Æstretfordæ's center. She has fulfilled a tale of lore, as written in the Kilstoneflyte's history, by allowing the Sword of Domesius to serve again. Be it known that from this day and according to our law, I give this symbol of the Kilstoneflyte to our new Huntress. May it serve her well in seeking honor and glory for the dragon flytes of Æstretfordæ. She gives her blood freely by the acceptance of the quest, and by her blood oath gives the blood of the one called Nall as well."

Holding the Sword of Domesius in her left hand, Yávië offered her right wrist to Faera, allowing her blood to flow into the Urn of Pledges for the final time.

Willowort came forward and lifted the Urn of Pledges above her head as she bestowed upon it and all it served the Blessings of the Ancients. She carried it before each Matriarch, allowing them to dip a talon into the blood and apply it to their foreheads. Then she turned and threw the ancient stone bowl onto the rocks of the field, where it shattered and spilled the blood for all to see.

"Guardians, step forward that I may introduce the new Hunter and Huntresses to the dragon flytes of Æstretfordæ."

With a great cacophony of bellowing and wing flapping, the dragons gave their approval, all save Sybeth who had slipped unseen beneath the sea before the casting of the blood.

That evening as they relaxed, exhausted from the ordeal, the Guardians spoke of Sybeth's behavior, asking Rydén what had caused the great sea dragon's reaction.

"She has not liked me from the day we met. She only pledged me to uphold the law and save her flyte from doom—at least that is what she told me. I don't care. I really don't like her either. We will do what needs to be done, but we will never be more than wary enemies. I fulfilled her quest—that is all that really matters, isn't it?"

The Dance of the Damned

Beyond the sight of Guardians and Ancients, dragons gathered in great numbers. The dragons of destruction, discontented by the decree of the Ancients and the law that bound the dragons of Æstretfordæ, had been summoned by a dragon of the sea—a dragon bound by law to the Guardians and the Ancients but a dragon about to break a pledge bond, something that had never been done before.

Sybeth watched the gathering of those willing to break the law of Æstretfordæ—the doomsday dragons. She weighed her chances of victory against the four dragon flytes that still felt honor-bound by acceptance and completion of quests and the spilling of blood. In her opinion, they were all fools.

The mistral dragons had passed their test. They had attacked and killed Azaeria's mate, Aerodorn, without a second thought. It had been done swiftly and at Sybeth's request. Now she would test the strength of the death dragons, Dahrea and Dielmor. They were covered in the filth of rotten meals, their stench nearly unbearable. Even with the breeze, their foul odor hung over the sea.

Sybeth addressed the gathered dragons:

"Dragons of Æstretfordæ, are we so weak that we allow ourselves to be dictated to by frail Ancients and foolish Guardians? *No!* I say we are *not!* Mohrica and Maeldroce of the Kaosflyte struck the first blow with the killing of the wind dragon Aerodorn. Now it is time to strike a swift second blow. I call on you, Dahrea and Dielmor, to cripple the Emeraldflyte by dispatching their Matriarch. Adra's mate is known for his stupidity and his undisguised hatred of the Guardian Nall. He will be quick to hold the Guardian responsible. We will plant a seed of guilt in Nall. Even he will believe he has failed Adra! We will weaken both the Emeraldflyte and the Guardians by our success.

"The new Hunter will be looking forward to his first flight with Adra. Because of Ardane's rudeness, she will choose to fly alone, giving you the opportunity to drive her from the sky and kill her."

"We are willing to kill Adra, Sybeth, but what part will you play in this game?" Dielmor asked.

"For now I must look innocent. I must play to the new Huntress Rydén until I win her trust. Then we will attack the four remaining flytes and their foolish Guardians. We will cleanse Æstretfordæ of all but dragon-kind. Then *we* will write the law." Sybeth answered.

"We will watch from the hidden safety of the Northern Mountains, allowing the klenzingkytes to call us once they spot Adra in flight. We will take Adra and her Hunter at the first opportunity," Dahrea promised, with the glittering light of hatred in her eyes. "There should be no life for dragon-kind who swear bonds with the likes of Guardians and Ancients."

While both Rydén and Yávië had already experienced a dragon flight, Nall had not and spent the night in restless anticipation of his inaugural journeys with Adra and Ilvaria. Each would take him to the flyte's chambers and introduce him formally to the flyte members. He knew that Adra had come alone, leaving Ardane behind because of his intense dislike for Nall. Perhaps it was just his manner to be rude and hateful and it truly had nothing to do with Nall personally. If that were true, there might be some hope of mutual respect in the future. Adra seemed to believe it. She had said Nall would be able to gain Ardane's respect. When he finally fell asleep, Nall's dreams were filled with flytes of dragons.

"Nall!" Rydén called, seeing her brother's morning rush from his bothie. "Where are you off to in such a hurry?"

"I am meeting Adra this morning. Going to the Emeraldflyte. How about you? Are you off to visit Sybeth?" Nall shouted back.

"Never, unless it is specifically decreed by Willowort." Rydén laughed.

Nall smiled and waved, wondering what it was Rydén disliked so much about dragons.

His breath caught at the sight of Adra resting in the field. She seemed so at ease, so unconcerned with the business of the Matriarchy. Seeing Nall approach Adra rose to her full height, a towering mass of elegant beauty. Her scales caught the early rays of the daystar and shimmered green and yellow.

"Come, Hunter, you sleep too much. Let us be about the business of the Emeraldflyte." Adra lowered her great head and neck, allowing him to jump lightly to her withers as if he had been born to it. Then, with a giant wing stroke, she lifted them into the glorious morning air and circled once around Meremire, allowing him to wave to Rydén far below.

"We will cross over the Wastelands before heading north," Adra advised. "I saw a flight of klenzingkytes there and I wondered what poor beast they are waiting to devour. No death dragons were present with them, so there should be no call for confrontation. I would not wish ugliness to ruin our first flight."

Only half listening, Nall scanned the valleys and hills below. It was amazing to see Æstretfordæ's beauty from high above. How could a day be more perfect?

Their first strike came from above and behind, two heavy-bodied death dragons plummeted with folded wings, slamming into Adra like an arrow into the heart of a simplestag, tearing her wings with their talons and tossing Nall from her back.

Unable to grasp what had happened, he made an unsuccessful attempt to slow his fall by flailing his arms. Recollecting his last headlong fall into the icy crevasse, Nall suddenly remembered the dragon scale shield he carried on his back and, grasping it tightly, pulled it over his head.

Adra fought for her life. She struck out with sharp talons, gouging a deep wound in Dahrea's thigh. She stretched out her neck and snapped her jaws down on Dielmor's wing as he swept past a second time, but Dahrea took advantage of Adra's extended neck and crushed the vertebrae, leaving her helpless. Dahrea and Dielmor watched Adra fall like a stone to the earth below, clearly broken and beaten, before flying away to lick their own wounds.

Nall was not as fortunate as he had been in his fall into the ice cavern. He landed with one leg twisted beneath him, hearing the bone break as he slammed into the ground. Though not terminal, it was extremely painful. As he raised himself to a sitting position, he heard the sound of an exploding forge somewhere behind him. Turning, he saw the torn and bleeding body of Adra.

He crawled to her side.

"Adra, what can I do? Tell me! I will do it!"

There was no response from the Matriarch, no last breath, no shudder of life. She had gone without a good-bye. Nall collapsed in pain and sorrow, wracked by the guilt of knowing that if he had just gone with Ilvaria today, Adra would still live, safe at the Emeraldflyte. If only he had been less euphoric. If only he had recognized the danger in a flock of klenzingkyte with no sign of death dragons. If only he had known that there are *always* death dragons with them. If only . . .

"*When a dragon dies, someone must take responsibility for its heart shard, otherwise the dragon remains trapped upon the earth with no hope for the soul's release. If you ever come upon a dying dragon, speak the words of the spell to free the shard and carry it to the safety of the flyte.*"

The words of the lesson flooded back to Nall and he spoke the words of the spell and began searching for Adra's shard. Already her body was turning into the soft dust that would blow it to the four winds, leaving the shard behind. There it was, emerald green and pulsing steadily. Nall lifted it to his heart and wept uncontrollably, washing the heart shard with his tears.

"*Nall,*" he heard Adra's soul whisper, "*do not weep. I go to hold a place among the stars for Ardane. Do not allow his anger to defile you. A day will come when he will understand. Until that day, I will remain with you.*"

The sound of rushing air startled him and then he heard the sweet voice of reason.

"Nall!" Even when she was screaming, her voice still gave him comfort.

Yávië dropped to his side. "Azaeria saw Adra fall! What happened? Are you hurt?"

Too sorrowful to waste energy responding, Nall simply said, "Death dragons, I smelled them."

Seeing his twisted leg, Yávië placed her healing hands upon him, taking the pain and repairing the broken bone. She knew his sorrow was too great, and that she could not take it from him; only Willowort, or revenge, could comfort a sorrow so deep.

"Come," Yávië urged, "we ride to Meremire. We must tell Willow and the others of the attack."

Helping Nall onto Azaeria's broad back, Yávië whispered a blessing for Adra's soul and gently touched the heart shard in Nall's hands.

Nall looked down at her. "My fault," he said. "I should have known."

"Nay, Nall, it is the fault of those who dealt her death. Together we will hunt them down, but first we must go to Meremire."

The Price of Solitude and Sorrow

Adra's death and Ardane's wrath had left Nall trapped within his sorrow. He would not allow Willow to take it from him and would not give it up to the Lake of Lost Memories. He could not give it to Adra as he had given his memories of desire for a life with Yávië. The pain would make him stronger—pain always did. At night, Nall slept a dreamless sleep with Adra's heart shard clutched against his own. His dreamless sleep was a gift from Adra, even though he did not realize it then.

Nall heard the calls of the dragons of the IIzenflyte, and he heard Rydén and Yávië call to him, but he wanted no part of it. He wanted solitude and revenge, a revenge forbidden by the Ancients. *Why?* They would not answer; they only spoke of finding the guilty. He *knew* who was guilty—their stench still haunted him.

Finally, Nall left Meremire, his friends, and the wisdom of the Ancients. He also left the dragon calls and headed deep into the Wastelands. Hidden from the world in a room created by age and time, Nall sat like a stone in a chamber of black crystal so smooth it appeared like lightning glass.

As immobile as if he were a part of the cavern, Nall's eyes were closed as he sat cross-legged, frozen in time. His chest was bare, save for the age-old designs of the art of sorrow along the right side, over ribs and continuing along his right arm to his wrist.

Nall slowly drew back his eyelids to reveal deep amber pools of golden light, staring into the darkness at three, small pools of molten stone. The stone heaved and rolled as if it were alive, waiting to be called.

The golden glow within Nall's eyes intensified, lighting the room so brightly that shadows were cast on the walls and floor. He sat within a circle, a line of ancient symbols radiating out to each of the molten pools. From each pool, the path of symbols climbed the walls, meeting at the top of the domelike cavern.

The symbols began to glow red-hot and, as if called by their master, the pools sent forth tendrils of molten stone along the lines of symbols to the very pinnacle of the dome. The stone began to roil and ripple and quiver and change within the pools, finally rising up from the depths like a long arm reaching skyward. A perfect sphere rested at the tip of each molten arm.

As the molten arms receded, the spheres remained above the pools, their surfaces rippling like waves on the shore of the Azure Sea. Then the surfaces calmed, becoming as smooth and glasslike as the walls of the cavern and reflecting the flickering world around them. As Nall continued the incantations of the Ancients, the spheres began to change again, forming intricate lines along the smooth surfaces with ancient symbols appearing within the lines. Only the powerful magick of the Ancients could bring forth such symbols. Nall had grown powerful, strengthened by his pain.

"Nall? Are you there?"

Rydén's crystalline voice shot through his mind, disrupting his concentration. The spheres began to lose density as he fought to control them.

"Nall?"

Her voice came again, and Nall's head drew back as he let out a bellow of anger that shook the walls of his cave. As the spheres pulsed and shimmered, threatening to return to the earth, he gave one last incantation to pull them from the pools into his lap, where they lay immobile. Together with the dried root of a verdant tree he had discovered in the cavern, he placed them in the satchel at his side and stood up.

"Nall! Your presence is required by the Council. Please answer me! I know you are locked beneath these stones."

"Rydén, I am not locked within the stones. You are locked outside the stones. It is as I wish it. I have no use for the Council."

"Nall, please. We need your help. A plague of darkness has seized Æstretfordæ. The dark dragons scorch the land and terrorize Meremire. Please come. Yávië and I need you. You are bound by a blood oath to her. Will you let her fight alone?"

Yávië. In all his days in the darkness, Nall had not spoken her name. He had neither called to her nor allowed her probing thoughts inside his head. He knew she sought him; he heard her calls, but shut them out. Outwardly, these were signs of a blood oath betrayed, but he knew they were not. His sorrow and pain were meant for him alone; he could not burden Yávië with them. His only contact had been with the Ancients' magick within this cave, and he had pulled it deep within himself, using his anger and pain to focus on the magick. He was acquiring knowledge for the day when he would seek justice for Adra.

Nall sat silent, wishing Rydén away.

"Nall, I will not go away. I have sworn an oath to bring you to the Council. I am no longer weak, and I am no longer a child. I will drag you from your chamber if you do not come willingly."

With a flash of angry energy, Nall burst from the cavern to stand before his sibling.

"Is it your family obligation to annoy me? I told Willow and the Council that I would return when I felt my work was done. What can possibly be so urgent that you feel the need to threaten me?"

"Look around you, Nall! While you locked yourself away in your pool of self-pity Æstretfordæ has been torn and blackened by the very dragons you detest. Our dragon flytes are attacked at every turn, and the Ancients now hide beneath the earth for safety. The death dragons are actively hunting us, and Ardane has withdrawn his support, taking your seclusion as a sign of guilt and shame. Sybeth has moved her flyte, and we have not seen a sea dragon in an age. What should I have done? Allowed Æstretfordæ to fall because you are filled with sorrow and anger? No, I will not do that. I will not betray Yávië, even if you choose to do so," Rydén snarled.

At last Nall looked up. The sky was faded and gray, the daystar clouded by the drifting black soot of dragons' breath. In his mind he could see the smoldering remains of Meremire. Great storms raged above the Crimson Fields and the Northern Mountains. The Halcyon Ice Fields were impenetrable, assaulted by fierce blizzards brought on by the mistral dragons.

His eyes returned to Rydén.

"Have you brought a mount?"

Nall and Rydén rode ahead of the raging storms, flying low to remain undetected. Their arrival at Meremire was grim. The Ancients crept from beneath the ground, their faces tear-stained. Yávië had gone to beg the help of Ardane, but she had not returned, nor had her young dragon mount, Aero of the wind dragons.

Beneath the earth, the Council convened. Willowort described the years of Nall's absence: Ardane's anger, Rydén's growing strength and wisdom, and Yávië's power as a warrior and sorceress. Willow's eyes grew moist again as she told of the dragons' attack on Meremire: death, mistral and animus dragons sending great wind storms to destroy the bothies; the mental assault of the animus dragons leaving Guardians and Ancients clutching their heads in pain.

The Tree of Creation was scorched and withered. If the dragons were not stopped, Æstretfordæ would soon return to the inhospitable, barren wasteland it was in the time before remembering.

Willowort paused in her tale and looked solemnly at each of them. "It is time to calls on the Guardians of Æshardæ."

As the Ancients nodded in agreement, Nall and Rydén looked at one another in bewilderment. There were other Guardians? There was another world? Why had they never been told?

"I see that you wonders why we did not tells you," Rosie spoke. "There was no way to tell, no foretelling of the dragons' hatred. Æshardæ is a mirror world—the same, but not the same, protected as we is by its Guardians. Two is strong and one is young and not too learned. In times of deep troubles the worlds calls upon each other for strength. Deep beneath Meremire is the door, the ancient mirror between our two worlds."

"Like you two," Willow added, "Sōrél and Näeré is siblings from the first life, but they is twins—one male, one female—still, alike as two berries on the prickleberry bush. Sōrél is very powerful and wields the Bow of Ages; Näeré is a sorceress and casts spells of the mind. She can drop a dragon from mid-flight. They should compliments you very well."

And so the Guardians of Æshardæ were called and passed through the ancient mirror into the world of Æstretfordæ.

Rydén stood stunned by the beauty of Sōrél and Näeré. Willow had said they were twins, alike save for their gender, but it seemed impossible that two could look so alike, yet so different. Both had dark hair, almost black and amazing sapphire eyes—deep wells with the spark of goodness shining clearly within—framed by luxurious lashes. Their auras implied great strength and power, and pulsed more brightly than did either her own or Nall's. When they smiled, they lit up the underground chamber with their guilelessness and purity. Like Nall, Yávië and Rydén, their physical strength was evident in their well-defined musculature and ease of movement, as they strode with graceful vigor from beneath the earth of Æstretfordæ.

"Our Ancients honor you and your request, Willowort. Rosewort, Grumblton sends special regards to you, and wishes to share new healing methods when next you meet."

Sōrél addressed Nall and Rydén. "It is my understanding that a Guardian is lost. The one with whom you share a blood oath, Nall. You did not answer her call. She went to seek assistance from your dragon flyte and she will have met with whatever anger they feel for you. While I do not know the details of your Matriarch's fall, I do know that there is bad blood between you and her mate, and I do know that it was your sworn pledge to Adra to serve as Hunter to her flyte."

Nall bristled and felt his arm rise in anger.

Sōrél held up his hand in peace.

"Nay, stay your hand, Nall, for I speak the truth. What is done is done. Now it is time to make it right. I have entered your blood oath's dreams, and I have seen her sorrow and her passion before the Lake of Lost Memories. As Guardians we are brothers, Nall; let that not be forgotten."

"Rydén, your dragon flyte is missing? Do you know why?" Sōrél asked.

Rydén felt her face flush. Of course she knew, but she wasn't about to tell this bully.

"I have no idea, Sōrél, no idea at all," she lied.

Näeré laid her hand on Nall's arm. "My brother is blunt, but not unnecessarily. He fears for the Guardian called Yávië, as he is bound to her through the past. Do not think too harshly of him. His heart is gentle and kind, as is yours."

"Rydén, why does the Matriarch wish you dead?" Näeré asked abruptly.

"She foresees the death of one near to her and believes I will be the bringer of that death," Rydén spoke truthfully, against her intent.

She stared at Näeré, vowing to watch this one closely. This Guardian could force the truth from her against her will, and the less anyone knew about Rydén's relationship with Sybeth the better.

Without conversation, the four Guardians prepared to leave Meremire in search of Yávië, their distrust and lack of respect for one another obvious.

"I should go alone," Sōrél declared. "Perhaps that would be best."

"No!" Nall shouted. "And do not suggest it again! I am here and I am aware of my failings, but as you so graciously reminded me, you heartless son of a bane boar, it is time to make things right."

Rydén hid a smile, thoroughly enjoying the power play between Sōrél and Nall. As she packed her satchel, she took a brief look into the smooth surface of her polished brass mirror, watching as her lips became just a bit fuller and her eyes widened a little more, intensifying their emerald color. Maybe she would grow beautiful enough to win Sōrél's heart.

"Aero, it's Aero!" Brundlewort called.

Aero stood on trembling legs, breathing heavily amid a clattering of scales. "I come for Nall," he gasped. "Yávië has sent me."

Nall placed a calming hand upon the young, wind dragon. "Where is she, Aero? Where is Yávië?"

"Ardane holds her within the Emeraldflyte. I fear he is tormenting her as revenge for the death of Adra. He does not know Dahrea and Dielmor attacked you. Why did you not tell him, Nall?" Aero's gaze was intent and accusing. "My Huntress suffers because you did not come."

Nall hung his head, "I know, Aero, I will make it right, I promise I will."

Glancing at Sōrél, Nall asked Aero, "Can you carry me to her?"

"I can carry you as far as the Emeraldflyte, but she is deep within the caverns. You must seek her there on foot." The dragon replied.

Nall nodded. They had a plan.

"Rydén, Näeré—you remain here and keep the Ancients safe until we return. Sōrél, will you accompany me to the Emeraldflyte?"

"Nall, you do not have the strength to stop me," Sōrél replied, smiling to ease the prick of his words.

Sōrél whistled, summoning Azaeria to him. He leapt to her back, his thoughts urging her upward. Carrying Nall, Aero quickly followed on the heels of his mother and and the Guardian Sōrél. With luck, Yávïe would be free this very night.

At the outmost edge of the Emeraldflyte, the wind dragons landed silently, allowing the Hunters to dismount.

Azaeria spoke wordlessly to Nall and Sōrél, "*We will await your return, Hunters. Bring Yávïe to safety. Blessings of the Ancients on your search.*"

Yávïe lay on the floor of the cavern where Ardane had tossed her, hair and face streaked with dirt and blood. She wanted to cry but was too angry. Why was Ardane so incredibly stupid and what had Adra ever seen in him that made her take him as a mate?

She had called to Nall, but he had not answered. Perhaps Rydén would come for her? But then Rydén wasn't really very brave around dragons.

Ardane's words played over in Yávïe's head, "Huntress, I cannot kill you, but I can keep you here and torment you every day for as long as we both exist . . . and that could be a very long time."

He had allowed the youngest of the dragon-kin to batter Yávïe and drag her through the halls of the great flyte, before tossing her into this small cave as if she were the foul remains of a meal. Tears welled in her eyes as she wondered what had become of Aero, so young and inexperienced in combat. Hopefully, he was not seriously wounded and had flown to Meremire. Then at least the Ancients would know where she was, and that Ardane had imprisoned her.

Yávïe examined the door to her cell and sighed when she saw that it had been constructed from dragon scales, Æstretfordæ's strongest material. She moved back into the corner, curled into a ball and tried to rest, knowing it was only a matter of time until her next torment.

Xander, the downy flier crept to her across the chamber and buried himself beneath her chin. These dragons didn't even leave enough leftovers to harbor butterpillars and he was getting very hungry, but still he refused to leave his Mistress.

Nall and Sōrél slipped into the main flyte chamber. The odor was sharp and pungent, and the snores of sleeping dragons were loud enough to cover what little noise the Guardians made as they crept along the wall. They descended deep into the caverns of the Emeraldflyte, listening at every turn and darkened cave, wary of wandering patrols.

"Nall!" whispered Sōrél. "This cave has a door of dragon scales; perhaps there is something valuable within, something as valuable as a Guardian."

Together they forced back the dragon bone bolt, wincing when the door scraped the ground.

"No, Ardane . . ." came a soft voice from inside the cave.

Nall rushed forward and fell to his knees, gathering Yávië into his arms.

"What have I done?" he cried out.

Nall brushed Yávië's hair from her face and looked into her eyes.

"Yávië, I am so sorry. I will kill Ardane for this." Nall said, overwhelmed with contrition.

Yávië smiled and her eyes glittered with tears.

"I had hoped you would find the time to come for me. Rydén is so afraid of dragons," she whispered.

Yávië's arms reached around his neck, as Nall lifted her from the filthy floor. She gazed over his shoulder at the shadowy figure by the door.

"You are real, and bear my Truth," she said before slipping into unconsciousness.

Sōrél watched as Nall murmured comforting words to Yávië, then slipped out of the chamber and headed back to Näeré and Æshardæ. Nall continued speaking soothing words of care and concern to Yávië. This Guardian was his blood oath and he had failed her, not intentionally but that did not make her suffering any less painful. Ardane would die for this—Nall would see to it as soon as Yávië was safe with Rydén and the Ancients.

"Perhaps you would like to kill me now!" Ardane thundered as he approached Nall and Yávië. "Or perhaps I will put two Guardians in my dungeons instead of one – more toys for the young dragons to play with on rainy days."

He stopped a dragon's length in front of Nall. "Put my prize down, Guardian. To win her you will have to kill me."

"Ardane, what you have done is despicable. If you wish to torture someone, torture me. I was with Adra when she died, Yávië was not."

"Your blood is the same as far as I am concerned. Torturing one is as good as torturing the other. However, torturing both will be even better. I will be happy to comply with your request, Guardian. Torturing you will bring me great pleasure and satisfaction."

Nall felt warmth on his chest—Adra's heart shard had begun to pulse. He touched it with his fingers, drawing Ardane's gaze to his chest.

"You stole Adra's heart shard?" Ardane bellowed, causing dust to fall from the ceiling. "How dare you murder her and carry her shard."

"Death dragons killed Adra, Ardane. My only shame is that I did not come to tell you when it happened. If you doubt me, ask Azaeria of the Suunflyte—she saw Adra fall and came to our assistance. Adra died at the talons of Dahrea and Dielmor in an unprovoked attack."

Ardane breathed deeply, seeking the scent of deception on this Guardian, but he found none. Though he detested these loathsome Guardians, in clear conscience he could not punish those innocent of the crime. While Nall had not protected Adra, he had not directly caused her death.

Ardane's eyes pierced Nall. He turned away and spoke to the Guardian over his shoulder, "The Emeraldflyte's new Matriarch is Azrea. Call on her if you have need of this flyte. Do not bother me again, Hunter. Take your blood oath and leave this place." With a snarl, he moved into the shadows.

Nall did not require a second invitation to leave the Emeraldflyte. He gently gathered Yávië against his shoulder and headed for the clearing where he knew Aero, Sōrél, and Azaeria waited.

Hurry, Hunter!" Aero implored. "My mother has already gone with the other Hunter."

"I wonder why . . . ?" Shrugging, he leapt to Aero's back, holding Yávië tightly lest he lose her again.

Crystal Prisons

Aero shot upward like a grass cat whose tail had been stepped on, his great wings sweeping through the air to lift Yávië and Nall ever higher. The dragon banked to the right in a long, arching turn before leveling out in the direction of Meremire.

A sudden blast of wind hit him from the side, throwing Yávië from the security of Nall's embrace, plummeting both toward the rocky earth below. The air grew dark. The turbulence of the wicked wind increased. As though flotsam, Yávië and Nall were catapulted upward and then, just as suddenly, held captive in a spiraling descent.

Nall sent Aero a silent message: *"Take Yávië and go! Go now!"*

He saw Aero nod his head and swoop down toward Yávië, pulling up as he passed beneath her unconscious form. Seeing her safely on Aero's back, Nall turned to face this new threat.

"What are you? Show yourself!" Nall hung poised above the scorched earth.

Nall's clothes began to flutter and rustle, as if now pursued by a gentle breeze. In the back of his mind he could feel a presence, though he still saw nothing beyond the dark and stormy sky.

"I . . . am . . . Maelsssssstrom . . ."

The voice was attenuated, wispy and devoid of gender, as if the wind itself had been given the power to speak. Nall's eyes widened as the breeze around him became a howling wind. In front of him a form began to take shape, the ethereal form of a featureless woman, reaching toward him. Her hands stroked his face like ribbons of spider's silk and long, caressing tendrils of air played over him.

"What do you want?" Nall asked, pulling his head away from the searching wind.

Nall sensed the wind welling behind him, rising upward.

"Greetingsss . . . Guaaaardian . . . Ssssybeth. . . sssends . . . her greetingsss . . . to you . . . all . . . "

From the corner of his eye, Nall saw a flash of amber light no larger than a grain of sand slip along a wisp of wind toward him. Suddenly he felt something tugging at him, as if his very core were being pulled into an airless void.

With a quick incantation, Nall surrounded himself with a barrier, staving off the wind but briefly. The Maelstrom shrieked and pounded against the barrier, creating tiny cracks through which small tendrils of air flowed, pulling apart and smashing the obstruction.

The wind curled around him but he resisted, shooting upward and away from the Maelstrom. Angered, the Maelstrom intensified its efforts, heaving great boulders across the sky at Nall and following with bolts of lightning and deafening thunder that reverberated around him.

With great effort, Nall forced energy from his body to disperse the wind around him, but there was no victory to be had here. Nall could only send his talismans to safety and avoid the tiny crystal for as long as possible, hoping Rydén and Yávië would have had time to reach a safe haven.

The twinkling light rushed past him in the wind, pulling at his clothing. Nall dodged it. Over and over the Maelstrom played with him, using its force to hurl him into the path of the crystal it meant to be his prison. The sky had become an obstacle course as the Maelstrom uprooted trees and boulders from the ground below and tossed them in his path.

Nall was furious, knowing that Sybeth was somehow to blame. He rushed at the Maelstrom and passed through the center of the swirling wind beast. A sudden, sharp pain struck him and he realized the Maelstrom had finally succeeded; his body contorted and shuddered as the greedy crystal consumed him.

Nall no longer remained. He had been erased as surely as a word in the sand was wiped away by the waters of the sea. In his place, the tiny crystal pulsed with amber light. Gathering the crystal to its core, the Maelstrom wailed in victory, forming a whirling funnel. The howling wind rushed off in search of other Guardians.

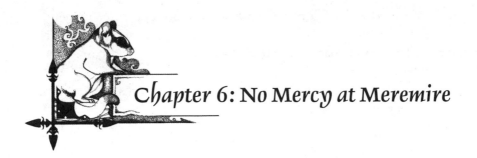

Chapter 6: No Mercy at Meremire

Rydén paced the room. Things were not turning out as she had expected. Yet again, Nall was nowhere to be found. Yávië was here, but she had not regained consciousness. And, worst of all, Sōrél and Näeré had just left. No good-bye; nice to have made your acquaintance—just gone. She had hoped to get to know them better, and to use Näeré's friendship to get closer to Sōrél, but now there seemed no hope of that.

When Aero had arrived carrying Yávië, he told of some sort of storm taking Nall, some dragon tale, most likely. Yávië had been bruised and bloodied, so something had certainly happened while she was with Ardane. Rydén had no intention of following up to find out just what had happened.

She sat. Taking her bane boar bristle brush she began to brush her hair. It was full and lustrous, and seemed to be getting prettier every time she looked at it. She let out a chuckle. Perhaps she should loan her mirror to Yávië. She could certainly use it after her visit with Ardane.

Rydén paused and listened, sure she had heard something outside her chamber. It was probably just one of the Ancients checking on Yávië. She supposed she should check on her too, but it was quite boring to sit next to someone who could not even carry on a conversation.

Rydén smiled, remembering how forceful she had been in her quest for Nall, telling him she would pull him from his cavern. His only concern had been for Yávië, though. She would have been foolish to believe anything else. They seemed so close since the blood oath, even though their relationship never crossed the line to become more as she had expected.

There was that sound again—like a gust of wind rushing through the tunnels. It was possible that the wind had become strong enough to find its way to the caverns, but not likely. Rydén went to the door and leaned against it, listening carefully. No sound at all.

She slowly opened the door and looked out into the corridor, but there was no one there, Ancient or otherwise. She decided to take a walk outdoors before getting ready for sleep. She would check in on Yávië on her way to the surface.

Yávië tossed restlessly, her dreams interrupted by deep feelings of unease and the physical aches of her bruises. Rosewort sat in the corner mending Morgwort's jacket and keeping one eye on the restless Yávië. She worried over Aero's story of the wild winds, and the fact that Yávië would want to search for Nall as soon as she awoke.

The door opened a crack and Rydén peered around the corner.

"I will sit with her awhile, Rosie," Rydén offered.

"Aye, calls me if she wakes. We need to talk to her." Rosewort gathered her mending and stood up, placing a cool hand on Yávië's forehead, smiling as she stilled under her touch.

Rydén smiled with automatic politeness as Rosie left, thinking, "No one ever cares when I don't feel well."

She sat on the floor next to Yávië's pallet and peered at her, noticing every cut and bruise.

"I really hate dragons, Yávië. Now maybe you will understand why."

Yávië's eyes opened wide and she grabbed Rydén's wrist. "Run, Rydén, we have to run."

Yávië struggled to rise, but Rydén pushed her back.

"No, Yávië, we need to stay here. Nall is missing again, and Aero is telling stories about the wind blowing him away."

"Rydén! It is true. I remember. Aero saved me. Nall sent me to Meremire with Aero, but Nall stayed to fight some sort of wind storm."

Rydén looked at her and then turned away.

Yávië shook her arm. "Rydén, we are in danger! Look at me!"

Rydén turned back and looked into Yávië's eyes. She saw fear there, real fear, and she had never seen Yávië afraid of anything.

"Rydén, I cannot *feel* Nall. Do you understand me?"

In those few words Yávië had managed both to terrify and mobilize Rydén. She understood exactly what Yávië meant. If she couldn't feel Nall, he did not exist. They were tied by a blood oath, always in contact.

"Can you walk, Yávië?" Ryden inquired of her injured friend.

"Yes, I will get dressed. Run and summon Aero. We will ride to the cliffs above the Azure Sea and hide there with the Suunflyte. They are strong and can provide protection. Go now, Rydén, I will be right behind you," Yávië said as she threw off the coverlet.

Rydén raced from the room, almost knocking Rosie over.

"We are leaving, Rosie. Yávië and I are leaving. She remembers what happened to Nall and he is gone!" she called back over her shoulder as she fled.

Yávië dressed quickly, throwing things into her satchel and calling for Xander. She placed the Sword of Domesius into the scabbard on her back and raced into the corridor. Rosie stood there, stunned by Rydén's words. Yávië bent down and hugged her.

"We will be back as soon as it is safe. There is something wrong with the wind. It took Nall. I cannot feel him, Rosie; he is gone."

Xander raced toward her, launching himself into the air and landing on her shoulder as she raced away to join Rydén who stood watching Aero, her eyes wide. She screamed for Yávië. Aero bucked and plunged, bellowing as the wind whipped around them. His form was shifting as the wind blew, his scales stretched and trailing into the wind.

Yávië leapt onto his back and stretched out her hand to Rydén who reached up and grabbed it, but her grip faltered. As Yávië watched in horror, Rydén was swept into the sky on the whirling winds.

Rydén screamed, but the wind did not hear. It tossed and battered her, spinning her around until she could not tell sky from ground. Suddenly, the winds pulled back and let her fall. At the last minute, threads of cool air wound themselves around her, pulling her back into the sky. Then the wind gathered itself and formed a shape, a dragon's shape, and the breathy voice of the wind finally spoke to her.

"I . . . am . . . Maelssstrom . . . sssent by . . . Sssybeth . . . to end your ussselesssss . . . life . . .

Rydén felt a tug and looked to see the wind pushing a tiny crystal ahead of it. The pain was agonizing as it pulled her little by little into the tiny prison. Finally, like Nall, there was no trace left of her.

The Maelstrom squealed gleefully and raced off in search of its final prey.

Into the Minds of Men

Aero raced ahead of the maniacal wind, weaving among the heavily wooded valleys of the Northern Mountains.

"Just get us to the flyte. We should find safety there," Yávië encouraged Aero, knowing deep inside that it was not true.

She had been watching the world below and the sky above and knew that with the loss of Nall a much heavier darkness had settled over Æstretfordæ. Just moments ago, the far edges of the world seemed to have grown even darker. Yávië knew that must mean that Rydén was gone, but where? How could Guardians suddenly just wink out, disappear completely, taking large pieces of Æstretfordæ with them? She wished she knew, and feared she was about to find out.

A loud wailing came up the valley behind them and Yávië knew that she was doomed. She refused to put Aero in direct danger, so she eased him to the ground with her thoughts.

"Aero, go to Azaeria. Tell her we are gone and to return to the earth until we summon the flytes again. Can you do this, Son of Aerodorn?" Yávië asked the dragon.

"Huntress, I fear for you. Have you not seen that the earth falls into shadow?" Aero replied, skittering sideways in unease.

"I will fight, Aero. I will not go easily, and I promise I will return. Now go. Fly like the wind and do as I ask. Dragons should not question their Huntresses," she chided him.

Placing her face against his lowered neck, she took heart from the fact that she would be sending the flyte to safety.

Not wishing to be caught on the ground, Yávië rose into the dark sky and was instantly struck by a blast of icy wind.

"What are you?" she called. "Why do you pursue me, a Guardian of Æstretfordæ?"

The wind raged around her, but she steadied herself and shouted, "You cannot kill me, and you cannot hold me, for I am not weak like those who went before me."

"I . . . am . . . Maelssstrom . . . ," the wind hissed. "Fed by the dragon Ssssybeth, I have grown sssstrong . . . "

"Sybeth!" Yávië snarled back.

The wind rose up and towered over Yávië. It drew back and then darted forward, holding something out in front of it on a long tendril of sooty air.

Suddenly, Yávië knew the danger. She knew what had happened to Nall and Rydén, for in the wind she saw the tiny creation crystal, the only prison strong enough to hold a Guardian; a prison stronger than dragon scales, a prison that could be as permanent as death. And with the Guardians gone, the world would fade, for the Prophecy was not complete. Æstretfordæ would darken and sleep. No topaz star would light the days, nor would anything live within its fields or seas. The dragons would lie dormant, and the Ancients would sleep below Meremire until the Guardians returned.

She swung away, feeling the tug of the crystal. What fear and anger Nall and Rydén must have felt. She knew that neither would have had time to prepare for summoners, but she would have to if they were to survive and be freed.

Yávië fled the Maelstrom and raced in among the Giant Stones. Using her power to change, she poured herself into a crack, becoming one with the stone. Silently she thanked Mallowort for the gift of the stone, given so long ago. It would not stop the Maelstrom's evil plan, for the crystal would draw her in one grain of stone at a time. But it would give her time to search for those who could call for her release, so that she in turn could release Nall and Rydén. She knew they would have sent their talismans to safety, a Guardian always did. She would seek the Maelstrom and from it, she would find their prisons. She would be the One.

She permitted her mind to empty and began to search the heavens for familiar souls who could be reborn to call on her in their dreams, seeking her wisdom and her aid, freeing her from the crystal prison.

There was a flicker in the universe where three men, familiar yet not remembered, were slumbering deep within the stars; men from a world called Ædracmoræ, unaware their realm had passed out of existence long ago. By her intervention they would become her saviors and leaders of the races she would one day create.

As Yávië began the resurrection invocation, she felt the pull of the crystal but it did not distract her. As the only remaining Guardian, there was no more important quest in all her life than the touching of the minds of these three men. *"Maloch, Xavier, Galen . . . come, come and awake in the darkness of Æstretfordæ."*

With the last words of the calling, she felt the final tug and passed beyond awareness. The light of the topaz star faded and Æstretfordæ fell into a silent darkness, to sleep until Maloch, Xavier and Galen cried out in the dreams of their resurrection.

The Dreams of Men

The awakening of the three men was gradual, almost imperceptible. Like the early mist of a long forgotten world rising to meet its morning star, the sleep of death left them. As they slumbered within space and time, they had been called by a voice as pure and sweet as that of a nightingale, a voice from his past.

Galen, the first to recover from the death sleep, stood on trembling legs, his eyes taking in the surrounding area. A plethora of emotions raced through his mind: surprise, wonder, the joy that always accompanied rebirth into the world, the courage natural to a man, and a sudden, cold fear. This was not the world of his birth. On the horizon, where a topaz star should have been rising, there was only blackness. What light there was seemed to emanate from the nearby rocky outcrops. Beyond this meager light he could see only darkness, black as death. He dropped to his knees as a deep weariness overwhelmed him and he began to dream.

Maloch shifted restlessly. Somewhere in the back of his mind, a familiar sound was trying to rise to the surface of his consciousness. Dark eyes opened reluctantly as the dusty dryness in his throat became unbearable. He reached for the water bag at his waist and gazed out across the landscape realizing that, with the exception of the few meters of earth on which they lay, there appeared to be only darkness. A few paces from Maloch, the form of Galen was faintly visible in the heavy gloom. There was no morning, noon or night. Only deep shadow surrounded them. Indeed, there was no longer time, only darkness and exhaustion that returned him to a dreaming sleep.

Awaking to a mind-numbing fear and an agonizing headache, Xavier made an unsuccessful attempt to raise his head. As an empath, he should have felt a telepathic connection with Galen and Maloch, the souls to whom he had been tied for many lifetimes. But unless they were both near death, what he felt did not come from them. The pain he felt came from something—or someone—trapped in a very small space. He could feel the pain of the walls closing in around them. "Galen! Maloch!" he croaked. As he lapsed into unconsciousness, three fleeting thoughts came to him. *Wrong world; no time, you will serve to call my summoners . . .*

The three men returned to a bottomless sleep, and although this was not the slumber between lives, it was just as deep. As their sleep intensified, their dreams fell into the black abyss and a tiny light pulsed within the darkest corner of space and time.

Their dreams called to the Guardian.

Maloch fell through timeless space, his stomach lurching at the descent. No time. How could it be? His life was grounded in the phases of the moon, the daystar's rise and set, the seasons, and the ages. It was inconceivable to be in a state of timelessness. A splash of scarlet, violet, and then startlingly brilliant, white light struck him like a fist. He found himself firmly planted on solid ground. A ground covered with crimson grasses and a rainbow of other flora. Trees with braided trunks, each section as thick as a man's waist, soared into the brilliant topaz sky. Movement caught his eye, and he whirled about to confront whatever threat might be approaching.

A woman, tall and slender with raven hair falling over her shoulders and cascading down her back, glided toward him. As she neared, Maloch could not help but notice that her pale skin reacted to the light with the iridescence of a butterfly's wings. She stopped before him, smiling a smile so dazzling that his heart constricted and his breath came in short gasps.

"I startled you?" she queried. "But you summoned me. Why should you be surprised at my arrival?"

Maloch remained silent, fearing that his response might send her away. Her violet eyes were wide set, framed by thick ebony lashes.

While the opalesque quality of her skin should have seemed unnatural to him, strangely it did not. She lifted a slender arm, and with tapered fingers brushed her hair from her eyes. Maloch realized that the gentle breeze that stirred her hair and clothing did not touch him. It seemed simply to be a part of her.

"Maloch? I have come for you. Your call has rekindled my light, though it remains dim. I can change what you request and repair the timelessness. Is that still your desire?"

Hearing her voice speak his name brought on another bout of breathlessness. Who was this woman? How had he called her, if indeed he had at all?

"I don't remember . . ." He let the unfinished thought slip out.

She smiled again, so beautiful it made his heart ache.

"Do you still desire this?" There was urgency in her voice now.

"Time? Yes, I cannot exist without time. It is part of planning; of knowing when to wake, work, eat, sleep . . . I am lost without time."

She took his hand and held it palm up in hers. "Time has been returned to you in the rhythms of this place. Others call me now and I must leave you. Rest here until my tasks are completed. You will know when the needs of the others have been met. I have prepared a dwelling for you over there." She gestured over his left shoulder. "Rest."

With that, it was as if she had never been. The landscape remained, but where nothing but crimson grass and braided trees had stood, there was now a small rectangular house.

Maloch went to lie down.

Xavier pressed his temples and wished he had become a healer instead of an empath. The headache was mind numbing. He thought he heard someone call his name, but through the pain, he could not be certain. He laughed, and the pain increased.

"Xavier."

This time he was almost positive he had heard someone speak his name. It was not the voice of Maloch, or Galen. It was soft, like that of his sister. He jumped as a cool, dry hand touched his forehead. Before him was the face of the loveliest woman he had ever seen. Her silver hair was cropped close to her head, her skin the color of water in a deep forest lake on his first life home. Light shimmered beneath it, giving it a lustrous sheen. Her eyes, however, were the most remarkable feature about her. They were filled with swirling emerald and gold light, like the scales of the rainbow fish he had seen in the pools at his training center.

He realized his headache was gone, and assumed she must be a healer. "Thank you." He spoke with great gratitude and sincerity.

"What is it you seek, Xavier? Your mind seems clouded." The woman's voice flowed over him creating a sphere of peace.

"I am an empath, connected to two others. Well, I was connected to them. It seems I have 'lost' them. I had a headache, a monstrous headache, and then they were gone."

Her hand passed gently over Xavier's brow. "If you follow the path you will come upon one you seek. The other is still calling. Once all three are reunited, the connection will be repaired."

Xavier turned and glanced in the direction she had indicated. The landscape was no longer dark but filled with topaz light. A small path wended its way through a field of crimson grass. When Xavier returned his gaze to his healer, she was gone.

With a shrug, he moved off down the path.

Galen cowered, drenched in sweat, his eyes closed so tightly they hurt. A paralyzing fear controlled him, keeping him curled in a fetal ball. Darkness—there was nothing but darkness beyond the pitifully dim light that had illuminated the clearing where he awoke. His face and clothing were covered in his vomit. He knew that if he opened his eyes and "saw" into the darkness he would die. In fact, he was certain he would be killed in a manner so hideous he could not even envision it. Beasts—there were unknown beasts in the darkness.

He had heard them shrieking and screeching, and then the sound of their long sharp nails as they moved over the luminous rocks. Galen's fear was so great that he had soiled himself, something so shameful that he almost welcomed the death he saw coming . . . almost.

Something slithered near his feet, and he drew them up more tightly. "Let the death be a swift one, no matter how horrible, just let it be quick," Galen mumbled to himself.

"Why do you wish to die, Galen?" said a voice in his right ear in tones as pure as an exquisite carillon.

Eyes still tightly closed, Galen replied without hesitation, "I have shown fear."

"Galen, you are a hero to your people. Is it not normal that a hero, in his wisdom, be afraid? Does not fear give you an edge as keen as the slayer's blade? What is it you require of me, Galen? Why have you called for me? Take my hand that your fear may end."

Tensed, and ready to fight the demons he expected to see, Galen allowed his eyes to open. Before him stood a beast unlike any he had ever encountered. The face was flat and misshapen. One eye was swollen closed, and the other appeared gangrenous. Broken teeth littered its sagging mouth and oozing sores covered its exposed skin. A moan escaped Galen's lips and his eyes closed again.

"Galen, take my hand so your fear may end." The soft voice again requested.

How could that musical voice come from such an evil-looking being? Even in his terror and exhaustion, Galen could not reconcile one with the other. With a sigh, he opened his eyes and reached for the sharp-clawed hand that had been extended in his direction. Let the beast kill him, he was beyond caring. As he raised his eyes to face his death, he was surprised to discover he was no longer afraid.

The beast released its grip, allowing Galen to stand alone. One side of the creature's mouth rose as if in a smile.

"Your companions await you. Go to them. I have dispelled the darkness which covered you. Fear is no longer your enemy, but will be your strength from this day forward." The beast moved away toward the far horizon.

"Wait! Beast, what is this place?" called Galen.

Without turning, the beast responded, "It is your home. You are the ancient mirror in which I have seen myself. I am a summoner."

Galen watched until he could no longer see the beast or the trail it left through the tall crimson grass.

Then he turned and headed toward his companions.

Chapter 7: Awakening

No larger than a grain of sand, the crystal lay in the gloom among the debris. The energy within—the Guardian of the timeless space—had been held captive, the crystal's prisoner, for a man's eternity. At the dream calling of the first man, a small spark flickered within. By the calling of the third, Yávië's soul had reached its full brilliance.

From across the empty cavern, the three shimmering summoners approached one another: a young raven-haired beauty, a warrior woman with blue-green skin and close-cropped silver hair, and a beast of great ugliness and unrivaled strength. As they entered the circle at the center of the cave, each one raised its right hand toward the other. At the first touch of their fingers, the tiny crystal at their feet pulsed once, shattered, and revealed Yávië. Her ethereal summoners swirled about her before fading and taking their places within her soul. Kneeling, Yávië swept the crystal shards into her hand. Her warm breath caused them to coalesce, reforming into a tiny, perfect crystal. Carefully, she placed it within her bodice next to the sleeping downy flier, Xander.

Moving with quiet grace, Yávië approached the crystal pool at the back of the cavern that had held her for the ages. She leant forward to examine her reflection. Though her face remained unlined, as often happens with Guardians, her raven hair was now touched with silver. Her eyes still sparkled with a color that rivaled the thickets of wild violets, and her skin still showed the pale iridescence for which her kind were envied. Slowly, her full lips curved into a smile. It was still a smile that could stop a man's heart. Looking deeper, as only a Guardian can, she examined those others who dwelt within her. The warrior, battle ready, hidden just below her lovely surface; the beast she carried even deeper—caged, lest harm come to those she had sworn to lead and protect. Viewing her outer self again, Yávië was reassured to see the aura of her station glowing around her form, its pulse strong and shimmering. She was at last ready to venture forth to meet the men who had saved her.

Standing on a small hillock not far from where the three men worked, Yávië observed each with great interest. How different they were one from the other, yet each had the strength and wisdom to lead. Maloch, Xavier and Galen had accomplished much in the time since they had unknowingly released her. It was time now for her to give each of them the burden he would carry the rest of his days. Yávië turned to face the land of the giant stones and thought of the race of Stonemen living there. Next, her eyes sought the land beyond the Ebony Plains and the ten thousand Plainsmen who made their homes amid the fields. Her gaze then fell on the rugged canyons of the Crimson Grassland, sensing the fierce Wanderers who roamed them. Finally, the races of Men whom she had created, while trapped within her prison, would have their leaders.

Leaders of Men

"Maloch, do you remember my voice?" Yávië asked.

Maloch smiled as he looked up. "You restored time to this place. But you have changed somehow."

"Yes, Maloch, I was not whole when I helped you. You were only the first mirror."

"Mirror?" he questioned.

"An old tale from the distant past, and a long one at that. Let us talk of your future rather than my past. Maloch, you have an important role to play in the history of this place. I must ask a heavy sacrifice of you. I must ask that you leave your companions and lead a great people among the Giant Stones of the Northern Mountains. Your coming has been foretold and the people there await you. Are you willing to do this?" Yávië asked Maloch.

"How can I refuse? Without your help I would have remained trapped in a timeless void, perhaps for all eternity. How will I know these people?" Maloch replied.

"On the twelfth day of your journey you will see the first of the twelve Giant Stones. A stone sprite waits there to take you to your kingdom. Rule wisely, King Maloch, and ballads will be sung in your name. Rule foolishly, and you will fall." Yávië directed.

As she rose, Yávië handed Maloch a small crystal. "Keep this safe. Should a time come when you must call on me again, simply place it between your hand and your heart. It will summon me."

Xavier felt a tug at the corner of his mind. It was not Maloch or Galen but it seemed familiar somehow. He opened his mind and was drawn toward the center of a large copse of braided trees. A woman was sitting there, head bowed as if deep in thought.

"I feel that I should know you, but I don't recall why," Xavier said as he neared her.

She lifted her head and smiled. The memory of her losses—the pain—flooded in before retreating just as quickly.

"I am Yávië. I was of some small assistance to you when you first arrived here. Now I have come to ask a favor."

Reluctantly, Xavier asked, "What favor would you ask of me?"

"Far from here, across the Ebony Plains, there are people who have no leader. Their stories speak of a "mind crawler" who will come to lead them to strength and success. Xavier, you are that "mind crawler." I must ask you to assume their leadership to fulfill this prophecy. Can you meet this challenge?" Yávië asked.

Unable to respond, Xavier turned and looked into her sad, violet eyes.

"Is there no other way?" Within her eyes, he saw there was not. "I will accept, but I must ask something of you in return. Sever my connection to Maloch and Galen; otherwise I could not bear the separation."

"This I will do. As you cross the Ebony Plains, a bird with golden plumage will lead you to your destiny. Rule justly that stories of your wisdom will be passed down the generations."

She handed him a golden feather. "Hold this feather to your heart should you need to summon me. I will come."

Galen tossed in a restless sleep. Yávië watched from the edge of the room, lingering where the shadows were deepest. She had seen his anguish as he searched for Maloch and Xavier, calling their names repeatedly until his strong voice grew hoarse. He was the greatest of the three—the noblest. She smiled recalling the way he had reached for the beast's hand, no doubt expecting his arm to be wrenched from its socket. His fear had been palpable that day, but she had also seen the depth of his strength.

"Galen." Her voice was a mere whisper but it cut through him like the sharpest sword. He sat bolt upright, searching the darkened room for the beast.

"Stay. Do not seek me out until we have spoken. It is obvious that you remember our last encounter."

A coarse laugh preceded his response. "I am not likely to forget it. You saw me at my weakest, and still did not kill me."

"Oh, Galen, it was at your best and strongest I saw you. In spite of a numbing terror, you reached out and took the hand of the one you suspected would end your life. There could be no greater strength than that. I have changed much in the time since then. Your strength as the third to call on me allowed my escape."

She stepped forward into the starlight that filtered through the window.

"As you can see, most would not call me beast."

"What realm is this we have fallen into? A realm of magick it seems, rather than science; magick that makes maidens from monsters, and causes flesh and blood men to disappear without a trace."

"Magick? Perhaps. Power, certainly. I am Yávië, Guardian of Æstretfordæ—the place you now call home. By your need, you and your companions have released me from imprisonment, and now it is time for the rest of an ancient prophecy to be fulfilled. Maloch and Xavier have accepted my requests and gone on to their destinations. It is time for you, Galen, to do the same. Your challenge is the greatest. Maloch and Xavier have gone to people who already love and accept them as part of ancient lore, but you must fight for your kingdom among the Wanderers in the canyons of the Crimson Grass. This land is not, as your have believed, void of humanity.

"The Wanderers are a fierce people and bide their time in the canyons waiting to see what the sky has brought them. I have chosen you as their leader, but I will not cloud their eyes and make them blindly accept you. It is by their fierceness that they have survived while awaiting the leader promised them in the tablets of their history. You are that leader, Galen. You need only show them."

Taking a stone-bladed dagger from a scabbard at her waist, she extended it to Galen. "As the Topaz Star rises on the morrow, challenge the nomad waiting in the center of the copse. Use only this dagger.

He will cede the battle when you draw first blood. Lead them well, Galen. Make them a great and honorable people."

Galen took the dagger, turning it over in his hands. "And if he draws first blood?"

Yávië's gaze was steady. "You will be lost."

She stood and walked to the door. Turning, she whispered, "I have given the others a talisman to summon me. I give you my name, Yávië. You need only speak it aloud for me to hear."

"I have not agreed to do this, yet you act as though I have." Galen stated.

"Galen, if you do not, then I am lost. Bringing leaders to the three tribes is a condition of the Great Prophecies. While it is within my power to destroy worlds and cause strong men to cower, I cannot alter the conditions of prophecy. My faith is in you, Maloch and Xavier. The time has come for me to complete quests of my own, free others of my kind. May the grace of the Ancients be with you until next we meet."

The Maelstrom

On the fringe of the Ebony Plains, close to the border of the Wastelands and just above the small stone altar that Xavier's people had built in the light of the gibbous moons, Yávië sat and let her mind drift back to the time before her captivity. Joyous days spent with Nall and Rydén. How she missed them! Nall, broad-shouldered, his amber eyes like bottomless pools of honey—the wells of his soul; his dark hair catching and reflecting the light of both day and moon as through a shimmering prism, his mirror images imparting strength and sadness to his countenance. And Rydén; her rich auburn hair, her emerald eyes so charged with electricity, and her silken voice that no man could resist. Outwardly, she was so young and innocent, but there were dark secrets hidden within her. Carelessness and pride had caused them all to be imprisoned, sentenced to the long silence, unable to escape until the chosen men called out to Yávië. All three Guardians shared in this catastrophe, and they would not be caught again. The long captivity had served an unintended purpose, that of increasing Yávië's strength and creative power.

Yávië's struggle to achieve the release of Nall and Rydén would be long and arduous, but not impossible. Already the pull of their talismans was growing stronger. She had accomplished the first tasks of the ancient prophecy, and this had brought back her strength and increased her power, although she knew it would not reach its full potential until she was reunited with the others. While she had remained trapped in her crystal prison, this planet's star had been set ablaze and the world reclaimed with the first man's calling, an indication that her powers were indeed great. By the calling of the third man, the world had been populated with the three tribes by her will alone. This required an extremely well-controlled power; a power of the mind far superior to that of the Maelstrom's winds. Yávië would set off in search of the evil wind with the rising of the Topaz Star.

Yávië's thoughts then strayed to the men: Galen, Maloch and Xavier. Their quests had just begun as well. Each had an important part to play in the Prophecy of Men. Each would be rewarded or defiled according to his leadership. But the men would make their own way, rise to power or fall to ruin without Yávië's help. It was her task to free the summoners needed to release Rydén and Nall. Each required three talismans: Nall, the stone dagger, golden feather and Gaianite crystal; Rydén, the silver Iaito, sorrowful woman, and emerald dragon. However, before she could seek these out, Yávië would have to defeat the Maelstrom.

Raised from the four winds in the times of the Ancients, the Maelstrom controlled the elemental air. The wind beast could fashion great storms containing powerful electrical charges that could sap Yávië's strength and slow her search unless she dealt with them. With the defeat of the Maelstrom, she would grow even more powerful and reclaim the strength of a Guardian.

Closing her eyes, Yávië created a veil of stealth and silence, increasing her weight by six hundred stones so that she would not be buffeted by the strong winds she could hear ahead of her. Finding the Maelstrom had been a simple task. Its pride was great and it delighted in tormenting the world's population with its terrifying storms. Yávië had followed the path of the storms and now neared the Maelstrom's lair. It must be lured inside and trapped there, within the very crystal where it had held her prisoner.

From beneath her cloak, Yávië drew out an old and heavily filigreed bottle. It was small and delicate, the opening large enough only for a single grain of sand. Still cloaked and silent, she slid between the casement rocks and into the Maelstrom's lair. Placing the bottle on a small ledge, Yávië settled next to it and turned herself to stone. Here she would wait for the wind's return, knowing that no being of air could resist slipping into the smallest of entrances like the one in the bottle. The Maelstrom would never suspect that it could be trapped; it was so certain of its might.

Hours passed before Yávië heard the banshee wail of a mighty wind rushing through the cracks and fissures along the canyon walls. The Maelstrom raced into its lair, traveling over every surface, tendrils of air caressing the roof, walls and floor like the fingers of a woman caressing a lover—gently, tenderly. Yávië shuddered inwardly at the touch. Abruptly, the Maelstrom ceased its examination of the lair and the air became deathly still. The Maelstrom had discovered Yávië's gift.

Haltingly, it sent small gusts of air toward the bottle, distrustful of this beautiful gift. Little by little, the wind gained courage and began to slip in and out of the opening, but never placing its entire center in the bottle. As if unable to decide on the bottle's safety, the Maelstrom formed a small dervish, and then, as Yávië had hoped, after a brief pause to consider what gifts might be inside, poured itself into the bottle.

Yávië placed the crystal that had once held her prisoner into the top of the bottle. With a quick summoning from her hand, she drew the Maelstrom into the crystal, murmuring the incantation that would seal it there for an eternity. However, unlike the Maelstrom, she did not leave the crystal lying in its lair to be found by the Maelstrom's summoners. Instead, she placed it gently beneath her tongue, where it dissolved, sending the Maelstrom's elemental strength coursing through her body along with its knowledge of the location of its prisoners.

At her center, Yávië felt the Guardians stir within their crystal prisons, hoping the wait need not be much longer. For the first time in a great many passages of the Topaz Star, Yávië spoke aloud, "I am coming, Nall! I am coming, Rydén!" Then she headed off in search of the Ancients.

Chapter 8: In Search of Talismans

The Lake of Lost Memories

The Ancient sat on the moss beneath the dramm bush which, despite its lack of loftiness, could have been a giant braid tree for the shade it offered. At less than five hands in height, he was quite diminutive. Unlike the Guardian, his skin had wrinkled and resembled nothing so much as poorly tanned hide. Though juggling seven golden balls above his head, his hands were folded in his lap.

"Sit, girl." He spoke quickly, with a purr like a grass cat.

Yávië sat. Following the commands given by the Ancients was always a wise choice since failure to do so often resulted in bruises or broken bones—easily healed, but painful all the same.

"Why do you still call me girl, Morgwort?" Yávië was sincerely puzzled by his refusal to notice she had long ago become an adult.

"Since you are not a boy, you must be a girl," Morgwort responded with a wicked grin.

"Well, there are varying degrees, you know. Older boys are men and older girls are women. I qualify as an older girl," Yávië explained.

"Very well, old girl, what brings you here?" Morgwort purred.

Smiling and knowing very well she had lost the battle for womanhood, at least in the eyes of Morgwort, Yávië began her tale, ending with her search for the talismans of Nall and Rydén.

"Pretty girl, Rydén. Sour puss, Nall," reflected Morgwort.

Not far off the mark, thought Yávië, at least from his perspective. He had taught each of them spells and incantations when they were all very young. Nall never wanted to study and Rydén spent most of her time trying to make herself even prettier.

Morgwort lifted a finger and pointed at Yávië. "You were pretty too, but almost too old to teach." Laughter burst forth. "You *were* an *old* girl!"

"Very funny! You know very well that I am a grown woman! I passed the Trials of a Guardian, Morgwort, long, long ago." Suddenly she felt old. Time was slipping by, leaving Nall and Rydén still captive.

"Morg," Yávië said, slipping into a more familiar tone, "I must search the Lost Memories. Nall left his golden feather there."

"Cannot do it!" Spittle flew from his mouth as he shouted. The balls he had been juggling dropped to the ground. "Lost cannot be founds. By the Rules."

"I know, Morg, but it was the safest place he knew to hide something so important. There must be some way to recover it. Please help me."

Yávië formed a tear in her mind and let it fall through her lashes and roll slowly down her cheek. She recalled how Morgwort had always grown soft and gentle at the sight of a tear from his "girl" students, and felt ashamed for deceiving him.

"Yávië, do not feel sorrow. I will see. I will see. You must wait here while I consult the others. I will return by starset." He got to his feet, looked at her once more, and shuffled off toward the nearby longhouse.

Yávië wasted no time. As soon as Morg was gone from her sight, she dashed down the crooked path that led to the lake. She dropped to her knees at the water's edge, careful lest she touch the water. She quickly dug a small hole in the sandy soil, placed a smooth Ebony Plains pebble into the hole, and covered it with a piece of spider cloth.

"Within the Lake a memory hides, along the currents, wild it rides, deep, deep, deep it hides, return the memory while time abides."

She watched as a slender finger of water slid up the shore and into the hole, soaking the cloth. It withdrew, taking the stone with it and leaving behind a golden feather. Tucking the feather into the tunic beneath her cloak, she hurried back along the path and resumed her seat in exactly the place she had been when talking to Morg. While she awaited his return, her mind drifted off into thoughts of long ago.

"Yávië." Morgwort gently shook her by the shoulder. "I am late—could not be helped. I argued long, but still the Rules do not allow finding memories, only losing them. I am sorry, girl. I wanted it for you."

Yávië smiled at him, guilt causing her sadness now.

"I am sure I will find another way." she lied. "Now I must search the Sea of Sorrows. When we are all together again, we will return to you. Blessings on you, Morg, until we meet again."

Morgwort watched her walk away. "Silly old girl not fool me. Golden feather I do see." In his eye a tear glistened.

The Sea of Sorrows

It is said that the Sea of Sorrows was created by the tears of those who had lost loved ones. Yávië knew that one of Rydén's summoners alone could have cried that many tears. Tears of sorrow and anger still resided deep in Rydén, although they were rarely seen and buried as deep as the beast within Yávië herself.

Surrounding the sea were many souls who had cried for so long they had been entombed in the salt of their own tears. Over time, nothing was left but salt figures shining in the light. It was among these that Rydén's talisman would be found.

Yávië opened her mind, seeking Rydén's talisman. A sudden vision caused her to gasp. Salt merchants, harvesting the salt of a crying woman! Rydén's woman! Setting off at a steady pace, Yávië headed in the direction the vision led her. What she saw on her arrival caused her to fall to her knees and weep uncontrollably. The harvesters had taken most of the talisman, leaving only the glistening salt feet. Yávië rose and gathered what was left of the talisman into a small satchel. Now she must find the harvesters to buy back the rest.

One would imagine buying salt would not present much of a challenge. After all, it was the goal of the salt harvesters to sell salt and they weren't very particular about buyers. However, unless she located the harvesters before they reached their encampment, all of the day's salt would have been consolidated into one large lot, making it very difficult to locate the specific salt she required.

Using her ability of far sight, Yávië scanned the horizon, locating a small group not far off to the south. It was not a direction in which she wished to travel, since her next destination lay to the north, in the land of the Stonemen. Sighing, she conjured a set of silvery wings and set off after the harvesters. Setting down just out of their sight, she dismissed the wings. It would not do to approach salt harvesters looking like anything out of the ordinary.

Thinking her clothing into a drab gray, the color of the surrounding stone, and her eyes to brown, Yávië approached the closest of the group.

"Brothers in the salt, I wish the harvest of the Ancients upon you," she greeted them respectfully.

"Sister in the salt, may the wounds of your journey heal quickly," responded an elder harvester. "May we offer salt?"

"Indeed, I seek a special salt as required by the Ancients. It must be harvested from the Sea of Sorrows. Have you such salt?"

"Sister, you are in luck. We are just returning from a day's harvesting at the sea. Do you wish to divine the salt?"

Yávië became suddenly wary; it was as if her change of clothing and eye color were insufficient disguise for this harvester. Deciding to use honesty, she asked, "What gave me away, harvester?"

"Your glow was seen in the sky before your arrival. We are not Merc Salters, but Galenite Wanderers. We simply seek salt for our settlement. Galen has spoken of you. It is said you are the only Guardian here." The elder stated.

Hesitating, Yávië decided to continue honestly.

"The salt I seek is part of a talisman for the sister of one with whom I share a blood oath. I can easily divine it and pay you for it in crystal shards. Unfortunately, you will need to continue harvesting to replace the salt, but if this will be a satisfactory arrangement I am willing to pay for destroyed salt as well."

In the process of divining, all salt not belonging to the talisman would be lost.

"By Galen's pledge, we will enter this pact with you. I will lead my people behind the stones so that your light will not blind them." With quick command to his group, he moved them away.

Yávië closed her eyes in a moment of concentration, reopening them upon the bags of salt left before her. An amaranthine glow, subtle at first, but quickly growing to a brilliant flash began in her violet eyes. It was followed by a sharp crackling, which left a single bag of salt at her feet.

She placed the salt collected earlier beside the single bag, her lips moving in mussitation as she condensed and combined the two with her incantation. After slipping the bag inside her cloak, Yávië placed eight crystal shards in its place, more than sufficient repayment for the day's harvested salt. Moving off to the north and the cities of men, she called, "Blessings of the Ancients on the Galenites!"

Two Perfect Crystals and an Air Machine

Nall's second talisman was a Gaianite crystal identical to the one Yávië had given Maloch. They were, in truth, two halves of the same whole. The fact that Nall's talismans were indistinguishable from her own was unusual, the result of the blood oath sworn in their youth. Nall's crystal lay hidden within the center of Maloch's kingdom, which meant that during its recovery she could spend a day advising him as there had been whispers of discontent among the Malochians. It seemed their ruler was proving less acceptable than she had expected.

As Yávië instructed, Maloch had set off in search of the Giant Stones and there the promised stone sprite had become his guide, entertaining him with its tales of release by the Guardian, Yávië.

When they reached the last of the stones, the sprite stopped, explaining that it must stay within the realm of the Giant Stones. It had pointed ahead to a dust-filled shambles of a town, telling Maloch that was his kingdom. In that instant, Maloch's heart plunged. A kingdom? It was barely a town! Rutted dirt roads were the only streets, houses were constructed of mud and grass, and the people were dirty and disheveled.

"Well," Maloch had thought, "perhaps I can change all of this."

The people received him with awe and respect and he promised them a great city if they would work hard and allow his guidance.

In the beginning, excitement and enthusiasm drove the people. They obeyed Maloch's every direction, eventually creating the wondrous machines he imagined in his mind. Streets were paved and soon lined with neat houses and shops. Machines had been built to make life easier and more pleasant. Machines cooked, cleaned, watered and harvested. The Malochians loved the new city and its marvelous machines, but they grew tired, wanting to enjoy what had been created, rather than continuing to create.

Maloch would not be stopped, however, and he kept his factories manned night and day, with workers both willing and unwilling. Murmurs of dissent fell on deaf ears, and the machines became larger and more complicated.

The sky above the Malochian city became more and more clouded and the waters more polluted with the dust and waste of manufacturing. Now the skies above were permanently gray.

It was apparent that word of Yávië's approach had already reached the city. The Malochian banners were flying and the technological advances were evident along the streets. Machines for ground travel moved noisily along the wider avenues. There were also machines dispensing currency, machines making cloth and bread—even machines making candy were visible in merchant windows. Time recorders were visible on every wrist, with larger versions prominently displayed on the walls of buildings. Maloch seemed to have saturated his people with technological marvels— which was perhaps the problem. The tribe given to Maloch was one of simple people without the knowledge of such wonders. He may have expected more rapid progress than they were able to absorb.

Arriving at the portal to Maloch's throne room, Yávië slipped inside behind several subjects who seemed to be having a heated argument about a machine, a flying machine, no less.

Maloch was certainly driven. She saw him, hair splashed over his forehead like a waterfall as he leant forward over a table, intent on examining a carved wooden model.

"It *will* work!" he shouted. "It will, trust me that it will." In a more reasonable tone, but one that still held a hint of frustration he went on, "In my dreams I have seen tens of thousands in the sky at one time." He continued, "I know it will work."

Yávië then stepped forward.

"Yávië! I have needed your council; I have, but did not wish to summon you from your quests."

"Today I am here and we will sort out your problems. Perhaps I can help you see them from a different perspective—the perspective of those you rule. Come. Let us spend time together. Tell me of your wondrous machines."

While Yávië could be exceedingly stern, she sensed that with Maloch, gentleness and jest worked best. She allowed him to tell her of the machines, what they did, and how they did it. She teased and cajoled him into agreeing that perhaps flight beyond the boundaries of the Malochian sky might best be put off for the present. As dusk began to filter the topaz light to a dusty brown and torches flared, she asked for the return of her talisman.

Uneasily, Maloch took it from the amulet he wore around his neck. "Have I so offended you that you refuse me your council in the future?"

"Nay, Maloch. Though you did not know, you have actually held talismans for two Guardians. I trusted you enough to keep them safe. I need only the crystal of one with whom I share a blood oath. Mine will remain with you always," she said, laying her hand comfortingly on his shoulder.

Once in her hand, the Gaianite crystal began to shimmer with a blood-red light. Gradually, the light at its center became darker—a dividing line between the two halves. The stone split without a sound, leaving two perfect crystals, Yávië's and Nall's, nestled side by side.

She handed Maloch the Gaianite crystal that would call her and smiled kindly at him. "Maloch, I am fortunate indeed to have saviors such as you, Galen and Xavier. Try not to push your people so hard. Change is always difficult, but easier when spread more thinly. Your machines are wonderful and have brought great prosperity to the Malochians. Always remember you are the one responsible for this.

"I must leave you now to search for an emerald dragonstone, but I promise a joyous return when my companions are both free. Blessings of the Ancients upon you and your people, Maloch."

Maloch watched Yávië fade into the distance. Her council was wise. He would concentrate on improving the existing machines rather than attempting to construct new ones. Perhaps, he thought, he would build just one air machine, to see if it would work. And with that thought, a small elemental fire demon, living in a nearby torch, slipped inside Maloch's mind, taking up residence and creating discord.

Maloch grabbed his temples, pressing against the debilitating pain. His arm swept across the worktable, sending plans cascading to the floor. As he sank to his knees, the pain began to subside.

The Dragonstone

To find an emerald dragonstone, one must first locate a dragon, not just any dragon, but a particular dragon. In this case, the particular dragon was Eonis, the emerald sea dragon who held Rydén's talisman. Since it was not wise to approach the sea dragons on foot, Yávië called upon Aero, son of Aerodorn, wind dragon of the Suunflyte.

His arrival was spectacular as always; roaring in like one of Maloch's out-of-control machines, shimmering as oil on water, so transparent that she could see the pale light of his giant heart beating at the center of his massive chest. He slowed at the last moment, dropping gently as a marsh fly onto the sand beside her.

"Greetings," his voice thundered in her head. Knowing that his voice deafened most, he rarely spoke aloud to any other than dragons. *"It has been long since you called upon me, Huntress. What is our task?"*

"What, no formalities? "None of your, 'Suunflyte and Honor of the Ancients' repertoire?" Yávië queried. "Very un-dragon-like, don't you think?"

Aero's brow furrowed, causing air to shift along his form. *"I am anxious to be about the business of my Huntress."*

She flung herself against him reveling in the billowing, pillow-like softness of his airy scales.

"Such nonsense! You forget I can see that ghostly light you call your heart, Aero. I can see it and feel its beat as if it were my own. I remember when you first ventured forth from that leathery egg, my friend. Huntress, indeed! When have you ever paid the least attention to my direction?" Yávië laughed.

He gave a soft "shuff-shuff" sound, the dragon's equivalent of a laugh.

"Then perhaps it is the adventure for which I am anxious." The young dragon admitted.

"Well, you are in the right place. You and I are off to collect something from the sea dragons . . . emerald, sea dragons. Are you stout enough for an adventure of that nature, my windy friend?" Yávië asked.

Lowering his body and extending his neck so that she might mount his broad withers, he spoke aloud, "Direct me, Huntress. Your thoughts are mine as well. I have never met a sea dragon I couldn't drown."

He rumbled with delight deep within his scaly body, causing Yávië's jaws to knock against one another.

"I had forgotten the wonder of dragonflight," she thought to herself as she rested her head against Aero's broad shoulder and watched the landscape slip away beneath them.

Soon the sea dragons were fishing below them. It was a joy to watch them as they ascended from the depths only to dive again; large enough to eat even the greatest fish in the sea, they scattered frenzied schools before them.

She touched Aero's mind lightly, suggesting they might come to rest on a small isle near all the activity.

"I will just have to hope they don't eat me before they hear me out," she muttered.

"I will not allow that, Huntress."

In spite of his inexperience, Aero looked very serious, and quite capable of protecting her from any threat they might encounter.

"Walk to the edge of the water and let them see us. That will give us some idea of our welcome." Yávië directed.

Aero did as requested, leaving enormous tracks across the sand. When he reached the water's edge, he allowed himself to be become visible to the hunting members of the Sailflyte. All action ceased and the sea dragons turned as a group, all eyes on Aero and his passenger.

"Speak, wind dragon," thundered their hunt master.

"Honor of the Ancients upon you and your flyte, Eonis." Yávië felt Aero's scales rise; not enough to imply threat, but sufficient to show courage and strength. "My Huntress comes on a quest for your Huntress Rydén."

Eonis's good eye narrowed and his weight shifted. His scales rose, showing the green sea beneath. It was not a display of threat . . . yet.

"Why does my Huntress not come herself?" His tail lashed once in a show of displeasure.

"Eonis, Rydén would come to you if it were possible. You must know that. She is in trouble and needs your stone." Yávië allowed pleading to creep into her voice, knowing that a show of strength would bring a battle without a victor.

"I have heard rumor of this, but did not believe my Huntress weak enough to be captured and imprisoned. Perhaps her right to lead this flyte should be challenged?" His head lifted and tilted to view Yávië with his good eye. "Perhaps I should challenge you as well?"

Yávië felt Aero tense beneath her and soothed him with her mind.

"Is your emerald dragonstone not the talisman of Rydén? Is it not a symbol of the respect she has shown your flyte? Dare you challenge the Guardians, Eonis? Have we not been given dominion over you by the Ancients?" Yávië allowed her voice to grow bold.

A show of strength for a show of strength, a threat for a threat—dragon's diplomacy, a game of chess—it was child's play to Yávië.

Eonis drew his head back, nostrils flaring in pretended offense, before lowering his gaze and deferring to her. Lifting a great claw, Eonis plucked the tiny dragonstone from between his eyes and held it out toward them. Leaning forward over Aero's shoulder, Yávië took it from him—a perfectly shaped emerald dragon, one of Rydén's talismans.

On the shore near the Azure Sea, Yávië bade Aero farewell and went in search of the master stone forger who held Nall's stone dagger.

The Stone Forge

Only one of the Ancients was capable of forging in stone. Mallowort often stated he had tried to teach others the art, but no one actually believed it. He enjoyed being the only one with this knowledge, and it was unlikely that he had truly attempted to share it. This was why he was entrusted with Nall's dagger. Yávië knew that it would have been reforged by now, hidden inside a larger blade—perhaps a sword or carving knife.

Mallowort's encampment lay cradled within the tangled roots of some of the largest braid trees. As Yávië entered the adjacent clearing, she couldn't help noticing the absence of a forge.

"Mallowort! You old curmudgeon! What have you been doing with yourself?" she called out.

Silence. Beginning to get annoyed and a little bit alarmed, she called again, "Mallowort, are you ill? Or are you just hiding out in there because you know I don't fit?"

When there was still no response, Yávië knelt down and peered into the open doorway. She detected shadows from a flickering lantern and the smell of roasting meat.

Hearing a rustle behind her, she stood and turned. There, looking scruffier and crosser than ever, stood Mallowort.

"What do you wants? I'm intolerably busy; don't have time for visiting, so just be off with you! Out of here, now! What? Are you deaf? Go, go now, away! Don't make me bust you with this stick!"

Unable to control it any longer, Yávië burst out laughing, then gave a sharp cry as the stick smacked her soundly on the knees.

"*Ouch*! Stop that," she said, backing away slowly and rubbing her knees. "What is it you're so busy with anyway? You don't even have a forge."

"Hmmmmph! Shows you don't know nothing! I got one, you just can't see it!"

"An invisible forge? Why would you need an invisible forge?"

"Fool girl! For makin' invisible things, of course!"

"Of course," she replied. "I knew that." Wondering what he was really up to, she decided to inquire about the dagger. "Mallowort, do you remember the dagger Nall gave you? To keep safe for him."

"'Course I remember! Do you think I am some addled old fool? Show respect, whelp! Or don't talk at all, that would be even better."

Mallowort started toward the door of his bothie, but Yávië stepped quickly into his path, blocking the way.

"No, you don't, old man. Not until you answer my question. Do you remember? Do you remember where it is now?"

"Bah, I knows where it is," he chuckled. "It's you that don't know."

"True, and that is why I have come to you—to ask you where it can be found. I must have it back." Yávië stated.

"Then you will have to build a forge. I'll have to get it out from the handle that it's in." Mallo said nodding his fuzzy white head.

"Handle? You put Nall's dagger in a handle?"

"Said to hide it, didn't he? So I did—in the handle." He pointed to a wooden door with a large ornate stone handle. "Forged it and carved it up myself." Mallowort beamed.

"Mallowort, I don't know how to build a forge!" Yávië wailed.

"I will teach you. Apprentice is what you will be. My apprentice." Mallo chortled gaily. "Seven seasons."

Sweat ran down her face, dripping from her hair as if she had been in a rain shower. This was to be her final test – to build a forge alone without any direction from Mallowort. Seven bad-tempered seasons. Unbelievable.

She knew he was watching her work, shaking his head and making nasty little noises, sniffing each time she made a mistake, if indeed she had made any.

As Yávië stirred the mixture, she added prickleberry tea to the clay and sand instead of water, just as Mallowort had instructed ten thousand times during her "apprenticeship." He said it aided in making her forge weather resistant—not that there had been any weather to worry about in months.

She could still hear his voice. "First gather up twelve prickleberry leaves and burn off the spines over an open fire. Cut them and boil them in a pot for five turns of the shadow clock. Then strain the liquid through the skin of a chale tree. Keep the tea and throw out the pulp. One bone bucket of prickleberry tea, one bone bucket of clay slurry, one bone bucket of sand and two bone buckets of hardwood ash. Mix it with an armload of longgrass. Build the base of cinder stones four hands square. Make it stout; keep the forge opening small to hold the heat."

Wiping her brow Yávië put the final touches to her forge. It looked perfect, but only the fire would tell.

"The first few heats will be a little slow, but once the crucible is hot you are ready to go." That little rhyme Mallowort chanted to her with every new build. She hoped it would hold true this time.

Yávië carefully placed the prepared charcoal, banking it as she had been taught, and finally lighting the kindling with a waffle root match. She held her breath, slowly releasing it as the kindling caught and began to heat the coals. She did this three times over the next three days, hardening the crucible to make it ready for the dagger.

Mallowort stood by Yávië's side as she placed the oddly shaped, intricately carved handle into the forge. She glanced sideways at him, furtively, so he would not notice. The smile on his face lit him up like a candle. She knew he would call her a master at the forge.

A clap of thunder cracked overhead, and rain began to pelt the forge. It hissed and snapped, but the forge held. The prickleberry tea offered the waterproofing that Mallowort had promised. She turned toward him and asked softly, "How did you know?"

Mallowort looked into her eyes and said with a smile, "I am this piece of the Prophecy."

At that moment, a bolt of lightning struck the forge tossing pieces of the structure in all directions. As the dust settled around them, turning to mud in the rain, Yávië saw that Nall's dagger lay exposed between the two halves of the now broken handle.

Dobbinwort's Furnace

As exceptional as Mallowort's skills were at stone forging, it was to be Dobbinwort's turn in the art of silversmithing. After a brief stop to collect it, the damaged Iaito, which had been carefully tended by the Ancients of Meremire during the captivity of the Guardians, was now in Yávië's possession. Wrapped in a soft cloth woven from the webs of spiders, the two pieces rested one on either side of her waist.

Tales of the Iaito led back to the Ædracmoræ stories, a legend among one race of people there. How it came into the possession of the magickal man who had given it to Rydén was unknown. Yávië only knew that it was one of Rydén's talismans, and was therefore needed for her release. Blood as old as the ages remained sealed in the cracked hilt, adding to the sword's mystic properties.

While many smiths might repair the Iaito, only Dobbinwort could replace its magick. Without that, it was just another sword.

Dobbinwort made his home in a small village of the Ancients far out on the Ruby Sea. His bothie was constructed of the bones and shells of creatures living beneath his feet, as were most of the buildings of the township. What set Dobbinwort's apart was the large ornamental sign above the portal: "Dobbinwort's Supernatural Sword Shop". It always gave Yávië a giggle when she read it, for most of his swords were really quite ordinary. Only those specially commissioned by Ancients or Guardians were truly "supernatural."

As she stooped to enter the doorway, a deathawk swooped at her from its nearby perch. "Still haven't taught that hawk any manners, I see," she said laughingly.

"By the soot of my chimney, Yávië! It is Yávië, isn't it? It has been so long I could bes wrong," shouted Dobbinwort.

"Yes, indeed it is the Yávië you recall, though older and wiser, 'tis sure. I've come with work for you, Dobbinwort; if you have time for it, that is."

"Time? Time for you? Of course, of course. What you needs, girl? And how's that downy flier?"

Deciding not to risk a battle over the "girl", she looked around cautiously and leaned closer to whisper. "I have need of a repair . . . a magick repair, Dobbinwort, for Rydén's Iaito. Xander is well, as you can see for yourself." The small flier peeked out from inside her shirt at the mention of his name.

"Rydén! How is Rydén? Where is Rydén? I haven't seen Rydén in . . . well . . . I don't remember when I saw her last! Why doesn't she bring the sword herself? How did she break it? Not taking good care of it, I see," Dobbinwort rambled on.

Quickly placing one of her hands against his mouth and a finger to her lips, Yávië whispered, "This should be kept secret."

"Oh! A *secret*!" Dobbin mumbled through his covered mouth. "You want the fulgor furnace! You want Dobbinwort to put the supernatural back in that sword! I know it! I *know* you do!"

Removing her hand and wiping it on her cloak—it had gotten quite wet with all his sputtering—Yávië replied, "Indeed I do, dear Dobbin. As only you can do."

"A fortnight it will take." He spoke in a hushed voice, apparently agreeing that this was definitely a secret commission. "A fortnight; no less and no more. Return for it then." He clutched the wounded sword to his chest. "Such a shame, such a shame. Very pretty sword. I will make it better than well," Dobbin promised.

"Tell no one you have it," Yávië cautioned. Knowing very well that she would remain within sight of the Iaito, she sank down on the tiny chair next to his workbench, crossed her feet at the ankles and her arms over her chest, and allowed her head to rest against the wall. "Begin your magick, my old friend, and wake me in a fortnight."

"Yávië, Yávië, looky here! All done, *see*!" Dobbinwort beamed proudly.

Yávië reached out and took the sword in her hand, turning it left and right, admiring the weight of it. Light rippled across it, the surface shimmering like a Topaz Star-dappled sea.

Dobbinwort blew out the lamps, leaving the shop in darkness but for the glowing sword. "Look inside."

Lifting the Iaito, Yávië looked into the blade. There she saw the swirling stars of a hundred universes.

"Very good magick for Rydén," whispered Dobbinwort with a sly smile.

And the last talisman needed to free the others. With a hug for Dobbin, Yávië set off once more to visit Maloch and his machines.

Chapter 9: The Summoning

Summoning of Nall

Nine long seasons! Yávië could never have imagined her quest to recover the six talismans could take so long. Of course, her unwilling apprenticeship to Mallowort had not helped, but she had certainly learned the art of stone forging!

With her ingestion of the Maelstrom, Yávië had learned the location of Nall and Rydén, but reaching them would be complicated and require some assistance. Nall's release must come first, for Yávië could feel his sorrow increasing, his light growing pale, and the shadows on his soul growing deeper. Should his summoners grow so dim they offered no reflection, the union of the soul with the body would crumble, leaving Nall shattered beyond repair.

Maloch and his machines would provide access to Nall's prison in the tubes beneath the Trembling Sea.

"A machine that goes beneath the sea?" Maloch looked at Yávië quizzically. "Why would you believe I had such a device?"

Yávië turned and faced him. "Have you not learned yet that I see all you do? That I know what you build, when you succeed and when you fail? That I know your thoughts and hear every word you speak? Do not play games with me, Maloch. I am in no mood to play."

Maloch hung his head, but she felt his deception, knowing that before long the next phase of the Prophecy would begin, ripping at the world and causing it to bleed. This day, however, she need not waste time on what could not be changed. This day her energy must be used to release Nall.

"Show me the machine," Yávië instructed Maloch.

Maloch complied, but the chill of unrest flowed from him like the breath of the Southern lands covered in snow. Yávië did not waste time chastising him again, allowing the dissension to grow—as it must in order to fulfill the Prophecy of Men.

"You will take me," Yávië instructed, climbing into the machine moored beside the ramp leading into the water. While she no longer trusted Maloch, she preferred him to be with her rather than above her.

Undeniably, the machine was a marvel. Its framework was fashioned from the ribs of some great fish, and covered in a metallic fabric woven from the scales of sea dragons. A large window of lightning glass spanned the bow of the craft, allowing her to see the underwater world into which they swiftly descended. A dazzling array of fishes and other marine creatures schooled and darted this way and that. A flyte of sea dragons hailed, as they swept by, obviously comfortable in the presence of the craft.

Maloch handled the undersea machine expertly. He controlled their speed and direction with the light touch of his hands on the levers.

"Your machines are truly wonderful; they must give you much satisfaction," Yávië complimented him.

Maloch turned and faced her, smiling for the first time since her arrival. "They bring me great pride," he answered.

Great sadness lay behind the smile she offered him in return, for from his pride would come his fall.

Guiding him with her mind, Yávië brought the craft to a cleft in one of the great underwater mountains of the Trembling Sea. She knew that once this place had been the home to Sirens released during the creation by the Ancients . . . Sirens who had perished in battle with the Maelstrom. The ground around the mount remained littered with their bones.

Then, on the left, Yávië saw the doorway to Nall's tomb. Her heart swelled and her throat tightened, constricting her breathing. Nall's light was so very pale, his umbra so dark. "Precious Ancients, let me not have come too late," she wept.

As Maloch brought his machine inside the cavern, they began

the ascent to the dry chamber where Nall was waiting. As the top of the craft rose above the waterline, Yávië leapt out, pausing only long enough to dismiss Maloch.

"Maloch, you are free to go. I have no further need of you this day." With that, she rushed headlong into the center of the cavern carrying her Staff of Souls.

Her lips moved in silent incantation, holding Nall's soul within his body by sheer will. Yávië quickly removed his three talismans, placing each at its appointed location: Dagger to the North, Gaianite crystal to the South, and golden feather to the West. She positioned herself to the East. Raising her slender arms, her voice then rang out loudly, echoing within the cavern walls. Yávië's eyes never left the crystal prison inside the center circle, as she began to recite the names of the Sojourners.

"Abaddon, Adorne, Aerial, Alandon, Amdahl . . . Deron, Dagnar Glarunga . . . Ileana, Kalmac, Karngul . . . Udûne, Uftak, Uglúke, Uinn, Uinenili . . . Yal, Yavna, Yavnnë . . . Zamînl, Zerok, Zirockzegel."

"Hear me, Most Ancient Travelers." The tap of the staff was loud against the rock. "Come forth, summoners of Nall." Again, the tap echoed through the cavern. "Beware the wrath of the Ancients if you fail him!"

The staff struck for the third time, followed by a brilliant flash of blinding amber light. As her eyes cleared she saw them there—Nall's summoners. Each of them raised his right hand and stepped forward into the circle that held Nall's prison. Fingertips touched and another flash of amber illuminated the walls of the cave. With the startling sound of a thunderclap, the crystal prison shattered, leaving in its place not three summoners, but one Guardian. Nall stood momentarily before collapsing to the cold, stone floor.

"*Nall*!" cried Yávië, feeling the pain of his captivity. She knelt at his side and placed her hands on either side of his face, allowing strength to flow through her and into his body.

"I wept for you, Nall. I was so frightened. Your light was so pale." Yávië's eyes fixed on his face, as Nall raised his head.

"And Rydén?" he inquired, his hand now strong on her arm, eyes a blaze of amber.

Summoning of Rydén

Despite his great protestation, Yávië left Nall in the care of their old teacher, Morgwort, and headed south with great haste. Having the successful completion of her quest within her grasp drove her forward to the great glaciers of the Halcyon Ice Field. It was there that Yávië felt the pull of Rydén's light, steadfast and strong.

As the ice came into view, a feeling of unease settled over her, followed by the hint of another's pain, faint and far off. Changing direction, Yávië headed for a distant crevasse, which split the great glacier beneath her. Focusing her senses on the faint pulsations, she crept to the edge, lay flat, and peered down. Below her, on a snowy shelf, lay a great ice dragon. His breathing was shallow and each exhalation cast forth great, billowing clouds of steam. The shadow of his heart beat slowly within his glass-like chest. A deep shudder passed through his body, causing his icy scales to ring like a king's fine crystal.

Yávië looked about for a way to reach the dying dragon, as images of Aero with his young, airy strength filled her head. She could not let a dragon die alone. Pulling her Staff of Souls from her pack, she began to cast steps into the side of the crevasse. Moving cautiously, she lowered herself down to the dragon's head. "*Brother Dragon*," she sent her wordless message to him.

While the great head remained motionless, he opened his eyes and allowed his gaze to settle on her. "Maloch's dragons," he moaned through clenched jaws. "Beware his dragon flyte; they have no

166

Matriarch, no souls." Yávië knew in that moment that Maloch had completed his flying machines—they were the soulless dragons of which this ice dragon spoke.

"Guardian? Will you carry my shard to the Matriarch of the IIzenflyte, so that it does not remain here alone?"

She stroked his cool, broad head and nodded. "But not too soon. I will stay with you and we will speak of the Ancients and the creation of the dragon flytes that you may rest peacefully in the Great Hall."

With his death came great responsibility. To care for the soul of a dragon was a duty as heavy as that of a blood oath. In accepting this responsibility, she accepted it not only for herself, but for Nall as well. Because of their blood oath, they were considered as one Guardian by the dragon flytes. Her failure would be Nall's failure as well, so she must not fail. Gently she spoke the words that would release the dragon's heart shard.

The dragon's massive body collapsed in on itself until only one piece remained—the shard of ice containing his soul. Yávië gently placed the shard in her water flask where it would melt and release the soul into the cool water. It would remain there until she reached the IIzenflyte.

IIvaria, Matriarch of the IIzenflyte, was waiting when Yávië arrived outside the flyte's entrance. Dusted with snow, she was invisible until she stepped forward, elegant and regal, a true flyte Matriarch from the time before remembering. IIvaria retained all of her flyte's wisdom from the time of the Ancients' release of the dragons. Each name, age, hatching and death was inscribed on the tablet of her soul. It was now time to add another, that of IIzenglad, her first born. Though she did not speak of it aloud, the message passed through the flyte that there would be retribution.

Following her brief and sorrowful stop with the IIzenflyte, Yávië sped quickly toward the ice caverns where Rydén remained. As day turned to night, she kept a steady pace southward.

As the Topaz Star rose above her, she came abreast of the portal to the cavern. Pausing momentarily to clear her mind for the task ahead, she broke through the snow covering the opening and stepped inside.

As she had done for Nall, she placed each talisman in its appointed place, stepped to the East and called forth Rydén's summoners.

With the recital of the Sojourners' names, a peace fell over her, a peace she had not felt in nine long seasons. With each strike of her staff, the peace grew deeper.

The talismans brought forth the summoners, who stepped forward with arms raised. Yávië wept with joy when the crystal holding the captive fractured with a blinding emerald light, leaving Rydén standing before her. The Guardians' power filled them, and she knew that Nall was feeling his sister's freedom even as she witnessed it, feeling the power that would come with the gathering of The Three.

Gathering of the Three

Resting against a wall high above Maloch's workroom, Nall watched the men and women of Maloch's tribe rush to and fro below him. He found their behavior amusing. They made him think of an insect after a trail of breadcrumbs is disturbed, but the focus of his interest was a sandy-haired man who barked the orders and caused all the scurrying about. Pushing off from the wall, Nall drifted slowly to the center of the room, moving between the strange contraptions suspended from the ceiling on heavy rope and large metal hooks. Then, turning sharply on his heel, Nall returned to the far side of the room. He continued to scan the people at drafting tables, as they sketched nervously for this demented inventor. Occasionally he would drop from his resting place above them to look at the drawings of the war machines the lunatic Maloch had them imagining.

Nall remained a spectator this day. He had not yet recovered sufficiently to manipulate the more complex of a Guardian's abilities. In fact, the simple act of hovering above this massive room and remaining cloaked had proved difficult, even though it should have been a simple enough task. Despite his dislike for Maloch, as he continued to observe, Nall found himself admiring—at least to some degree—the man who was so driven and single-minded that he could not even see the discontent of his people.

"*Now that takes skill.*" Nall thought, laughing to himself.

Right now Nall was supposed to be under the watch of his old teacher Morgwort. Even though it was with Yávië's best intentions,

Nall felt far too old to be left in Morg's care. Dealing with Morgwort, even when Nall was in peak condition, was a trying experience and being "looked after" during this weakness constituted an unspeakable horror.

The final insult had come when Morg offered his fallowass as transportation. Nall's vision of himself seated upon the foul-smelling, evil-tempered and unkempt beast had driven him to call upon a dragon to carry him away from the unreasonable little Ancient. Since he sensed a disturbance in the nearby city, he decided he might as well pay a visit to the man Yávië called Maloch.

It appeared that Maloch had done well. His city was heavily fortified and it was difficult to find a place where a dragon could land unnoticed. Nall had decided it would be best if Azrea remained a fair distance from the city, allowing him to slip in from Maloch's throne room.

Dropping in from above, Nall settled at Maloch's side and watched him intently from within the cover of his veil. He sensed the man's frustration and anger at everything around him, but most of all towards Yávië. He resented the simple people he had been asked to lead, hated their ignorance and plodding nature, but his deepest hatred came from the fact that Yávië attempted to restrict his creations. Nall felt his blood heating with fury at this stupid man's lack of respect and honor.

Nall raised his hands to Maloch's temples, hovering there as he thought how easy it would be to crush Maloch in that instant—so easy to simply dissolve his mind into a gelatinous slime. Or perhaps it would be better just to open the walls Yavie had so carefully built to protect Maloch from past nightmares. Sighing, he dropped his hands. This man was part of the Prophecy, and although despised, Nall would not break it. "*Bound by prophecy before I was summoned,*" he thought bitterly.

Another and darker thought also stayed his hand—that killing Maloch at that moment would be murder.

He was growing weary of listening to the man's volatile thoughts. They blasted him with hatred and discontent. Nall was on the verge of erecting a wall around Maloch's mind to contain the wickedness when something within the man's memories hissed. It spoke with a fiery crackle and seemed to be feeding Maloch's fury. Nall drew back, shocked. All this time, there had been a presence in Maloch's mind that Yávië had not noticed?

Sliding deeper into Maloch's consciousness, Nall sought the elemental fire demon. He wove his way among memories and dreams, finally arriving at the barrier the small entity had constructed around its hiding place. He watched as the demon piped a steady stream of evil into Maloch's mind. Thoughts of dark destruction and chaos reached Nall—strange machines of dragon scales releasing fatal flames. These were the dreams of Maloch. Nay, not dreams, but Maloch's future. Nall heard the fire demon whispering delightedly at the coming terror of Maloch's war machines, Maloch's great mock dragons. An image appeared within Nall's worried mind—the image of a hangar in the rock, built into the mountainside behind Maloch's fortress. Suddenly Nall sensed the attention of the demon.

Nall had been discovered lurking in Maloch's mind.

Maloch seized up, screaming in pain as the demon's flame flared. Clutching his head, Maloch screamed to the guards, "Go . . . protect the hangar, for we have been discovered. Prepare the dragons, save them . . ."

Nall fled, calling for his dragon mount as Maloch's guards raced to do his bidding.

From his position on the dragon's broad back, Nall scanned the area. Despite the fact that many guards had been drawn to the hangar, they did not seem particularly prepared to deal with a threat. Bows were flung carelessly to the side and swords were sheathed. He grinned. Maloch's men had little respect for their mad leader. Perhaps some of these people could be saved.

With silent instructions, Nall directed the dragon's attack, dropping from its back to stand in front of a group of Maloch's men. Casting off his veil, he watched the looks of terror spread among them. With a nod of his head and a wave of his hand, Nall sent a wall of force toward the startled men, pushing them away and flinging them in all directions.

A stream of acidic dragon's breath rained down from above as the accordant dragon obeyed the Hunter's instructions. The stone and wood of the giant building bubbled and boiled. Barrels holding the crystal fuel of Maloch's machines burst like thunder, filling the hangar with flame and destruction.

As the dragon circled back toward the Hunter, they heard the call of Maloch's horns summoning troops to meet the threat—too late. As a throng of Malochians raced toward the failing hangar, Nall leapt once more to the great Matriarch's back and wondered if any good would come of this small victory.

Upon Nall's arrival back in Meremire, Yávië raced into his welcoming arms.

"Morgwort tells me that you were quite impossible during your stay with him." Yávië pursed her lips to hide a smile. "Now why would you want to cause an old man such trouble, Nall?"

Nall snorted, "Crazy old man. It is difficult enough to bear him when one is full of health. Can you imagine him when he is *caring* for you? I simply had all I could stand, and went off to do some work. I was feeling fit enough. Look at me, Yávië. Don't I look fit?"

He did indeed look fit. His health had returned and in spite of his pretended annoyance at Morgwort, he seemed in good spirits.

"Yes, you look quite fit, which is well for there is a storm brewing. The Prophecy is soon to be fulfilled for the men of this world."

"Yávië, I saw Maloch while you were away. Watched him. He has built his flying machines in the image of the dragons,"

"I know, Nall. The first-born son of Ilvaria and Ilgrond told me just before his death. He was mortally wounded by one of Maloch's machines. Soulless, he called them. The Ilzenflyte intends retribution. A war is coming. As foretold in the Prophecy, we must choose a side. You must gather the Emeraldflyte dragons and attack Maloch's machines before they leave his lands. Rydén must use the Sailflyte to destroy the sea machines, and I must go to Galen." Yávië spoke.

"Did I hear my name?" Rydén asked. Her beauty and youth were stunning, yet her eyes and mouth were soft with sadness.

"Morgwort is in some sort of a maelstrom himself, spouting about machines beneath the sea, mechanical dragons, and the general doom of war. I will, of course, assume he is right . . . as always. So, where is it I am needed?" Rydén continued.

Nall reached out and put his hand on Rydén's shoulder, "You, little sister, are needed in battle—a place well suited to you. Yávië requests that you take that motley group of so-called dragons and put an end to Maloch's sea machines. I hear Eonis is feeling a bit testy and may require your firm hand," he teased.

Smiling, Rydén concurred, "Eonis does require my firm hand, but he is one of the fiercest, even with only one eye. I will be off to the Trembling Sea and summon him. Maloch's sea machines days are numbered." With that, she returned the way she had come.

"Rydén, we will meet at the Council of the Ancients once this task is complete! Honor and glory to you!" called Yávië.

Rydén lifted her hand in acknowledgement.

"Honor and glory, Nall! Yávië! May the Ancients guide your flytes until we meet in Council," her voice floated back to them.

"Why is she so distant?" asked Nall, worry furrowing his brow.

"Because she is young, and for some reason her soul is much heavier to carry than either of ours." Yávië placed a comforting hand on Nall's arm.

"Remember, she has control of a flyte of sea dragons. She is neither weak nor foolish, Nall."

As Aero landed with a whisper of scales at her side, Yávië leapt lightly to his withers.

"Until the Council, Nall!"

A Call to War

Yávië again stood in the shadows of the man Galen's bedchamber, watching him as he slept. The years had treated him well and he was loved and respected by his people. He had led them from their wandering to stable settlements and brought them from poverty to wealth. Of Yávië's three chosen leaders he had been, by far, the most successful. Even though she knew the Prophecy by heart, she liked to believe these mortals chose their own fates, and to some small degree, perhaps they did. After all, if Maloch had followed her directives there would have been no soulless flying machines, no dead ice dragon and no impending war. Building them had been his decision, hadn't it? It was as if he were driven by some demon. Shaking her head, Yávië stepped closer to Galen's cot and whispered his name.

"Galen."

Even after all the years of safety and security, he was up in a flash, eyes wide and stone dagger in hand.

"Is it your intent to slay me or summon me, Galen?" Yávië asked in jest.

"Yávië? You have come with news of Maloch? Aero was here warning of possible trouble with the IIzenflyte to the south. What is it that Maloch has done? The IIzenflyte have never been a threat."

"One of their own, the firstborn of IIvaria and IIgrond, has been slain by Maloch's infernal flying machines. Whether it was intended, I do not know. But I do know that the IIzenflyte plan to

174

seek retribution against him, and I do not believe they will seek it through the Council of the Ancients.

"I have come not just to bring you news, but to prepare you for the coming war. The dragons of the Suunflyte are at your disposal, and I believe you will also have the support of the IIzenflyte. Nall will coordinate an attack on Maloch with the dragons of his accordant flyte. It is Nall's hope that he can at least disable some of the flying machines still hidden within the mountains. Rydén and the Sailflyte will destroy the sea machines. You and I, Galen, will prepare for war."

Chapter 10: Dragon Storm

The Challenge of Ardane

Nall watched as Yávië soared away on Aero until he could no longer see her and then silently whistled for Azrea. Unlike the wind dragon, she was not silent. He heard the beat of her leathery wings long before he caught sight of her. She was Matriarch of the Emeraldflyte, an accordant or empathic bloodline that had evolved from the Earth dragons. She did not land lightly, but with a crash that sent nearby boulders tumbling. Azrea and her flyte would certainly put the fear of the Ancients into Maloch.

Extending her long neck, she greeted him with her smoky salutation, "Welcome home, Hunter."

Azrea and Nall traveled swiftly on the great winds to the domain of the Emeraldflyte. Azrea landed on the ritual gathering ground of the dragons, extended her head to the sky, and bellowed three times. The world around them vibrated and birds rushed up from the forests below.

Within moments, the world was alive with responses to Azrea's call. The wind became charged as the sound of hundreds of wings taking flight filled the air. Like breaching sea giants, the dragons rushed up the sides of the cliffs, arched, then landed firmly on the plateau. Scores of emerald green behemoths posturing and snapping at one another surrounded Nall and Azrea. In the skies beyond, a hundred more circled the gathering site.

An angry bellow preceded the last dragon. With staggering might, Ardane, Lord of the Emeraldflyte, came to rest in front of Nall and his dragon Queen, Azrea. The dragon's imposing bulk and flamboyant entrance silenced the others. Placing one of his great talons in front of him, Ardane stared down at Nall.

"You . . . " he rumbled. "What brings you to our land?" His eyes pierced Nall, as if trying to burn him.

Nall cocked his head and stared up at Ardane. "I do not have time for this, Ardane. I know I could not have changed enough for you to forget my image, let alone my scent."

Of all the dragons in the flyte, Ardane was the only one with whom Nall still had to posture and joust to obtain compliance.

"Ardane! Do you challenge me, the Hunter of the Emeraldflyte?" Nall's voice thundered. "You know of the pledge! You know that the first born of the Ilzenflyte has been slain! You know the battle approaches and we must stand ready!"

Nall was no longer simply addressing Ardane, but the entire flyte.

"Grand words for such a small creature!" Ardane bellowed.

"You think I speak lies, Ardane?" Nall said, matching Ardane's tone. Slowly, Nall rose from the ground to stare into the eyes of Ardane.

Ardane lifted his scales and bared his teeth, but still he dared not touch Nall.

"Do not be foolish, Ardane," said Nall. "Despite our differences we are, and always will be, equal in strength, and a battle between us would result in victory for neither. You know as well as I that if I had commanded it this conversation would not even have taken place. I respect you, and so I let you speak. But this game is growing tiresome, Ardane. Time is precious and we cannot afford to waste it."

Ardane sat snarling at Nall.

"Maloch's soulless machines lay inactive. It is time for us to strike. So Ardane, do you seek to sever the pact of Adra?" Nall said, placing his hand over his chest.

Below it glowed something green, pulsing through Nall's hand. Adra's heart shard, her very soul, had been entrusted to Nall. A collective thunder came from the flyte around them, then all placed their right talons forward, heads bowed low; all except Ardane.

"I have kept this shard, Adra's very soul, because I failed her. It has sung me to sleep on many nights and kept the pain from my heart, but perhaps I have been too selfish in retaining it.

"I should have seen long ago how much you needed this," Nall said, taking the emerald shard from his neck and holding it by the golden chain he had woven for it.

Looking into Ardane's eyes, he spoke, "You, Ardane, are now keeper of Adra's soul."

Drifting closer to Ardane's great skull, Nall placed the shard on the dragon's head. Ardane's eyes closed for a moment, as the shard touched his scales. The whole dragon flyte seemed to be holding its breath.

When his eyes opened, they were ablaze with angry fire.

"You dare, little one, to question a dragon's honor! *No!* You will not break this pact so easily, whelp. At the end of this battle, Adra's soul will be yours again. I will not dishonor my dead mate's pledge!" he roared as he launched himself into the sky. "On now, my kin! We will fight and win against these soulless machines!"

Around Nall and Azrea, the dragons of the Emeraldflyte took flight and followed their Lord. As Ardane vanished from sight, Nall chuckled and walked back to Azrea.

"That blowhard," said Nall, laughing. "So many ages and now the bad blood is finally starting to fade away."

"I never thought it would happen," replied Azrea as she watched the flyte follow Ardane toward the horizon.

Nall hopped on Azrea's back, and they leapt off the plateau— following the great flyte at Azrea's fastest pace.

A Trust Betrayed

The dragon Eonis met Rydén at the shore of the Trembling Sea. He was edgy, knowing full well that Aero's Huntress would have spoken of his earlier disrespect.

"Huntress," he said, extending his neck.

"Eonis, we have a task to complete. I expect you wish to apologize for your rudeness to Aero's Huntress, but we don't have time for it now. So just save it, will you?"

As a dragon Huntress, Rydén had been taught well in the art of dragon diplomacy. While she knew an apology was the thing furthest from his mind, a deliberate dismissal of her charge's unacceptable behavior would leave him off balance, right where she wanted him.

In a further attempt to shame him she added, "Take me to your mother."

After a backward glance, he dove beneath the sea, forming a diving bubble between his scales to keep the Huntress safe on the deep dive to the flyte's home.

To walk into a dragons' flyte was an overwhelming experience. Cavern walls towered over all. The sleeping ledges were vast fields of stone and at the far side of the chamber, Sybeth and Sygarnd lay relaxing on theirs. Eonis padded on dripping feet to stand in front of his parent and Matriarch, lowering his Huntress to the floor before her.

"The Prophecy of the Men is coming to pass. The strength of your flyte is needed. A mortal has overstepped his bounds, causing the death of the firstborn of IIvaria and IIgrond. He has also placed machines beneath the sea that are a threat to this flyte. They are shielded with sea dragon scales. Which of you allowed this?" Rydén asked tersely.

Sybeth drew herself up to her full height, towering above Rydén. This was a serious accusation, for the law of the Ancients forbade the use of dragon scales by any save dragons or Guardians.

"Why do you think it was allowed? Why could the *man* not have stolen them from the scale pile?" Sybeth challenged.

Rydén shook her head. "I may have been captive in a crystal, but I was neither blind nor deaf. I heard a dragon's voice freely give the scales, Sybeth, and I saw Maloch take them from a dragon's claw."

"And did you recognize this dragon's voice, Huntress?" prompted the great dragon.

"Nay, but I am certain that you did," Rydén replied sharply.

Sybeth moved from her ledge, allowing her tail to brush Rydén's legs, causing her to stumble.

"What if I did, Guardian?" She put her face up close to Rydén's.

Rydén steadied herself. "You will mete out a swift punishment to any involved, or see this flyte destroyed."

From within her cloak Rydén drew a crystal, round and clear as glass. Holding it out before her, balanced on three fingers, she asked, "Do you recall this, Sybeth?"

Sybeth pulled back her head and bellowed in terror. It was a creation crystal, capable of entrapping an entire dragon flyte.

Hearing the dragon's thoughts, Rydén chuckled, "Oh, not just any creation crystal, Sybeth, but the Sea Dragons' creation crystal. It will destroy your flyte without harming the others. You choose. The traitor . . . or the flyte."

With an anguished roar, Sybeth's mate, Sygarnd, sprang from his ledge and closed his great jaws over Eonis' neck, twisting and snapping, leaving Eonis broken and bleeding on the sand of the flyte's floor.

Rydén knelt near Eonis' head. "I have time for that apology now," she whispered into his ear as the last of his light ebbed. There would be no one who dared to gather this dragon's heart shard.

"Call the flyte, Sybeth. I will explain my plan," Rydén commanded.

Death of a Dragon

The attack on Maloch's mountain workshop had not gone as Nall intended. Unfortunately, the initial assault had alerted Maloch to the fact that his air machines were no longer secret. By the flyte's second strike, a large number of the machines were already in the air or preparing for launch. Many had already fled the area.

Nall had not been prepared for the machines' defenses. Maloch had managed to build a flame launcher using the gases produced by fermented dragon's dung. The gas was held within a yingass bladder and then forced out over an open flame. While it did not do excessive damage, it created a distraction among the dragon flyte, causing them to swerve and fly lower than normal. This enabled the catapults on the ground to toss heated boulders with remarkable accuracy.

From Azrea's back, Nall watched as her acidic breath—weapon of the accordant dragons—spread over her targets like a perfectly projected beam, dissolving scales and exposing the fragile cores of the air ships.

Both damaged machines and wounded dragons plunged to the ground. Nall saw Ardane arch his neck and bellow as his breath peeled away the framework of a machine, then, using his immense weight as a battering ram, collide with the remains to send the resulting fragments plummeting to the earth.

Below them still stood the catapults, armed and ready to fire.

"Azrea," Nall shouted to his dragon mount, "We have to destroy the catapults. They are more dangerous to us than the air machines!"

Azrea did not reply, but simply banked and pulled her wings close to her body. Suddenly the ground was rushing toward them, but just when it seemed there would be no way to avoid death on the rocks below, she extended her wings to make a crash landing on the ground.

Nall ducked to avoid the catapults' heat, but Azrea strode forward with acid bubbling up from her throat. She launched a stream of acid across the catapults, leaving them in ruins as their operators fled screaming, though not before several had launched their burning boulders.

An agonizing howl pierced the air. Both Nall and Azrea turned as one, staring into the sky. Nall's heart constricted as it had not done since the day the Maelstrom imprisoned him. Ardane was dropping from the sky in an uncontrolled spin, a massive wound in his chest.

Azrea gave a roar unlike anything Nall had ever heard and shot into the air. Remaining low over the ground, she sped toward the rapidly descending Ardane. The earth shook as Ardane's body crashed down. Azrea could barely control her speed as she slid to a halt on braking talons.

Nall disappeared from Azrea's broad back and reappeared at Ardane's head. He knelt, immediately aware that Ardane's breathing was very shallow, and his eyes were growing dim.

"Ardane," Nall said quietly, brushing his hand against the dragon's thick, scaly hide.

Ardane coughed and blood flowed over his tongue.

Azrea approached, a rumbling deep in her throat, nuzzling Ardane as she wept a dragon's tears. "Nall will heal you, my love. He will," she growled deeply, denying the truth.

Ardane shifted his head until he was looking directly at the two of them. "Do . . . not deny the truth, my Queen."

Despite his pain, his voice was strong and dignified. He looked at Nall.

"My time has come. And nothing, not even the Guardians, can stop it. For all their power they cannot heal my death wound."

Turning to gaze on Azrea, Ardane spoke to her heart. "My heart, my soul, you will, indeed you *must* go on. You must continue to lead the flyte. Our clutch is un-hatched and our offspring will need a mother and a father. You must take a new mate, Azrea. Even in your sorrow you will do what you must."

Ardane wheezed. With every word, he was growing weaker.

"Nall, you must take my heart shard—and that of Adra—to the Well of Viileshga. You will know what to do."

Nall looked at Ardane gravely, "Are you sure?"

Ardane gave the soft "shuff" of a dragon's laugh. "Is an emerald green?"

Azrea stroked her dying mate as he gave a final shudder. His breathing stilled, and his eyes grew cold.

As Nall spoke the words to free the heart shard and lifted his hand from Ardane's side, the body gradually turned to stone. The stone cracked into dust and blew away in the wind. Left lying at Nall's feet were the pulsing emerald heart shards of Adra and Ardane. He lifted them, his eyes filled with a sorrow that quickly turned to rage. Raising his eyes to the sky, he began to ascend, amber energy flowing over him like the reflection of light on the crystal surface of the Sea of Sorrows.

Nall rose, screaming, into the sky. His hand extended out, holding the remaining air machines motionless. With his mind he began to rip and tear at the machines, causing them to buckle. He ripped the gas bladders open in fiery explosions, as burning pieces floated down around him.

"Maloch!" Nall screamed. "You will die this day!" With those words, Nall vanished, leaving only a fading amber haze in his wake.

Between the wreckage of an air machine and the man he sought, on a battlefield far from the one where Ardane died, Nall appeared.

Yávië stood there, staring at Maloch. Looking up she gasped, "Nall!"

Nall's body was rippling with amber energy. His breathing was ragged, and echoed as if it came from a great depth.

"You! You, little *Wort*!" Nall staggered, his body drenched with sweat. His hand hovered in front of Maloch's face, "I . . . I will see you to your death."

Nall's body seized, doubling him over and dropping him backward to the ground at Yávië's feet, where he lay convulsing. As his body finally relaxed, two pulsing emerald dragons' heart shards fell from his open fingers.

Beneath the Trembling Sea

Rydén gazed at the dragons gathered before her. The air was thick with their breath and the sound of their shifting bodies. They were a delight to behold, their beauty stunning. Unlike the insubstantial appearance of the Wind Dragons, or the massive bodied Earth Dragons and Fire Dragons, the Sea Dragons were delicate. Their scales were specialized for travel under water, the outer scales almost leafy—like the great leaves of the underwater forests. Encumbered on land, they were remarkable in the sea, gliding along at great speeds and delighting any rider. Unfortunately, where Rydén was about to take them only danger and the possibility of death waited.

"Damn Maloch," she exhaled.

The plan was simple. Maloch would not expect an attack from the sea dragons. They had never given any indication of threat. There would be no threat now, only direct aggression. Led by their Matriarch, they would destroy all of Maloch's ships. Sybeth held Maloch responsible for the betrayal of Eonis, and Rydén had done nothing to dissuade her from that belief.

Returning scouts reported five machines underwater within the Trembling Sea and one docked at the ramp near the workshop. Rydén's eighty-dragon flyte would form six war groups of eight dragons each. The remaining thirty-two dragons would provide a distraction by pretending to hunt near the shore of the Malochian city. Rydén's only hope was that the underwater machines had no weapons, for if they did there was bound to be sorrow at the end of the day.

Sybeth and Sygarnd, with the four chosen hunt leaders, would each lead a hunting group. As the decoy hunt departed, the six attack hunts went to their assigned machines. From Sybeth's back, Rydén remained in contact with the hunt groups using her mind to guide and control them. A coordinated attack was imperative if they were to bring down the machines.

At her signal, the dragons broke off their hunt pattern and began systematically to ram the machines. The sounds of clashing scales and splintering bone framework soon filled the air; the mingling of human screams and dragon calls deafening. One by one, Maloch's machines sank to the bottom of the sea.

Rydén felt the fear and pain of the drowning men and swore against Maloch, "If Yávië does not kill you, I will."

Sybeth gave a bellow to recall her flyte and the dragons dove, returning to the flyte grounds beneath the sea. They were safe, and for that, Rydén was grateful. A shudder passed through her, as she sensed Nall and Yávië were not as fortunate.

A Prophecy Fulfilled

The dragons of the IIzenflyte answered Yávië's call and hundreds had assembled in the fields outside Galen's settlement. IIvaria paced restlessly in front of her flyte, eager to repay the murderer of her firstborn.

Across the courtyard, the dragons of the Suunflyte were assembled. Instructions had been issued and they impatiently awaited the call to flight.

Galen stood next to Yávië. In the twilight, they gazed across the fields, ripe with men and dragons prepared for war.

"How does this end, Yávië? I cannot see how any good can come of it." Galen spoke softly, so as not to be overheard by his nearby men. "I don't want my people to die, yet how can I prevent it?"

Yávië sighed deeply and turned to look at Galen. "You are a great leader, Galen. Look at them. Men and dragons ready to follow you into battle, ready to die for a leader they believe in."

"Well, the men perhaps, but I really believe the dragons are here for you, Yávië. Aero is the only dragon I have ever spoken to," he teased.

Yávië laughed. "I summoned and they came by the dictate of the Ancients, but I believe their true desire is a good fight; dragons are like that. Of course, for IIvaria and IIgrond it is more personal, their son was lost. It is good to see you still have your sense of humor."

She stepped forward and every head turned toward her.

Speaking aloud for the sake of the humans present, and sending her thoughts directly to each dragon, she spoke in a calm, clear voice.

"We have come to fulfill the Prophecy of Men. A man has broken the laws of our land by building war machines and using dragon scales as shields. He has," she looked at IIvaria, "taken the life of an ice dragon, and caused the deaths of his own men in a battle with the sea dragons this very day. This man has betrayed his tribe, the Ancients and the Guardians. It is time for us to rise up against him."

Galen came to her side. "Galenites, we have an important role in the Prophecy. As foretold, we will join with the Guardians and the dragon flytes to overpower one who was once a friend. Many may die, for that is the way of war. But if we die, it will be with strength and honor. Blessings of the Ancients on us all!"

Galen stepped back, deferring to Yávië's command. Raising her arms, with palms upward and eyes closed, she covered her troops with a veil of protection and gave the signal to mount for flight. She could sense both the unease of the inexperienced riders and the impatience of the dragons. Today would be a trial for both.

Aero lowered his great head toward Yávië, his eyes locked on hers. "Huntress, my blood runs hot, as does that of my brethren. We will not fail you this day!"

Yávië's answer was a sad smile as she leapt to his withers.

To see three hundred mounted dragons rise in a single moment is beyond imagination—wondrous airy, wind dragons amidst the glittering ice dragons, all calling with deafening voices in the excitement of flight; the most aggressive of them lashing out with talons and snapping at those next to them in anticipation of the battle.

As they rose, Yávië sensed movement on the far northwestern horizon.

A voice shattered the quiet of her mind, "*Why were we not summoned, Huntress?*"

A spontaneous smile crossed the face of Yávië. It was the unmistakable, gravelly voice of Faera, Matriarch of the Kilstoneflyte war dragons.

Slowing the wind and ice flytes slightly, she prepared a response for the offended matriarch. As Faera flanked Aero, she released a burst of flame and smoke, displaying her obvious displeasure.

"Blessings of the Ancients to the Kilstoneflyte, Faera," Yávië responded. "You were not called to battle because your flyte's name is not written on the scroll of the Prophecy of the Ancients."

Turning quickly, and matching Aero wing stroke for wing stroke, her massive head no more than a few hands from Yávië's, Faera replied with the stone-like implacability that only a dragon can exhibit. "Then I will change the Prophecy and allow the Ancients to fall where they will. What can it matter? Did you intend to win without us? Of course you did! I see it in your eyes, Yávië, and feel it in your soul. Now you will win with us! A war requires war dragons!"

Giving a long, low bellow, she called her flyte into a new position, regrouping to the east of the ice dragons.

All that remained was to bring Maloch to his knees.

As Maloch's mountain fortress came into sight, Yávië got her first vision of the flying war machine. Built in the image of the dragons, it was large but not as large as a true dragon. Like the underwater machines it was constructed of bone—not the bone from some great fish, but the bones of dragons. The machine flew with the power of Gaianite light crystals, giving it endless power, and it had superb shielding with the use of dragon scales. However, a point of weakness gave them hope. Beneath the structure lay the entry portal, unshielded to allow easy entrance and exit to the machine. It was here the dragons would strike: blowing, freezing and burning through the unprotected area. While a single dragon could not break through the portal, a coordinated strike of fire, ice and wind would shatter it. Without the arrival of the war dragons, this could not have come to pass. Yávië smiled again at the wisdom of the war dragon Matriarch.

From within the mountain, the machines began to rise. Certain death awaited those within them who had put their trust in Maloch. At Yávië's signal, trios of dragons began to pass below each machine, ice dragons with their freezing breath, followed by war dragons and their fire. Finally, the ethereal wind dragons cast their breath to shatter the portals and destroy the machines from within. The cacophony was deafening.

Sensing Maloch's presence, Yávië quickly summoned Faera and Ilvaria to her side, guiding their path beneath his machine. Following closely, she directed Aero's breath and watched as the doorway shattered, throwing the machine into a downward spiral. The three dragons trailed the craft in its descent, landing nearby on the fractured earth. IIvaria thundered toward it, frost from her frozen breath hanging in the still air. Guiding Aero, Yávië placed his body between IIvaria and Maloch's broken air ship. Shaking her head and soothing IIvaria with her mind, she turned toward Maloch. Just as she started to speak, a movement near IIvaria caught her eye.

Nall! His anger was so fierce it caused her to take a step away from him. Moving toward Maloch, uttering words she could not comprehend, he collapsed at her feet.

Maloch drew back his hand, a silver dagger clutched ready to strike Nall.

"Stay your hand, Maloch! If you do not I will kill you!" The words were spoken before the thought had formed.

Yávië nurtured her hatred toward Maloch, and felt the beast within her push against his prison. A snarl escaped her lips and her features slowly shifted. Backing away with horror on his face, terror in his eyes and a scream in his throat, Maloch tripped over a dragon's scale, landing hard on his back.

As Yávië approached him, a great, clawed foot stopped her forward motion. "Nay, Huntress. His death is not yours to deal."

Aero's cool breath caressed her cheek.

Blinking, Yávië's eyes came back into focus, feral features softening. "Maloch, it is indeed your lucky day. You owe your life to this dragon."

She dropped beside Nall. Placing her hand on his heart Yávië allowed her unspent power to fill him. Permitting relieved laughter to bubble up from her center, she smiled and pulled Nall to his feet.

"And you, Nall, owe your consciousness to this . . ." Her words cut off as Maloch threw himself against her.

Fully recovered, Nall grabbed Maloch's arm, flinging him to the ground. "In my version of the Prophecy, you die!" he cursed.

Placing a hand on Nall's arm, Yávië addressed Maloch. "You have evil in your mind, Maloch. Evil you could have cast off, but chose not to. Because of this, the Ancients have decreed your eternal imprisonment."

Hatred crossed Maloch's face. A voice not his own spoke with a sound so vile it burned in the air around them. "I am *all-powerful! My machines are great!*"

"Your machines are dead, Maloch." Drawing a crystal from within her cloak, Yávië said, "A prison for you and your followers."

"No!" croaked Maloch, falling forward on his knees, gagging and retching.

"Not . . . my . . . people!" He gasped as if unable to breathe. He fell to his side clutching his head.

"The . . . people . . . have . . . no . . . guilt!"

Foul smelling vomit rushed from his mouth, spraying his crushed and battered air machine. There, within the vomit, lay a small flame, flickering faintly toward extinction.

"De . . . mon!" cried Maloch, throwing himself toward Yávië and the empty crystal.

Opening her mind, Yávië swept Maloch into the crystal, speaking the words that would hold him there for eternity.

Turning, she hugged Nall, sliding Adra and Ardane's soul shards inside his tunic.

"You should be happy, Nall. Maloch's prison will remain in the care of Morgwort. Can you imagine it? Eternity with Morg."

Laughter released their tension and flowed around them, with the "shuff, shuff" of the dragons joining in.

Calling Aero aside, Yávië caressed his wind-scaled neck. "Thank you, old friend. I would have failed without you."

Then she called the flytes, offering praise and then dismissing them to return to their resting places. To Galen and his men she extended the invitation of the Ancients. A great feast would be held in Meremire following the meeting of the Council.

Chapter 11: Justice of the Three

Arriving in Meremire as the daystar set, Nall and Yávië met Morgwort outside the Hall of the Council.

"Rydén arrived yesterday—no damage for her flyte," the Ancient told, nodding his head in agreement with himself. Glancing covertly at Yávië, he tugged at her sleeve. "You bring Maloch the machine maker to Morg?"

She smiled and answered, "I did, but he will remain in my custody until the Council formally states otherwise. Why are you so anxious to examine him, anyway?"

"To make machines for good. For bringing water, for long-life fire, machines for good," Morg stated, grinning his nearly toothless grin. "I will picks his mind clean through the ages."

As they stepped into the Hall, Rydén ran to them, clutching Nall tightly. "Nall, I am so sorry to hear of Ardane's death. I know he was difficult for you, but . . ."

Nall held up his hand, shaking his head and closing his eyes. Soon he would make the trip to Viileshga, but for the moment, there were more pressing matters on his mind. The decisions regarding Maloch's tribe had to be made – difficult decisions that demanded his full attention. With a sad smile, Nall led them to the Council.

Morgwort waddled into position to the left of Rosewort and the right of Dobbinwort. As he took his seat, Rosewort stood to address them.

"As the Prophecy foretold, the machine war was brief, but not without cost. The machines' master is condemned by the Prophecy and cannot be saved. His people will be sentenced according to the Guardians' wisdom." She sat and nodded to Nall.

"Honor to the Council of the Ancients," he began, considering his next words carefully. "Maloch had many people. Some followed him, some expressed objection to the war machines, and some were innocent of the knowledge. It is hard for me to speak of this, for Ardane's life was lost because of Maloch's pride and greed. But Morgwort says good can come from machines, and that he will use the knowledge to help the whole of Æstretfordæ. For this, he will need those with knowledge of the machines. My vision is of three parts. Those who followed Maloch should be scattered to the four winds. Those who objected should become the builders of the new machines, and the innocents should be entrusted to Xavier and become one with his tribe." Bowing, Nall stepped back.

"Honor to the Council of the Ancients," Rydén spoke as she stepped forward. "My vision is of enslavement to the tribe of Galen for those who followed Maloch blindly into war. For those who protested his evil actions and for those innocent of knowledge, I see them melded within the tribes of Galen and Xavier. While my flyte did not suffer injury, that of my brother did. I feel that enslavement for those responsible is just punishment." Bowing, she took her place next to Nall.

"Honor to the Council of the Ancients." Yávië bowed her head silently, allowing her raven hair to fall forward around her face. "I lack the wisdom required here. Without a dragon's guidance I would have failed the Prophecy and Maloch would be dead."

Nall stepped forward and put his hand on Yávië's arm. "According to that dragon, you chose to save my life at the expense of his. I would consider it a wise decision."

Yávië looked up at Nall, tears flowing freely. Throwing herself into his open arms, she wept shamelessly. Finally, she drew back and smiled through her tears.

"Your life and mine are one, Nall. I chose our lives over his, but I truly would have killed him if not for Aero's intervention. Surely the Council cannot allow this to pass without censure?" Yávië pointed out.

"If I recall correctly, only moments before you threatened to slay Maloch, I had done the same. Had unconsciousness not intervened, Maloch would be dead by my hand," Nall spoke truthfully.

"If the two of you is finished, we would like to hear Yávië's recommendation. Maloch is not dead, and the first Prophecy of Men has been fulfilled, as it was told." Willowort reminded them.

Regaining her composure, Yávië addressed the Council. "It is my vision that the minds of the Malochians be rewritten; as their creator, it is my place to do so. I do not believe that Ancient Morgwort will require their assistance, as he has Maloch with whom to spend the ages. I request that these souls be reclaimed within Galen and Xavier's tribes equally. I do, of course, defer to the Council's decision." She bowed before the Council and stepped back to join Nall and Rydén.

Looking kind and wise, the wisdom of the ages pooled in her eyes, Willowort then stood. "Guardians, you serve Æstretfordæ with strength, wisdom and honor. We will discuss your recommendings, and speaks of the decision when the daystar rises. Until then, we will feast and celebrate this part of the Prophecy's fulfillment. Soon the quest for Truth will require your strength and devotion."

"Galen's tribe has arrived." Rosewort added, smiling.

Indeed Galen had arrived—bringing not only his own people, but Xavier and his people as well.

Yávië was almost vibrating with excitement as she brought Galen and Xavier to meet Nall and Rydén.

"Nall, Rydén," she called, "meet Galen and Xavier."

"It seems we should already know one another, Galen, as we have fought a war together," Nall said, before turning to Xavier. "Have we met before? For some reason, your name and face are known to me."

"We spoke long ago in a vision," Xavier responded with a nod.

Rydén smiled shyly under her auburn hair, her eyes glittering with mischief as she welcomed both men to the feast.

"The music starts soon; perhaps I will ask you to dance with me," Rydén added, speaking to both, but looking at Galen.

"Xavier's musicians are very good, but I do not believe they play music for dancing," Galen replied, giving Rydén a stiff smile.

"Oh, we Ancients will provides the dancing music," Morgwort added, with a slap on the back for Nall.

"I don't dance, Morg," said Nall, glancing around to see if anyone thought he should.

"Then you better gets on a dragon and flies out of here before Rosie and Willow shows up. They say everybody dances," Morg laughed. "Too late! There they comes!"

Dobbin, Brundle, Weezel and Willow began to play and their music was sweet with flutes and lyres, and definitely made for dancing.

Rosie grabbed Nall and sashayed around the fire with him, much to his embarrassment and to the discomfort of his aching back and knees. Yávië laughed with glee at Xavier's solemn bow and accepted his hand, following Nall and Rosie around the fire.

"I guess that leaves us." Rydén looked up at Galen. "You wouldn't leave me all alone, would you? That would be very ignoble of you. Come," she said, slipping her hand into his and pulling him toward the others.

The Decision of the Council

They sat in the Council chambers, awaiting Willowort's arrival. Seated apart, Yávië was deep in thought over the past night's festivities. Rydén's attentions upon Galen made her uneasy but she was not quite sure why. Galen was a grown man, and Rydén knew all the rules of Guardianship, so there should be no danger there. Still, her mind would not rest.

As Willow entered the chamber and took her seat, Rydén glanced knowingly at Yávië. "Now what was that about?" Yávië asked herself.

"The decision's made. We weighed each recommendations careful, and 'tis decided that what's best is to allow Yávië to wipe the minds of the Malochians. Then she can places them half each with Galen and Xavier.

"Maloch will remains in his prison under the watch of Morgwort for all his days. Yávië, you can gives him to Morg at the close of Council.

"With the ending of the war and the capture of Maloch, a part of the Great Prophecy has been fulfilled.

"It was a dark time when the Guardians was lost to us. Now begins a new time of light; a time when the search for the past Truth will begins. Dragon evil still abounds, and it is time for the second calling of the Guardians of Æshardæ to helps us. The deaths of the dragons Aerodorn and Adra will be avenged and the ones responsible punished.

"Keeps the law and be mindful of temptations." Willowort stood, looking at each Guardian in turn as if searching their hearts for signs of betrayal, before making her way out of the chamber.

Morgwort hurried toward Yávië, anxious to begin his research into Maloch's machines. Yávië almost felt sorry for Maloch. She handed Morg the tiny crystal, smiling as he rushed off toward his newly constructed longhouse, complete with a workshop, and then turned to Nall and Rydén.

"I wonder what it was Willow was searching for within us?" Yávië asked.

"I was curious too," Nall agreed.

"Oh, I think she was just wondering how much fun I had last night," Rydén said with a wicked smile. "Isn't that what you were wondering, Yávië?" she added with a toss of her hair before walking away.

"Yávië, what is wrong with her?" Nall asked, obviously bewildered.

Yávië laughed, "Don't worry, Nall, she is just being Rydén. Shall we go to meet the Guardians from Æshardæ?"

Nall cringed; he had not forgotten his last meeting with the Guardian Sōrél.

Wondering at his expression, Yávië asked, "What is it?"

"Nothing, just some pain from all that dancing. Come, let's make them welcome in Æstretfordæ."

Yávië's Heart

"**N**all! We meet again," Sōrél said as he approached them. "I see our lady has been recovered from the dungeons of Ardane, and her long sleep within a crystal as well."

He lowered his voice and looked deep into violet eyes. "Are you well, Yávië?" he asked, his fingers brushing hers.

Electricity shot through her as if she had been stung by a gall wasp, and her hand jerked back involuntarily.

"I have seen you . . ."

". . . in a dream," Sōrél finished for her. "I have seen you as well. I was also with Nall when he rescued you from Ardane's lair. He did it quite well."

Looking to Nall, Yávië whispered, "Then he gave up his freedom so that I could reach Meremire safely."

"Where is Näeré?" Rydén asked, stepping up behind them.

"Rosie required her for some reason, but she should be along soon. I understand I missed the opportunity to dance with you, Yávië." Sōrél whispered.

Feeling her face flushing, she answered, "I only danced with Xavier; I needed his empathy."

Rosie and Näeré suddenly appeared through the doorway. Rosie seemed to be pushing Näeré ahead of her.

"We thoughts we heard your voices," Rosie said brightly. "Nall, could you take Näeré up to the fields? She needs to talk to the Wind Dragon, Azaeria."

At the mention of Azaeria's name, Yávië offered to take Näeré.

"Nay, nay, Yávië, you need to take Sōrél to meet Galen. He waits near Morg's bothie. Get now, all of you, gets."

She shooed them ahead of her as if they were a flock of wood hens.

Yávië felt her heart grow heavy as she watched Nall and Näeré.

"Why so sorrowful, Yávië?" Sōrél asked. "He loves you, you know, but he is a little foolish."

"How dare you!" Yávië hissed. "You know nothing of Nall, nothing. He is . . ."

Sōrél held up his hand to ward off her angry words as he pulled her near.

"He did not come when you called. He broke a blood oath. I was called, Yávië, at Willowort's request. I came to find you."

Her eyes blinked and a single tear fell.

"No, that cannot be." She looked confused, and Sōrél felt a pang of guilt pinch his heart.

"It is true," a soft voice added. "The Council sent me for Nall, but he could not be bothered. He chose his self-pity over your blood oath. If it were not for Sōrél, you might still be lying in the filth of that dungeon. Sorry, but sometimes the truth is difficult to take."

Rydén smiled at Sōrél. "Perhaps I should take you to Galen. Yávië isn't looking well."

Yávië ran. She did not care where as long as she was far from those who so coldly conveyed those painful words. Finding herself outside Rosewort's bothie, she grabbed the door and flung herself inside. Dropping to the floor, she hugged herself as if to ward off a wintry cold.

Rosie knelt down beside her and held her tight.

"Oh, Yávië, don'ts be sad! Think of all the goodness. Nall is good and kind. His sorrows at the loss of Adra were great; he should not be shamed for it. He cares much for you, you knows it. Remembers the warnings of the Teller of Prophecy, Yávië, remembers them. And, Yávië, Sōrél cares deeply for you. Sōrél sees only the law and to him there can be no reason to breaks a blood oath, but . . ." Rosie rocked Yávië gently, wrapping her in a warm coverlet.

"But Rosie, I cannot bear it, something is not right." Yávië whispered as she drifted off to sleep within the hold of Rosie's spell of deep sleep.

Rosie and Willow held hands and looked down on Yávië.

"This gots to stop," Willowort snapped from the doorway. "This gots to stop soon. I will tells Sōrél to takes her on the morrow. He will keep her safe and shows her things to keeps her mind away from here. Set her on the search for the Truth."

Rosie nodded. "But for now, just lets her dream."

In her dream, Yávië stood in the center of a great domed garden. She looked up at the falling water, one of many falls cascading hundreds of feet into the garden pools— the Xavians had built a beautiful place. People passed around her, but she remained unseen except by the children, who, in their innocence, could pierce the veil of mist as long as she allowed it. She smiled at them. They often hid behind their parents in shyness when they saw her. There was a gentle tug at the back of her mind alerting her to the presence of another Guardian. Turning slowly, Yávië saw him leaning against a chale tree—so natural, so relaxed. He stood taller than she, a good head taller. His hair was the deepest chestnut and his amber eyes were cast downward at the stone dagger in his hands. He smiled a smile that told her he was up to no good.

"So, no embrace for your old friend?" Yávië quizzed.

Nall looked up, his eyes as bright as the night stars and he held her gently.

"It is good to see you again, Yávië," he spoke, his voice quiet.

"And you, Nall. You have grown." Yávië smiled.

He chuckled at her remark.

"This is the beauty you wanted to show me? The gardens of the Xavians?"

"Shhh," she hushed, putting her finger to her lips. "Come and see."

Nall felt leaden and awkward following Yávië's graceful form as she took his arm and led him through a long, wide hall into another garden where there were many people and, thence, to a small courtyard and a group of Xavians, elegantly dressed in flowing robes.

"Listen, Nall, just listen."

Nall stood transfixed by the perfection of the Xavians' voices, so exquisite was the intonation of their beautiful utterances.

He turned to Yávië, smiling. She looked into his eyes, which were as deep as drowning pools; eyes of sapphire . . .

But the face she perceived before her was no longer that of Nall. It was Sōrél's smile that filled her vision. It was Sōrél's eyes looking back at her with kindness and concern, his head tilted slightly as if questioning. His warm hand moved around hers.

"Come, Yávië, I want to show you something," he whispered.

Dance with a Demon

While Yávië dreamed, Rydén left Sōrél with Galen and then headed out toward the fields with Valia. The grass cat stayed close to her as they moved at a slow run. Since her release from the crystal, Rydén had felt the need to stretch at every opportunity, as if the ages spent within the small space had left her still feeling confined. Valia forged ahead, her long body swiftly covering the ground to the center of the field before collapsing and rolling in the grass.

"Silly cat," Rydén teased, rubbing Valia's soft underbelly to hear her purr.

Around her a song erupted, melodious as a carillon. She looked around for the source of the sound, but saw nothing.

"Rydén!" a voice called to her. "I need your help."

"Remember me?" the Siren asked, sitting down next to her.

"No," Rydén lied.

"It really doesn't matter, since you will do my bidding anyway. I know you will – you promised, Rydén. I remember it well. I see you have grown very beautiful, though not quite as beautiful as you had hoped, it seems."

"There is a very handsome man at stake, Rydén—a Guardian like you. A perfect match if it weren't for Yávië." Syria laughed, her voice like the tinkling of chimes.

"What is it you need, Siren? Just say it and go," Rydén snapped.

"Why, I need a dragon killed. Just a small one, not too difficult a task for a Guardian like you."

"A dragon?" Rydén looked at Syria. "Sybeth?" she added hopefully.

"Aero, son of Azaeria and Aerodorn," Syria smiled.

"*No!* I will not do it!" Rydén shouted, "He is a Wind Dragon and no threat to anyone."

"Oh, I think you will, Rydén. I really think you will."

The Siren ran her finger along the side of Rydén's face, leaving a long scratch.

"That one will heal. The next one may not," Syria hissed.

Stunned, Rydén held her hand to her face and watched Syria walk away.

"Do not make me wait too long, Rydén. Something quite ugly might happen to you," the Siren called back.

Rydén sat frozen.

Nall. Nall would help her. Perhaps they could kill the Siren. She would have to think up a reason, but Nall was often distracted and would not question her too deeply.

Yávië! That was the answer. If Yávië were the one being threatened, Nall would spare no weapon. When Rydén burst into Nall's bothie with blood on her face, he would believe anything she said. She just had to make sure they saw no one before they left to hunt the Siren.

Racing to his hut, she banged on the door and dashed inside. The bothie was empty; it was yet again as if Nall didn't exist. It seemed he often disappeared without telling anyone these days.

With a deep sigh, she stroked her blood soaked cheek and headed off in search of someone else to help her.

Rydén felt somewhat ill. It seemed her vanity was about to cost Aero his life. Too late for remorse, the Siren had said. How could it ever be too late to acknowledge an error in judgment? That was all it had been, after all. She really did not need any greater beauty, for she was already beautiful. She could have killed that trybrac and reclaimed the Pearl of Perception alone, even if the beast had been awake, she was certain of it, so she had not even needed the Siren's help.

It was unfair for Syria to expect her to kill Aero, Rydén considered making a deal with the death dragon, Dielmor. She remembered his hatred from her training. He was a perfect choice for a task such as this, and Rydén would remain innocent of the Siren's foul desire. What would Syria care as long as the deed was done?

Approaching the lair of the death dragons without gagging was impossible, but Rydén tried to exhibit the outward certainty and strength expected of a Guardian. Standing before the flyte entrance, she hailed the smelly beasts.

"Dahrea, Matriarch of the Direflyte, honor of the Ancients upon you."

"What brings you here, Guardian?" Dahrea exhaled her foul breath over Rydén.

"I come seeking Dielmor on behalf of the Guardian known as Nall."

"I remember you, whelp!" Dielmor challenged, "Have the Ancients not ended your miserable life yet?"

"Nay, Dielmor, they put great stock in my wisdom, as well as in the wisdom of my sibling, Nall. We seek your service. You will gain great favor with Nall by accepting this task."

"What is the task, whelp?" Dielmor snarled.

"A young wind dragon called Aero departs Meremire for the Suunflyte. Nall requests your help in ensuring that dragon never reaches the flyte. Surely this is not too difficult a task for one such as you, Dielmor?" Rydén challenged.

With a gusty laugh, Dielmor stretched out his neck and blasted her with the stench of rotting flesh, fire and ash.

"I accept this task with pleasure, whelp! Tell the Guardian Nall he is in my debt, and that the young wind dragon will be dead before the daystar reaches its zenith. Now take your foul odor from our flyte!"

Visions of Viileshga

Nall lay awake in the darkness of his bothie. In the days since the feast he had slept very little, yet each morning he rose with the same energy and vigor as if he had slept through the night.

He lifted Adra and Ardane's heart shards, watching as their pale light pulsed rhythmically. They were bound together by a golden chain and would remain that way for all eternity. He would make sure of that. As he watched them, he realized that his own heart beat with the same slow rhythm, as if it had slowed deliberately to maintain harmony.

He looked at the long, raised scratch along his forearm and remembered several days before. He had gone hunting with Hawk and encountered a bloodren, a small reptilian creature with sharp claws and a bad temper. Its attack had been swift and brief, leaving only the oozing wound as a reminder. It had not bled long; the blood seemed to coagulate quickly, leaving a series of bloody beads to dry above the gash.

He had been feeling angry recently, becoming enraged even by Rydén's foolish chatter over last night's meal. He had lashed out with angry words, seeing the hurt in her eyes and wondering at his own lack of control. Others had noticed, too. Yávië's look of concern still haunted him, and Sōrél's scornful look made him angry even now.

Nall had been keeping his thoughts from Yávië, who seemed more distant now, although he was not sure why. He did not wish to burden her with his recent concerns. There was no reason to draw Yávië into his personal cauldron of confusion.

Hearing footsteps, he dropped the shards beneath his coverlet and pretended to be asleep. Then he heard a soft chuckle.

"You pretends to sleep well, Nall," Rosie's gentle voice teased.

Nall opened his eyes, pushed himself up on one elbow and swung his long legs over the side of the cot.

"How did you know?" he asked. "I thought I was doing a fairly good job of feigning sleep."

"I knows you best of all, Nall. You can hides things from the others, but nots from me," Rosewort said, climbing up onto the bed beside him.

"Tells Rosie what's wrong," she prodded in a motherly way.

"I don't know, Rosie. I feel so angry and I find I don't trust myself to control that anger," Nall whispered.

Rosie looked at him gravely.

"Hmmm . . ." she trailed off, lost in thought. "Let me hears your heart, Nall."

Standing up, the little Ancient leaned forward and placed her ear against his chest, then pulled back and looked at him sharply.

"You beens playing with the bloodrens, boy?" she asked brusquely.

Without thinking, Nall lifted his arm and looked at the long inflamed scratch.

"Foolish, foolish, not tellin' Rosie and Willow when you are hurt! Them bloodrens is small, but they carries a powerful venom. No wonders you been feeling mean and ornery. I'll gets my healing bag and Willowort."

She hopped spryly off the cot and headed for the door, adding, "But it aren't just the bloodren's poison makin' you mad," she grinned. "I figures Sōrél for some of that responsibility."

Rosie and Willow cared for Nall very effectively, bossing him around and reciting incantations over him for two passages of the daystar. They even allowed Morg to visit and annoy him, to test his anger. Finally satisfied, they let him go to sleep.

Upon waking, he found himself alone with Rosie.

"Azrea and the flyte waits for you on the far side of the meadow. They arrived late last night. I think you are goings with them to the Well now. You won't be saying good-byes?" Rosie looked at him pointedly.

Nall whispered, "I wanted to leave quietly for the Well and take the sorrow with me."

"I wills say the good-bye to Yávië for you then," Rosie said, not looking at him.

Nall lingered in his bothie, turning Rosie's words over in his mind. His body still ached a bit, but she had assured him his blood was now clean. He threw on his shirt and leathers, pulled the strap of his satchel over his head, placed the dragon scale shield on his back and headed for the field.

The horizon carried a hint of gold as the topaz daystar began its ascent. Nall could just make out the forms of dragons resting in the field. It appeared to be the entire Emeraldflyte, and Nall wondered if they had come at Azrea's request, or in spite of it.

At Nall's approach, Azrea rose to her full height and stepped forward.

"I see you brought the whole flyte," Nall acknowledged.

"I could not have stopped their coming. They have attended my every step since Ardane's death," Azrea answered, lowering her head to receive her Hunter.

Letting out a bellow to her drowsy flyte, she pushed off with a leathery rustle, rising into the sky above Meremire.

As they banked away, Nall heard Yávië's call and saw her arm raised in farewell. He returned the gesture before looking forward to the difficult task that lay ahead, the placing of Adra and Ardane's heart shards at the Well of Viileshga.

As they approached the Well, Nall saw a woman, the one he had expected. Yávië had come to share the ordeal of parting with Adra and Ardane. Even though he had chosen to come alone, he regretted the decision. Sorrow should be shared; he understood that now. However, when he drew closer Nall realized the woman was not Yávië, but Sōrél's sister, Näeré. Smiling in an attempt to hide his sorrow and disappointment, he leapt lightly from Azrea.

"Näeré, what brings you so far from Meremire?" Nall asked.

"Nall," she whispered, drawing him to her in a gentle embrace. "You suffer so . . . and for naught. Yávië told me you were coming to Viileshga for the ceremony of the shards. I could not let you face this task alone. I have passed through the fire of this trial on Æshardæ many times. What you will witness will be with you forever. Your sorrow will be lifted, as will that of the dragon flyte."

Though she had released him, he still felt the warmth of her embrace and looked at her with a new respect. Then, feeling the gentle probing of her mind, he smiled and hid his thoughts.

Drawing back, she returned his smile, "You have avoided my probe. Do you think me a witch?" Näeré's smile broadened and she laughed heartily.

"We will see just how long you can avoid me, Hunter," she added lightly, as if it were a game.

Azrea shuffed at the two of them and Nall turned to her. He drew a cyliopendia root from inside his satchel. The gnarled and tangled root was all that remained of the ancient tree. Pulling the heart shards from his neck, he gently wrapped them within the root. Nodding to Azrea, he moved to the edge of the Well, followed by Näeré. Azrea gave a soft call, drawing the flyte to the Well.

As the flyte gathered and Nall prepared to speak, he felt a soft touch on his arm and looked down to see Näeré take his hand ever so tenderly, though her eyes never left the gathering flyte of dragons. A sudden need for Yávië welled up inside Nall and he almost drew his hand away, but as quickly as the need had come, it faded. Näeré's warm hand in his was the most comforting thing he had felt since the dragon Adra had drawn him to her and taken away his desire for the woman of his blood oath.

Taking a deep breath, Nall spoke, "In ages past, the great Willow tree brought forth the Ancients and they in turn breathed life into Æstretfordæ. Dragons were released from their long sleep and Adra and Ardane arose from them, the great leaders of the Emeraldflyte.

Pointing to the summit far above he continued, "Adra emerged there at the top of the falls, bringing with her the life waters of the Well; Ardane broke through below us, allowing the waters to return to the earth.

"A great blow was dealt the Emeraldflyte with the death of Adra, and then again with Ardane's death during the machine wars, but as the holder of their shards, it is my responsibility to see their deaths honored and their purpose fulfilled.

"As it is written on the wall of dragonian history in the chamber of the Emeraldflyte, with the passing of the two, their hearts will be placed within the Well, and the Well will be sealed forever. Adra and Ardane's hearts will remain in the Well, so that their souls may take their places in the heavens." Nall paused as the flyte rumbled in anticipation.

"But I will forge a new destiny for the Emeraldflyte this very day. The Well's life-giving energy will not be lost. In fact, it will grow even greater, for wrapped around these dragon hearts is the root of the cyliopendia! The verdant tree!"

The flyte roared as if in victory and Azrea gazed at Nall with appreciation. He felt Näeré's hand tighten on his.

Releasing Näeré's hand, Nall descended into the Well. Landing within the cavern, he walked with reverence to the water's edge. Holding the heart shards with great tenderness, he moved to the center of the Well, hovering just above the life-giving water. He gazed into the deep blue darkness that Ardane had dug and paused. Sighing, he wished Adra and Ardane one last good-bye and released the shards. They sank slowly, still visible within the dark waters, their lights pulsing in harmony. Without warning, the root around the shards erupted into life. Tendrils emerged from its sides, weaving through the water and plunging into the earth at the bottom of the pool. As the roots thickened, smaller ones sprouted, searching for a place to anchor, reaching deep into the life source and sealing the water's flow.

Watching the rapid growth of the root system, Nall returned to his place between Azrea and Näeré. As he settled there, the falling water slowed to a trickle and the world around them began to ring with the thunderous sound of the roots burrowing through the earth. The dragons of the Emeraldflyte broke, arising from their places near the Well and filling the sky.

A great trunk ascended from the center of the Well. As it burgeoned into the sky, roots from the cliffs shot out over the plateau, winding their way around the massive trunk and pulling it to the jagged edge of the precipice. The tree raked across the cliff, dislodging great stones as it grew toward the sky, twisted and gnarled.

Grabbing Näeré's hand, Nall leaped to the back of Azrea as she took to the sky. The great tree was engulfing the edges of the Well where they had stood only moments before. Below them, the forest seemed alive as the massive roots erupted from the ground like sea serpents, dislodging trees then plunging back beneath the soil. The roots ranged over great distances around the epicenter of the growth. The forest was in chaos as it gave birth to new life.

The great trunk shot into the topaz sky, ten dragon lengths above the lofty plateau. As its growth slowed, great branches thrust from the trunk, unwinding and casting shadows over the forest beneath. The sky filled rapidly with green as the branches grew leaves. As the tree's growth became imperceptible, a lush canopy formed above the ancient forest. The Emeraldflyte circled this new tree of life, a symbol of promise to the forest below.

The joyous calls of the dragons filled the sky. In Näeré's tight embrace, Nall sat at peace on the back of Azrea watching the great tree that he had helped bring to life. A smile lightened his features as he thought of Adra and Ardane's work being completed.

He hoped that Adra's spirit would help to guide these new protectors. Perhaps the life force within the great tree would be that of Adra.

"Soon," Nall whispered, "soon this tree will bear the first seed of the verdants, the protectors of our forests for ages to come."

Nall's heart was light. His sorrow seemed to have fled with the release of Adra and Ardane's heart shards. The great dragon Azrea, too, felt the fullness of heart that came from the shard ceremony. The daystar had warmed Azrea's scales and her riders were enjoying the womb-like comfort of the flight. Then, as they passed over the Crimson Fields, before turning toward Meremire, Azrea took Nall and Näeré by surprise and suddenly dove toward the earth.

"What is it, Azrea?" Nall called.

"A wind dragon is in danger. I sense his fear," Azrea roared.

A sudden updraft brought the stench of death dragons causing them to shudder, and bringing back a flood of memories for Nall.

"What are death dragons doing here?" Näeré asked. "Don't they usually inhabit the Wastelands where death and decay are plentiful?"

"Aye, but they are not scavenging this time. I sense this one hunts live prey," Azrea answered.

The wind dragon's long wispy scales trailed behind him as he passed below them at top speed, followed by the blackened death dragon. The smaller wind dragon was obviously young and inexperienced in combat, for not once did he roll to offer his claws to the opponent. The death dragon raked the back of the young dragon, causing a scattering of lost scales and a bellow of pain from his prey.

Azrea folded her wings and dove toward the two combatants, her neck extended and jaws open. As she sped past the death dragon, she snapped and ripped flesh from its side and her talons flew upward raking his face. She opened her wings with a loud popping sound and swung around to face him again. This time recognition flickered in her eyes and Azrea moved more determinedly, turning slightly above before diving again. There was no hesitation as she crashed into Dielmor, sending him spinning toward the grasslands below.

But Dielmor was not an easy challenge. He spread his wide wings and with great downward strokes rose toward the Matriarch of the Emeraldflyte. His eyes blazed with fury at her disruption of his sport with the young Aero. Dielmor was determined to rip Azrea from the sky, disemboweling her and feasting on her intestines before gulping down her heart shard, assuring the end of the Emeraldflyte.

As he arose and flew adjacent to Azrea, his eyes caught sight of the Huntress she carried. With fear in his heart, he quickly turned away. He was not quick enough, however, and the power of the witch's mind slammed into his body as if she had plucked a giant stone from the ground below them and hurled it into his side. His ribs caved in and his body fell into a downward spiral as he tried to right himself using his one, unbroken wing.

He felt Näeré's power follow him and knew that he did not have the strength to fend her off. Extending his good wing, he allowed it to slow his fall as he plummeted to the grass below. His body struck with such force that it created a huge impression in the earth. Sharp ribs punctured giant lungs, causing a great vent of steam to escape and form a cloud above his broken body.

Azrea approached, no longer aware of the Guardians she carried.

"Retribution," she hissed, "retribution for the damage you have done to my flyte, Dielmor."

Raising a large claw, Azrea placed it on Dielmor's side above his heart.

"Why do you hunt the wind dragon? I will not ask again. I will flay you alive, making what little time remains of your life one of agony and despair if you do not answer quickly," Azrea snarled.

Dielmor's eyes rolled in fear, not of Azrea, but of the Guardians now standing next to her.

Raising a talon toward Nall, Dielmor panted, "The red-haired one sent me to kill the wind dragon. She said it was your wish, that with Aero's death I would gain your favor." His eyes rolled again and he whispered in desperation, "Do not let the witch crush me."

Nall turned, glancing at Näeré, "Do not worry, Dielmor, I reserve that honor for myself."

He pulled his blade and plunged it deep into Dielmor's throat, watching indifferently as the dragon's rich blood soaked into the soil. Speaking the words that would release the dragon's heart shard as the dragon's eyes widened in terror.

"My shard!" Dielmor gurgled through the spilling blood.

"Do not trouble yourself, Dielmor; I will care for your shard!" Nall spat, staring coldly as the great dragon's eyes glazed over, and his body collapsed into a putrid pile of oily froth.

As they watched Dielmor's remains soak slowly into the ground, Nall reached down and grabbed the pulsing heart shard, flinging it carelessly into his satchel.

Näeré's eyes narrowed as she watched Nall. Turning to Azrea, she spoke softly, "Finally, you will have justice."

Two dragon lengths away Aero landed lightly. He was battered and sore, his breathing still heavy with fear.

"Honor and glory to you and your flyte, Azrea, Matriarch of the Emeraldflyte," he gasped breathlessly. "The Suunflyte will call you legend and sing ballads of your valor."

Nall approached, stroking Aero's glistening side. "Where is Yávië?"

"She is gone, gone with the Guardian called Sōrél, sending me back to the Suunflyte. I was journeying home when Dielmor struck."

PART II

Chapter 12: Ancient Mirrors

"Come, Yávië, I want to show you something," Sōrél whispered.

Yávie stared at Sōrél, "Is this another dream?"

"No, Yávië, no more dreams. Come with me. Willow has asked me to show you the mirrors."

Together they followed the underground path that led to the chamber of the mirror, beneath Meremire. Yávie was struck by its beauty. The mirror stood alone at the center of the chamber, its heavy wooden frame covered in the writings of the ancient Sojourners. The mirror itself was of polished bronze and within it Yávie could see her image beside that of Sōrél. She reached out and touched the surface with her finger, expecting it to prove malleable or fluid, but it was cool and unyielding.

"How . . ." she began as Sōrél took her hand in his, pushing them through the mirror, then quickly withdrawing his hand.

"You are not skilled enough to move through the mirror alone, but I can take you if you like." Sōrél offered.

"Where does it lead?"

"To the sister mirror on Æshardæ. Æshardæ was the first of the worlds inhabited by the Ancients and holds the mirrors to each of the six worlds." Sōrél smiled at Yávië's obvious amazement.

Yávie searched his face for the truth in his words and found no deception there.

"There are six worlds?" she repeated.

"No, there are seven. Æshardæ was inhabited first, Æstretfordæ last, with the others lying between. Yávië, do you truly not remember?" His voice was filled with hurt.

"Forgive me. I should not have asked. Willow expressly forbade it. I have no excuse beyond my own curiosity." His words were lighthearted, but the lightheartedness did not reach his eyes.

"Perhaps I should go now," Yávië began, but Sōrél placed a hand on her arm.

"Step through the mirror with me, Yávië. Come to Æshardæ."

Secrets of Æshardæ

As Sōrél and Yávië crossed into Æshardæ, the polished bronze mirror solidified and Æstretfordæ faded behind them, reflecting only their images.

"Come," Sōrél insisted, taking her hand, "the other mirrors are in here."

Entering the next room, Yávië's eyes became bright with wonder. From the top of the cavern hung crystal stalactites each glowing from within, and around the perimeter stood six perfect mirrors, each with a massive wooden frame that carried the words of the Sojourners. Each reflected her image as she examined them. Above each was a name: Æcumbræ, Æshulmæ, Æwmarshæ, Æstaffordæ, Ælmondæ, and Æstretfordæ. At the center of the mirrors was a pool of deep, violet water, shallow at the edges but becoming deeper as it neared the center. Sōrél stepped to the edge and then turned toward Yávië.

Her fingers stroked the name of Æstretfordæ lovingly.

"Will you take me home if I ask it of you?" Her eyes sought Sōrél's in the polished bronze.

"I will take you anywhere you want to go, Yávië. I will do anything you ask of me," Sōrél answered, his voice barely a whisper.

"Why?" Yávië asked softly.

"I . . . Yávië, I cannot tell you, it is forbidden to me," he said with his eyes lowered, breathing deeply.

"Sōrél, why do you weep?" Yávië said as she watched a single tear fall into the water.

He looked up, smiling sadly, "Because, like you, my heart has been broken, my Truth stolen from me."

"Let us return to Æstretfordæ. I believe Näeré and Nall have arrived at Meremire with news."

"Sōrél," echoed a masculine voice. "Grumblton says that I should return to Æstretfordæ with you. I will be studying with a Guardian there. One named Nall. Do you know of him? Have you met him?"

"Aye, I have had the displeasure," Sōrél replied tersely. "Come then. There is bad news at Æstretfordæ. Yávië, this is Zeth."

Yávië smiled to keep from laughing, for the young man before her was extremely disheveled. His fine, blond hair stuck out as if he had slept on his head. Bright blue eyes looked out from a slender face filled with excitement at the prospect of such an adventure. He was too tall for his clothing and his bony ankles and wrists extended below the sleeves of his shirt and trousers. As he moved forward, he tripped over his staff, catching himself at the last moment to avoid sprawling on the floor.

"Nall will be honored, I am sure," Yávië promised

Betrayal

Nall watched as Yávië stepped through the mirror, her hand in Sōrél's, and wearing a bright smile that touched both her lips and her eyes. He had never seen her so beautiful.

"Nall, what is it?" she said, suddenly solemn.

"Aero was attacked by Dielmor. Fortunately, Azrea was flying us to Meremire and we intercepted them. Before his death, Dielmor said it was at my command that he attacked Aero. He said that the red-haired Guardian came to him in my name. It was Rydén, Yávië. We believe Rydén was responsible."

"Where is Rydén? What has she said? Dielmor must have been lying." Yávië spoke with concern.

"No one has seen Rydén since the day Sōrél and Näeré arrived. She escorted Sōrél to Galen and then said she was going hunting with Valia. Neither Rydén nor the cat has been seen since," Nall shrugged helplessly.

"Where is Aero? Is he hurt?" Yávië asked.

"No, we arrived before more than a few scales had been lost. He was badly shaken. His youth and inexperience could have cost him his life. I sent him home under the escort of Azrea," Nall reassured.

Yávië moved to Nall, and embracing him tenderly, she whispered, "We will find Rydén, Nall, just as you found me within Ardane's dungeons. You and Sōrél call the flytes; have them begin a search for her. I will go to Sybeth and have her search the seas." She headed to the field to call Aero.

As she approached the Trembling Sea, Yávië noticed there were neither sea dragon hunts nor any young dragons playing near the exposed seamounts.

Easing Aero to a halt on the sandy shore, she dismounted and walked to the water's edge. Casting a spell of safety around herself, she dove into the sea, quickly heading toward the Sailflyte's lair. She thought it odd that there were no dragons between the surface and the cavern's entrance. Surfacing in the main chamber, she called to the Matriarch and her mate.

"Sybeth? Sygarnd?"

Yávië's calls were met with silence. She moved through the chambers one by one, but the only evidence of dragons were the bones of old meals scattered throughout the large resting rooms. Even the salty, acrid odor of the dragons seemed to be missing.

At the back of Sybeth's chamber, beneath her sleeping ledge, Yávië discovered a pathway leading deeper beneath the sea. Following it, she reached a fork and continued on to the left. Soon the hall ended, opening into a large cavern filled with collapsed rocks and remnants of old meals. She noticed the body of a trybrac at the foot of a tumble of rocks. It was long dead. The skeleton and a few bits of dried flesh were all that remained. An arrow extended up through the ribcage; the Guardian's arrow must have pierced the heart. The trybrac's three skulls had separated from the vertebrae and rolled away from the body. Yávië lifted one, staring into the empty eye sockets.

"It was sleeping when it died," said a Siren's sweet voice.

Yávië whirled around, blade drawn, to face the ancient threat.

"The tales were wrong," the Siren's voice flowed, reading Yávië's thoughts. "Not all of us were lost in the Maelstrom wars. I was not."

"You come seeking the Sailflyte, but they now lay hidden deep within the Azure Sea. You also seek the one called Rydén, but she is no longer the one you seek."

"You speak in riddles, Siren," Yávië snapped.

"I speak the truth, Guardian, as you will see."

With a pass of her hand, the Siren tossed the stones away from a wall to reveal what remained of Rydén. Her hair was wild around her face, her eyes sunken and yellowed and her mouth drawn into a snarl. Her beauty was gone and instead scabrous skin hung from exposed cheekbones. The flesh of her arms sagged and her gut appeared bloated where it was exposed through torn clothing. One arm was chained to the rock above her head and the other hung at her side, ending in a curled claw.

"Rydén failed me once, Guardian. I do not believe she will choose failure again. As you can see, it was costly." The Siren's laughter jolted Yávië out of her shock.

"Rydén!" Yávië choked back a sob. "What have you done to her?"

With a flick of her hand, the Siren released the chain that bound Rydén's wrist.

"Kill her, Rydén! Regain your beauty." The Siren demanded, pointing at Yávië.

Rydén rushed shrieking toward Yávië, her hands curved into claws, sharp nails extended.

A sharp crack of thunder rent the air around them, bringing with it Nall and Sōrél. Pausing in her headlong rush, Rydén peered from beneath her tattered eyelids at the two Guardians. Then, with an inhuman roar, she plunged forward striking Yávië and throwing her backward onto the jumbled rocks, the blade flying from her hand.

"Nall!" Yávië screamed in terror on seeing the weapon tossed to Rydén by the Siren. The blade was of hollow lightning glass and filled with the blistering acid of spell-cast slitherwort. This meant death to a Guardian, a cruel and painful death that no blood oath would stop. As Rydén's hand closed around the shank, Yávië whispered words to ease the agony of her own soul's passage to the never-ending sleep.

Rydén's body flew from Yávië and smashed against the wall behind her head. A Guardian's death arrow pierced her heart and pinned her to the stone.

With Rydén's death, the Siren's wail faded and was lost.

Through tears, Yávië sought her savior, but wept with deep sorrow seeing the Bow of Ages still drawn in Sōrél's hands, a second arrow nocked and Nall standing silently, hands empty, eyes locked on the body of Rydén.

Sōrél swept past Nall and gathered Yávië to his chest. Without a backward glance, he created a path of light to the surface.

Leaping to Aero's withers Sōrél urged the dragon toward Meremire. Over and over his mind replayed the scene of death—no, murder—the murder of a Guardian by his own hand. There had been no hesitation, no thought for Rydén's life, only unbridled anger at her attack on Yávië; only his fear of losing Yávië. His powers were great. He could have stopped Rydén without ending her life, but he had chosen a different path—the path of death—ending the possibility of future threat to Yávië. He knew he would face the Council without remorse, just as he had done before in the time beyond Yávië's remembering.

Willow and Rosie scurried around Yávië, wiping away tears and brushing her hair, telling tales of nonsense in the hope of a smile, but there was none. Sōrél had gone, and she could not look at Nall. Only Näeré's company seemed to soothe her and even that salve was brief, washed away by the tears that always came with the night.

Finally, nearly two weeks after Rydén's death, Yávië emerged from her bothie. She looked neither left nor right and did not answer Morg's delighted hail as he ran to get Willow and Rosie. Yávië strode purposefully across the field and disappeared beyond the prickleberry thicket on the other side. Nall's eyes followed her, but feeling the warmth of Näeré's calming hand; he made no move to intercept her.

Solitude

Yávië sat in the cavern where long ago Nall had sought solitude, the very cavern where he first failed to heed her call. She sat quietly, the language of the ancient Sojourners drifting through her mind as she sought some explanation for all that had occurred. Sōrél had killed Rydén, an act expressly forbidden by the laws of Guardianship. She had felt him leave Meremire, She felt his presence, then his absence as the mirror closed behind him. She no longer felt Nall. He might as well be dead. The bond of the blood oath was tangled somehow. It was no longer strong and clear but as twisted and muddy as old roots below the soil.

"Yávië," the voice called from deep within the cavern walls.

It was the sound of the very earth trembling, the voice of a Sojourner who had lived before the time of prophecy.

"I am here, Ancient One. I come seeking truth. I can feel my soul hardening, and I know that only your wisdom can prevent its death."

"I have stayed your death before, child, and I will stay it again. Long ago, the Truth was stolen from you; the time has come for you to take it back. Seek the cleansing waters of the seven pools, Æshardæ, Æcumbræ, Æshulmæ, Æwmarshæ, Æstaffordæ, Ælmondæ, and Æstretfordæ in the order of the arrival of their Ancients. When the Book of Ancients is yours, seek the Fortress of the Dragon Queen. It is there you will find your truth. With this touch, I give you the gift of purity and the power of the Book. Use both wisely."

Yávië saw a pulse of violet light. It began at the apex of the cavern's domed roof and flowed down the walls along the lines of ancient language, through the pools of molten rock, and into the circle where she sat. Flowing over and around her, it purified her soul and gave her power over the Book of Ancients. The rumble stilled and the voice and light were gone, leaving Yávië alone. She wondered how she would get through the ancient mirrors without Sōrél. She recalled his words: "I will take you anywhere you want to go, Yávië, I will do anything you ask of me."

"Why?" she had asked. Now she knew why, for in her heart she knew that he held the answers to the truth of her past.

Yávië's return to Meremire was met with silence. She knew the Ancients watched her, but none approached and none spoke. She went to her bothie and gathered her belongings, calling softly to Xander who was sleeping in the hood of her cloak. Bleary eyed, he crawled out and jumped to her shoulder, nuzzling her before slipping inside her tunic and returning to his daydreams. She left nothing, for she did not plan to return to this place. This thought caused her eyes to water and she blinked away tears.

"No more tears for Yávië," she told herself.

She lifted the Sacred Sword of Domesius from its soft scabbard, watching her reflection upon its scarlet blade. Soon she would draw on its formidable power; soon she would call upon its dragon magick. She replaced it and lifted it over her head, allowing it to nestle against her back. The hilt was in easy reach at her left shoulder.

She placed the stone dagger of her calling in its place at her waist, gathering her talismans and placing them in a spider cloth bag around her neck.

As she turned to leave, Nall appeared in her doorway. He seemed ill at ease as though unsure why he was there.

"Nall," she whispered, trying to smile and failing miserably.

"Yávië, I am so sorry . . ." he began, but his voice broke and tears began to flow.

She held him close, resting her head in the hollow of his shoulder. His strong arms closed around her and his tears mingled with hers as they stood in silence, no words left to speak.

Gently Yávië pushed away, and without looking up, she left her bothie at Meremire for the last time.

Nall did not follow. While Yávië sought the cleansing waters of the Seven Pools, he and Näeré would train the young Guardian Zeth for the trials that Näeré said lay ahead.

Yávië entered the passage that led below Meremire and followed it to the room containing the mirror to Æshardæ. She stood for a moment, looking at her reflection in the shimmering bronze, then, closing her eyes, and taking a deep breath Yávië stepped through into Sōrél's world.

The room was empty except for the mirror, but Yávië recalled Sōrél pulling her into the next room, the room with six mirrors arranged in a circle around the violet pool, the first of the seven pools.

She paused to listen but on hearing nothing, continued into the room with the pool. It was also empty of life, so she went directly to the water and, after placing her cloak with the sleeping Xander near the mirror to Æstretfordæ, she stepped into its coolness. As she reached the center of the pool, the water closed over her head and she drifted downward. As her feet touched the bottom Yávië pushed off, rising back toward the surface.

When her head broke the surface of the water, a pair of dazzling sapphire eyes locked onto hers and a hand reached out, pulling her from the pool and wrapping her in a warm cloak.

"The time of our trial begins, Yávië. I am yours to command as long as you will have me," Sōrél promised.

Chapter 13: Preparation

Personal Appearances

Nall released Zeth's head, allowing him to pull back from the barrel of water, gasping and choking.

"Why did you do that?" Zeth choked out.

"Personal appearance, Zeth, is important. Each day begins with a small regimen of personal care as another chance may not present itself during the day," Nall proclaimed, handing Zeth a brush of bane boar bristles.

Smiling at Rosie as she passed he added, "Besides, the ladies like us to look our best."

Rosie tittered behind her hand, then held out Zeth's new trousers and tunic, each measured carefully to fit his lanky frame without leaving bones exposed. Nall had insisted on it.

Taking the clothes, Nall continued, "Beginning on the morrow you will meet me at star rise, fully dressed and well groomed. We will begin with sparring, followed by hunting and dragon mastery. Do not be late, and do not disappoint me. Today is your last day of freedom, so I suggest you use it wisely."

As Zeth finished smoothing back his soaking hair, Näeré rounded the corner of the bothie.

"How handsome you look, Zeth!" she smiled.

Zeth turned scarlet and Nall grinned at Näeré.

"What are you up to? Either of you care for a hunting partner?" Näeré asked.

"I fear Zeth is far too busy with his grooming detail, but I am at your service, milady," Nall responded with a deep bow and was rewarded with her sultry laughter.

"I will fetch my bow and meet you in the field."

They ran effortlessly, each with thoughts unshared. Nall slowed first, catching sight of a simplestag ahead of them and sending the thought to Näeré, watching her slow a few paces in front of him. Turning, she dropped to a crouch and waved him forward with a smile. She seemed always to smile in his company, and he in hers. He knew his heart was always a little lighter in her presence. Rydén's death had taken its toll, though oddly enough he felt no anger toward Sōrél, perhaps because in his dreams it was he who killed his sister, not Sōrél. He still missed her, the Rydén of long ago, but not the Rydén of the Siren's song.

Näeré sat on the grass behind the cover of brush. She patted the ground beside her, raising her eyebrows slightly and winking at Nall. He crept forward and sat next to her, staring ahead at the oblivious stag.

"Shall we eat him for our evening meal, or allow him his freedom?" Näeré whispered.

"Eat him," Nall replied. "It will take many such stags to fatten Zeth."

"Then you will have to catch him first!" Näeré stood and shouted, "Run!" at the now terrified stag.

Nall jumped up and was after the stag before Näeré had time to laugh. Her eyes followed him as he raced after the fleeing meal. By the time he returned, empty-handed, she had gathered several grosshare and a large wood hen to make up for her foolishness.

Flinging himself to the grass, Nall looked up at her, wondering at the way she constantly probed his mind, always looking for a way in, some little crack he had neglected to seal.

"What is it she searches for?" he wondered.

"Feelings," she answered with her back still toward him. "I am a witch you know. The Ancients are polite, applying the term 'sorcery' to what I do, but it is simply witchcraft, the ancient art of witchcraft. Slipping tendrils of thought into a man's mind and driving him mad." She offered him her hand and pulled him to his feet. "Are you mad, Nall?"

"Sometimes when I am with you I believe that I am," he answered with a silly grin.

"That will do for the present. Now carry these hares, so you will look like a hunter when we return and I will not have to tell your apprentice how you allowed the stag to go free," Näeré teased. "Let us go feed Zeth for we must ready him for our trials before my brother returns with Yávië."

Sword Play

Nall grabbed the end of the cot, sending it and its blanketed occupant sailing into the opposite wall.

"Star rise! That is when that Topaz Star breaks its bond with the night sky and bursts above the far horizon! Do you know nothing?" he stormed.

Zeth had snatched his cover and was now cowering behind it.

"Nall?" Näeré called, her sweet voice breaking through the crimson veil of his anger.

She peeked around the corner and into the room.

"Oh my! Zeth, here in Meremire we usually sleep on the cot, not under it! Nall, I wondered if you were interested in having me spar with Zeth this morning, but it appears he is not quite dressed." She gave a girlish giggle that made Zeth turn scarlet and caused Nall's heart to flutter.

Näeré gave a wave over her shoulder and called back, "I will be waiting in the meadow—and Nall, see that Zeth remembers to bring his sword today. I think that would be a great help."

"Why does she do that?" Zeth asked.

"Not why, Zeth, but how does she do that? She always seems to know when your life needs saving." Nall allowed himself a short laugh.

"Get dressed and be sure your hair is combed. A lady awaits our arrival." Nall tossed Zeth his clothes. "I will be at the meadow. And don't forget your sword."

Forcing himself to walk slowly toward the sparring field, Nall watched with wonder as Näeré went through her morning sword play. Her head was high and the sword swung rhythmically on the upstroke, backstroke, parry and thrust. Her arms were strong and smooth, her motion fluid. Starlight sparkled on her hair and her aura pulsed brightly with each swing of the sword.

"Isn't she beautiful?" Zeth whispered behind him.

Without taking his eyes from her, Nall agreed that she was indeed.

Näeré smiled at them and asked, "Who is first? Why not you, Nall, a demonstration for the apprentice?"

Approaching warily, Nall drew his sword. "Do not make me look a fool."

"Nall," Zeth called, "I will return straight away. I seem to have forgotten my sword."

Ignoring Zeth, Nall circled Näeré, never taking his eyes off hers.

Her eyes sparkled in anticipation, deep sapphire pools in which an unwary Guardian could drown. One lapse in concentration and he would be lying on his back with her sword at his heart. Winning delighted her, and it took all of his strength and focus to best her.

"Nall." Her voice was a whisper.

His eyes narrowed as their swords rang against one another, hers sweeping his to the side. His backstroke was met with force and cold metal scraped as the swords slid, blade to blade. She spun quickly, bringing her blade low and sweeping it beneath his leap. With a great overhand swing, she forced him to his knees and into a backward roll. He brought his sword up in a strong backhand slice, but she met it with fierce resistance. Again and again the blades collided, the field ringing with each strike. Suddenly she stepped back, placing her sword on the ground in submission and nodding her head in the direction of the bothies.

"Your pupil has arrived. Actually, he arrived some time ago, but was enjoying the demonstration, as were Morg, Dobbin, Weezel and Rosie. Save some strength for the hunt. Willow wants a stag." Näeré gave him a wink and a smile, grabbed her sword and headed toward the gallery of spectators.

"Zeth!" Nall bellowed—a big grin belying his ferocious tone. "Get out here!"

"Nall, I think my sword is too heavy," Zeth offered after another disastrous sparring match where he had nearly been decapitated several times for not raising his sword.

"I think your arms are too weak," Nall replied. "Perhaps after hauling home a stag or two they will be stronger."

They traveled at a slow jog, which was all that Zeth was capable of after several bouts with the sword. Näeré had been kind to Zeth, only knocking him to the ground twice. The memory made Nall smile. Zeth always seemed so surprised that Näeré could best him.

Signaling Zeth to stop, Nall pointed ahead, holding his finger to his lips as a reminder that one did not shout when one saw the prey.

In a low whisper, Nall instructed Zeth in nocking the arrow and holding the bow steady, then breathing in and holding the breath during the final aim and release. He watched carefully as Zeth applied the instructions. He actually seemed to be improving. Now if he could only learn to raise his sword.

The arrow flew and stuck the stag just in front of the heart, causing it to stagger and fall before getting up and racing off into the brush. Nall shook his head and started off after it, an arrow nocked to finish the kill.

Dragging the large buck back to Zeth, he guided him through the bleeding and gutting, and helped get the stag settled on Zeth's shoulders. Zeth only stumbled once on the return to Meremire, eliciting a "fair job" from Nall, which was high praise indeed.

During the meal, Nall announced that the stag stew was from Zeth, bringing smiles and praise from everyone. Later, as Nall and Näeré sat at the fireside after everyone else had gone, Näeré slipped her arm through his and told him what a kind thing he had done in building Zeth's pride over the hunt.

"If I had known it would make you proud of me, I would have done it yesterday," Nall teased.

"He really is improving, Näeré. He only missed a heart shot by a few thumb widths, but he is disastrous with the sword."

"Perhaps it is too heavy," Näeré suggested, bringing a strange look from Nall. "Tomorrow he can try mine. It is a bit less leaden, and the magick in it will give him a lift and be good for his fragile male image." She lowered her eyes, looking at Nall below her thick lashes.

"Are you saying I have a fragile image?" Nall asked, bristling slightly.

"Nay, Nall, there is nothing fragile about you," Näeré laughed, jumping up and heading for her bothie.

Date with a Dragon

"**N**ever calls a dragon, Dragon!"

The stick thudded against Zeth's shoulder.

"Address them by the flyte or theys name!"

Another thump of the stick for emphasis as Brundle instructed Zeth in dragon diplomacy.

"Nall is goin' to takes you on your first flight today and you better knows how to address your mount!"

"Yes, I will Brundle. I will remember," Zeth stuttered, expecting another whack.

"Go now. Meets Nall in the field. Aero is the dragon's name, Aero, *not* dragon!" Brundle said with one last blow to drive the point home.

Nall stood waiting, his hand unconsciously stroking Aero as he spoke to the dragon.

"Zeth is very green, so he will make mistakes. Try not to lose him between here and Xavian City. If he falls, just swing around and try to catch him before he hits the ground."

Nall shook his head, wondering if the dragon flight was such a good idea. Probably not, but Näeré wanted to see the Xavian gardens, so it seemed a good time to introduce Zeth to the main mode of transportation.

Hiding their smiles, Nall and Näeré watched Zeth attempting to mount Aero. For a dragon, Aero was being quite patient. Following the formalities, he had extended his airy neck for Zeth, rolling his eyes as Zeth grabbed his scales and tried to climb aboard hand over hand. Suddenly the pinches and pulls had become too much, eliciting an involuntary shake from Aero which flung Zeth across the field, end over end.

At last, Näeré dismounted and gave Zeth a leg up, which helped some—at least it allowed him to clamber as far as Aero's withers and get himself positioned for flight.

"Remember, think him up," Nall reminded. "Don't shout at Aero or pull on him, just think him up."

Nall and Näeré silently commanded flight and were airborne. Zeth, however, remained on the ground with Aero. Nall swung Azrea around and sent Aero a silent command, resulting in a rush of airy wings and a breezy lift-off from the field. They heard Zeth squeal before he tumbled to the ground.

"Let me try," Näeré offered, swinging her mount around and landing next to Zeth's prone form.

Dismounting, she spoke to Zeth in words that Nall did not hear and then they moved side by side to Näeré's mount. After some small commotion, they were both mounted on the Matriarch Azaeria's broad back.

"Perhaps it is best that Zeth be in the company of a more experienced rider for his first outing," Näeré shouted to Nall as Azaeria surged upward past him.

Nall nodded, his eyes narrowing at the sight of Zeth's arms around Näeré's trim waist. Then he laughed at the wide grin on Zeth's face. The awe of dragon flight had struck. It was a good sign, one that would encourage Zeth to try harder.

Chapter 14: Cleansing of Sorrows

"The voice told me to seek the cleansing waters of the seven pools. Then, when the Book of Ancients was mine, I should seek the Fortress of the Dragon Queen. The Sojourner said the Truth was stolen from me. What does it mean, Sōrél? I know you have some part in it," Yávië said.

"Yávië, I can only be with you, protect you, and guide your path. I am forbidden to give you the answers to your questions," Sōrél answered with a deep sigh. "It is not the way I wish it, but the way it is decreed by the Sojourner of whom you speak.

"A river flows beneath the seven worlds. It only surfaces in seven pools—one on each world. It is those pools you seek. You have found the first, and by its water the first of seven sorrows has been taken from you. You must be pure and free of any unhappiness that evil might use against you before you touch the Book of Ancients," Sōrél explained.

Yávië let out a short laugh. "Only seven sorrows? It feels like I carry many more."

"The Sojourner has granted you great power, but given you a heavy burden as well. The first of the pools, the one on Æshardæ, has posed no barrier to your task, but some of the remaining six will be difficult to find and those worlds will harbor many dangers along the way."

"But you will journey with me, Sōrél, as my defender and my shield?"

"Yes, Yávië, I will travel with you on your journey, but sleep now, for on the morrow we will begin the search for the pool of Æcumbræ. You will need to be well rested, as will I."

Sōrél watched as Yávië gathered her cloak around her and spoke to her small downy flier. He knew that for the duration of her quest he would not sleep again. He would watch and serve as her defender and her shield. His only hope was that those who tried to stop her this time would not be Guardians.

"Wee one, I will need your night eyes," Sōrél said silently to Xander. *"Your Mistress is in danger; there are those who wish to keep her from completing her task. The nearer she comes to the end of her quest, the more powerful her enemies. My strength is great, Xander, but four eyes are better than two. Will you help me?"*

"You are the slayer of a Guardian. Will you slay my Mistress?" Xander asked, placing a small hand-like paw over Sōrél's heart.

"I share a timeless union with your Mistress," Sōrél answered, his heartbeat never wavering. "No harm will come to her by my hand. Tonight we may rest, for there is safety here."

"I will lend my night eyes," Xander chirped, and set off in search of a meal.

Æcumbræ

The room was dark and dusty, containing only the mirror con-necting it to Æshardæ. The frame was damaged, as if attacked by someone in great anger, scarring the wood in an attempt to erase the ancient words.

"Who . . ." Yávië began, but Sōrél held a finger to her lips.

"We are not alone here, Yávië. Terrible danger lurks within these walls and we must make haste if we are to avoid it. Follow closely, for the pool you seek is far from here and we must not pause along the path."

Taking her hand, he placed it at his waist and gathered his shirt, folding it into her fist.

"Do not let go, Yávië. I would rather take your hand in mine, but the bow does not allow that freedom."

He drew the bow and nocked an arrow, keeping the bowstring taut. Then he set off through the darkness at a quick pace.

The banshee's wail was sharp within the cavern. Sōrél pushed Yávië down behind him as he sent the first arrow flying, pinning the creature to the wall. A second and third rapidly emerged, screaming the blood-curdling wail of the deathshade. Sōrél was a master of the bow and sent arrows in quick succession impaling his enemies and fixing them to the chamber walls.

"Run with me, Yávië!" he demanded, racing through the darkness as if it were daylight.

In her panic, Yávië did not notice Xander's tiny face peering out from her shirt, nor did she hear his silent direction.

They burst out of the cavern into bright light and tangled undergrowth, sending Xander ducking into the darkness of Yávië's tunic.

"There Yávië, up ahead in the circle of trees, the pool is at the center. Run! Do not look back."

Yávië ran. Slipping through the trees, she saw the pool of shimmering emerald water. There were no shallow sides, just a deep, dark pool. She started forward but felt a tug at her center.

"Sōrél!" she called, turning and racing back the way she had come. Sōrél was just outside the circle of trees, firing arrows without apparent aim. Yávië drew her blood-red sword and stepped to his side.

"I told you not to look back," he spoke through gritted teeth.

"I did not look," she said, slicing through a deathshade before pushing it back with a thrust. "I just came."

As the last deathshade fell, Sōrél turned, grabbing Yávië roughly by the shoulders. Her eyes widened in surprise.

"Yávië, when I tell you to run and not look back, then run and do not look back. I cannot allow you to be harmed."

He felt her shiver under his hands and lightened his touch. Her eyes were bright in the aftermath of danger and her skin was flushed as she breathed heavily from the exertion of the run and the battle with the deathshades. She was more beautiful to him than any star set he had ever seen, more precious than all the jewels he had possessed.

He dropped his hands.

Then, taking her hand lightly in his, he led her to the pool. She removed her cloak and slid Xander into the hood before handing it to Sōrél. Then, placing her hand on his shoulder, she stood on her toes and kissed him lightly before jumping into the water.

As the water closed over her head, she saw light flicker about her. The light seemed to be drawing something from her, perhaps a second sorrow.

Æʃhulmæ

Æshulmæ was the polar opposite of Æcumbræ—the cavern in which the mirror sat was well lit with wall torches. The light flickered and danced on the bronze surface of the mirror's face and the wooden frame was polished to a high gloss. The chamber was void of life. Sōrél had chosen the dark of night for their visit so they would not meet Æshulmæ's Guardians.

They moved quietly down the wide, well-lit hallway and up the passage to the exit near a group of bothies. A finger to his lips cautioned Yávië to be silent as he invoked the veil of mist. Beyond the cluster of huts lay woodlands much like those of the Northern Mountains on Æstretfordæ.

Xander's night eyes guided them and his keen sense of smell gave ample warning of trouble ahead.

In the meadow, where the pool reflected the night's starlight, there stood a Guardian. Sōrél's heart sank as he drew his bow.

Yávië's hand touched his arm and she shook her head.

Silently, he cast a thought, "*I cannot risk it, Yávië.*"

"Let him raise his hand against me before you decide, Sōrél."

"I cannot risk his call of alarm, Yávië. Trust me," Sōrél whispered.

The arrow struck the Guardian in the chest and he fell silently, save for the soft rustle of dry leaves when his body met the forest floor.

"How can I trust you, Sōrél? You kill my kind indiscriminately."

He took her hand and lifted it to his heart. It beat slowly and steadily.

"I cannot lie to you, Yávië, it is not possible. If any Guardian sees you come to one of the pools, they will know what you are doing, and they will strike you down rather than allow you to complete your quest for the Book of Ancients. The Book has been hidden since the last epoch of the Sojourner. It is believed to be a danger to the Ancients and the Guardians, and any one who attempts to claim it is a threat. Can you trust me, Yávië? Can you trust that I will never harm you, that I will commit any act required to keep you safe?"

He removed his hand from hers, but she did not pull back. Her hand remained on his heart, feeling the blood course through his veins.

"What is it you know, Sōrél? Why do you protect me so fiercely? Yávië asked, her voice barely audible.

"You will know when you reach the Fortress, Yávië. You must learn the Truth there, must take it back from the one who holds it."

"I need to know now, Sōrél. How can you refuse me truth that is mine?"

"I can refuse you because you still belong to Nall," Sōrél whispered curtly, then immediately contrite. "Forgive me, Yávië, that was cruel and that is not in my true nature."

"You have no reason to be repentant, for you speak the truth. I am bound to Nall as surely as if by chains. We share a blood oath, one he no longer honors, but one with which I must live or die. I am bound to him beyond that, bound by my heart, a fate that is even crueler than the blood oath and has caused me much more pain. Do not be sorry, Sōrél, for that fate was not of your making, but of my own."

Yávië's tears fell, and Sōrél longed to comfort her, but there would be no comfort here, not until the Truth was known and the blood oath with Nall released. And it would be released. By magick or by death, it would be released.

Sōrél waited silently, allowing Yávië her sorrow, the sorrow he had caused by his angry words. While he waited, he hoped that Nall was drowning in a barrel of boiling oil—or falling in love with Näeré.

He watched Yávië step past the fallen Guardian and lay her cloak beside the pool, then sink beneath its amber waters to shed the third sorrow.

Æwmarʒhæ

Yávië slept within the bough of a large chale tree as Sōrél crouched upon a nearby branch keeping watch. She slept a dreamless sleep, and the shadow of Nall seemed to have left them, at least temporarily.

Sōrél used his ability of far sight to keep an eye on Æwmarshæ's Guardians and Ancients, determined not to have a repeat of the slaying on Æshulmæ. The pool lay beneath the tree where they rested, and there did not seem to be evidence of any guards, but he would wait until Xander woke and gave the all-clear before allowing Yávië to approach the water.

"Brother?" Näeré's voice filtered into his daydream.

"Aye, Näeré. I am here."

"Is Yávië safe?"

"You know that I would allow nothing else, Näeré."

"My, you are bad-tempered. Have you considered a nap? I imagine your eyes are quite bloodshot by now. Where are you?"

Sōrél laughed aloud, causing Yávië to stir in her sleep.

"You can find my mind, yet you do not know where it is? Sweet sister, just what kind of witch are you?"

"I know you are blocking me, Sōrél," Näeré pouted. *"One would think you did not trust me."*

"Nay, I trust you Näeré, but I do not trust the company you keep."

"Zeth? You do not trust Zeth?" Näeré teased.

"Oh are you keeping company with Zeth these days?"

"Yes, but only to be close to Nall, brother."

"Tell me he is not the devil I believe him to be," Sōrél said.

"Oh, Sōrél, if you were not so jealous you would see him for what he really is, a fine man, strong and brave. He is also quite funny on occasion, something I appreciate after spending time with a cantankerous fool like you. Eventually, Sōrél, you will like him."

Again, Sōrél chuckled, causing Yávië's eyelids to flutter.

"Always such an optimist Näeré; I hope you are right. If you value him, keep him far from her as she completes her quest, for I will not hesitate to kill him," Sōrél admitted.

"A shame then, Sōrél, that I would be forced to kill you, and we would have a nasty mess on our hands. Enough talk of death. Tell Yávië I wish her good fortune and a Guardian who is not as unreasonable as you."

He felt Näeré fade from him and knew she had discovered his location. He dearly hoped she did not tell Nall.

Xander crept from his sleeping place and raced to the pool, taking a quick drink and watching for any sign of threat. He returned to Sōrél and his Mistress, reporting no sign of danger.

Sōrél dropped to the ground and lifted his arms to catch Yávië. He quickly set her on her feet, for the temptation to hold her was very great. Together they walked to the pool and he watched her dive beneath the water, cleansing yet another sorrow.

He did not speak of Näeré or Nall.

Æstaffordæ

"This has always been my favorite world," said Sōrél. "In ages past, there was a great battle leaving the land without the voices of men or enchanted. I spent the days of my deepest sorrow in silence here. It helped with the healing. It is peaceful and without threat, unless someone has learned of your arrival here."

"Sōrél, why did you not have your sorrows taken by the Lake of Lost Memories, or by one of the accordant dragons?"

Yávië seemed more at ease here, less shadowed by the past, or perhaps the cleansing from the pools was truly making a difference to the weight of the sorrows she carried.

"It is not allowed. I must bear my suffering as punishment for my actions."

"Punishment? By whom are you punished? The Council?" Yávië asked.

"Nay, by a far greater power than the Council of Ancients, Yávië. My transgressions are great. One day I hope to be absolved, but as yet I have seen no sign of forgiveness."

"Might you tell me your transgressions, or is that also forbidden?"

"It is a part of the Truth you seek. Come; let us walk to the fountainhead. It is beautiful and will soothe your worries concerning lost truth and my transgressions."

Sōrél held out his hand, fearful that she would not take it, but she held it to her heart.

"I know that you are here, within my heart. I know not why or how you came to be there, but I know you linger, waiting for something. Understand this, Sōrél. My heart wells at the sight of you each time I wake, but it also shivers at the power of your bow and the depth of your anger. Like Nall, you hide dark secrets. I cannot live in darkness, for I am light."

Smiling at her comparison of him with Nall, he pulled her to him and hugged her tightly, causing her to squirm away and look up at him in confusion.

"Come, my light, let us see the fountainhead," Sōrél said with a smile.

They stood upon a rocky outcropping several dragon lengths above the sapphire pool. Æstaffordæ's topaz daystar crept slowly toward its zenith, creating a play of light and shadow within the heavy forest.

"Shall we climb down, or do you wish to enter from here?"

"I wish you to enter with me," Yávië said softly, not looking at Sōrél.

"I cannot, Yávië. You know I cannot."

"I do not believe that, Sōrél. Somehow, you and I are tied to this place. I do not know how, nor will I ask and have you deny me an answer, but I can feel it and I know that it is true."

Sōrél's eyes glistened and his heart hammered in his chest. Yávië knew they had been here, even though she did not know how or why. He took her offered hand and stepped with her to the edge of the outcropping. With a glance of confirmation, they leapt into the pool together.

Another of Yávië's sorrows left her heart, as did one of Sōrél's many.

Ælmondæ

The odor of death hung in the air above Ælmondæ. Ash and smoke filled the sky and the scream of death dragons assaulted their ears. Sōrél and Yávië had remained veiled since stepping through the mirror, passing beasts of indescribable ugliness and the bodies of the dead they had ravaged. The ground was littered with corpses and the dying; klenzingkytes flew among the dragons, their hoarse voices adding to the pandemonium.

As they came nearer the killing field, Sōrél paused to cast a shadow spell, creating a deeper protection against the sharp eyes of the evil ones around them.

Stone cold, without light
Hold the shadow of the night
Carry it through light of day
Out of sight and out of way
Spirits of the night
Lords of the shadows
Guide our path
Envelope us in thine cloak of darkness

Darkness covered them in a dense cloak and they moved as silently as the shadows.

"*What happened here?*" Yávië probed Sōrél's mind.

"*The chaos of the Dark Guardians reigns here, Yávië. This place was condemned to unending death by the Sojourner. Only the Truth will release this world from its dying agony. Your truth, Yávië.*"

249

The pool of Ælmondæ lay amidst a pile of fallen rock. Its water was stagnant and foul smelling, the shimmer of death oil floating on its surface.

"How can such a pool cleanse my sorrows?" Yávië asked. *"This place only adds to the sorrows I already carry. How could anyone condemn a world to this horror?"*

"I know only that this is the final pool before our return to Æstretfordæ, and that the dangers in this place are small compared with the dangers that await there," Sōrél answered.

Yávië stepped to the edge and, willing her mind away from the stagnant pool, allowed the fetid waters to close around her. As she drifted downward, the blackness slowly cleared, revealing the still pure depths of the pool of Ælmondæ. Lights erupted around her, glittering like fire crystals and drawing out the sixth sorrow. As she returned toward the surface, the untainted waters followed, driving back the foul darkness and leaving the pool pristine.

Sōrél gasped as Yávië emerged from the pool, her aura colliding with the surrounding rocks and pulsing with a deep violet radiance so bright that it all but hid her image. He knew there was no longer any way to hide her light, that it would draw the wicked as surely as a flame draws a buttermoth. The battle cry for truth had been sounded, the lines drawn, and the combatants chosen. Sōrél prayed to the Sojourner Alandon that this time he would allow Yávië to succeed.

Grabbing her hand, they fled back to the mirror and to the safety of Æshardæ.

Return to Æstretfordæ

Yávië lay in the chamber of mirrors, exhausted but unable to sleep. Tomorrow they would return to Æstretfordæ, a place that Sōrél said held great danger for her. He told her they could trust no one, that they must assume all were against them. She wondered how long he had lived believing this to be true.

She knew she was growing more powerful. She could feel the power coursing through her body, even as she rested.

Soon the last sorrow would be lifted and the search for the Book of Ancients would begin. Where it was or how to find it she did not know, but she trusted the ancient Sojourner to guide her steps. As her eyes finally closed, her mind called to her blood oath in great grief and solitude.

Nall jerked awake and stared into the darkness around him. They were coming, Yávië and Sōrél, but there was a vast emptiness ahead of them. A heavy gloom hung over them like a death pall, yet he sensed Yávië's life force was strong and true. "What has Sōrél done to her?" he whispered to himself in the night's shadow.

"We must pass into Æstretfordæ when the Ancients sleep, and while Nall and Näeré are away. Näeré will lead Nall from Meremire to protect you, for Nall cannot be trusted with your safety until the Book is in your possession. Then you will be strong enough to draw him to you. I know that you have called to him. He is aware we are coming. Näeré is his only hope of safety now, Yávië. She loves him and will not allow him to cross my path. She is well aware of the danger," Sōrél said with fierce passion.

Yávië placed her hand on his arm and searched his face for some sign of promise for the future, but could see nothing beyond the misery and contempt of the moment. She raised her hand to his face, watching her light in his eyes.

"I cannot see your soul, Sōrél. Why can I not see it?"

His eyes closed and he pulled the warmth of her hand into his memory, to store it for a time when it might no longer be offered.

"Like your truth, Yávië, my soul was taken—flung away beyond hope of reclamation. Now only a stone lies in its place. But it is good that it is gone, for it leaves me with nothing else to lose."

Her gaze was steady, though he did not see it and her breath warm and sweet against his lips. "Then I will share my soul with you."

His arms closed around her and he held her to him, but he did not open his eyes for fear that she was just a dream.

Näeré's bright eyes smiled at Nall above the dragon scale shield, her sword held loosely by her side.

"Are you coming or not?"

"You beat me to a pulp, and now you want me to go hunting with you?" Nall laughed.

"You were never in any danger—you had your shield to protect you," Näeré replied, adding, "I thought perhaps it might be time to dispose of that filthy dragon's heart you carry. We can return through Xavier's woods and bring home a meal for Zeth."

"Lead off, milady. I am more than ready to put an end to what little is left of the death dragon Dielmor."

Together they traveled to the distant Wastelands, a trip that would keep them from Meremire through the daystar's passing and return.

"Nall?" Näeré's voice was quiet, serious, unlike her normal teasing banter. "I must tell you something."

Nall looked at her grimly. "That Sōrél returns with Yávië?"

"Nay, Nall, for I do not care what Yávië and Sōrél do. I care only what you do. I know that your heart is bound to Yávië, but I must tell you that I intend to take your heart. You will not come easily, for your honor is too great, but I will steal your heart— all of it—leaving nothing for any other."

Nall glanced around, surprised to find that they were nearing the southern edge of the Trembling Sea.

He paused in confusion. "I seem to have wandered astray."

Näeré smiled the smile of the grass cat that has captured the bloodren. "Nay, Nall, you did not wander. I led you. Come, we must reach the undersea cavern where you were held within the crystal."

With a cast of her hand, she enveloped them in a cocoon of air and they plunged beneath the sea to the dry sand where Yávië had arrived with Maloch long ago. Holding Nall's hand tightly, Näeré led him toward the cavern of his prison.

They entered and stood together silently as Nall recalled his imprisonment and release. He turned to Näeré, his eyes aglow with passion.

"None can find us here," she murmured. "We are safe and free from duty's call. Stay with me, Nall, and I will bind your heart to mine. I will share the fire of my soul with you."

With her fire in his mind, he could only whisper, "You truly are a witch."

Nall woke from his dream with an intense feeling of heat at the center of his chest. There was no cavern, no aftermath of passion, just the fire he had built before they went to sleep last night, nothing more. He glanced across the fire at Näeré. Her cloak covered her; dark hair lay tangled around her face and lashes rested against the blush of her cheek. Quietly he stood and slipped to her sleeping form. His hand reached out and gently brushed the hair back from her face. Though he could not say it, he loved this Guardian beyond all else.

"You will not come easily, for your honor is too great . . ." Had she really spoken those words to him, or had he dreamed them too? It did not matter. He was not free to accept her heart, not now, perhaps never, and as for his honor, it seemed to have failed him. No, not failed him, but failed Yávië. He wondered how he could have ignored her calls, began to wonder if it had been his doing at all. Something was wrong, very wrong with their blood oath.

He looked back at Näeré to see her smiling sleepily, her sapphire eyes glowing with mischief.

Shaking his head he said, "The daystar will be past its zenith before you rise."

Sōrél lifted Yávië and stepped through the mirror into the cavern below Meremire. He was not surprised to find Rosie waiting there, her small wrinkled face somber.

"I cast the sleepings spell. None will wakes until long after star rise. You must hurry with her. Take her to the pool beneath the great cyliopendia near the Emeraldflyte's lair. The spirit of Adra will lets her pass, but only her, nots you. Sōrél do not make it harder, let her goes alone. Nall and Näeré are far to the west. Näeré will keeps Nall safe until you calls them. Aero waits. Go, go now." She reached up and touched Yávië's hair, casting the sleep upon her to keep the light dim.

Sōrél did not need Rosie to tell him to hurry; he knew the importance of the seventh pool. When the seventh sorrow was lifted, Yávië would be given the location of the Book of Ancients and the power to use it. That power would draw the evil already gathering here on Æstretfordæ, but beyond that, it would call the evil from the other six worlds. The power of that evil had grown significantly since the last battle for the Book was fought. Sōrél only hoped that the power of those on the side of the illumination had grown to match it.

Making small breathy sounds, Aero approached, intent on touching his Huntress.

"She rests, Aero, for the challenges ahead. I need you to be fleet and carry us to the boundary of the Emeraldflyte. Yávië will go alone from there."

Sōrél's throat tightened with fear at those words, but he knew Rosie's knowledge surpassed his where the search for the Truth was concerned and he would abide by her instructions.

With the sleeping Yávië in his arms, Sōrél mounted and guided Aero into the night sky. Looking back, he saw the dangerous trail of light they had cast upon the wind. Leaning forward, he urged Aero to fly faster.

As Nall and Näeré reached the Wastelands, Nall felt a strange tug at his center. He looked to the east and saw a pale light trail in the sky.

"Yávië?" he whispered, causing Näeré to turn.

"Nall! Look at me!" Näeré demanded. "Yávië is no longer your responsibility, but soon she will need your strength as an ally. Do not fail her. We must destroy Dielmor's heart shard before Dahrea can take it from us. Come."

Nall looked back toward the East, pulled as he had always been by Yávië. He felt Näeré's warm hand in his and in a moment of absolute clarity knew that she spoke the truth. Yávië was not his responsibility; she never had been. The blood oath had been Yávië's failure, not Nall's; it was never meant to be.

He drew the devil's shard from his satchel and placed it on the flat rock at his feet. Pulling the dragon scale shield from his back, he held it above his head like a forge hammer and let it fall, smashing the heart shard and grinding it into a dust so fine not even Dielmor's mate would be able to collect it from the four winds that now swept it away.

Grabbing Näeré, he planted a kiss firmly on her warm lips. Her eyes widened momentarily and then narrowed in mischief.

"Perhaps you will come more easily than I thought," she said, her lips curving into a smile.

"Perhaps I will, Witch," Nall agreed, hiding his smile before turning back toward the east. "But first we must see Rosie."

At the boundary of the great forest, home of the Emeraldflyte, Sōrél fussed over Yávië like a dragon matriarch over her clutch.

"Take the bow, Yávië."

"Sōrél, listen to yourself. You will have me so burdened with weapons that I will not even be able to reach the pool for the weight of them. Please, do not worry so. The Emeraldflyte is strong here in the forest. Nall has blessed this place with the spirit of Adra and Ardane. I have the Sword of Domesius and it will serve me should the need arise."

Touching his heart lightly, Yávië added, "Do not mistake what I say. Your care for me is precious to my heart, but your fear is unwarranted in this place."

Yávië made her way to the heart of the Well of Viileshga, toward the cyliopendia that now held the heart shards of Adra and Ardane.

The great tree was just as Nall had left it. So much had happened since that time. Yávië felt tears welling but brushed them aside. How would she ever make up for the hurt and sorrow she had caused Nall?

"*Yávië*," a voice rumbled through her head, "*why do you seek the pool?*"

"I follow the quest for the Book of Ancients. I must be cleansed in the pool before I am allowed knowledge of the Book. May I enter the pool with your blessing, spirit of Adra?"

"By the seeking of the Book you bring great misery on yourself and others. It has been done before. How do you hope to change the past?"

"I seek the Truth that was stolen from me, no more, no less."

The great tree sent out a tangled branch to touch Yávië's heart.

"The Truth lies here," the voice said pointedly.

"Nay, great one, it should lie there, but it does not. I will take it back from those who stole it from me," Yávië whispered.

"You seek the Fortress of the Dragon Queen as well. Only death lies there, dormant, but festering. We fear no good will come of it, Huntress. Can you promise the safety of the one called Nall?"

"No, I cannot promise he will remain safe, for much depends on his own choices. But I can promise that I will do my best to protect him."

"You speak with great wisdom, Yávië, Huntress of the Suunflyte. To promise his safety is not possible. Go, touch the water within the deep and cleanse your seventh sorrow. Then take the Truth from those who hold it from you. A door lies beneath my roots to the west that will lead to the witch's lair; you will find the pool there."

"Blessings on you and the forest you protect, Adra."

Yávië climbed through the tangle of roots to the passageway below the mighty tree. She recalled Nall's tale of his battle with the haruspex and the taint of the precious Well. Because of his strength, and that of Adra and Ardane, the Well had been purified and the forest given a great protector.

Following the downward path, she came to the chamber where the witch had built her hovel of bones and skin. Nothing remained of it, but Yávië could see it as clearly as if she had been there with Nall. His thoughts were once again hers; the blood oath binding them was restored. She did not stop to wonder how—or why—but rather, stepped quickly to the pool that now lay at the center of the small cavern. The water was crystal clear and a frost hung over it. Looking up, she saw the tangled roots of the great tree had lifted from the water to allow her passage. Silently, she thanked Adra and Ardane for their wisdom and compassion.

As she sank beneath the water, she heard Nall call her name.

The Confession of Rosewort

Nall and Näeré stood before Rosie, their fingers as entwined as their hearts. Rosie gave a sad smile before backing into her bothie and waving them to follow.

They sat on the floor beside her cot as she spun the tale of darkness. It was a tale of betrayal and theft, of hatred that was so strong it surpassed time and space. She told Nall of Näeré's love for him, of her sacrifices from the past. Näeré was embarrassed. She grimaced and called Nall "fool," but could not remove the grin from his face or the love from his heart. So, finally Näeré kissed him, causing Rosie to titter and Nall's smile to grow even wider.

Then Rosie spoke of the betrayal by the Dark Guardians and their pursuit of Yávië across her world, of Sōrél's anguish when Yávië was lost to him. She spoke of his punishment for breaking the laws of Guardianship, and of the theft of his soul by a Sojourner. She told of the terrible suffering when he discovered that Yávië was alive, but without memory of him, and of how he could never tell her. She spoke of Sōrél's anger at what he saw as Nall's betrayal of Yávië. Lastly, Rosie spoke of the Sojourner's call for Sōrél, holding out the hope of redemption if he could see Yávië safely through her quest for truth. It was the Sojourner who had pulled Yávië from death and sent her to slumber among the stars until the Ancients summoned her. Rosie said she had called Yávië to seek the Truth, to be reunited with Sōrél, never imagining the girl would pledge a blood oath to Nall. She asked them to understand Sōrél's rage at seeing Yávië's heart bound to another.

Willow called on Sōrél and Näeré to free them from Æshardæ and bring them to Æstretfordæ in the hope of bringing the memories back, but only Yávië's quest for truth had brought them to this point. The Truth was much more than just Yávië's memories of Sōrél, or Nall's memories of Näeré. The Truth would bring all knowledge of the past to them, allowing Yávië to change it and enabling a past evil to be overturned.

Now there was a greater problem. To find the Truth required the opening of the Book of Ancients. Guardians of the law felt this posed a danger by giving too much power and knowledge to one Guardian. The Dark Guardians wanted the Book for themselves and would come for it soon. Many would try to stop Yávië before she reached the Truth within the Fortress of the Dragon Queen. Soon Yávië would call on Nall and Näeré and they would be required to choose. Would they uphold the law of the Guardians, or the Truth of Yávië? Rosie did not know the answer, for the Prophecy is written without an end. Not even Willow knew.

The door opened on six small, leathery faces huddled outside Rosie's bothie. A tall, gangly Guardian stood behind them wringing his hands.

"Rosie, what shoulds we do?" asked Weezelwort, just as he had so long ago at the first summoning of the Guardians.

Rosie smiled and tears ran down the deep lines on her face. "We just has to waits. We just has to waits this time, Weezel."

Nall, Näeré and Zeth sat near the dying fire as the new day approached. All night they had discussed Rosie's tale and the dilemma of the Book of Ancients. The law clearly stated that no Guardian should quest for it. To do so meant a death sentence.

As Zeth left them and headed to his bothie, Nall whispered in Näeré's ear, "I hope Rosie has a spell for him before we need him in a fight."

Näeré gave a low chuckle then took Nall's hand, her expression grave. "What will you choose, Nall? I will follow you."

Nall lifted his free hand to Näeré's hair, fingering its softness. He touched her face, wondering at her beauty and finally pulled her near, letting her rest against his chest.

"I know Yávië." He spoke with certainty. "She would not abuse the power of the Book. I doubt she truly seeks its power, but she must know the Truth, just as you and I must know. When we are called we will go. We will follow this path to its end, regardless."

Silently, he planned to leave Näeré at Meremire.

"*Näeré.*" Sōrél's voice called softly within his sister's mind.

"*Yes, Sōrél?*"

"*We have left the seventh pool. On the morrow, we will follow the path that leads to the Book. We will be on the cliffs below the wind dragons' flyte in five days. Will you come?*"

"*Aye, Nall has chosen to fight with Yávië.*"

"*Good, he chooses life,*" Sōrél replied gruffly.

"*Sōrél, you are such a buffoon! If anything happens to Nall I will pick my teeth with your bones! How does Yávië stand your company? I would certainly have killed you by now,*" Näeré fussed.

Sōrél's laughter rippled through her mind. "*Passion becomes you, Näeré. Do not lose it. Safe journey, and be watchful, for I have felt Aléria's presence. She has grown stronger, Näeré, much stronger, and she travels with Talonmet and Gorn. Warn Nall as well.*"

"*Concern for Nall? Really, Sōrél, you continue to surprise me.*"

"*Nay, Nall can take care of himself, but I do not wish my bones between your teeth.*" Before his voice faded from Näeré he added, "*And by all that is holy, have Rosie cast a spell of strength over Zeth before you leave Meremire!*"

Chapter 15: The Book of Ancients

Sōrél observed Yávië as she returned from the seventh pool, the exquisite features of her raised head, her posture projecting the power and threat residing just beneath the surface. Yávië's sorrows had lifted, freeing her to be the Yávië of Sōrél's past, the Yávië before the last battle that had torn their world apart. As always, her beauty made him catch his breath, but far more than her beauty, her soul inspired him as a Guardian of the Truth, a defender and shield of Yávië.

Her voice lifted him further when she told him, "I have been given the path to the Book of Ancients."

"The Guardians of Darkness seek us even now. I have seen a vision of them. There are three, two men and a woman. They travel with the dragons Sybeth and Dahrea and they plan to summon the darkness of Ælmondæ. We must go quickly to recover the Book, for their power will be greater than ours until we have it," Sōrél told Yávië.

With her heart she summoned Aero.

"We must be swift, my dragon pledge. You will carry us to the core of the Wastelands where we will seek the Book of Ancients."

As they swept into the night, Yávië called on Nall.

"*By the binding of our blood your strength grows with mine. By the power of my heart, I call on you one final time, Nall. I know Sōrél has called you to the cliffs of the Suunflyte beyond the fourth day, but I beg you to intercede on my behalf within the Wastelands where you will see my light. Nall,*" her voice caressed him, "*come to me. Without you I will fail.*"

In the darkness of the bothie, Nall turned to Näeré . . .

"Yávië calls us to the Wastelands,"

. . . and all thoughts of leaving her behind fled his mind, for he understood the value of her sorcery.

"Zeth! Awake and dress, for we are called to battle."

Nall stepped back, allowing Rosie to make her incantations over Zeth, granting him strength and power over the sword.

"Rosie, send him to us when he is prepared. See that he is dressed and armed before he reaches the fields."

Näeré stood in the field among the dragons. With swift authority, she cast the spell for warding off Evil and for strength in battle over all of them. She carried a staff Nall had not seen before. It was long and crooked, with the emblem of the dragon's head upon its top. The eyes within the headpiece shone with the light of a thousand fires.

She rushed to him across the field.

"The three of darkness approach the Wastelands from the west; we will arrive at our destination only a short time before them. You grow stronger, Nall. By Yávië's strength and the blood oath you share, you grow more powerful even as she does. This is a battle already fought and lost that must not be lost again. Zeth draws close, Nall. You should speak to him before we leave, but do it without delay. "

As Nall approached Zeth, the weight of accountability hung heavily about him. Zeth was not ready to meet anyone in battle, but there was nothing to be done for it—every arm was needed.

"Zeth, we serve the Truth. If you join us, all will be against you. This battle may not be won, but we must fight it on the side of justice. Do you swear your allegiance to Yávië, or do you swear against her?"

Nall's hand tightened on the blade at his waist, and in that moment he understood Sōrél's passion to protect Yávië, for he knew in his heart that if Zeth swore against her he would slay him without thought.

"Nall, my allegiance is to you and those you serve," Zeth responded without hesitation. His voice and body were strong with the gift of Rosie's spell.

"Come, then. We ride to the Wastelands to meet our foes."

Yávië felt the call of the Book from within the rocks of the Wasteland and eased Aero to the floor of the canyon. Her senses tingled with the presence of evil, and she silently urged Nall to hurry. She would be most vulnerable during the reading of the Book, and required the strength of those who served the Truth to keep her safe.

Sōrél knelt before her, ancient passions coursing through him.

"Tell me Yávië, where is the door to the chamber of the Book?"

"Below us, beneath the flattened stones. I can feel it call and we must hasten. One called Aléria can also feel its pull. Soon she will see my light."

Sōrél raised his hands, pulling the flattened stones from the entrance below them and flinging them aside. There lay the opening to the chamber of the Book. Grabbing Yávië's hand, he raced ahead—her aura casting light around them as bright as the daystar.

They descended to a hall with seven exits, pausing only long enough for Yávië to point the way before pushing forward and up the stairway winding along the wall. The stairs were narrow and stained with the blood of yesterday's battles—battles they had lost. Sōrél heard the scuff of boots on stone below and drew his bow. Pushing Yávië ahead of him, he continued up the steps, but moving backwards.

"Go Yávië. Go quickly. Find the Book. I will face our enemies."

This time Yávië did not look back, but sped up the stairs to the immense room at the top, the room of the Book. As she entered, she heard the vibration of his bowstring and the whiz of the arrow, followed by the sound of tearing flesh.

The room held seven tables, each supporting an ancient tome covered in the dark scarlet blood of ages past, dusted with time. Without hesitation, Yávië moved to the first book on her left and passed her hands over it, seeking the words of the Sojourner. Nothing. She continued to the second book with the same results. At the third book, her hands flew up as it slowly raised itself, the cover opening to reveal the dark, empty pages contained within.

Nall, Näeré and Zeth arrived in the canyon to find it empty, with a deep opening at its center.

"They have gone to the chamber of the Book," whispered Näeré. "Let us follow swiftly."

With weapons drawn, they raced up the stairs calling to Sōrél and flinging emerging deathshades from the steps along the way. They heard an arrow strike above them, pinning a screaming deathshade to the wall across the cavern.

"Sōrél!" called Näeré as she burst over the top of the stairs.

He lifted a hand to stop them, his eyes fixed on something ahead. It was Yávië, the Book of Ancients open in front of her, hands flowing along its pages and, in a brilliant light, lifting the missing words.

Her voice was clear as she read the ancient words in the language of the Sojourners.

Skal-at maór runar rista, bat veror morgum manni,
Sa'k a telgou talkni bat hefr lauka lindi nema raoa vel kunni.

They were words not spoken since before the memory of Ancients. They were words of power and promise; words to call the rightful Dragon Queen to her truth, words that would bring about the final gathering at her Fortress.

Es of myrkvan staf villisk; tiu launstafi ristna, langs ofrtrega fengit.

As she spoke the final words, Yávië turned to them. She lifted her arm lazily and, with a turn of her hand, sent the deathshades that were creeping up the stairs behind them into the darkness of oblivion.

"We must return to Meremire to prepare for the battle for the Truth. It is my sister Aléria who hunts us."

"I do not think you will be leaving this place, Yávië," the Dark Guardian Gorn said with certainty from the stairs below them.

Näeré's mind pulsed and sent Gorn crashing to the floor below. She moved in front of Yávië and raised the dragon's head staff. Electricity crackled in the air and a charge of light flew toward Gorn's chest, missing by a thumb's width as he rolled away.

"Sweet Näeré, were you not imprisoned on an uninhabited world with your poor excuse for a brother?" Gorn taunted.

"Yes, Gorn. I believe I killed *your* brother to receive that sentence, and I will gladly accept the sentence again for killing you. You will not be allowed, Gorn, to harm Yávië. I will pluck out your heart and feed it to Sōrél."

"Sōrél," Gorn spat. "Do you still hide behind women's skirts? Allowing your sister to fight your battles? As I recall you arrived too late last time we met."

"No, Gorn. This time I hide behind you," Sōrél whispered from the shadows as he drove his blade between Gorn's ribs.

"Come quickly," he called to those above him on the stairs, "we must return to Meremire. We are fortunate Gorn came alone; he will not make that mistake again. Already Aléria heals his wound," he said, indicating the slowing flow of blood from Gorn's side.

In Meremire Rosewort and Willowort fussed over the Guardians, feeding them and casting spells of strength and safety at every turn. Yávië was cloistered away somewhere. Not even Sōrél was allowed to see her, which did not improve his already foul humor.

"Sōrél! *Sit*!" Näeré commanded from her place next to Nall. "You are driving us mad with your pacing and mumbling. Do something useful and tell us what you know."

Sōrél stopped in front of his sister, looking first at her and then at Nall, causing Nall to prickle instantly. Näeré pinched him, hard.

"Stop! Must I supervise the two of you as if you were children? We do not have time for your posturing. I mean it!" she glared at each of them in turn.

Unable to stop himself, Nall began to laugh. He laughed until tears poured down his cheeks and his sides ached. He looked up at Sōrél who was doubled over, hands on his knees and laughing just as hard.

"Is she always like this?" Nall choked out.

"Indeed she is. I hope you understand how bad your life has become since your entanglement with our precious Näeré," Sōrél replied, wiping the tears from his eyes. "She is a 'wicked' witch."

At that remark, Näeré sprung at him, knocking him off balance and throwing him to the ground with her sword drawn and at his throat. This threw Sōrél into a new fit of laughter, leaving Näeré rolling her eyes and kicking dirt on him.

Looking at each of them she said, "The two of you are truly mad! You deserve each other!"

With that, she stomped off, leaving the pair howling with laughter.

"She is beautiful when she is mad," said Nall.

"Aye, and she is always mad," Sōrél responded as he brushed the dirt from his clothing.

Suddenly he looked directly at Nall. "I am grateful for your help. I did not believe you would assist Yávië, but I misjudged you and for that, I am regretful.

Nall felt a quick sarcastic retort rising, but restrained himself. Instead, he replied simply, "You did not know me."

Together they sat in silence and watched the fire's dying embers.

Yávië sat smiling at Näeré. Her description of Nall and Sōrél's foolish behavior brought the first smile in a very long time.

"Näeré, you are so good for Nall. He has carried a great weight for so long. I want so much for him to be happy. You seem to bring lightness to his heart, something I was never meant to do," she said, lowering her eyes.

Näeré took Yávië's hand and said with simple certainty, "You did not know you loved my brother."

Continuing, Näeré said, "Soon you will give Sōrél back his heart, I have no doubt of that, and when you do, you will be free to release Nall of the blood oath. Then I will release him of the spell I cast to gain his heart, and we will see if he still cares for me."

Yávië chuckled, "Näeré, he never needed your spell in the first place. You forget I see his heart quite clearly; it is bound to you as if by chain but it is his doing, not yours."

Näeré stood, blushing. "I will send Sōrél to you. He is quite beside himself at the separation, and you have much to talk about."

An Innocent Betrayal

Beyond the borders of Meremire, Aléria planned the death of her sister Yávië and the Guardians. Meanwhile, the death dragons had gathered and, under the spell of a shadow veil cast by Gorn, were waiting.

Aléria sat beyond them, prepared to open the gateway to Ælmondæ that would flood Meremire with darkness. Within her mind, she saw Sōrél enter Yávië's chamber and drop to his knees beside her, resting his head in her lap as she stroked his hair.

"I will kill you Yávië, my sister," she swore again.

Talonmet placed his hand on her shoulder. "Soon Sōrél will writhe in agony staked to the plains of the hell that is Ælmondæ, his intestines strung up for the marsh flies. I promise you Aléria; this time he will not escape."

"Sōrél, they are very near. I can feel Aléria as if she were in the room with us. She will kill you this time." Yávië spoke with fear.

He smiled at her as he looked up from his place at her feet and touched her face, smoothing the furrow between her brows.

"Nay, Aléria cannot kill me, Yávië, for I am already dead. As dead and soulless as a deathshade, do you not recall?"

Placing her hand on his chest, she reminded him, "No longer, Sōrél, for a small part of my soul is here. Soon I will restore your spirit; I will have that power."

His smile was sad, and frightened her.

"Do not fear for me, Yávië. You must concern yourself with greater things. I will be safe."

"Promise it. Look into my eyes while my hand lies on your heart and promise it to me."

In the same way she could not promise Nall's safety to Adra, Sōrél could not promise his to her, for there was no written ending to the Prophecy. Instead, he held her through the darkness and into the light of day.

Zeth heard the morning bird's call—one he did not recognize—and headed toward the sound. He found a woman who rivaled Yávië's beauty. He stopped, staring intently as this creature dazzled him with her smile and took his hand, holding it to her heart.

"Guardian, I need your help. I am seeking one called Nall. Do you know of him?"

Grateful that her request was one he could fulfill, he told her of Nall. Then he told her of Yávië, Sōrél and Näeré, of the quest for the Book of Ancients, of the evil Guardians called Gorn and Talonmet and of Yávië's plans for them to leave Meremire on the morrow for a battle at the Fortress of the Dragon Queen.

"You are very strong, Zeth," the woman whispered to him. "Come with me. I want you to meet someone."

"Näeré, have you seen Zeth?" Nall asked.

"Nay, not since just after star rise. He was at the edge of the meadow, practicing his sword work."

Nall walked toward the meadow and saw Zeth pushing through the brambles near the trail out of Meremire.

"By the Ancients, where have you been? There is much work to be done. Wipe that stupid grin off of your face and help Näeré take stock of the weapons."

Nall shook his head, wondering what was wrong with his young apprentice.

Yávië stared at Zeth in horror.

"She looked just like you, only her hair was white, but her eyes were exactly the same," Zeth stuttered. "She was right over there. She wanted to know about Nall."

Sōrél's fist slammed into Zeth's jaw, knocking him down, then a sword suddenly flew past Sōrél, hilt first, and smacked Zeth squarely between the eyes, rendering him senseless.

"Now, just exactly what is the problem?" Nall asked over Sōrél's shoulder.

"The evil is here at Meremire. Young Zeth has just returned from courting it, though he cannot be held entirely to blame, for it was in the form of a woman quite capable of toying with an innocent young Guardian's fancy. Still, now they know our plans and Meremire is threatened. They will attack by night, as they believe we will be waiting until morning to depart."

"Gather the Ancients. We will send them to Æshardæ and have them seal the mirror. We will leave immediately for the Fortress. Yávië, you know the way. Yávië?"

Sōrél placed his hands gently on her shoulders.

"Yávië? We are going to leave now. Come say good-bye to Rosie and the others. You and I will go to Æshardæ and get them once this is over. Yávië?"

"Why does she hate me so, Sōrél? Why does my sister hate me? You were never Aléria's. Were you?" Her eyes lifted to search his.

"No, he was not," Näeré answered Yávië's question. "May we go now, before we find her sitting at our fire?"

She looked between Yávië and her brother and felt her heart grow cold at the sudden memory of the last time Yávië asked that question, just before sending Sōrél away, leaving only two Guardians to protect her at the Fortress—two had not been enough.

Näeré struck Yávië with a resounding "smack," leaving her cheek staining red and her eyes with tears welling up. Slowly she raised her hand to her face and looked at Näeré.

"Stop it! Stop it! I won't let you do this again!" Näeré shouted in a fit of rage.

Yávië's eyes narrowed and her voice grew quiet. "I could kill you."

"Yes, you could," Näeré cried. "But please don't kill my brother again."

Yávië blinked.

"I did not kill Sōrél," she said uncertainly.

"Yes, Yávië, you did; as certainly as if you had pierced his heart with the Sacred Sword of Domesius. You drove him away so that he could not protect you. He died a thousand deaths—a million—thinking he had failed you. Don't do this, Yávië," Näeré sobbed, turning away. "Please, don't do this."

Nall took Näeré into his arms, holding her tightly as she wept. Above her head, he looked at Yávië and Sōrél with unbridled fury.

"Tell her the truth, Sōrél. Whatever it is, tell her the truth," Nall said his voice tight with anger.

"She will not believe me," Sōrél whispered sadly, looking at Yávië, "Just as she did not believe me last time."

He turned and walked toward the meadow.

"No!" Yávië screamed, but it was too late.

Talonmet's arrow struck Sōrél high in the chest as Aléria's laughing voice floated across the field toward them.

"Yávië, you fool! This time we won't even make it to the Fortress."

With a snarl of rage, Nall pushed Näeré to the ground, out of harm's way. He nocked an arrow as he ran across the field toward Sōrél's body. The first arrow hit Talonmet in the throat; the second went through his eye. Suddenly, the cloaked dragons were exposed and in chaos at the unexpected furor. A hundred pairs of wings beat the sky in a frenzy to escape Dielmor's killer. His final arrow struck Aléria, pinning her leg to the side of her dragon, Dahrea, as they moved out of range and into the night sky.

With a sigh, Nall dropped down next to Sōrél.

"Should I tell Yávië you're alive, or would your prefer to remain dead?"

Sōrél grimaced. "Perhaps you can ask her if she intends to kill me herself, before Rosie and Willow invest any healing on me."

Yávië could not breathe. Her mind told her she had failed Sōrél again. Aléria had called her fool. A fool because she believed the lies of a sister over the truth of Sōrél? His eyes had held no guile. Why had she not believed him?

Näeré stood before her, cheeks still wet with tears.

"He was never Aléria's, Yávië. He was only yours."

"Could somebody help me here?" Nall called, "before Sōrél requires one of Yávië's blood oaths."

Malevolence at Meremire

The mood was grim. At Nall's insistence, Zeth remained confined to his quarters. Sōrél fidgeted under the care of Rosie and Willow, and Yávië fell under the intense scrutiny of Morgwort. Nall and Näeré had not spoken to any of them since the fiasco.

"Yávië, how could you makes the same mistake twice?" Morg asked disbelievingly.

She sat with her head in her hands.

"Morg, tell me why I didn't believe him, why I still don't. I know there is a reason. I am not the fool my sister thinks I am. I would not doubt him without reason."

Morg looked very uncomfortable.

"Yávië, sometimes we see something and thinks it is one thing when it is really something else."

Yávië stared at Morg.

"Are you saying I saw Sōrél with Aléria?"

"No, I am not saying that because Rosie'd kills me if I did."

"But, Morg . . ."

"Maybe I better gets Rosie," Morg nodded, heading for the door.

Yávië's eyes clouded over as Rosie came in.

"Don't gives me that look, girl," Rosie fussed. "Morg gots a big mouth."

Then she softened and climbed up to sit next to Yávië.

"Has Sōrél dones anything to hurt you, Yavie, while you beens with him?"

"Nay, Rosie, he has only cared for me tenderly, but we aren't talking about now, are we? We are talking about something long ago, something that hurt so badly I will never see past it. Is that true, Rosie? Is that what we are talking about?"

So Rosie told a story of long ago, and Yávië listened.

Yávië slipped into the room where Sōrél lay sleeping. Willow looked at her and "hmmphed" before hurrying out the door.

Slowly Yávië slid to the floor next to his cot and rested her head on its edge.

Taking a deep breath she spoke, her voice quivering through her tears, "How could you love one such as me? I have betrayed you twice, believing my eyes and not my heart —or yours."

Sōrél's hand slid over her hair and around her shoulders.

"I did try not to love you, but failed. Next time you try to make me go, I will not do it. I will simply stay and face your wrath. Rosie and Willow's healing hurts too much to do anything else."

Raising her eyes to his, Yávië saw the honor there; the honor she refused to see in her hurt and anger. Aléria had known her well, known exactly what to do to place Yávië in a position of vulnerability. Just take Sōrél, or make her think she had—Aléria was right to call her a fool.

Chapter 16: Fortress of the Dragon Queen

Gorn laughed as Aléria and Talonmet shared their tale of the killing of Sōrél. Aléria's wrath had now been transferred to Nall,
since she believed Sōrél dead and Yávië incapacitated by sorrow.
Talonmet promised to end Nall's life at the first available moment,
even while still aching from his own wounds and the healing of his
flesh.

Aléria shared her visions with them.

"They will take the Book to the Fortress. Even without Yávië,
they will believe they have some power to reverse their past mistakes.
We should be wary of the one called Nall, for he has shared a blood
oath with my sister and may carry much of her strength. His love
for Näeré weakens him, but I do not know how much. If he learns
it was Talonmet at the Fortress in the past, his anger will overcome
that weakness. This is all I know. I will remain alert for Yávië's pulse,
though without Sōrél to sustain her she will most likely take her
own life. My sister is weak,— as she has always been where her *love*
is concerned. The one called Rosewort has betrayed us to her, telling
her that the vision of Sōrél and I was nothing more than a vision. I
will plant the seeds of doubt in Yávië's mind again if she arrives with
them at the Fortress."

Gorn smiled and said, "Call the darkness, Aléria. Send it to
Meremire for the Ancients that remain there."

Turning to the south, Aléria lifted her slender arm. Striking
downward, she created a breach in the fabric of time separating

Ælmondæ and Æstretfordæ, allowing the chaos of darkness to pour toward Meremire, bringing with it the odor of decaying flesh and smoke.

The death dragons of Ælmondæ circled above Meremire. In their midst swarmed the scavenging klenzingkytes, but there would be no carrion for them there, as the Ancients had fled with Zeth to Æshardæ, and the Guardians of Truth had already begun the journey to the Fortress. There was nothing to do but raze the small collection of bothies and burn the fields of crimson grass and prickleberry bushes—a barren waste where Guardians had once been summoned.

The hateful horde then turned toward Xavian City and men.

Xavier sat within the garden watching children play in the pool below one of the many waterfalls. His mind was at peace, as were his people.

He recalled the feast at Meremire and dancing with Yávië. Her mind had been consumed with sorrow and worry and he had felt concerned. He knew the Guardians' laws were harsh, and not kind to gentle hearts such as hers.

It had been welcome to spend time with Galen and saddening to learn of Maloch's treachery. Xavier was scheduled to visit the city of the Galenites within the fortnight to discuss the exchange of a group of agriculturists for a team of artisans.

Children's laughter reached him, bringing a smile to his usually sober face, for though Yávië had encouraged it, Xavier had not taken a wife.

Life on Æstretfordæ had brought him many blessings, the blessings of the Ancients.

Saranol interrupted Xavier's pleasant thoughts. "Xavier, there is a darkness on the horizon towards Meremire. Come; tell us what you think it is."

As they stood together watching the long shadows race toward the city, fear seized Xavier's heart.

"Flee!" he shouted. "Take the people and flee to Galen's fortress."

As the Xavians left the mighty city, the walls collapsed, melting into their minds and leaving behind a barren plain of blood-red grass blowing in the gentle morning breeze.

It had been Brundlewort's idea to extinguish Yávië's light, at least indirectly. He had recommended traveling only in darkness, and Sōrél recalled that the light was very dim when she slept. It was a difficult task convincing Yávië to allow Rosie to cast a sleeping spell, for she feared there would be need of her along the way.

"How will you know where to go?" she asked Sōrél.

"You will tell me."

"But how? If I am asleep . . ."

"Näeré will read your thoughts when it is necessary and if there is danger I will wake you," Sōrél assured her.

"I do not like it," Yávië said, shaking her head emphatically, "but for your safety I will allow it."

"Then I will kiss you once before you sleep, so that you will recall it upon waking," Sōrél promised.

He grew solemn and gazed deeply into the violet pools of her eyes.

"Yávië, I must warn you that Aléria will try again to drive a wedge between us. She will cast dark shadows on what you believe, sending visions of deceit into your heart and mind. I will not leave you again, regardless of your wishes."

Yávië took a deep breath before answering him, "I cannot promise I will not succumb to her treachery. She is strong and knows my many weaknesses." She placed her hand on his heart. "Only know," she said, "that what I believe under her hateful deception is not what I truly believe. Keep yourself safe and I will return to you."

"Näeré, you must keep the Book, for no male may touch it," Yávië continued, handing Näeré the hard won tome.

After accepting the promised kiss from Sōrél and falling under Rosie's spell, Yávië slept.

Within the Blinding Light, Darkness

The Guardians stood on a bluff overlooking the entrance to the lower Fortress. Its gates were sealed and covered with a wild and thorny growth of slitherwort.

Sōrél stood holding Yávië, fearing to wake her. Once she awoke, they would no longer be hidden. The Guardians of Darkness and the hellish horde they had released on Æstretfordæ would turn from whatever evil they pursued and rush to stop Yávië at the Fortress.

Nall felt the same fears. Very soon, there would be no turning back. In fact, from the moment Rosewort had summoned them, they had been headed toward this dark place.

"*Nall?*" Yávië's voice whispered in his mind. "*You could just kill us. Then take Näeré and leave this place. Go to Æstaffordæ where you can keep her safe. Kill us before Sōrél wakes me, for then I will be too powerful.*"

Nall shook his head as Näeré watched him closely. Sōrél held his blade protectively over Yávië's sleeping form.

Shaking his head again, Nall said hoarsely, "It isn't Yávië, is it?"

"Nay, Nall," Näeré replied, "it is her sister. Close your mind to her, as you did to me, for her mind is strong and she will use yours against you."

Turning to her brother Näeré said, "Come, and let the end begin."

Sōrél woke Yávië with the words he had been taught by Rosie. Brushing her lips with his to remind her of his last kiss, he watched her faint aura grow brilliant as her eyes opened and she smiled up at him.

"We will need a key, Yávië, as quickly as possible," Sōrél told her.

Taking the Book from Näeré's hand, Yávië went to the entrance below them, her lips moving silently in conjuration. As she approached, the dense covering of slitherwort drew back, withering and curling in on itself as if to escape her light. Beneath it were the heavy doors stained dark with blood. She raised her hand and the doors opened inward, releasing cold, stale air.

Pausing, Yávië allowed Sōrél, Nall and Näeré to enter ahead of her and then followed close behind them. She closed the doors.

"It will not keep them out, only slow them momentarily." Yávië said.

As they moved forward, the walls around them began to wail.

"*She lives!*" Aléria screamed, slashing Talonmet with her dagger. "You did not kill Sōrél! I should gut you and bleed you myself!"

Gorn slapped her with enough force to throw her to the ground.

"I will not allow your lack of restraint to cost us victory, Aléria. You can gut and bleed as many as you please when the victory is ours again. Now call your horde, for we move to the Fortress to end this. There must be no survivors this time. *None*. Is that clear to both of you? I do not wish to return."

Snarling at Aléria and Talonmet, Gorn then turned his dragon mount toward the light bleeding into the sky from deep within the Wastelands.

Aléria threw her hands up, sending the doors of the lower Fortress shattering against the rocks

"Death has come, Yávië!" she shouted into the darkness.

Gorn grabbed her arm and shook her.

"I warned you, Aléria; I will not allow you to ruin our chance for success. We must end this; they must not have another opportunity to best us."

Glowering at him, Aléria jerked her arm away.

"And I will not let you stand in the way of my killing her this time, Gorn. She will not have you. No matter how dead Sōrél may be, she will never want you. You did not allow me to crush her last time, which is why we are here again. It was not my doing."

"Nay, not your doing Aléria. It was done by the Sojourner you call Father." Gorn shook his head at Aléria as he headed for the stairway.

"Talonmet, open the well within the hall of mirrors so that Sybeth may enter there," Gorn called from the doorway, "and Aléria call the horde to us."

Turning of the Horde

Galen saw the Xavians racing towards his gates long before they were near enough to call for help. He hastened from the fortress with an armed detail to search for the cause of their headlong rush to his city. Urging the people within the safety of his walls, Galen finally located Xavier among the last to enter.

"By all that is holy, Xavier, what can be so frightful that you have abandoned the city?"

"Come, let us go to your battlements and I will show you," Xavier panted.

From high atop the walls of the fortress, Xavier pointed to the coming darkness. Sky and land were filling with the gruesome cries of the hideous legion as it rolled toward them.

"Move the women and children below ground. Have the men join me at the garrison," Galen directed the soldiers around him.

"I have a gift from Yávië that may be suitable for this occasion. She told me there were secrets, forbidden to me, but I think I do not mind breaking a few of Æstretfordæ's laws in this instance. Let them jail me if we live," Galen confided in Xavier.

"How strong is the collective mind of your men, Xavier?" Galen asked.

"We have never used our minds for anything but good, Galen, Never anger, certainly never war," Xavier replied.

"It will be for good this time as well. In fact, I think it would be very good if you could crush a few of those beastly creatures headed our way. What do you think? Can you do it?"

Xavier hesitated, wondering if indeed their minds could be channeled to cause damage to the approaching nightmare.

Nodding, he replied, "We will try. To try is preferable to death."

As they entered a large hangar, Xavier gasped.

"I thought they were all destroyed."

"They were," Galen smiled, "at least technically."

"And you know how they work?" Xavier asked in amazement.

"As do many of my men," Galen assured him. "Morgwort taught us. I suppose laws are meant to be broken sometimes."

"You gather your men and work up a mind trick, while we get these machines into the air."

As the horde reached the walls of Galen's fortress they were met with Maloch's fire-spitting, flying machines and a devastating mind force that crushed and flattened them.

Xavier had to admit killing such evil beings did seem to be a good thing.

Then, as quickly as they had come, the horde turned away, flying, running and crawling toward the great light strobing over the Wastelands.

Within the Maze

Yávië and her Guardians stood within the Great Hall, looking about at the remains of what must once have been its splendor. The tattered, heavy tapestries still clung to the walls, which soared on four sides to meet the vaulted ceiling. The stones were held together with crumbling golden mortar, and the floors were of beaten earth with remnants visible here and there of the straw that had once covered them. Against one wall, a massive fireplace still held ancient ash.

The entrances to eight circular towers were evenly spaced along the walls. They were five dragon lengths tall, with walls as thick as a dragon's girth. Winding stairs hugged the tower walls.

Beyond this central hall lay a maze of twists and turns, and it was here that Yávië must find the great tower where the Truth was held.

"We will meet them here," said Sōrél. "They must pass this way to reach the keep, but we will not allow them to get that far. Find the Truth, Yávië; for once it is yours. The darkness will hold no power over us."

She went to him and held him close before turning to Nall and Näeré.

Handing Näeré the Book, she whispered, "Keep him safe."

Then she disappeared into the interior of the great Fortress.

Yávië moved quickly and with certainty for she knew that the Truth lay locked within the Fortress keep. Her light sent shadows falling along the walls in front and behind. She passed great sleeping chambers containing elaborately carved beds, rotting feather mattresses and silken canopies and curtains. This had once been a fine palace for some ancient Dragon Queen.

Suddenly, a hand pulled her roughly into a side chamber. There was a well at its center and six mirrors stood around the perimeter, covered in the dirt of time. The cover of the well had been lifted and placed against the wall. Sybeth emerged from the well, her wicked eyes blazing.

"It seems I am to have the pleasure of killing you—a pleasure your sister had hoped would be hers!" Sybeth said, dragging her talon along the floor next to the well.

Yávië turned, looking not at Sybeth, but at the one who had dragged her to this chamber.

"Talonmet, I assume, since I know you are not Gorn, and even Aléria could not cloak herself so effectively. Finally, I recall the Guardian who betrayed us when last we came here. Näeré was blamed for your death, as well as that of Gorn's brother."

Sensing Sybeth's movement behind her, she swung towards the Matriarch and with a sweeping movement, ripped her head and neck from her great shoulders sending it rolling into the passageway.

"For Rydén," she said with satisfaction. Her gaze returned to Talonmet, reveling in his terror.

"Is it your place to kill me now?" Yávië asked.

But Talonmet had already fled down the passageway toward Näeré, who would tear out his heart and feed it to her brother.

Glancing back at what was left of Sybeth, Yávië promised, "Do not worry, Sybeth, Nall will come for your heart shard."

She paused at the steps to the keep, closed her eyes and sent a silent message to Sōrél.

"Allow Aléria to pass, for it must end here."

Then she started up the steps towards the Truth.

They had positioned themselves among the tower entrances, out of sight, but with a clear view to the Great Hall and all the entrances and exits. Nall held the western corner, Näeré the center, and Sōrél— as was his right—the doorway to the keep.

At the sound of running footsteps, their tension increased.

Talonmet burst into the Great Hall, calling to Gorn and Aléria. His eyes were wide and he spun around in a panic, looking for help from the Guardians of the Dark.

Näeré stepped forward, clearly visible, and gave Talonmet a sweet smile. "Not who you had hoped for, is it?"

Her mind gripped him in a throat hold and pushed him up the wall, squeezing ever so gently, just enough to cut off his breath and make him gasp.

"Did Yávië tell you I would rip out your heart and feed it to Sōrél? I told her to tell you that if she saw you first." She tilted her head questioningly.

"Oh, you cannot speak? There. Is that better?" she asked, releasing her hold on him just a bit. "Surely now you can answer such a simple question."

It was at that moment that Gorn and Aléria walked into the room.

"What have we here?" Gorn asked. "A beautiful young woman— while you are not Yávië, you will do for now."

Nall threw his blade, pinning Gorn's arm to the wall as the dark horde flooded into the Great Hall.

With a twist of her mind, Näeré left Talonmet lying on the floor, his neck broken, hoping that Aléria would not repair it too soon. She slammed the nearest deathshades into the walls, watching as her brother deftly fixed them there with arrows fired from the entrance to the keep.

Nall raced to the far wall and searched for Gorn, but he had vanished, leaving only the blade behind, still buried deep within the wall's mortar. Drawing his sword, he began to beat back the demons from Ælmondæ.

Gripping them with her mind, Näeré held the beasts, allowing Nall to sever heads or torsos as he chose. The howling of death grew louder.

Together they backed toward the entrance of the keep, where they would hold the horde away from Yávië as long as they could.

Suddenly, Aléria stood before Sōrél, a smile playing at the corners of her mouth. He wanted so desperately to smash her. His hands gripped the Bow of Ages tightly; an arrow was nocked, the bowstring taut . . . it would only take a quick release and she would be gone.

Lowering the bow, he met her eyes and gave her safe passage, watching her evil smile grow.

With a toss of her head, she raced for the eastern end of the Fortress, seeking Yávië.

Sōrél hoped Yávië knew what she had asked of him and he sent a silent plea, "*Aléria comes. Don't talk. Just kill her.*"

Then he returned to the task at hand.

Yávië moved slowly among the items in the keep: ancient relics from the long forgotten days of the Dragon Queen, silver bowls and chalices, tattered remnants of the Queen's robe lying upon a carved stone throne. Her mother's robe. To one side of the room rested a magnificent stone dragon; it sat on its haunches, scales flared and tail wrapped around its lower legs and feet. The neck was drawn back, the elegant head thrust forward with its jaws open and teeth exposed. The jewel on the forehead was coated with dust and grime, its color invisible. One foreleg was extended, the claw palm up. In the dragon's palm with the claws curled around it lay a small globe of violet and sapphire. The colors eddied and swirled, constantly changing, drifting apart, and then rushing together.

Fascinated, Yávië leaned forward to examine the sphere more closely.

"Do not touch it, Yávië." Aléria's voice hissed behind her.

"I have earned the right, Aléria. Do you not believe I have?"

"I believe you have earned nothing, Yávië. You have simply taken what is mine, as you can see."

The vision exploded within Yávië's head: Aléria held tenderly by Sōrél, words of promise and words of love flowing over and around her.

Then the words changed.

"Yávië, do not believe her lies."

They were no longer words within her mind, but words within the keep. Sōrél stood at the entrance, bow drawn and arrow nocked. But this time he did not hesitate and let the arrow fly, past Yávië and into Aléria's hateful heart.

"Take the orb, Yávië. It is yours, the Stone of Truth."

Tilting her head, she looked at Sōrél and smiled, "Yes, it is."

She held out her hand to him. Together they stood before the stone dragon and watched the colors play within the small globe. Yávië touched it gently with her fingertips, watching the colors separate and combine before finally melding into a deep indigo.

"What will happen if I take it?" she asked.

"You will be the possessor of the Truth, the One with the power to right the wrongs of the past, to restore balance to our worlds, to end the darkness. Trust your heart, Yávië. Do what you must do."

Gazing past Sōrél, Yávië saw Nall and Näeré step into the room. Nall carried Talonmet's body, which he dumped unceremoniously on the floor.

"Aléria has a legion of death dragons waiting for us outside the Fortress walls, so I guess if you are going to do this, it had better be now," said Nall.

Näeré slapped him lightly for his nonsense and held out the Book.

"You will need this, Yávië."

Opening the Book of Ancients, Yávië spoke the words of wisdom that would unlock the Truth. Though not being held, the Book lay open before her. As she spoke, the indigo orb rose above the dragon's claw and toward her waiting hands. As it nestled in the cup she had created for it, the colors slowly separated and left the orb, curling up her arms – violet to her right and deep sapphire to her left. The light flowed like water, covering her in glistening color, crossing toward the opposite side and combining once again into indigo. Yávië's light pulsed brightly with the light of the Truth. Her hands reached for Sōrél and the color traveled over him, shifting slightly to sapphire before returning to indigo. Together they rose from the stone floor into the middle of the room.

Spellbound, none noticed Gorn as he slipped in behind them. No one noticed as he drew the blade of death. With a scream of rage, he threw the blade straight toward Sōrél's heart, but it never made the mark. Yávië held Gorn's gaze, watching him as the blade hit the target she intended, the one who had again attempted to steal the Truth.

Gorn, the last of the Dark Guardians, lay dying on the floor.

As the color faded from Yávië and Sōrél, they dropped lightly to the floor. Yávië's aura pulsed brightly, as did Sōrél's, the pulses answering one another's slow and gentle rhythm.

"There is a set of mirrors here within the Fortress. Perhaps it would be best for us to use them," Yávië suggested.

Together the four hurried toward the chamber of the mirrors.

As they entered, Nall saw Sybeth's remains, and leapt into the well, diving deep for her heart shard. As he rose, he held it up and gently proclaimed, "for Rydén."

Helping to pull him from the water, Yávië hugged him tightly and whispered in his ear, "You will always be my heart, but you are no longer my heart of hearts." She smiled as she stepped away, allowing Näeré a moment to fuss over Nall.

Yávië whispered with a sudden unease, "The darkness slips away and fades. Dahrea returns with her foul flyte of death dragons to her lair beneath the Ebony Plains, but somewhere there remains a seed of evil. We must return to Æshardæ with the Book of the Ancients, for I must see Willow and Rosie."

Beyond the heavy Fortress walls the trailing remnants of Aléria's dark horde fled the brightness of the Truth. Not even Ælmondæ would harbor them as the brilliance of Yávië's light pushed beyond Æstretfordæ, illuminating all in its path and driving darkness before it, as Galen's shepherds would drive a herd of domestic simplestag.

Sōrél pulled a piece of ragged tapestry from the wall and wiped the years of grime from the Æshardæ mirror until its gleaming bronze reflected their images.

"Yávië, only you can pass through the mirrors in the Fortress. Go to Æshardæ and bring Zeth and the Ancients back to Meremire. We will travel overland and meet you there."

"No, I will not leave you," Yávië replied, eyes wide.

"Yávië, you will never leave me. Now go. Go to gather the Ancients. Your light will keep us safe even though we are apart."

He gave her a quick embrace before gently pushing her through the mirror.

Sōrél gave Nall and Näeré a crooked grin. "Shall we go to meet Dahrea? She will have fled the light, returning to her lair below the Ebony Plains. We can catch her and her spawn where they will least expect us."

With a flick of his wrist, he sent a stone flying toward Nall. "A gift for you."

Resting in Nall's hand lay the death dragons' creation crystal. Nall smiled. "Let us put the demons where they belong."

Dahrea had led the Direflyte of death dragons into its chambers deep below the scattered rocks of the Ebony Plains. Here they would be safe from the radiant, cleansing light of the Guardian with the Stone of Truth.

Sybeth's violent death at the hands of this Guardian had reached Dahrea through the fleeing deathshades; it would not be wise to be above ground and in the path of the Guardians. The deathshades also said the one called Nall had come for Sybeth's heart shard, leaving Dahrea with a feeling of great unease.

As the Guardians crossed the Wastelands toward the Ebony Plains, they remained low, hugging the uneven terrain in the hope of avoiding any klenzingkytes still lingering. The filthy scavengers had developed a fondness for the death dragons and the remains of their meals.

Nall glanced below, seeking an entrance to the Direflyte lair, but Näeré's sharp mind located Dahrea's distressed thoughts before him.

"I will show her distress!" Nall warned viciously, fingering Sybeth's heart shard.

Bringing their dragon mounts to the ground, Sōrél cast a heavy cloak of shadow over them as they approached the entrance to the lair.

They crept along the ash-filled passageways, nearly gagging at the stench of rotting flesh. Sōrél turned and looked over his shoulder, silently calling Näeré forward. She would lead, since she would be the first to sense the dragons' thoughts.

At the first large chamber, they found no dragons, merely the remains of a few bane boars. Crossing the room, Näeré motioned them toward a right hand passage, whispering that it would lead to Dahrea's sleeping ledges.

Not far down the passageway on the left was a dragon scale door. Nall paused to listen and then turned to Sōrél.

"Someone is crying behind this door. Help me open it."

Together they pried the door from its heavy leather hinges, exposing a dank and filthy prison room. Several women and children were huddled in the corner, afraid to look at what might be coming through the door.

Nall approached quietly, whispering words of comfort. These were clearly Xavians, and by their appearance, they had not been there long.

"Tell me of your capture," Nall instructed the woman closest to him.

She fell into his arms, sobbing. "They came upon the city: deathshades, dragons, and hideous beasts I did not even recognize. They chased us from Xavian City towards Galen's fortress. Most escaped, but we were unable to outrun them. The deathshades carried us here to the dragons' den. We knew the dragons would feast on us when they returned."

Nall eased the woman from his arms, looking at Näeré, "Will you take them out? Have Azaeria, Azrea and Aero take them to Galen. Sōrél and I can continue to Dahrea's chambers."

Näeré gave a curt nod and beckoned the women and children to follow quickly and quietly, leaving Nall and Sōrél to deal with the murderous Matriarch.

They forged ahead, the heat and moisture becoming more intense as they neared the Matriarch's chamber. As they reached a small rocky outcrop near the entrance to her bed, they ducked and waited, listening intently.

A sudden breath against his neck caused Nall to spin, dagger drawn, but it was only a smiling Näeré.

"I could have killed you, Näeré!" he said, clearly horrified. She merely smiled and calmed him with her thoughts.

"I would never allow you to kill me, Nall, for I would miss you too desperately. The Xavians are away safely, and our mounts will return for us straight away."

Sōrél rolled his eyes at them, "If you two are quite finished, could we get on with this? There will be hell to pay from Yávië when she discovers what we have been up to, and I will be on the receiving end of her wrath! I would prefer we were in Meremire when she returns from Æshardæ."

Näeré quietly opened her mind to the thoughts ahead of them. Dahrea sent grim and fearful dreams toward her, filling her head with chaos.

Looking at Nall and Sōrél, she motioned them forward.

"The dragon sleeps. If we enter quietly, surprise will gain us an unfair advantage," Näeré grinned. "I have always preferred unfairness when dealing with death."

Still cloaked in shadow, the three Guardians entered Dahrea's chamber and stood before the sleeping ledge where she lay. Nall removed Sybeth's heart shard from his shirt and placed it on the ground at his feet. Then he withdrew the creation crystal and held it in his left hand, lightly balanced on three fingers. With his right, he lifted his shield and handed it to Näeré.

He looked at Sōrél and nodded. The cloak of shadows disappeared, revealing the three Guardians.

"Dahrea, I bring a gift!" he called loudly, causing the great dragon to waken and pull back, sending a spontaneous blast of hot breath just above their heads.

Dahrea's eyes squinted down at them and then fell to the heart shard on the floor.

"You bring me Sybeth's heart shard, Hunter? I do not offer haven to the likes of sea dragons within my flyte."

"I believe you have been providing Sybeth safe haven here for a very long time, so why would you not offer to care for her shard? How unkind of you, Dahrea."

"Actually, I bring a better gift than that, one that will last a lifetime. At least your lifetime," he said, slowly moving the creation crystal back and forth to draw her attention to it.

Her eyes grew very wide, and she drew back further.

"There is no need of threat, Hunter. We have returned to the earth from which we came. We offer no threat to you or the one who carries the Stone of Truth."

"Unfortunately it is too late to withdraw, Dahrea. It is too late for regret and too late for you and these beasts you call your flyte. The one you speak of could crush you with her words. I prefer to use a shield."

At that, Näeré brought the dragon scale shield crashing down on Sybeth's shard, crushing it into powder, the motes drifting lightly as dust through the cavern.

Dahrea bellowed as the creation crystal began to glow in Nall's fingers. Her bawling became louder and more terrified as the crystal began to draw her body toward it, beginning with her tail. Her head lashed and she attempted to reach the Guardians with snapping jaws, but the crystal did its work too quickly and her cries were engulfed as she disappeared within the glowing sphere.

There was a thunderous sound as dragons came to their Matriarch's defense—too late. As each entered the cavern, they joined her in the crystal prison where they would remain through the ages.

Nall placed the crystal in his satchel and took his shield from Näeré.

"Sōrél, we may be in Meremire in time for the evening meal. Perhaps Yávië won't even have missed you."

Sōrél's grimace indicated something very different.

"Yávië needs us." He spoke with certainty. "Näeré, go to Meremire. Nall and I will go to Ælmondæ through the mirror at the Fortress."

"*Yávië, get up!*" he cried silently. "*Remember the Sea of Flames! You have the power. Save yourself. Call the sea, Yávië, call the sea. Be there when we come for you. Be there, Yávië!*"

Chapter 17: Yávië's Truth

Yávië stepped through the mirror and into the cavern on Æshardæ. She suddenly smiled at the realization that she had never been above the caverns—firstly, she had been too fascinated by the mirrors and later, during her quest for the pools, too frightened and tired to think of Æshardæ as anything other than the chamber of mirrors.

She hurried to the door and looked out onto Æshardæ for the first time.

Suddenly, Yávië was surrounded by Ancients shouting her name and smiling. Through the crowd of weathered faces, she saw the most precious of them. Rosie came toward her with outstretched arms, beaming a smile that could have lit the world as well as its star. Yávië hugged Rosie, whispering over and over how happy she was they were safe.

Drawing back, and still beaming through her tears, Rosie piped up, "These is all the Ancients from them other worlds you went to. They was hiding here with Grumblton. But now they can go home, Yávië, because you brought the light."

She crushed Yávië in her short arms again and Yávië returned her hug.

"But all is not done, Rosie. I sense the need to return to Ælmondæ."

Rosie pulled back and looked hard at Yávië. "Don't go there alone, waits for the others."

Taking Yávië's hand, she pulled her toward the caverns and the mirror that would return them to Æstretfordæ.

"Rosie," Yávië argued, "I can go to Ælmondæ from here. The mirrors are here. There is no need for me to return to Æstretfordæ with you. Take the Ancients and go through the mirror. Nall, Näeré and Sōrél should already be there. Just tell them to join me on Ælmondæ; Sōrél can bring them through the mirror."

Rosie grabbed Willowort and called to the others as they went to the mirror that would take them to Æstretfordæ and Sōrél.

Return to Ælmondæ

As Yávië had expected, Ælmondæ had not returned to the light, though it did appear that the death dragons and other beastly visions were not present—at least not for the moment. A foul odor still hung in the air and the ground was covered with the slick slime of death.

The spread of Yávië's light increased and drove the darkness back, leaving purification in its path. She watched it in wonder.

Shaking her head, Yávië continued toward the pool where she had given up her sixth sorrow. She was sure it would be the key to Ælmondæ's cleansing.

Nearing the pool, she caught the scent of smoke, though not that of the dying embers she had passed but rather, as if its source was a new fire. Looking behind her she gasped in horror for rising from a fissure in the earth was an enormous being covered in flames.

It shook its head and roared. Fire imps were falling and leaping from the hole that served as a mouth, rushing at Yávië and howling in madness.

Yávië doused herself using a water spell, warding off the burning imps and flames the beast now flung at her.

The fiendish fire beast lashed out with tendrils of flame and smoke, surrounding Yávië in heat and choking ash. She again cast a water spell, raining a waterfall over her body.

In an attempt to pin her down and keep her from the pool behind, the flames poured through gullies and around rocks. As she turned to dive into the pool, a long arm of flame turned it to boiling steam hissing from the depths.

Shielding herself with another torrent of water, she raced down a narrow canyon. The fire beast followed, embracing her in the heat of the abyss.

Yávië cried out for Sōrél and Nall.

Again and again she cast spells of water and ice, wind and mist against her enemy, but still no one came. They had not returned to Meremire as they had promised.

Exhausted and blistered, and with no defenses left against this ancient enemy, Yávië allowed herself to fall into the dreamless sleep. Pulling her soul in tightly, she waited for death.

A cool breeze blew in her mind, lifting her hair around her face and cooling her flushed cheeks.

"*Yávië, get up! Remember the Sea of Flames. Call the sea, Yávië! You have the power. Save yourself. Be there when we come for you. Be there, Yávië!*"

Sōrél's voice brought strength, causing her heart to beat rapidly and her withering soul to unfold.

Suddenly a second voice spoke, older than time, wiser than the ages—the voice of her past.

"*I have given you life, strength, and the power to change the past, my daughter. You need no one, for you have the power of the Book and the Stone of Truth. Call the sea, Yávië!*"

Yávië slowly rose from the ground and stood tall and straight, her mind clearing, her breathing steady and sure. The elemental fire being howled with rage at the sight of her rising.

With tremendous effort, she cast a drenching spell, sending cooling water over her burning body. Her aura flashed brilliant violet and she felt the power flow from her center, rushing out in a wave of force toward the demon, throwing it into a spinning ball of flame.

Yávië turned to face south and called the Sea of Flames.

The blood-red sea rose from its bed, towering above the surrounding landscape, before rushing toward Yávië and the devil flame.

The wall of water coursed through the bitter landscape, cleansing Ælmondæ of the death and damnation that covered it, rushing forward to extinguish the demon.

As the sea struck, the beast of flame gave a final guttural scream, its flaming image sizzling and popping as the water doused its fire. Great ramparts of steam burst forth from the deep crevices where the water flowed, seeking every remnant of the evil fire.

Birthright

With a flash of energy, Sōrél and Nall returned to the Fortress. Sōrél raced up the winding staircase to the keep, urging Nall to meet him at the mirror. There in the keep lay the jewel of Yávië's birthright, placed long ago in the forehead of the stone dragon. He removed the stone and polished it as he headed for the chamber of mirrors.

Grabbing Nall's arm as he raced by, Sōrél held the glittering violet stone before them and leaped through to Ælmondæ.

The world was awash with firelight. Ahead of them flames leaped and danced within the rocky canyons. As they reached a small knoll they saw the beast and Yávië before them.

Sōrél stopped Nall, and together they stood and watched the child of the Sojourner drive the hell beast to its grave as she called a torrent from the sea. Water flowed around them, sizzling where it touched the death and decay that lay upon the ground, cleansing and renewing.

Light raced out from Yávië's form, dispelling darkness and driving death before it. As the sea receded, the damp ground brought forth a new carpet of greenness, sending out tall shoots that became great trees with trailing vines of rainbow flowers. They watched her arms rise up and her fingers flash as herds of simplestag sprang into the fields and birds flew into the cerulean sky. She steadied the daystar and positioned it to warm the new growth. Low on the horizon, she returned the two rocky crescent moons to orbit and irradiate with their soft night light. Around them a soft breeze gathered to dispel the final, lingering acrid reminders of the damnation from Ælmondæ.

As Yávië's brilliant aura dimmed, Sōrél bade Nall wait as he went to her. He extended the violet jewel to her, its braided chain dripping from his fingers.

"I used it to come through the mirror at the Fortress, but it is yours, Milady. Do you recall it?"

Her eyes welled with tears and she closed his hand over the stone and held both to her heart.

"I remember."

She turned to Nall and repeated softly, "I remember."

Sharing of the Truth

Their arrival at Meremire was met with jubilation and many questions. Galen and Xavier had sought news of the dark horde and its origins and Morg was describing the flying machines and their intricacies to the visiting Ancients. There was no discussion about the broken laws.

Yávië used her powers to restore the beauty of Meremire and the bothies lost to the horde, before creating a great feast to feed them all.

It was long after nightfall before the four Guardians were left alone by the fire.

"Yávië, will you tell us of the Truth?" Nall asked.

She reached across and took his hand before saying very gently, "You were a Guardian in the service of my mother, the Dragon Queen. My truth is also yours."

She fingered the chain holding the violet stone that Sōrél had placed around her neck, telling her it belonged there, how it was her birthright as the reigning Dragon Queen.

Smiling sadly, she began the tale of how they had come to be among the Ancients of Æstretfordæ.

"Many lifetimes ago, before we lay slumbering among the stars of the universe awaiting the call of the Ancients, we shared another life—a life of idyllic pleasure and joy among the citizens of Ædracmoræ.

The Fortress was strong and within it lived my family. My mother, Queen Ya'vanna was wed to an immortal from a time unknown, a man of creativity and peace, in harmony with the universe. Twins were born to them—Aléria and I—and we grew up under their tutelage and safety until the death of my mother . . ."

Yávië then began the recalling of their Truth.

Long Ago . . . Æðracmoræ

Ya'vanna watched as her husband created flowers among the weeds. She smiled and called to her daughters.

"Yávië, Aléria, the sword master is ready for your lessons."

She saw Yávië look up and wave. She was an extraordinary beauty, with a will more stubborn than any man would tolerate, much less accept in a wife, but her own father had once said the same of her. Aléria hugged her father, waved to Ya'vanna and trailed off after Yávië toward the training field. She knew they would have no trouble finding a suitable match for Aléria—half the eligible young men in the kingdom wanted her hand, for she was the first born and would one day be Queen.

Alandon—the King, though he refused to use the title—crept upstairs and placed his hands over his wife's eyes.

"Now who would this be?" Ya'vanna asked playfully. "An odd man from an unknown place trying to wriggle into the Queen's good graces by bringing her flowers?"

She turned to take the flowers he offered. "How goes creation today, beloved?"

The crooked smile appeared that had charmed her so long ago.

"I have delivered the most amazing beast: small, no bigger than the hand, with remarkable night vision and the ability to sense danger from a great distance. I thought I would give him to Yávië."

"Husband, you dote on her. Time approaches for them to wed, and Yávië has no desire . . ."

Alandon reached out and cupped his wife's soft face, "Oh, Yávië has desire. She desires the Captain of your Guardians."

"Sōrél?" Ya'vanna asked in surprise. "What makes you believe this, Alandon? His loyalty is beyond question."

"Loyalty is not the issue, Ya'vanna. Love is the issue. Do you not recall your father's voice when I asked for your hand in marriage?"

Ya'vanna laughed in spite of her concern. "That was an entirely different issue. I wished to marry outside the kingdom—outside our world. My father forbade it. He thought that as a Sojourner you would whisk me away, never to be seen again."

"The problem now is that Aléria also fancies Sōrél," Alandon added, smiling to hide his dislike for the man who led his wife's Guardians.

"And Sōrél's position in this triangle?"

"I do not believe he is yet aware he is being courted."

Yávië and Aléria fought one another fiercely, as neither could bear losing. The sword master watched with great concern, for their battles were becoming more violent. While Yávië was more skilled, she seemed less likely to inflict serious damage. Aléria's control was far more fragile.

Blades clashed, ringing loudly in the still air. Yávië countered every one of Aléria's blows, enraging her.

"Give up, Yávië! Just give up before I am forced to hurt you!"

Yávië laughed. "I will never give up! So why don't you just place your sword before me and walk away, Aléria?"

"Never!" Aléria responded through gritted teeth, continuing to beat Yávië back savagely.

With a stroke of sublime skill, Yávië's blade swung beneath Aléria's, causing her to lose her grip and sending the sword flying, blade first, into the earth.

"Let us call it a day," sword master Maloch recommended, shaking his head.

Galen Remembered

The Queen's Guardians Näeré and Rydén watched Yávië as she slipped through the forest. She was silent—a perfect hunter. Unlike Aléria, her sister, she had listened well to their instructions and polished her skills with daily hunts on her own.

A rustling put them on alert and they quickly veiled themselves. They continued to watch their charge, ready to intercede should the princess require assistance.

Yávië stood silently poised, hand on her quiver, ready to nock an arrow should the need arise. The scent was male—acrid, but not entirely unpleasant. She had become familiar with it in the past year's training. Snatches of sound reached her ears. This one was at least attempting to move quietly, but it was evident he did not have the gift of silence. Leaves rustled just past the nearest copse of trees. Perhaps he was stalking the boar she had seen pass by earlier.

Suddenly she heard the shout of feral beasts as their heavy bodies crashed through the dense brush. She nocked an arrow, ready for whatever might come. Four of the beasts rushed forward, surrounding the now visible human. He would be killed swiftly—no mercy here for humans, nor any living creature for that matter. Without further thought, she let fly the first arrow, followed rapidly by three more. Each hit its mark in the throat of a beast, dropping them instantly—just as well, since even a wounded feral beast could be dangerous to a fragile human. The man stood stunned. Yávië's bow was still drawn, and a fifth arrow nocked.

"You won't need that, I hope. I mean no harm. I was . . ."

"Tracking one of the Queen's boars?" she queried.

"Yes, how did you know?" the stranger asked.

"I have the gift of far sight . . . and I saw the boar ramble by not a few moments ago. I think he is long gone by now." Yávië lowered the bow, replacing the arrow in her quiver.

"May I ask the name of my savior?" the man asked, his mouth curving upwards.

"Your tongue could not grasp my true name, so you may call me Yávië. May I ask why a man is wandering alone, stalking a boar, in a place where he is considered a poacher?"

"Poacher? And you are not?"

Laughing lightly, she tossed back the hood of her cloak. "I will ask you who I am."

His dark gaze lingered upon her too long for comfort. She felt uneasy and tense, and put a hand on the dagger at her waist. He seemed to sense her unease and spoke quickly.

"I am Galen of Æstaffordæ, milady. You have put me in your debt, and I take an oath to repay it."

Unable to stop a chuckle from reaching her lips, she taunted him, "You intend to save *my* life? It is not likely I will need saving anytime soon, for my mother's Guardians are never far away."

"As that may be, it is still my oath and my intent. I am an honorable man," Galen responded.

"I accept your debt and the honor of your oath, whether there ever be occasion to repay it or not. It is refreshing to meet an honorable man; most I have seen were far less. It is best if we be off, others will soon be looking for those feral beasts. Safe journey, Galen of Æstaffordæ."

She set off westwards at an easy jog. Suddenly, she turned and shouted, "You, Galen of Æstaffordæ. Have you, in your wanderings through my forests, come across the one called Sōrél?"

"Nay. And I am sure I would have recalled had I met one of the Queen's Guardians."

Releasing the veil that hid them from Yávië, Rydén turned to Näeré and whispered, "It seems your brother is in high demand with the young women of the court."

Sōrél watched the young woman approach. She was one of the Queen's daughters, but which one he could not tell. Only when they spoke did they give their identity away. Yávië was always serious and intense, while Aléria was flirtatious and lighthearted.

"Perhaps you would have time today to give me some advice on ranged weaponry, Sōrél," this one said, her eyes lowering and a smile lingering on her lips.

"Nay, Aléria. I must attend the hearing of a poacher, but I believe Zeth is free."

"Another day, perhaps. I find that Zeth does not have the experience that I require." Aléria pouted.

"Be cautious, Captain," Nall advised, watching Aléria walk away, "that one is a danger."

"Aye, I fear what you say is true, Nall."

The man stood with his hands tied at the waist—another poacher. This was becoming a frequent problem as prey sought the relative safety of the Queen's woodlands.

"The penalty for poaching is a serious one," Sorél advised. "Why did you risk it?"

"Sōrél! This man owes me a life debt, and I intend to collect on it at some time in the future. Please release him," Yávië called, racing toward them.

"Milady, only your mother can request the release of a poacher, for it is she who has been wronged," Sorél responded, bowing courteously.

"I do request it, Sōrél," Ya'vanna spoke from behind her daughter. "We certainly do not wish to imprison one who owes a life debt to my daughter," she added, smiling at Yávië.

Sōrél called to Yávië as she left, "Milady, would you care to accompany us on a hunt tomorrow?"

The Queen's eyebrows rose, causing Sōrél immediate regret, though he covered it well by adding, "Your personal Guardians have told of your prowess with the bow. Your skill would be helpful in returning a fine simplestag for your mother's table."

Casting a glance at Ya'vanna, Yávië accepted the invitation.

A Reign of Chaos

Beyond the Fortress walls, Aléria sat mounted on a young dragon. Holding a satchel filled with gold and jewels, she awaited the Guardians she had summoned.

Gorn and Talonmet appeared, wary at being summoned by the firstborn of the Queen.

"I require something killed," Aléria said, her voice loud in the stillness of the evening. "Are the two of you for hire? I have heard that you are, and that you poach on my mother's land for those fearful of doing it themselves."

"What trick are you up to, Milady?" asked Gorn. "Does the Queen now send her children to interrogate the Guardians?"

"The Queen does nothing but laugh with my father and give my sister what she wants. I am the strength of our bloodline. With your help I will be Queen of Ædracmoræ and when I am perhaps you will become Captain of the Guardians in place of Sōrél."

"Why would you replace Sōrél? He has earned the respect of his garrison," Gorn asked.

"He has not earned my respect," Aléria said, tossing the bag of riches at his feet. "Will that buy your service to none but me, Gorn?"

Feeling the heft of the satchel, he smiled slowly. "Milady, this will buy you many lifetimes of loyalty from both of us and many of our friends as well."

"You will murder my mother. Tomorrow. I want it done tomorrow.

When my mother takes her morning ride, she will be alone. I have waited far too long for what is rightfully mine. Lord Abaddon has promised his support, promised his dark magick and the armies of the abyss. Do this, Gorn, and one day I may make you King."

The Queen's wounded body was found in her woods, the victim of a poacher's arrow. The wizard healer was called, but it was too late. Smug behind spurious sorrow, Aléria watched her sister suffer with the loss of their mother. Traitorous Guardians conducted a perfunctory search for the Queen's murderer, while Sōrél and those loyal to the crown sought the truth behind her death.

Aléria's coronation came swiftly following her mother's funeral and Alandon retreated, abandoning Yávië to her sorrow and Aléria to Abaddon's dark mentoring.

Yávië tried to support Aléria, but her sister's decisions were corrupt and hurtful to the citizens of Ædracmoræ. Yávië's heart ached with the loss of her mother and father and the wanton disrespect of the new Queen. Each day cloaked Yávië in deeper darkness, sorrow left her weak and fretful.

She began to spend even more time honing her skills as a huntress and more time with sword master Maloch and the Guardians who protected her. She avoided the fortress and camped in the woods. Eventually, Nall approached her with his suspicions of betrayal and an oath of protection.

"Milady, it is rumored that our Queen's death was not due to a poacher's arrow, but to the arrow of a Guardian—one who has sworn allegiance to your sister. Two Guardians spend riches they should not have, and talk of favors that should not be owed by one in service to the crown. There is talk of Sōrél's replacement as Captain of the Guardians. His successor is believed to be the one responsible for your mother's death as ordered by Aléria."

"Why would my sister want to kill our mother?" Yávië asked in confusion, her eyes filling with tears.

"To be Queen," Nall stated.

"But she would be Queen anyway. Upon her twentieth birthday, the crown would have passed to her. My mother had no wish to rule beyond that time, and I was no threat. It has never been my desire to rule Ædracmoræ and the seven kingdoms."

"Nay, but you do have a desire that has planted a seed of hatred in Aléria's heart."

"What desire?" Yávië asked. But as her eyes found Sōrél approaching with Näeré, Rydén and Zeth, she knew her desire.

"Yávië, you are no longer safe here," Sōrél insisted. "The Guardians do the bidding of your sister and Gorn, the new Captain of the Guardians. It is their intent to kill any who do not swear allegiance to them. You have our oath of protection. The five of us have sworn to protect you as long as you have need of us."

Yávië was only aware of the fact that Sōrél had used her given name, something he had never done before.

He wrapped his cloak around her and lifted her to his shoulder, soothing her with his warmth and the faithful beat of his heart.

"Näeré, are the dragons ready?"

"Aye, Sōrél. They await us at the border of Æstretfordæ."

Together the five Guardians and the young woman they were sworn to protect made their way from the Fortress of the Dragon Queen to the highlands far beyond.

There, hidden among her protectors, Yávië became a Guardian and vowed to take her revenge.

A rumor soon reached the highlands that Aléria had taken the counsel of her Sojourner uncle, Abaddon, a Sojourner with the ability to call the hordes of darkness from the very abyss. She was said to have built a great army within the borders of Æstretfordæ, an army she intended to use to hunt down those she called traitors and murderers—her sister and five Guardians hiding in the North.

The horde brought death and destruction to Ædracmoræ, and no living being was safe from the brutality. Farms and townships were burned to the ground, animals and citizens slaughtered and eaten. The search for Yávië ranged over the whole world and kept the Guardians running to stay just ahead of certain death. Chaos reigned, and her name was Aléria.

Yávië cried out in sleep that was fitful and filled with nightmares. Sōrél held her and promised to restore what was hers. He promised his heart and his soul and, amid those promises, a bond was formed, one that linked them for eternity.

As Alandon watched the destruction of his wife's world, a deep hatred grew toward Aléria. From his haven, he watched Yávië become strong. He saw Sōrél forget his past and pledge himself to her. Finally, Alandon decided to destroy Ædracmoræ leaving behind a means to recover it if Yávië would only deny Sōrél.

Alandon gathered the three dragon Matriarchs whose pledges to his wife had long been honored, and with them he traveled to the North, to the deep caverns of Yávië's hiding place.

Sōrél came forth to meet them, alone and unafraid.

"Sire," he acknowledged coldly, "your daughter weeps for you; your betrayal stings her like a fire."

Alandon smiled, without denial. "My betrayal? What of yours, servant? I have come to give the only gift I have. A second chance. Will you allow my daughter that?"

"I have pledged to Yávië, and will defend her to my death—and yours, should that be necessary. I will protect her from the wickedness you hide behind your smile, for as many lifetimes as I am gifted by the gods."

"What you and I did long ago is of no consequence now. You will never rise to power over my house, never be more than just her Guardian. Yávië will deny you when she finds out who you are and what you have done. Your end is near."

Before Sōrél could answer, Yávië raced from the cavern and flung herself into her father's arms, all pain and sorrow forgotten, if only for a moment.

"Why did you leave me, Father? Aléria has lost her mind; she damages Ædracmoræ beyond hope of repair. She has released an unholy darkness. Why?"

Alandon held his daughter without answering. No answers could change the deeds of his past.

"Yávië, I cannot stop this flood of evil, for it has spread too far. Aléria has become strong. Her hair pales with her wickedness. But, I can stay the loss of your soul and help you to change the outcome of the final battle during your next life. You will be called as a Guardian during the time of the Ancients. Follow your heart then, Yávië, and you will come to the Truth."

Gesturing to the three dragons waiting patiently behind him, he explained, "The three matriarchs, Adra, Azaeria and Faera have pledged to your mother and to you for eternity. When you are next summoned, they will be there to assist in your quest. This world will be torn asunder, unrecognizable to you on your return. Only by questing for the Truth will you revive the past."

He hugged her tightly and ordered Sōrél to bring the other Guardians to him.

Drawing a large pentacle on the ground, he placed Yávië and Sōrél at the center, Nall to the West, Näeré to the East, and Rydén and Zeth to the South. Alandon then took his place to the North.

Taking a thin golden thread, he bound it around them, tying them together for eternity. Then he began his incantation:

"Guides of the journey of the dead, hear my plea:
That the spirit of these Guardians will follow thee.
Let it be that no harm to them may pass
Or worry break across their travelers' trail.
Lead them to their slumber hidden in the stars,
Opportunities for rest to them afford,
That in their haven may abide
Safety, peace and love.
Guard them from all evil.
Let enter
No trepidation,
No anguish.
Keep them until they are called once more.

"Your return is assured. You must now go to the Fortress to fight your final battle. It is one you cannot win. This time."

He removed the golden thread and held Yávië once again.

"We may not meet again, my daughter, but I will always be with you. The Book you will seek is hidden in a place you will call the Wastelands. The Stone of Truth lies in the palm of the dragon's claw."

Calling Sōrél aside, Alandon reminded him, "You are a servant of the House of Dragon Queen. Do not forget it. Protect my daughter, Sōrél of Aaradan, but do not forget your place."

"I hold her more precious than my own life, Sire. No harm will ever come to her while she is in my care."

"I leave you with the Bow of Ages. Its power will kill even a Guardian, should the need arise."

"We returned to the Fortress under cover of darkness, creeping beneath the walls as if we were common thieves, and there we fought the battles we could not win before being called to slumber among the stars.

"Aléria filled my mind with false visions of Sōrél's betrayal and I sent him away. Without his strength and protection, my sister, Gorn and Talonmet were the stronger and we were slaughtered.

"My father thought Sōrél had failed me because of Aléria's trickery, holding both he and Näeré responsible.

"In a final act of rage and anguish at the loss of my mother and me, he rent the very fabric of Ædracmoræ, tearing it into seven planes connected only by seven ancient mirrors. Näeré and Sōrél were sent to Æshardæ to wait for our calling and the chance to make things right," Yávië continued.

"And that is how we came to be together once again, my friends— called from slumber as promised by my father," Yávië finished.

"And here we are," Nall said with a wry smile.

Näeré hugged him and agreed. "Yes, here we are but this time we have won!"

"Have we?" Yávië asked. "Where there was once a single world of peace and beauty, now there are seven, each incomplete without the others."

Sōrél pulled Yávië to her feet and danced her around the fire. "You expect far too much from one night's work, milady. Could your weary Guardians not rest for a night or two before you decide to quest for the rebirth of Ædracmoræ. I love you, but you are a cruel task mistress."

Yávië tossed her hair, smiling and enjoying the moment of freedom from worry.

"Perhaps I should be content to be free of sorrow for a fortnight before I require that you do my bidding again."

Nall gave an "hmmmph" and said, "She is going to be impossible now that she is a Queen!"

Chapter 18: Reunion

Yávië sat with the Book of Ancients open on her lap, reading her father's words. Hidden among the ancient incantations lay the history of his people—her people—a race now long gone. The Guardians had agreed they would do whatever was necessary to restore the world of Ædracmoræ, but she was uncertain of the wisdom in doing so—there was grave danger in the quest for rebirth. While her heart longed for her old home world, her soul sought only the safety of the five sworn to her.

As she closed the Book, Willow slipped in, doing a little curtsey and causing Yávië to smile.

"Willow, please don't do that, it only makes me want to giggle."

"You is a Queen, Yávië, and there's protocols," Willow admonished.

"Not among friends, Willow, never among friends."

Willow glanced at the Book on Yávië's cot.

"What are you thinking, girl?" Willow said, suddenly forgetting her "protocols."

Yávië sighed. "I am thinking about how much I love each of you."

Willow nodded. "The decision's a hard one."

"Willow, I have restored the seven worlds, and six are ready for a race of Men. I am going to repopulate each with a single race, and I ask that Rosie call Guardians for them. Would she do that for me?"

"Aye, Yávië. Your plan's sound, but I sense it will not satisfies you for long. You will want to see Ædracmoræ again."

Yávië's eyes glistened with tears as she whispered, "It is our home, Willow."

To each of the new races Yávië gave the name of their home world, touching the heart of one who would lead. She gave each leader a talisman to call her and then Rosie called forth Guardians to serve as their protectors.

Among them was an auburn haired beauty that Rosie called Rydén, a Guardian with the gift of a new soul void of vanity and a bond to her first life sibling, Nall.

No evil shadows fell on the summoning of the Guardians, as no klenzingkytes remained. In their place, Yávië gave the magpies and deathawks the duty to keep the worlds pristine.

To guard against betrayal, Yávië placed a piece of herself within the soul of each new Guardian, just as Willow had suggested. On the morrow, they would begin training with the Ancients and preparing for their dragon quests. She smiled at the precious memories she shared with Nall. Rydén would have no recollection of her treachery, but also no memory of those shared times on Æstretfordæ. Her memories would be of her service to the Dragon Queen of Ædracmoræ.

While Yávië watched the summoning, Näeré smoothed Nall's memories, erasing the sorrows of his sister's past betrayal and death. He would remember her as she had been at Ædracmoræ: strong and loyal to her Queen and charges.

Sōrél took Yávië's arm in his.

"Yávië, the good Queen," he breathed into her hair.

"Why do you say it? I have been Queen for too short a time to tell whether I am good or bad."

"Nay, I see the witchcraft my sister weaves around Nall. You do a kind thing for him and without it I do not believe he would trust Rydén again, regardless of her soul's condition."

Yávië allowed herself a small smile. "Nall is still my heart," she teased wickedly.

"And you are mine," Sōrél said, sealing it with a kiss.

"Have you heard the voice of the seventh?" Yávië asked him suddenly.

His eyes became serious. "Nay, I have not. But he will come when you ask. He owes a life debt, as I recall."

Rosie came before them and presented Rydén, Guardian from Ædracmoræ.

"This is Yávië, daughter of Ya'vanna and Alandon, and Sōrél, the Captain of the Guardians."

"I once served your mother, Princess. It is my honor to be in your service."

Smiling at all the formality, Yávië held up a hand. "I spent too much time with you during the dark days of Ædracmoræ for us to stand on ceremony. I am simply Yávië. Your service is well remembered, Rydén. I recall you and Näeré taught me to hunt."

Rydén smiled her enchanting smile. "You are a fine Huntress. What is this place called?"

"We call it Æstretfordæ; we rest here until we are again called to serve Ædracmoræ."

Yávië looked up and saw Näeré with Nall. Their eyes met and Näeré gave a subtle nod as Nall began to run.

"Rydén!" Nall shouted, lifting her off her feet and swinging her around. "You have arrived! It is like our days on Ædracmoræ, the six of us again!"

Yávië whispered to Näeré, "You are a remarkable sorceress."

Tempering of Time

Willow, Rosie and Morg stared at Yávië in disbelief.

"But you only just founds out!" Morg hollered.

"Morg, I am not giving up the crown, I am merely not accepting the responsibility of my birthright . . . for now."

Willow shook her head as Rosie continued to look worried.

"I only wish to leave the Book and the Stone of Truth in your care until the time comes when I can lead Ædracmoræ. My father trusted you with our calling, now I want to trust you with the artifacts of my birthright. There is much to be done within the seven worlds. There are Guardians to train, new races to supervise, stags to hunt, and bane boar to fight." She watched their faces but found no sign of understanding.

"I want to be with Sōrél," she said, at last seizing their attention. "I am trained to be a Guardian, and it is where I am needed most."

Rosie looked up and smiled grudgingly. "You will stays at Meremire when you are here in Æstretfordæ?"

"Aye, Rosie, this will always be our home for as long as you are here."

Suddenly she had three sets of arms wrapped around her and tearstains on her leathers. Kneeling, she hugged them back and shared her tears with them.

As they turned to leave, she called to Rosie, "I need your help, Rosie."

Rosie waited, watching her suspiciously.

"Can you temper time, Rosie?"

"Aye, but it's not a goods idea. Some things might gets out of order."

"I need Galen to recall a past life. Can you do that and not get things out of order?" Yávië asked.

"Maybes I can. I don't suppose you wants *him* to knows we're doing this does you?"

Yávië smiled, for she knew that Rosie did not refer to Galen, but to Sōrél.

"No, Rosie, I don't want you to tell him. He will think it rash of me, see it as hurrying the future. But it is not, truly it is not. I have waited too long already."

Rosie made a face, but agreed to Yávië's request. "You'd best be with Galen when he remembers."

Aero made a tight circle before setting down in front of Galen's gates.

Yávië directed him to wait and ran into the Galenite city.

"Yávië!" Galen cried when he saw her, "What brings you to us?"

"I have need of your help, Galen. I have come to collect on a promise you made to me long ago."

She watched him carefully, waiting for the flicker of recognition in his eyes.

"You are the Queen's daughter; I met you in the woods. But . . . "

"It was a lifetime ago, Galen. You pledged a life debt to me. Do you remember?"

"Aye, I recall as if it were yesterday. How is that possible?"

"Galen, soon I will need you to join us as our seventh Guardian. You must prepare someone to take your place here. Will you do this for me?" Yávië asked gently. "Will you honor your pledge?"

"I am a man of honor, Yávië. I owe you my life. I will be ready when you call me."

Within the Wastelands where the Fortress stood, Yávië cast a spell of avoidance, leaving the way to her home forgotten to all but seven.

She stood in front of the great, stone dragon and watched as Sōrél replaced the jewel of her birthright.

"Are you sure, Yávië?" He asked as he stepped back and took her hand.

She nodded. "It is not the time for a gathering of these worlds. I will know when that day comes and will call upon the Guardians to complete the seven quests."

"I have seen it, Sōrél; I have seen the day of Ædracmoræ's rebirth. On that day, you and I will return to reclaim the power of my father. On that day, I will accept this legacy and not a day sooner. For without Ædracmoræ I have no kingdom, and I cannot restore it while I carry my father's gifts of power."

Sōrél raised his hands to her shoulders. "You are the Dragon Queen, Yávië, whether or not the jewel hangs at your heart."

They joined the four waiting Guardians. There were now six of them, six who would soon be seven—the seven Guardians of Ædracmoræ.

Release of the Blood Oath

They gathered once again at Meremire to witness the release of Nall and Yávië from their blood oath.

Yávië held Nall's hand and smiled up into his amber eyes. "We have waited long for this. When next your blood is filled with the poison of the slitherwort, another will have to save you."

Nall laughed and answered quickly, eyes bright, "The witch has promised to care for me as long as I do not annoy her."

Yávië turned to Näeré. "Care for him well, witch, for he will always be part of my heart."

Hugging her, Näeré whispered, "And my heart of hearts."

A great crowd had gathered. The Ancients of the seven worlds with their Guardians, the six new races of Men, the Xavians and the Galenites had come to witness the magick release of a blood oath. The great dragon matriarchs, Faera, Ilvaria, Azaeria, and Azrea were also present to see the one become two.

Willow and Rosie approached them, looking as elegant as an Ancient can, and dressed in scarlet finery. Gold shawls covered their heads and shoulders, and each carried a casting staff complete with a stone dragon's head and violet jewels.

"We's only goin' to do this once," Willow fussed. "When next you get into a fix likes this you will be stuck with it."

Both Nall and Yávië hid their smiles, stepping into the circle as Rosie directed, their hands clasped tightly to one another.

Before them was a table carved of willow wood. A candle in a dragon head holder stood upon the table. Beside it rested a thin golden thread and a stone bowl filled with water from the Lake of Lost Memories.

Rosie lit the candle and Willow began the casting to free the hearts of Nall and Yávië.

"Single candle burning bright
Bear two, yet be one
Yávië and Nall
Nall and Yávië
Wrapped up tight
Let them come undone
Unleash the spirit of the blood
Unleash the spirit of the heart
Unleash the spirit of the soul
Let no small piece remain ignored
As I build this partition
What was once one will now be two
When the candle's burning's done."

She held the golden thread above the flame as it burned through, leaving two golden cords, one in each hand. She thrust each of the burning ends into the bowl and the steam rose as the water doused each.

Kneeling, she used her staff to dig two holes at opposite sides of the circle. She buried one thread in each, dividing the remaining water over them.

"Now we just waits," she said.

As the candle's flame flickered and its last light faded Nall and Yávië separated, freed of the blood oath that had bound them for so long.

Willow and Rosie waved their staffs with a flourish to bind the separation.

Willow proclaimed, "Where there was one, now there's two: Nall without Yávië, Yávië without Nall.

Rosie hugged each of them and led them from the circle, allowing Sōrél and Näeré each to claim a heart.

As the music began to play, Yávië smiled and said to Näeré, "I believe Nall would appreciate you asking him to dance before Rosie comes for him."

"Aye, once in a lifetime is enough dancing with Rosie." Nall agreed, pulling Näeré off into the crowd of merrymakers.

"And you, milady? Would you like to dance with the Captain of the Guardians?" Sōrél asked Yávië, bowing deeply.

Agreement on the Promise of Ædracmoræ

Yávië and Sōrél sat back to back, resting against one another in companionable silence.

"I spoke to Willow about Ædracmoræ."

"Is it possible, Yávië?"

"She says that the task is mine to claim, and that my father has hidden a Book of Quests, which we will require before we begin. We must also call for the seventh Guardian, he who has pledged a life debt to me."

Sōrél pulled Yávië to her feet. "Then let us tell the others, Yávië, and begin the quest to restore Ædracmoræ."

"I suppose this quest is ripe with danger, and that you have no idea where the Book of Quests is hidden," Nall said with his usual charm.

"If it were easy, anyone could do it," Näeré teased.

"Aye, every quest is dangerous and I do not know where the Book of Quests lies, but I do know where the search begins. We must travel far beyond the Wastelands, beyond the great ocean of the west to an unknown land that remains in shadow and untouched by my light.

"As with the dragon quests, we must travel as mortals; Morg has constructed a ship of sails to carry us across the water and Rosie will cast a spell to grant us the strength of the wind."

"Will the dragon flytes support this quest?" Rydén asked.

"The three flytes bound to the Dragon Queen will each send a hunt of two, plus Aero, making seven, to accompany our quest, as promised by Alandon," Sōrél said.

"What weapons may be carried?" Zeth asked, fingering his bow, the only weapon he had truly managed to master.

Yávië sighed, "We will be limited, for I have renounced the power of my birthright until our quest to restore Ædracmoræ is complete."

Nall mumbled, "Do you really think that wise, Yávië?"

Yávië placed her hand on his arm. "Nay, Nall, wisdom has been swept from me in the quest for Ædracmoræ, for if I keep my power I must give up the search. I cannot allow the seven worlds to remain divided without asking the quest of you, and therefore must renounce my birthright."

She continued, "Sōrél will carry the Bow of Ages, Nall has his sword and bow and holds the dragon scale shield of the Emeraldflyte, Rydén possesses the Iaito, Zeth his bow, I have the Sword of Domesius, and Näeré wields her mind as our sorceress.

"We will retain our ability to heal, but our enemies will know our weaknesses. The rebirth of Ædracmoræ will draw whatever evil lies beyond us."

Näeré looked at Yávië with concern. "My vision shows this quest requires seven. We are six."

"Aye, Näeré, your vision does not fail you. Willow and Rosie will call the seventh if we are agreed to quest. I will not ask it of you but once, and your refusal will carry no harm. Speak you, aye or nay, and the matter is done."

The chorus of five "ayes" brought the heat of quest to Yávië's heart. The Guardians stood for the Dragon Queen and Ædracmoræ, Galen of Æstaffordæ would be called to serve his promised life debt.

The Summoning of the Seventh

Remaining veiled, Yávië shadowed Galen as he rode to Xavian City. She had given him the bullram he rode at the feast following the machine war. A fine animal, strong and intelligent, it was a mount fit for a king. She turned her gaze towards the man who accompanied him, Kade, Vice Counsel of the Galenite government, a good choice to replace Galen.

"Replace Galen." The words seemed harsh, but the time had come for Galen to join the Guardians and accept the place he had chosen when he swore his life debt to Yávië.

Together they had planned the death that would send him to slumber, waiting to be summoned by Rosie. His people knew that he had been called to serve the Guardians and the change in leadership was expected.

"Did you think I would allow you to do this alone, Yávië?" Sōrél's whisper startled her.

"Rosie told you?"

"Nay, Galen did. He feared his death would lie too heavy on your heart . . . and he knew that I was an unfeeling son of a bane boar." he smiled. "Let me do this, Yávië. He will feel no pain."

"You do not condemn me for this?" Yávië said, surprised.

"Yávië, I stand with you whether you are right or wrong."

"Am I wrong this time, Sōrél?" Her eyes glistened with uncertainty.

"I have no answer. You must follow your heart."

Her arms went around his waist and her head rested on his chest. "But you are my heart of hearts—where would you lead me?"

"I would lead you on a quest beyond the waters to the west," he said, looking down on her.

As she stepped away, he drew the Bow of Ages and sent an arrow cleanly through Galen's heart.

The fortnight following Galen's death seemed very long. Kade had arrived at Meremire bearing the news and requesting the right of mourning.

The Guardians had spent the week among the Galenites, sharing their grief and conducting the ceremony of the pyre, ensuring that Galen's soul would ascend to its rightful resting place in the universe.

Yávië was glad she had been spared the taking of this life, and once again, she found herself marveling at Sōrél's willingness to carry all her heavy burdens.

The calling of the seventh Guardian required the presence of the six; Rosie would cast the binding spell over all of them once Galen arrived. Yávië recalled standing with the Guardians in the pentacle long ago on Ædracmoræ; she remembered the sound of her father's voice as he bound them for eternity and she remembered the warmth of Sōrél's hand gripping hers. Now there would be seven.

With great care, Rosie gathered the elements for the calling of the seventh Guardian, for not only was this one being called as a Guardian, he was being transformed from mere mortal to protector of the Queen. There could be no errors.

She drew a pentacle, then a large circle with seven smaller ones inside. Galen's circle was at the center, with three above and three below it, each one overlapping the others.

Each Guardian had given a gift to provide Galen with the strength he would need for the transformation. Rosie blessed the calling with the herbs of truth and oils of wisdom and called the Guardians to take their places.

Yávië's circle was at the center top, bound on the right by Sōrél's and the left by Nall's. Zeth's circle lay at the center bottom, linked right and left by Näeré's and Rydén's.

The Guardians each knelt at their place and Rosie began the ceremony.

As the ancient words tumbled over them, each understood the importance of this summoning. Their circle would be closed, completed by the seventh. They would begin the quest for Ædracmoræ's rebirth with the coming of the morrow.

Carefully Rosie placed the tears of the dragon mothers in Galen's circle, followed by the gifts of the Guardians. A deathawk's heart for strength and far sight, a grass cat's whiskers for speed and stealth, an arrow from the Bow of Ages for marksmanship, blood from the handle of the Iaito for strength of sword, an incantation to ward off fear, and the breath of Yávië to bind him to her soul. Next came the Ancients' seven gifts: quickness of wit, veil of mist, stone heart against a wicked woman, healing spell, diplomacy of dragons, beast speak, and a spell against shadow bane.

Rosie bound them all with a golden thread and for her final binding, called Galen to her.

"Child of mine, who once was man, Guardian of Ædracmoræ, I calls you forth from sleep within the stars. Come, child, come quick to me," called Rosewort, swiftly passing her hand above the center circle, "and let no shadow cover you."

In a blinding flash of perfect white light, the seventh Guardian arrived.

"I calls you Galen, cause you is," she added, wrapping him tight within the spider's silk to keep him warm that night.

Looking at the others she said, "We'll sleeps here tonight to keep him safe."

Yávië moved and knelt near Galen, smoothing back his hair with her fingertips. "I am sure you will think long and hard before you swear another life debt," she spoke softly to his sleeping form.

In the early morning light, Galen went to Willow for his clothing. Brown eyes, she told him, required deeply tanned leathers.

As the Guardians welcomed him among them, Rosie called Yávië to her.

"I have never seens more purity in a Guardian, never—excepts in you," she said softly. "Galen is meants for something very special, Yávië. Watch him close."

Yávië looked at Galen. He was smiling, proud to be with his new friends, and with a new strength and vitality radiating from his startling white aura.

"Who are you really, Galen of Æstaffordæ?" Yávië whispered.

There was no awkwardness in Galen, no uncertainty with weapons. His motions were smooth and efficient as he sparred with Sōrél and Nall in the early morning light.

"He is very strong; good with the sword and well beyond mere adequacy with the bow," Näeré said, watching over Yavie's shoulder.

"Though I doubt he could beat Sōrél's accuracy or you in a duel of swords," she added, smiling. "Perhaps we should see."

Turning with a startled laugh, Yávië asked, "You want me to beat him in a bit of sword play, do you? What of his fragile male . . . "

"I do not believe Galen to be fragile. Look at him. Only your aura pulses more brightly. It will be good for him, and you are the best among us," Näeré urged.

Yávië removed her cloak and handed it to Näeré.

"Remember, you asked for this. If I get In trouble, cast a spell and knock him unconscious," she said as she headed toward the practice field.

All swords lowered as she approached, her own sword drawn, its scarlet blade gleaming.

"I have been asked to lend a new perspective to the game. Näeré believes that you may be able to best me, though she would not say so outright," Yávië said, gazing curiously at Galen.

Sōrél and Nall looked at one another and then back at Näeré who was doubled over with laughter.

"I don't think Näeré meant . . ." Nall began, and received a swift punch from Sōrél.

"Come, Nall. We should give them some room for their practice," Sōrél said, pulling Nall away.

"What were you thinking?" Nall asked Näeré, "Yávië will kill him, and then what will we do?"

"Oh, I don't think so; I think he can match her," Näeré said, smiling mischievously.

The ringing of swords returned their attention to the field.

Yávië drove Galen back, battering him with strong forehand strokes.

Smiling at him, she whispered, "You are not trying, Galen."

"Nay milady, I fear death."

"I think you fear nothing." Yávië returned with a vicious thrust that caused Galen to leap backward, barely avoiding disembowelment.

He rushed forward and their swords clashed high, blades grating as they slipped toward the hilt. She quickly circled her blade and knocked his away before delivering a wicked backhand swing.

Their swords locked repeatedly, and Yávië disengaged him repeatedly, always beating him back with her return strokes. Galen caught her with a swift thrust, causing her to somersault away and return with a strong forward strike.

"Who are you, Galen of Æstaffordæ?" she asked, causing him to trip and allowing her to place her sword at his heart. Withdrawing her sword, she held it high in victory, winning the cheers of those watching. She replaced her sword in its scabbard and helped him to his feet.

"You cheat," Galen said, smiling.

"Indeed, I will do anything to win." Yávië winked at him.

Sōrél swept Yávië off her feet and swung her around. As he released her, Nall seized her to do the same.

"I knew you could not best her," Nall swore to Galen as he slapped him on the back. "She is a formidable swordsman."

Sōrél looked inquisitively at his sister, noticing the glance and nod that passed between the two women. He wondered what he had missed.

Far from Home

Looking dismal in the pouring rain, the Guardians stood outside Willow's bothie, their cloaks pulled tightly around them and hoods drawn up.

"Is it a bad omen, Rosie? Is it?" asked Dobbin excitedly. "If it's a bad one I don't wants them going yet."

"Waits for the rain to go before you leaves," Weezel suggested.

"Nay, it is only weather, Dobbin. We have all seen rain before," Sōrél reassured them.

"Morg'll meets you at the ocean's edge with the boat. The dragons are helping him hauls it there," Willow promised. "He'll goes with you."

Rosie brought morning buns wrapped in oiled paper to keep them dry. Willow gave Nall a satchel filled with dried stag meat and said he had to share it, which brought smiles all around.

Yávië noticed Rosie pulling Galen aside and whispering in his ear, but was not quick enough to catch what she said.

"Rosie, are you telling secrets?" she asked lightheartedly.

"No, fair lady; she was giving warnings," Galen laughed.

Yávië looked at Rosie with a more serious expression.

"Warnings I should be aware of, Rosie?"

"No," Galen answered, "actually they were warnings about you."

Yávië raised her eyebrows and looked at them sternly.

"Say your good-byes, for we journey as far as the borderland this day, regardless of the weather," Sōrél called to them.

There were many hugs and tears, for all knew it would be a long time before they returned to the safety of Meremire.

As they departed, Yávië looked over her shoulder at the tiny Ancients waving in the rain. She looked at her Guardians—strong, brave and true every one of them—and hoped her dream was not folly and that one day she would again rest in the Fortress of the Dragon Queen.

Chapter 19: The Dragon's Crown

The rain continued throughout the day, keeping everyone wet and uncomfortable. The decision to use the bullrams had been a good one, for while they were a bit malodorous and not as glorious as dragons, they were steady and sure-footed on the rain-slick road.

As they reached the border of the Crimson Plains, Sōrél called a stop to set camp for the night. Galen and Nall built a warming fire beneath a stand of stones and the seven of them huddled down to a cold supper and a long wait until the daystar's rising.

Day broke clear and calm. Galenites who had come to see Galen as a Guardian lined the road along which they would pass. He was clearly pleased to see them and he had a warm grip for all who offered their hands.

Suddenly Zeth's bullram took offense at the crowd, bucking and bawling until Zeth was tossed unceremoniously to the ground amid the laughing Galenites. Dusting himself off, he joined in the laughter and raced off to capture the rapidly disappearing beast.

Nall laughed, and he and Näeré both shook their heads. Zeth had made a great deal of progress, but in bullram riding he was not proficient. Leaving the Galenites, they entered the Ebony Plains where they spent their second night. Yávië and Sōrél wandered off in search of privacy to discuss the coming ocean voyage. None of them had sailed a sea, though Rydén and Yávië had spent time beneath one.

"Willow is sending Morg with us for a reason. He has never accompanied us before. Rosie was telling secrets to Galen, though they both made light of it when I asked what they were talking about," Yávië said with concern.

"You worry too much, Yávië. Morg is quite a skilled sorcerer and his presence should be a comfort. He is also the boat's builder, and will have the knowledge to repair it if need be. I hear he modeled it after some of Maloch's designs using dragon bone and scales," Sōrél said, taking her hand as they walked among the ebony stones.

"What do you know of the place we seek?" he continued.

"I know that of all places on all the seven worlds, it is the only one my light could not reach. I believe Morg may know more, but he has not shared it with me." She hugged Sōrél fiercely. "I worry so that I am endangering the six of you unnecessarily. If I could do this alone, I would."

"I know Yávië, but we would never allow it. We are sworn, and our oath binds us to you always."

"What's more, I enjoy death and dismemberment," Nall spoke, stepping out from the stones to their right, "as long as they are another's. Galen is no longer in camp and this concerns me. Shall we take a look and see what he is doing?"

"Yávië, return to camp. Nall and I will look for Galen," Sōrél said.

Yávië headed slowly back to camp, wondering what Galen was up to and why Rosie felt so strongly that his purpose was more than just that of seventh Guardian. When she reached the fire, she found Galen sitting with his back against a stone. The others were gone.

"Nall thought you were missing," Yávië said off-handedly. "They have gone to look for you. Where are Näeré, Rydén and Zeth?"

"Perhaps they also thought me lost," Galen spoke quietly, all the while looking directly at Yávië with the same intensity that had made her uncomfortable so very long ago.

"Who are you, Galen of Æstaffordæ? Who are you really?" she asked for the third time.

"I am a common man who swore a life debt to a beautiful princess a lifetime ago, nothing more."

A smile spread slowly from Yavie's lips to her eyes. "I do not believe there is anything common about you, Galen. I will discover who you are before our quest is through. I promise it."

Galen's response was a nod of agreement.

Nall and Sōrél stared at Galen from the nearby stones.

"He drew us away on purpose to be alone with her." Nall's tone was accusatory. "I do not like it."

He looked at Sōrél, adding with a knowing smile, "From the look on your face, you do not like it either my friend."

Sōrél glowered at Nall, then at Galen and finally at Yávië before striding purposefully toward the fire.

"When you leave camp, take someone with you, and let me know where you are going. I am responsible for the safety and success of our quest. I do not take kindly to being led on a wild boar's chase."

"No harm was intended," Galen answered. "I merely walked the perimeter of the camp. I was restless."

"I have seen your restlessness. Next time take Nall." Sōrél nodded curtly as Naeré, Rydén and Zeth returned with a large simplestag.

"We bring a meal," Näeré called out. "Zeth was too hungry to get by on cold rations again."

The air was thick with discord. Her eyes sought her brother. Shaking her head, she cautioned, "Not again."

"He is up to no good," Sōrél fumed to Näeré.

"Nay, I do not think that is so. I believe he is here for a purpose deeper than ours, but I do not believe it is negative. He is frighteningly pure, Sōrél, as pure as Yávië. She has no interest in him, other than to know who he really is. Do not seek trouble where there is none, Sōrél. It will only serve as a distraction, and we cannot afford to be distracted."

At Yávië's approach, Näeré smiled and returned to her place at the fire, sitting close to Nall and sharing with him the story of the hunt for the stag.

"Sōrél," Yávië said gently, "you were rude. There was no need."

"Aye, there was; he should tell us where he goes."

"That is not why you were rude," Yávië continued, taking his face in her hands and forcing him to look at her. "What do you see, Sōrél, when you look at me?"

"I see the truth," he whispered, breathing deeply. "I see no reason for the fear I feel."

She looked up at him and nodded. "Next time look at me before you become fearful. We are seven, we are one. Only together can we accomplish our task. None will ever claim my heart but you. If you do not believe that, Aléria may as well have won. Speak to Nall, for he shares your fear. Galen must be trusted; it can be no other way."

She turned to go, but he held her for a moment longer, a moment of apology.

Returning to the fire, they feasted on stag and listened as Zeth told them nonsense of the chase for the bullram before they slept.

Deep into the night, Yávië woke Galen and urged him to follow her. Just beyond the fire's glow, she paused and looked deep into his eyes.

"What do you seek, Galen?"

"I seek that which I have not yet found." His voice was strong and quiet.

"Seek what you will, but do not mislead Sōrél by your actions. He is dangerous when he is fearful; do not give him cause for fear. Why did you bait him?"

"I test him. Soon you will be in danger. He must be able to protect you. If he cannot see past his jealousy he will not do his job."

"Why is it your place to test him?"

"Your father sent me," Galen stated bluntly.

Yávië blinked. "My father? He told me when I last saw him we would not meet again. Why does he still concern himself if he can no longer join me? Tell Sōrél why you are here. If you bait him again, I will kill you myself."

Without waiting for an answer, she spun on her heel and returned to the fire, placing a comforting hand on Sōrél's chest as he pretended to sleep.

Across the fire, Nall watched through half-closed eyelids, a smile tugging at the edges of his mouth. He would pay dearly to see Yávië kill Galen.

Nácré slapped the back of his head and said, "You would not," causing his smile to grow before her calming presence lulled him back to sleep.

Aero snuffed and nuzzled Yávië as if he had not seen her in ages. She chuckled and shared her thoughts with him as she slipped her hand beneath his lifted scales and scratched his tender skin.

"Huntress, the boat is a remarkable machine. Morgwort shared stories of its building as we dragged it here upon the sledge."

"That must have been a sight to see, five dragons pulling a boat on a sledge," Yávië said with sincerity.

By the time the Guardians had arrived, the boat was in the water, moored with heavy line to a stake driven into the sandy shore.

The boat was magnificent. Two dragon lengths from bow to stern, its framework was made of dragon bone, and modeled after the smaller craft Maloch had built and launched upon the Trembling Sea. It was covered in wind dragon scales, the lightest of all scales, over hides tanned and treated by the Ancients to resist water should any of the scales be lost.

Above the deck rose three masts with sails attached. The sails had been crafted by Willow and Rosie of the very finest spider's silk, woven so tightly and sewn so carefully that the seams were practically invisible. So light were they that even the gentlest of breezes would be caught, propelling the craft across the great expanse of water.

The figure of a dragon's neck and head carved of a great braid tree rose from the bow, the ropy tendrils curled below and along both sides of the vessel. Atop the dragon's head sat a golden crown. Across the stern was the name, "Dragon's Crown"—it was, indeed, a beautiful sailing vessel Morg had given them for their voyage.

They moved supplies from the second sledge to the boat, storing them below the deck, as directed by Morgwort. He fussed and showed them where each item should be placed. When the last of the supplies was secured to his liking, he gave them a tour.

A great wheel attached to a rudder at the stern would help guide their direction. Morg described the way the boat would move gently to the left or right with a turn of the wheel. He showed them how to lower and raise the sails and pointed out the name of Yávië sewn into the large midsail. He showed them where the sleeping cots were, and how to use the pail.

"Wherever we go, they will sees us comin'," Morg said, clapping his hands in delight.

"What if we do not wish them to see us, Morg?" Nall asked, rolling his eyes.

"Then we just veils her in mist!" Morg shouted, thumping Nall with his stick.

Näeré laughed uncontrollably, hugging her sides. "Nall, will you never learn?"

"What?" Nall grumbled, "All I did was ask a question."

"Foolish question, *foolish*!" Morg replied, taking another swing at Nall's knees.

"It is going to be a long trip," Nall said, shaking his head and backing away from Morg.

"Aye, very long," Morg agreed with a cheeky grin.

"Perhaps you should learn to swim like a fish," Näeré teased Nall.

"I know how to swim. I just don't like being wet," he replied as Näeré pushed him over the side and then jumped in to "save" him.

The five, dry Guardians and their Ancient boat captain stood laughing at them as Nall and Näeré frolicked like children in the cool water of the gray-green ocean. Soon the dragons joined in, causing great waves to lap against the boat's sides and sending Nall and Näeré swimming for the safety of the shore, where they sat on the sand long into the night wondering what mystery lay on the other side of the ocean's vastness.

Across the Ocean Obscura

The morning was cloaked in fog, shutting out the rise of the daystar and bringing a feeling of desolation to both shore and sea.

Morg led them aboard again, this time pulling up the steep ramp they had used to come and go. There would be no returning to this shore for many days.

Nall and Galen pulled in the heavy bone they had used to anchor the boat, and Rydén and Yávië set the mainsail, while Zeth and Sōrél let the fore and aft sails fly. Morg stood short before the wheel and steered them away from everything they had ever known, into the Ocean Obscura.

"Legend says there's a land of shadow far across the sea, a land where nothing has substance, everything's made of fog and mist and shadow. They calls it Abaddon's Abyss. A netherworld filleds with pain and misery, a place that holds lost souls," Morg told them with a sad look. "But we'll be careful. Rosie and Willow'll be real mad if I don't brings you back."

The days seemed endless, each one so like the one before. It seemed impossible to tell one from another. They entertained each other with stories of the past, reliving the battle of the Fortress. Morg told tales of long ago, tales of Ædracmoræ's death as he had been told by Willow.

The legend said that in his fury Alandon had ripped the once spherical world into seven pieces and flung them away, leaving the seven parts drifting about the topaz star. The first Ancients on Æshardæ had built the mirrors allowing them to pass from one piece to the next and back again. Now the worlds still lay separate, seven giant puzzle pieces seeking a child's hand to make them whole again.

The dragons came and went, soaring above, or drifting sleepily on the surface of the water alongside the boat. The wind dragons rested in the clouds above them, keeping watch for danger, but danger never came, just endless days upon an endless sea.

Each night Xander would venture forth from his sleep within Yávië's vest and race about the deck and rails, leading Valia the grass cat on a merry chase. Nall's deathawk sat sleeping like a stone and Morg told more legends of the past: Ædracmoræ in its finest days, the seven races of men, and the Guardians who kept the law. He told the tale of Alandon's arrival and Ya'vanna's discovery of him in her garden. He told how her father had proclaimed Alandon the kingdom's sorcerer for his amazing abilities.

All had been well until Ya'vanna was old enough to wed. She would have none other than Alandon, and her father's fears were great. Alandon had come from a race of beings called Sojourners who were unknown to the king. He feared his daughter would be taken to a world far from home, but Alandon assured him this would never happen, for his race had fled a dying world and Alandon had become separated from the others. It was unknown what had happened to them, and he had found himself alone in Ya'vanna's garden. Eventually the king gave his permission and they were wed.

It was thought, Morg told them, that Alandon's people had created all the known and unknown worlds and all the beings on them, but no one knew for sure.

A dragon's growl seized their attention. Aero hovered beside them as he told them what lay ahead.

They emerged from the fog just long enough to glimpse land before the mist enshrouded them again—a beach of silvery sand with a backdrop of high, jagged mountains, black against the leaden sky. There was no sign of life, not even a whisper of movement, and the dragons reported nothing as they searched overhead.

They stood on a shore which no Guardian had ever touched; a place so dark not even Yávië's light had pierced it. Näeré sensed no danger, nor did any dragon. The land appeared to be devoid of living things, and there was not even a hint of sentient life forms beyond the dark and heavy foliage that covered its lower regions. The towering black mountains lay in stark relief against the foggy backdrop; barren and jagged, their peaks soared into the darkness.

Faera burned a path before them and Aero's brilliant heart light dispelled the immediate gloom as they made their way through the velvet shadows.

An austere plateau rose before them, desolate and harsh. The path became steeper, but they forged ahead holding tightly to a rope linking them together. Faera and Aero returned to the shore, now far below, where they would remain with the other five dragons unless called.

When the Guardians reached the crown of the plateau, they found it cleaved by an escarpment. A waterfall cascaded down its entire drop of ten, dragon lengths to an inland sea that lay far beneath them.

Gathering twigs and branches, they prepared the night's fire. Sōrél assigned a watch to each of them, making sure that Nall and Galen were paired. Näeré looked unhappy, but agreed to share the first watch with Zeth and Rydén. Yávië and Sōrél would take the more difficult middle watch, breaking their sleep, but allowing the others a full night's rest. Morg was allowed an uninterrupted slumber.

Näeré woke Yávië a little before the appointed time. Placing a finger to her lips, she beckoned her away from the others.

"Yávië, there has been no indication of trouble, but there are voices, silent voices from within the earth. They do not call to us, but merely babble without meaning."

Placing a hand on Näeré's arm, Yávië thanked her and went to wake Sōrél.

They sat at the edge of the precipice watching the water tumbling down into the blackness below. It was like the distant roar of thunder, drowning out Morg's snoring.

Yávië listened quietly to the voices drifting up from below—they were using the ancient language, the language of her father. Näeré was correct; they were not speaking to the Guardians or calling out to anyone, but rather a soliloquy of misery. The words described the wretchedness and torment of souls trapped within the bottomless pit of perdition.

She gripped Sōrél's arm tightly, moaning in pain.

"It is so dark there, Sōrél. I am afraid," she whispered.

"What is it, Yávië? What do you see?"

"He steals souls. Abaddon steals souls. Go, wake Morg!"

"There was tales of this long ago, one of evil who could grasps a soul as it passed on its way to slumber," Morg said, a frown deepening his wrinkles.

"Then we will just have to release them," Nall stated, "since we are here anyway."

Yávië laid her hand on Nall's shoulder. "One of them is my mother," she said, smiling sadly. "He has Ya'vanna's soul. I heard her voice."

"That is why my father called you, Galen," she said with certainty. "My father asked you to release my mother's soul for him."

Galen nodded.

"He also told me to uphold my life debt to you, or my own soul would not be worth anything, not even to Abaddon," he added, meeting the eyes of Nall and Sōrél.

The cliff face was a sheer vertical drop, offering little in the way of hand or footholds beyond roots and small bushes that had managed to survive the steep terrain. About two thirds of the way down, a large outcropping of rock would give them a resting place provided they could reach it safely.

"Why is it that when we quest we must travel as mortals?" Nall complained. "Why must everything be so damnably difficult?"

"It is my father's requisite, the requisite of *your* King," Yávië reminded.

"You are simply gnashing your teeth because you have been chosen to carry Morg," laughed Näeré. It had been agreed that a sling would be fashioned for Morg as his legs were far too short to descend safely. Nall would have to take him down to the base of the cliff.

"He had better keep his staff tucked away is all I can say. If he smacks me with it I will simply cut him lose and let him fall," Nall muttered.

Näeré hugged him. "No you wouldn't! Your ranting is far fiercer than your actions, but don't worry. I will keep your secret."

Sōrél led off, dropping over the cliff and grasping the first of the many roots they would rely on to secure them to the steep face. The others followed one by one, with Nall and Morg coming down last.

About halfway down the face of the escarpment, Sōrél discovered a crack in the cliff. It was large enough for a man to slip through and it seemed to extend far inside the cliff.

Shouting for the others to wait he slipped along the crack. Using the root torch Morg had given him, he peered into the darkness ahead. It seemed odd that a breeze seemed to be coming from within the mountain, but since the destruction of Ædracmoræ he had seen stranger things He sensed movement behind him and turned to see Yávië had entered the fissure. He shook his head, hiding his smile.

"Why are you here when I asked that you wait?"

"Because you told me I was the Dragon Queen, therefore I will do as I please. If you intend to continue much further all of us should accompany you. I don't want the group separated, Sōrél, not after the evil I sensed last night."

He nodded his agreement, pointing back the way they had come.

"Let us continue to the base of the falls. Nall cannot pass here carrying Morg."

They exited and continued down the face to the rock outcropping, waiting there for the group to assemble. All were dirty and exhausted, for the descent over the face of the escarpment had been strenuous, but they had progressed past the halfway point. The remainder would be easier than a return ascent, for which Sōrél hoped they would find an alternative route when the time came.

Näeré came to sit next to Yávië.

"Do you still hear them?" she asked.

"Aye, even more clearly than in the night. We are getting closer to this demon's lair, Näeré. I do not know how we will defend ourselves against such a monster."

"I think Morg and I can come up with some magick that will protect us against the loss of our souls. We spoke of it last night. We will need some herbs and roots, but they should be plentiful within the forest surrounding the inland sea," Näeré offered.

Yávië nodded, distracted by the ancient language pouring into her mind. Hundreds were pleading for peace and an end to their suffering. Images of herself on the floor of Ardane's dungeon came to her. The feeling of helplessness and despair had come swiftly and she knew these souls had been enduring their torment for a much longer period. She hoped it would be as easy as Nall's words had made it sound, ". . . we will just have to release them." She knew it was Galen's intent to free her mother and for that she was grateful. Her father had not forgotten them after all.

Sōrél called and they rose to continue. It was not much further to the base of the falls—less than three dragon lengths. A sudden ruckus caused everyone to look around only to see Nall being chased by Morg, stick raised threateningly.

"He says I am too fat!" Morg hollered, reducing everyone to laughter. Watching the short Ancient chase the long-legged Nall in and out and around them on the small rock overhang provided much needed relief, and they resumed the climb down to the base of the falls in lighter spirits.

Zeth offered, and Morg graciously accepted, a lift for the rest of the way. Nall helped him settle into the sling on Zeth's back, all the while dodging Morg's attempted blows.

"Fat! I will show you fat! A fat lip *you* will have, boy!" he assured Nall.

"Nay, you cannot reach my lips, you little gnome—only my shins will be bruised!"

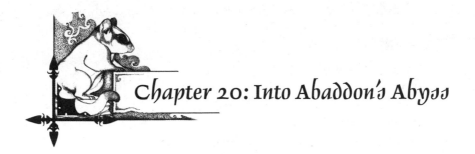

Chapter 20: Into Abaddon's Abyss

They set up camp on the sandy shore at the base of the escarpment and began gathering wood for a fire. Näeré and Morg went off in search of copperwort, baneroot, and shadowmoss to use in their protective spells against Abaddon's theft of their souls. They were quite certain they could protect the group.

Nall touched off the blaze and Zeth and Rydén went in search of prey for a hot meal. Rydén was sure something must inhabit the area, if only a grosshare or wood hen, and Zeth thought he had seen movement within the nearby forest.

Yávië could hear the voices very clearly now. They were individual utterances, no longer unfocused, but calling out for help. Her mother's voice was particularly clear, bringing back a flood of memories from long ago—memories of happier days, days of freedom without care, days spent as a young princess protected by those with whom she now traveled. But she was no longer a young princess; today she was as much a Guardian as any. She would help to free the souls trapped here and locate the Book of Quests as her father had promised her. No one would stop her—not even one who preyed on the souls of others.

The voices seemed to be coming from behind the falls and Yávië walked towards them.

"Yávië!" Sōrél's voice cut into her mind.

Turning, she saw Sōrél and Nall coming quickly toward her, concern etched on their faces. Behind them, Galen stood ready to assist.

She smiled to allay their fears before pointing and whispering, "They are there behind the falls. The voices call to us now. We must go to them."

"Nay, Yávië, not until Morg and Näeré are certain it is safe. This beast has your mother's soul; we do not want him adding yours to his collection," Sōrél said, taking her arm and attempting to draw her back in the direction of the fire.

Nall nodded emphatically and took her other hand.

"Let Morg and Näeré work their magick first, Yávië. That is best."

She allowed herself to be led, grinning at the two of them and shaking her head.

"Have I suddenly become a fragile flower that requires such careful tending?" she asked, swiftly turning to place her dagger at Sōrél's throat and trip Nall. Withdrawing the dagger, she went to meet Näeré and smiled as Galen quickly stepped back when she passed him.

"Why did she do that?" Nall asked rubbing his knees.

"I think we offended her with our protection," Sōrél said, sighing and smiling after her. "But she is very beautiful when she is fierce."

Näeré and Morg had gathered the objects required for casting the spell and were preparing to cast it once Rydén and Zeth returned.

"I hear your mother's voice, though I cannot understand her words," Näeré told Yávië.

"She begs us not to come," Yávië replied. "Over and over she begs it. What force can this be that she fears it so? And why has my father not gone for her himself?"

Zeth stumbled under the weight of the stag he carried. Rydén was beaming—it was the largest she had ever brought down. They hung it from a nearby tree, bleeding and gutting it, preparing it for the fire. The meal would not be cold tonight.

Morg wandered in. He walked in a circle around the encampment, sifting dust through his fingers and murmuring an almost inaudible incantation, his hands flying out every few steps. Then with his staff, he drew a circle around the fire and surrounding area.

Näeré told Yávië it was a spell of protection for the campsite and would keep them safe while they slept.

"We sleeps inside the circle," Morg stated, looking at each of them in turn. "Nobody leaves the circle from starset to star rise. The spell of souls we'll wait and does in the morn, so it's fresh when we goes into Abaddon's Abyss."

Then he called Yávië to him and made her sit before him.

"I know you hears your mother's voice. I hears it too. She says go home. This Abaddon is fearsome, but we is stronger all together. Promise me you won't leaves the circle, girl." He looked intently at her, searching her eyes for deception. Then he called Sōrél.

"Keeps Yávië close—I fears for her," Morg said. "Bind her if you must."

"*What*! You are telling Sōrél he may tie me up? How dare you!"

"I dares because you is in danger and it is my place to keeps you safe. My place and his," Morg said, pointing at Sōrél.

Yávië turned, giving Sōrél a look that would have caused a weaker man to bleed.

"You have a choice, milady—my arms or a rope." Sōrél smiled down at her.

"Do you think your arms can hold me?"

"Aye, I will remain awake and watch you as Rydén's cat watches your downy flier."

His words brought a smile to her lips that almost reached her eyes.

"I certainly get pushed around a lot for a Queen," she murmured over her shoulder, hiding the glance she shared with Näeré.

Morg assured them no watch was needed, but Sōrél insisted he would remain awake and keep watch over Yávië. He urged the others to sleep, as the morrow would require all their strength. He nodded to Nall and Galen, knowing they would get no sleep either.

Deep within the night they were awakened by the sound of souls wailing and calling Yávië's name. Sōrél sat wide awake, holding her firmly as she wept against him.

Purification and Protection

The still darkness of early morning found them bleary eyed and short tempered. Making quick work of morning buns and tea, they prepared for the casting of the spell of protection, which had to be completed before the topaz star broke the horizon.

Morg drove them into the water for cleansing with no thought of modesty. Cleansing was a requirement, and they had no time to waste. Morg's directions were clear—using the meadowfoam seeds he and Näeré had gathered, they were to begin at the tops of their heads and end with the soles of their feet. He supervised closely to make sure no one came away unclean. The water quickly became frothy, turning the area below the falls into a seemingly upside down world of fluffy, cumulus cloud-filled sky. As they dried themselves with spiders' silk and dressed against the morning chill, they were as clean as new fallen snow.

Since waking in the dead of night, Morgwort had not ceased his incantations. He knew that if they were not cleansed and protected, none would return to Meremire. The one below was as powerful as any he had ever known—as powerful as the Sojourner Alandon.

Taking care to keep himself within the shape as it was drawn, with the tip of his staff Morg carefully drew a large pentacle on the sandy earth around the standing Guardians. Näeré followed every line, blessing each with the herbs of truth and the oils of wisdom, her lips moving silently as she called on the strength of the ancient Sojourners to keep them safe.

Morg placed a candle at each tip of the five-pointed star, where the Guardians stood at their appointed places, each facing south. Yávië stood at the center of the central pentagon with Sōrél behind her at the pentagon's lower point. Nall stood in the right arm of the star, Rydén in the left, Zeth within its lower left point, and Galen in its lower right. Morg took his place at the topmost point with Näeré just before him in front of Yávië.

Using a stone mortar and pestle, Morg ground the copperwort, baneroot, and shadowmoss into a fine powder in preparation for its casting to the seven winds at the closure of the spell.

Checking one last time to make sure all faced the south, he instructed them to turn west thence, upon his subsequent commands, north, and thence east and then west, returning to the south. He began the incantation:

"I call to Abaddon, king of this evil horde,
Leader of the six and sixty legions,
Call up thine minions and order them down,
That none should set against us this day or next,
Bade them instead protect,
Protect us from the evil,
Protect us from those,
Those of evil will."

Morg struck his staff against the earth and all turned north. This was done twice more—from the east and the west—each time accompanied by the incantation to keep them from evil and protect their souls. At the last calling, facing south, Morg completed the casting with the following words:

"Abaddon, thief of souls,
Hear mine words, for I bid thee no visit,
Only that our quest be done."

With these final words, Morg tossed the dust of herbs and roots above each of the seven Guardians and thence, as all turned to face the south again, to be carried by the seven winds.

"The spell is done," Morg said, taking a deep breath and silently hoping it would be enough.

Together they left the safety of the pentacle and headed toward the waterfall where Yávië said the entrance to the abyss was located.

Into the Chasm

Behind the falls was a great stone arch covered with words carved in the most ancient language. They paused and allowed Yávië to speak the words, first in the language of her father, and then in the language of the Guardians.

The translation was grim; it warned all who entered Abaddon's Abyss. Nall remembered the words of the witch at the Well of Viileshga. In promising the wrath of Abaddon, she had sworn a fate that would make even an eternity of damnation and hellfire seem like paradise. Nall feared the time of that wrath was at hand.

Morg and Näeré led them into a velvety darkness. No voices cried out now. They had been stilled by Morg's spell against Abaddon. At least for the present his evil was held from them.

The passageway fell in steep descent, as if its builders could not reach the bottomless pit quickly enough. Its increasing warmth heightened the humidity of the air, and as they continued deeper down the path into the darkness of the earth, their torches cast only the dimmest of illumination. Suddenly Morg drew up short, holding his hand aloft to stop those behind him. He rapped his staff on the stone path seven times in quick succession and then once more. The head of the staff burst into brilliant light, exposing the horror that lay before them.

For as far as they could see, the floor of the immense room was covered with crystals as tall as a man, and just wide and deep enough to enshroud a soul within it. Those within the crystals pounded the sides to no avail. Their mouths were opened in screams of terror, screams that were silent except to Näeré, Morg and Yávië. Abaddon sent images of their greatest fears, endless nightmares of perpetual torture. Even during the infrequent lapses in his bombardment of them, their terror did not abate.

Yávië stepped forward, but was halted by Sōrél's strong grip on her wrist.

"My mother," she said in a hushed voice, "my mother is there."

She pointed to the right and down an endless row of crystals.

"She is held there, at the end. I must go to her."

Sōrél looked questioningly at Morg, who nodded. Sōrél released his grip, his stomach churning as he watched her walk forward.

Nall stepped back behind the others, his bow drawn and an arrow nocked. The others followed suit.

They followed Yávië, slowly advancing towards Ya'vanna's trapped soul.

Hearing Yávië cry out, Sōrél rushed forward and saw her kneeling before a crystal, hands flat upon its surface, faced pressed against it.

"Mother!" she cried, "How is it you came to be here? How can we release you and the others?"

"Yávië, go!" Yávië heard her mother's voice as clearly as she had as a child. "Go before it is too late and you become trapped within this nightmare."

But Yávië did not go. She stood, eyes large with fear and anger, and drew the Sword of Domesius. In the language of her father she cursed Abaddon and his minions—cursed the darkness and torment of his creation, cursed her sister and her father—before she called upon the magick of the sword and drew back to strike the crystal.

Galen's sword flew past her, its blade shattering the crystal.

Crystal shards flew, cutting and stinging those around Ya'vanna's prison, but the deed was done. Ya'vanna's image collapsed into a heap at Yávië feet.

The Guardians began to smash the surrounding crystals, freeing the captured ones within them. The wailing reached a deafening crescendo as their tortured, tormented souls were released from the crystals. Arrows flew and swords struck as the liberation continued for the hundreds of prisoners. The cavern filled with freed souls who began to ascend to the passageway and streamed along the path toward freedom.

Yávië knelt next to her mother's fragile form, the soul so weak it could not raise its ghostly image from the ground.

"Mother," Yávië cried, "Mother, please rise, you are free to go to your slumber. Go, please *go!*"

She looked up pleadingly at Sōrél, who made an unsuccessful attempt to gather up Ya'vanna's form, but it was too insubstantial to be carried.

A sudden clap of thunder froze the Guardians. A second caused them to surround Yávië and her mother. A dazzling white light filtered through the rock, illuminating the fleeing souls and drifting dust motes as it slowly made its way toward the Guardians. It swirled and eddied, casting the colors of the rainbow over them before it gained substance and then assembled itself into a familiar figure.

Alandon stood before them.

The others stepped aside as he moved to the pale soul of his wife. With a pass of his hand and the words of his people, he gave Ya'vanna substance, making her whole. His hand reached for hers and he lifted her gently to her feet, embracing her with the tenderness only a long lost lover can feel.

After a moment, he turned and grasped Yavie by the shoulders.

"Daughter, you were foolish to come here, but I cannot fault you. Together with these Guardians, you have returned your mother's soul to me. Now we must go. Your Ancient's spell of protection is failing and with its passing, Abaddon's fury will be cast against you."

Behind him, the darkness became more impenetrable. As had Alandon's light, the blackness swirled and eddied, finally forming a being of shadow and smoke, more insubstantial than the souls it had held captive. As the particles drifted and whirled a face appeared, a face of wickedness and fury, a demon of the deepest darkness— Abaddon.

"Alandon, why does it not surprise me to find you here fawning over your wife? You were always weak, always bound by the light, unable to see the power I had chosen in the darkness. Today you shall join me." Abaddon's voice was like rock on bone, grating and dusty as though drawn from the floor of the cavern itself.

Alandon pushed Yávië toward the Guardians, his eye contact brief but sufficient to convey his instructions. Galen gathered Ya'vanna and the Guardians fled. Nall grabbed Morg by the back of his coat as he passed, carrying him one-handed as he raced behind the others, headed for the passage and safety.

Behind them, they heard the thunder of Abaddon's duel with Alandon sending rock falling from the ceiling of the cavern.

"The *Book*!" screamed Yávië, tugging against Sōrél. "The Book of Quests lies in Abaddon's cathedral ahead of us."

"Nall, take them out of here. I will go with Yávië to claim the Book."

Nall nodded and raced after the others, clutching Morg to his chest as if he were a grass kit.

Sending a jagged bolt of lightning at Abaddon, Yavie's father crouched behind the remains of a broken crystal. He knew his daughter would not go, knew she would realize the Book of Quests was held within this despicable dungeon. He knew that she would go to the cathedral to claim the answers that only it could give to her questions on the rebirth of Ædracmoræ. Alandon marveled at his daughter's strength and thought before turning to drive Abaddon away from the Guardians and their Quest, that she would make a good Queen if she would only deny Sōrél and the House of Aaradan.

Abaddon threw a boulder, smashing the crystal where Alandon had hidden only moments before. Turning just before a bolt of lightning cut through him, he sent snaking tendrils of smoke toward his opponent, strangling him with acrid fingers. Alandon swept it away, blowing it back against him, slamming his enemy into the far wall as rock and debris tumbled to the cavern floor.

Grasping a jagged shard of crystal, Abaddon threw it at Alandon's heart as he spun away to avoid another lightning bolt. The crystal struck the cavern wall with the force of an earthquake, sending the wall of rock crashing down.

With sure footsteps, Yávië raced ahead of Sōrél. She knew exactly where the Book lay; her father had sent her a message while she knelt at her mother's side. He had also sent the ancient words that would open the crystal altar where it was encased. As she reached the towering crystal doors, she shouted the words of her father and, with a wave of her hand, cast them open.

The cathedral was immense. Carved from the crystal walls, it towered two dragon lengths above them. In front of the altar, a horde of Abaddon's demons stood before them, gnashing their teeth and spraying vile spittle from their maws.

Yávië drew her sword and charged, knowing Sōrél's arrows would strike before she reached them. Sword swinging, she slashed those the flood of arrows had missed, continuing through the slime of entrails to the altar.

Her hand gently caressed the surface of the altar before she lifted her arms and spoke the ancient language. The altar cleaved as if struck by a war hammer. As the two sides fell away, she saw the Book lying on a pedestal, just as her father had described.

She lifted the Book and met Sōrél's eyes. His look was grim but his nod gave her heart a lift.

"Are you coming, or have you decided you like it here?" called Nall as he surveyed the gore-covered floor from the fractured doorway.

"The place is coming down around our ears. It would be wise to make our exit now." He gave Yávië a wink before continuing with the news he knew she must hear, "Your mother is with Galen. I have sent them on to the boat. We are all who remain, and I think it is time even for us to take our leave."

Yávië agreed and put the hard won Book in her satchel and fled down the steps. With the deafening sounds of battle behind, Sōrél pushed Nall ahead of him as they made their way up the steep passageway. Suddenly Yávië slipped, sliding back toward them. Nall lifted her up and passed her to Sōrél, forcing them ahead in the direction of the dim light.

Without warning, a powerful tremor within the rock face threw them to the ground. Rocks cascaded down around them. They grabbed at those that were stable, climbing over and around them, always upward. Although the light was dim, there was still sufficient visibility for them to continue. Sōrél burst out of the mouth of the passageway with Yávië, gulping in great breaths of air and then turned to be sure Nall had made it.

He was nearly at the mouth when the darkness behind Nall

deepened and thickened. Sōrél dropped Yávië to the ground and raced back toward the passageway's entrance, his screams of anger uniting with Nall's screams of agony as Abaddon's vaporous hand extended deep into his center and withdrew the soul of Nall, leaving his empty shell crumpled beneath the falling rock.

"*No!*" Sōrél's voice was hoarse with pain and fury. He raced to Nall's fallen form, dragging it out from the still collapsing cave entrance. He crouched, holding Nall's body across him, and looked up into Yávië's glistening eyes.

"The cost was too great, Yávië," he whispered.

With a cry of anguish, Yávië fell to her knees beside him.

Galen and Näeré raced toward them from the direction of the forest, stopping abruptly at the sight of the three Guardians on the ground.

Sōrél knew he would never forget the sound Nall had made as Abaddon reached in and wrenched his soul away or the sight of Näeré, heartbroken with grief as her loss overtook her, shattering her soul as surely as if it had been ripped away with that of Nall.

Galen gently lifted Nall's lifeless body and placed it over his shoulder.

"We must go," he said softly, pointing toward the still disintegrating earth. "This place is failing and we cannot help Nall if we are dead."

Bereft and unaware of their surroundings, crushed and beaten by the burden of their loss, the sorrowing group staggered down the forest path, Rydén's wailing mingling with the screams of suffering that Sōrél already carried in his tormented mind.

As they fell upon the deck of the "Dragon's Crown" at anchor awaiting their return, they watched the island of Abaddon's Abyss crumble from sight, leaving only a vast and empty ocean before them.

Strength out of Sorrow

The Guardians dragged themselves into Meremire broken and beaten. Neither the release of Ya'vanna nor the acquisition of the Book of Quests offered any consolation to the heart worn travelers.

Rosie and Willow took charge of Nall's body, weeping copious tears of sorrow as they carried him to the cool caverns below Meremire where they would prepare him to await the return of his soul.

Morg had the difficult task of beginning to heal the shattered hearts and minds of his charges. He promptly put Yávië, Näeré and Rydén into a deep and dreamless sleep, and would have done the same for Sōrél if he had allowed it but, like Nall, he was stubborn and had chosen to carry the grief and guilt himself.

The silence was deafening. Where there had been light and laughter, there was now only shadow and sorrow. None met on the field for swordplay or called to the dragons that lay still in the meadow outside the wall.

On the fifth day of Morg's enforced sleep, Yávië emerged from her bothie. Her eyes were red and felt as if they had been rubbed with sand. Her hair was uncombed and her clothes hung from her body, for she had not eaten since the meal before they entered the chasm. She found herself drawn to the practice field where she sat on the wall, allowing the sun to warm her chilled body. Her mind was void of thought. She had been practicing allowing it to remain empty every time she awoke, even if only for a few moments, but she could no longer hold back the tear now making its way slowly down her pale, drawn cheek.

A hand on her shoulder made her jump. She had been expecting Nall, a smile ready for him, but her heart broke again as the memories flooded in and she fell weeping into Sōrél's waiting arms.

"Shhh." His voice was a whisper. "You and I must be strong, for if we do not lead them, the others are lost."

He rocked her gently, concerned by her frailness and deep sorrow.

"Come," I will brush your hair and then you will eat some of Rosie's broth. Later, we will work the swords together and perhaps Aero will take us to Xavian City to see its restoration."

As they walked toward her bothie, they saw Näeré trembling on unsteady legs outside the door.

Smiling sadly, Sōrél put his arm around her. "You come too, and I will brush your hair as well. Both of you need a bit of looking after and I have been appointed to do the job."

Rosie came quickly, helping Sōrél get the two women seated. She handed him a bane boar brush and she took one for herself, then they brushed Näeré and Yávië's hair until it glistened once again.

After a meal of broth and bread, Sōrél took them to the field where they drilled with the swords until the daystar drifted towards its slumber.

Later, as dusk began to settle, Sōrél called Aero, allowing him to sooth his Huntress with his soft "shuffs" and gentle rubs. He watched as her hand slipped naturally beneath the scales to scratch the dragon's hide.

Sōrél leapt up and offered her his hand. With only a moment's hesitation, Yávië' jumped up behind him and wrapped her arms around his waist, her hands upon his heart. Her face was warm against his back as they soared toward Xavian City and the empath.

The city glistened in the dying light—its beauty was worth the journey. Xavier came out to meet them, immediately holding Yávië and whispering into her mind, giving her strength and taking some of her sorrow to himself. They walked through the gardens and Yávië paused to touch the tree against which Nall had once leaned in her dreams.

She turned and looked up at Sōrél, her eyes bright with tears. "We must go for him. I know he is in great agony at the hands of Abaddon. We cannot wait."

Brushing the hair away from her face, he nodded his agreement, for he was uncertain whether he could speak without adding his tears to hers.

At the sound of clashing swords, Morg came running to the field, pleased to see Sōrél, Yávië and Näeré engaged in light practice. Willow and Rosie joined him at the wall.

"Sōrél's strong; he will leads them until she cans again," Willow said.

Rosie and Morg looked on with worried eyes.

Galen watched from the doorway of his bothie, nodding approval at the sight of the three Guardians practicing.

The sound of the swords brought Zeth and Rydén outside to see what the commotion was about and soon they joined in the sparring with Galen.

Sōrél drove them ruthlessly from star rise to star set each day. Exhausted, they fell into bed at night, sleeping without dreams or tears. Soon they would be ready to begin the search for Nall.

Yávië spent hours with Rosie, Morg and Willow trying to decide how to begin their search. With no remnant of Abaddon's Abyss remaining, they were at a loss. They decided to ask Ya'vanna.

"Mother, I need your help. We must go for Nall. We cannot leave him in Abaddon's clutches any longer. Can you help us with our search?"

"Oh Yávië, please do not put yourself in jeopardy. Nall would not wish it, you know he would not."

"Aye, Mother, he would tell me stay, not to risk my own life but I am his Queen and a Guardian as well. I will search until I have no breath left to do so. Will you help me or not?"

Ya'vanna wept quietly for the age of torture she had endured at the hands of the beast. Weeping for Nall, she decided to help her daughter save him.

"Far south, beyond the Halcyon Ice Fields, you will find him there beneath the ice."

"And my father, where will I find him?"

Ya'vanna looked startled.

"Did he escape Abaddon, Mother, or is he dead?" Yavie watched her mother's face for any shadow of untruth.

"I do not know, Yávië. I truly do not."

Yávië turned and left her mother in the care of the Ancients.

Without realizing it, she had gone straight to Näeré's bothie. Näeré should know before anyone—even Sōrél—if there was a hint of knowledge regarding Abaddon's location.

She knocked and opened the door to find Galen backing quickly away from Näeré. She saw the flush on Näeré's cheeks.

"Sōrél will kill you Galen, if I do not do it first," Yávië spoke with barely contained fury.

"I . . ."

"Do not compound your betrayal with excuses. Näeré, do you wish me to call Sōrél?"

"Nay, Galen merely attempted to comfort me, but I am not yet ready for comfort. As long as Nall suffers, so will I. You are kind Galen, and your heart is tender, but I belong to Nall whether or not he lives."

"He lives, Näeré, and I know where he is held." Yávië spoke quickly, her anger at Galen forgotten. Come, let us call the others."

As she passed Galen, Yávië placed her hand on his heart. "If I judged you harshly, I am regretful. If my assumption was correct, your days are numbered."

The Ancients, the Guardians and Ya'vanna all met in Morg's longhouse. As Sōrél paced he fired questions at Ya'vanna faster than she could respond. Yávië placed a hand on his arm to slow him. He covered her hand with his and apologized to Ya'vanna.

"We must find him soon. If Abaddon continues to torment his soul Nall will be weakening, and we must find him before his summoners are no longer strong enough to reflect in mirrors. Yávië, can you call him if we gather his soul in time?"

"Aye, his tie to me is strong, I can call him, or Rosie can. Näeré cannot because their hearts are bound," she added, staring her warning at Galen.

"Yávië, please. If you must take on this folly, accept the strength of the Sojourner; it is your birthright and will give you the power you need to accomplish this task," Ya'vanna urged her daughter. "If not for you, then for the others . . . and for Nall."

"You cannot win without it," she added softly.

In her mind, Yávië heard Nall's voice. "*Listen for once, Yávië, and take the strength you need to win, to live, to keep them safe.*"

Her voice was strong when she spoke. "We will leave for the Fortress at star rise. Sōrél, will you walk with me?"

As the others headed for their bothies, Näeré hugged Yávië fiercely, her eyes damp with tears.

Smiling, Yávië said, "Nall is still my heart."

"And my heart of hearts," Näeré answered.

Together Yávië and Sōrél walked to the field and sat on the wall.

"Is this another of my follies, Sōrél?"

"Nay," he responded without hesitation. "This will begin your greatest quest."

Awakening in silent darkness deep beneath the Halcyon Ice Field, Nall immediately recalled the agonizing terror of his soul being ripped from his body by the Sojourner soul-thief, Abaddon. He remembered they had come in search of an ancient tome, the Book of Quests, and had discovered Abaddon's Abyss filled with hundreds of captive souls. Of the seven trusted allies—six Guardians and a small wizard—who had escaped Abaddon's Abyss, Nall remained captive.

Searching his consciousness, he found the memory of the others racing to their freedom. As he became aware of his surroundings, Nall realized that the soul of Alandon, father of Yávië, lay trapped within a crystal cylinder not far away. Projecting his thoughts, Nall called to Alandon, "Yávië escaped with the others. She and your wife are safe, your lordship."

A sudden wrenching pain accompanied by images of death and mutilation assailed Nall's mind. The deep shadows surrounding his soul's prison grew heavier and long tendrils of smoky darkness curled about the crystal surface.

"If you wish to speak to someone Nall, speak to me." Abaddon's evil voice came like an unwanted caress. "There is no hope for you.

I have summoned your enemies from their slumber. They will serve me as do the demons of the dark horde."

A sudden thought flickered through Nall's mind, a thought from beyond the depths of the abyss. It was as a ray of purity and light and came from Yávië, offering a glimmer of hope. "*Nall, we come for you. We leave Meremire this day and will arrive within the fortnight. Be strong. Do not let the liar's images distress your spirit.*"

Taunting, searing laughter burned Nall's soul. "*Fools*! All of them, *fools*!" Abaddon roared. "They come as I have summoned through the wife of the captive Alandon. Did you believe they discovered the abyss without my allowing it? There is no hope for you, and now there is no hope for them. I will rip their souls from their bodies and, like you, they will discover their greatest fears have become a reality. You, Alandon—my brother—you will grow as dark as me. The black seed of hatred that burns within you will soon consume your soul and destroy your precious heir and her Guardians. Never will Yávië be allowed to reunite the Seven Kingdoms—there will be no rebirth of Ædracmoræ."

Chapter 21: Peace Beyond Punishment

The sorrow of the days since the loss of Nall had taken its toll. The Guardians preparing to leave Meremire that dank morning were not the same as they who had begun the search for the Book of Quests two seasons earlier. Each now carried the weight of loss, though for some it was heavier than for others.

Näeré had grown more somber. Deep shadows remained beneath her sapphire eyes, and her sable hair lacked its former luster. Although Sōrél insisted she remain strong and pushed his sibling unrelentingly to hone her skills in swordsmanship and sorcery, Näeré's fortitude remained fragile. The hurt she carried ran deepest of all, and she felt as if her heart were missing. The loss of Nall's passion and strength had crushed her spirit, and only Yávië and Sōrél's continued assurances that they would reunite her with him could sustain her. Tears were never far beneath the surface, a constant reminder of her pain.

There was no friendly banter, no smiles or laughter—only apprehension. Failure in the quest that lay before them would cause them to lose Nall forever.

Yávië took the Book of Ancients and the Stone of Truth from Willowort and placed them in her satchel. She hugged Willow tightly, promising to return as quickly as they could. The other six Ancients stood with hands clasped, watching the transfer of the artifacts that Yávië would use to regain her power at the Fortress, their faces solemn and wrinkled as the dried mud of a riverbed.

From his dragon mount, Sōrél kept watch over Yávië, raven hair blowing back from her face in the gentle breeze, and violet eyes flashing with the obsession of the quest. Although Yávië had been released from the blood oath she once shared with Nall, she still maintained a deep and tender love for him. As for Sōrél, in his mind—as Captain—he should have been taken. His already deep desire to return Nall to the Guardians was strengthened by the grief of his twin and sister, Näeré, at the loss of her beloved. Glancing over his shoulder, he quickly assessed the others. Rydén, Nall's first life sibling, was well prepared and willing, her sword arm strong and true. Galen and Zeth were both powerful allies; Galen's life debt to Yávië made him honor-bound to protect her even if it required him to forsake his own life, and while Zeth still lacked some of the skills that would make him as strong as the others, his loyalty was unwavering.

Sōrél returned his gaze to Yávië and felt his heart seize. He swore again to protect her above all. Calling to her, he was blessed with her dazzling smile, the one she reserved only for him.

"Nall's homecoming is not far off. Do you hear me Näeré? We will soon return your heart of hearts; I swear it," Yávië said loudly enough to be heard by all.

She knelt to embrace the Ancients who had summoned her so long ago—the holders of the Prophecies and law—then turned and leapt to the back of Aero. Directing a thought, she sent her dragon mount into flight and he responded with a swift downward stroke of his shimmering wings that lifted them high into the sky. The other Guardians followed, carried by wind, accordant and war dragons—all bound to them by pledge and quest—each representing their highly specialized flytes. The wind dragons, light and ethereal to soar high above the others; accordants, physically and mentally strong and adept at easing the pain of men and Guardians alike, and the war dragons with their brute force and fire.

Circling once and waving down to the Ancients, the Guardians banked to the west toward the great Wastelands and the Fortress of the Dragon Queen.

Under Yávië's spell of avoidance, her former home had been hidden from all except the Guardians. As they approached the Fortress, she looked for evidence of the battle that had been fought there—the battle to restore the truth that had been stolen from her; leaving her without knowledge of her past, without knowledge of Sōrél. She allowed a flash of anger to flicker and then die. There was no time to waste on anger over those already defeated—it should be saved for the one who held captive the soul of Nall.

Leaping from Aero, Yávië held up her hand to stay the Guardians, save Sōrél.

"Will you accompany me?"

Sōrél dismounted, placing a reassuring hand on Näeré's shoulder before moving toward Yávië and taking her hand in his.

"Were we not just in this place?" he asked.

"Aye, Sōrél, as always, I cause you to do more than your share of duty."

"Milady, it is my honor to serve you," he said, lifting her hand to his lips. "I have sworn it again even as we awaited you in Meremire."

"You must stop, Sōrél, for I can be bound to you no more than I already am."

As they entered the remains of the lower Fortress doors, both drew their weapons and readied to defend themselves against whatever manner of evil might remain.

Sōrél nocked an arrow in the Bow of Ages indicating his readiness to Yávië. Together they made their way up the steps toward the Great Hall. Apart from the breeze that swept in from the Wastelands, creating dust devils that ran along the hard packed earth floor, there was no sound.

Yávië paused to touch a tattered tapestry, one of her mother's favorites. They entered the hall and Sōrél examined each of the eight tower doorways for threats, but none appeared. Still, he did not relax his guard. He watched Yávië, approving of the way she kept the Sword of Domesius held high and ready. He remembered that the Sword had been a gift from the war dragon Matriarch, Faera. It had been forged from Æstretfordæ's deep magma flows and infused with magick, making it a formidable weapon. In Yávië's hand, it made her an even more fearsome opponent. She was already a natural warrior. The instruction received from the Guardians while hiding from a sister intent on destroying her had not been wasted.

When he was satisfied that no evil lay hidden within the towers, Sōrél motioned for Yávië to approach the stairway to the castle keep. With backs against the wall, they eased themselves up the winding staircase, finally arriving at the keep wherein lay the violet jewel of Yavie's birthright.

The gem sparkled with power and brilliance, light radiating from the stone dragon's claw in which it rested. Sōrél placed its golden chain over Yávië's head with the stone resting on her heart.

"Do you have the Book?" he asked.

Yávië pulled the Book of Ancients and the Stone of Truth from her satchel. She opened the covers, allowing it to rest in the air before her, the empty pages awaiting her call.

In the ancient language of her Sojourner father, she invoked the force of the flame. As her strong, clear voice advanced, words began to appear on the Book's pages, then arise and flow toward the heavens.

"Spirits of my father's flame,
Draw near and hear my cry,
Evil rises and forms against me,
Thine enemies harm for me harbor,
And clamor that ill-deeds be done against me and my Guardians,
Ill-deeds to add to the iniquitous actions,
Of Abaddon and his minions of the dark,
I beg thee fold me in thy arms,
Whilst right be done and vengeance be wrought,
The flaming sword of retribution,
Be visited on Abaddon and his evil horde,
Let great pressure be brought to bear,
Upon their wicked heads,
So that their minds be weakened,
And mine strength be forged as that of my father,
These things I beg that I might serve as an anchor in the wind,
That I may reclaim the soul of the Guardian called Nall."

The air around them began to burn, and a fierce wall of flame appeared before Yávië and the Book of the Ancients. As it had once done, long before, the Stone of Truth sent its light to cover Yávië and Sōrél, binding and strengthening them for the battle ahead.

"I wish I had not released the blood oath," Yávië whispered, "for had I not, Nall would gain my strength as well."

Turning to Sōrél, she permitted herself a moment's comfort in his embrace.

"I heard his voice, Sōrél, at Meremire. He urged me to take the strength of my birthright and use it to protect us when we came for him. Do you think it was truly Nall?"

"If he has the power to contact any, it will be you or Näeré. I must believe he tries to reach us even as we try to reach him."

As they emerged from the Fortress into the dying daylight, the Guardians shielded their eyes against Yávië's bright aura and the dragons cast their eyes down in respect.

Näeré held out the heavy hooded cloak that the Ancient Morg had sent to contain Yavie's dazzling aura.

The Halcyon Ice Fields

Beneath the depths of the distant Halcyon Ice Field, the Sojourner Abaddon prepared for the Guardians. Upon his arrival at the icy abyss, Abaddon had taken the time to summon Yávië's enemies, including Aléria, from their death slumber. Having been killed by the Guardians at the final battle within the Fortress of the Dragon Queen, each held a deep and abiding hatred for Yávië, an emotion that brought an evil joy to Abaddon's black soul. Now, deep beneath the earth, the souls of Nall and Alandon remained trapped and in torment.

"Ah, I stand corrected Alandon. Sweet Yávië is heir to your wife's kingdoms. You renounced all claim to them as I recall," Abaddon's smoky voice rumbled through the cavern in a seemingly endless soliloquy. "It was no more than a flickering moment of weakness, a false attempt to cleanse your wicked soul.

"Alandon, I am speaking to you. At least give me the courtesy of a reply. Have I not been the perfect host?" Abaddon's laughter poured over Alandon and he sent dark images of Yávië dying at the claws and fangs of the demonic horde. Then, remembering his other special guest, Abaddon presented the same images to Nall, watching as the Guardian's soul writhed and attempted to withdraw.

"Nay, do not shrink from these beautiful portraits of the precious princess! Soon they will be real enough and I will be sure her entrails are smeared across your prison so that you can wake each day with their foul odor assaulting your nostrils," Abaddon laughed, squeezing Nall's mind until he heard the Guardian cry out.

"You will die here, Nall, Guardian of Ædracmoræ. You will never see your beloved Näeré again; never walk the halls of the Fortress. You will die here! Näeré sleeps in the arms of another; the one called Galen—but you surely already knew this. You are pitiful, Guardian— not even your woman waits for you.

"Aléria, come to me. Show yourself. There is work to do."

From deep within the shadows Yávië's twin approached Nall's prison.

"Hello, my love; we meet again. The last time you saw me I was not so beautiful, thanks to Sōrél, but as you can see, Abaddon's kindness has restored me."

The words came from a mouth that seemed so like that of Yávië' but was so utterly unlike hers. Yet Yávië's raven hair fell around Aléria's shoulders, and the same impossibly brilliant violet eyes were set beneath Aléria's perfect brows.

"Oh Nall, you disappoint me with your surprise. I see you have forgotten my true beauty. Did not the handsome Captain Sōrél tell you how alike Yávië and I are in every way? I will not disappoint you as you have disappointed me.

"Again you show surprise? What did you think Sōrél and I did when we pretended to hunt the stag long into the evening?" Her golden laughter—so similar to Yávië's—filled the cavern and Nall's soul, and the assault on his mind was swift, burning visions of Sōrél and Aléria. His soul writhed with anger at the betrayal, as he watched his Captain slide the dress from Aléria's shoulders, kissing her with the passion Sōrél had pledged to Yávië.

Shaking with fury, Nall swore he would kill Sōrél for his betrayal of their queen.

Another laugh, sharp as a dagger, pierced him and Nall found himself outside the crystal prison standing before a great altar of ice. He realized that though he wore no shirt, the cold did not penetrate his skin.

"What game is this, Aléria? Allow me to return to my solitude for even prison is preferable to your company."

"Always trying to be clever, Nall." Aléria's voice came from behind. "I will soon beat that out of you."

Nall spun to face her, feeling nauseous at her nearness.

She tilted her head, staring at him as a hungry hunter stares at a fat simplestag.

"My sister really is a fool," she said, sliding her fingers down the side of Nall's chest, following the art of sorrow painted there and sending an evil chill across his soul. "Had I known what you hid beneath those drab Guardian's rags you wore I would have tossed Sōrél aside as if he were a bloodren."

"Aléria, I did not summon you to toy with him! I have no interest in your private desires."

Dense darkness crept in from the shadows, shifting and changing as Abaddon reached Aléria's side.

"Why does his soul remain strong? Why is Nall not broken? Must I perform this task myself, apprentice?"

"No, Master," Aléria whispered, her eyes averted. "I only seek the best way to break him."

"He is a fool—headstrong and reckless—treat him as you would anyone of that weakness; enter through his heart, it is his weakest point. Tear the woman Näeré from him and feed her to the horde before his eyes, Aléria, lest I use you as an example to the others."

Aléria's eyes filled with rage. "I will tear his soul apart so that not even my precious sister will be able to summon him again," she hissed.

Gathering his strength, Nall spat, "You do not have the power to break me, Aléria. I did what had to be done, and there is nothing of me left for you to break."

"I disagree," Abaddon's venomous voice drifted back to Nall. "You are a clever Guardian Nall, but not clever enough. The wretched Alandon told you the battle was lost. Told you I would come for his beloved daughter Yávië. Yes, I know the truth, Guardian."

Long tendrils of darkness wound their way up the crystal prison holding Alandon.

"The two of you conspired to keep my brother's offspring from my grasp. Alandon relied only upon you, Nall, to make sure they escaped—you pathetic creature!" The darkness slipped around Aléria. "You threw yourself in my path, knowing that if I could not have Yávië I would take you, but you lose, Nall. Yávië will be my prisoner by star set on the morrow, and you will watch her torment all the rest of your days.

"It will bring me intense joy to watch you writhe and scream. You are strong, Nall, and the shattering of your soul will bring me the greatest pleasure. Once broken, you will do my bidding and, like Aléria, you will cower in my presence."

His voice trailed away as the darkness retreated.

Aléria gave Nall a look of defiance, a twisted smile on the mask presented by her beautiful face. "You will love me, Nall," she whispered, as she approached him.

"I will kill Näeré with our love.

Peace beyond Punishment

The crushing pressure, provoked by the vision of Näeré being held so tenderly by the Guardian, Galen, with his soothing words of comfort, was too much. Nall's soul crashed against the sides of the crystal that held him prisoner.

"Shhh, hush, I cannot bear to see you cry, Näeré. Nall is gone, separated from his soul. There is no hope for his return. I will care for you always," Galen's voice came, soothing Näeré—Nall's Näeré.

"*Lies! Galen lies! Näeré, no! I am here!*" Nall cried out. "Do not forsake me! I am here. I am always here. I would never leave you."

"Do you think she will wait, Guardian? Look around you. You are in the bowels of the abyss; no one will come to save you!"

Nall tried to close his mind against Aléria's evil. He murmured to himself over and over that he did not believe the burning visions, would never believe them of Näeré.

Näeré. Just her name brought Nall peace. He remembered asking her not to make a fool of him when they sparred before the apprentice Zeth, recalled how she always came, her voice soothing him when his anger threatened to overcome him. How could she forget him? She would not—no more than he would forget her.

Suddenly, Nall saw Yávië and Sōrél within the Fortress of the Dragon Queen. They had returned to reclaim the jewel, Yávië's birthright. They were in the keep—the jewel around Yávië's neck nestled against her heart. He smiled at the thought of them together. Happiness for Yávië; it was all Nall had ever wanted for her. He saw the shadow cast upon them, heard them cry out, and watched as they fell. He saw Sōrél's Bow of Ages in the hand of the Dark Guardian, Gorn; the satisfied look on the evil man's face as he stooped and yanked the jewel from Yávië's throat, placing it over Aléria's head. Nall listened to the laughter of Aléria as she once more proclaimed herself the Dragon Queen and called on Abaddon to collect the souls of the victims.

Nall weakened as he felt his soul wither and close in upon itself; he cried out against the torment and the agony of loss, but none heard him and none in Abaddon's Abyss cared.

Within the still, calm dream, a feeling of coolness came to his fevered cheeks and Nall opened his eyes to see Näeré standing before him, her cool hands caressing his face, and her warm lips touching his.

"I will never leave you, my heart of hearts," Näeré's sweet voice promised. "You will return to me, for Sōrél and Yávië swear it. Without you, I shall surely die; my heart is broken, my soul shattered until we are together again. Wait for me; we are coming. We leave the Fortress now and we come to you. Do not leave me Nall. I could not bear it."

Once again, he felt her hands upon him, her heartbeat next to his, and remembered the way his breath caught in his throat at the sight of her, for such was her beauty. A feeling of peace calmed his mind.

"Have you seen this, Nall?" Aléria screamed, sending fresh piercing pain into his fragile mind.

Nall's young apprentice, Zeth, was lying in a bothie, his skin a deathly green. The Ancient Rosie was rocking to and fro as she wept beside him. Though hushed, her words were audible within Nall's mind.

"It's the slitherwort poison. No one was there to helps him, none offered the blood oath. Oh, Nall where was you when Zeth needed you?"

The fever raged in Nall's soul, causing it to close more tightly against Aléria's horrors. Hallucinations took him to the gardens of the Xavians; he saw Yávië's graceful form as she led him to listen to the beautiful singing.

"*Nall,*" her voice within his mind was tender and kind, "*do not disappoint me when I come for you. I have traveled far. Näeré's sadness burdens her for naught, for we know that you are here. Do not fail me, my friend, for I could not bear it if you did. Wait for us. Do not let my sister's visions harm you. Close your mind to her. I listened for once. I come with the power of my birthright, the power to free you from the chasm and reclaim your soul."*

Even in his misery, Nall wondered at the thought of Yávië listening for once.

Then his sister's face swam before him; Rydén, sweet, sweet Rydén, her face radiant as she walked beside the sea. She turned toward him as a sea dragon rose behind. *Sybeth!* No. Sybeth was dead and gone; Nall had seen to it himself.

The dragon rose to its full height, water flowing from its leafy scales.

"Sybeth sent me," it hissed, before its jaws struck Rydén, tearing her head from her torso and tossing it down.

Nall moaned within his crystal, his soul tightly closed. All were gone from him; he was alone. They would not come for him, could not come for him. He had not been there when they needed him. He had failed them, one and all. Then a sweet, soft voice again brought the promise of peace.

"Sleep, Nall, within the walls I have built for you," Yavie's private words caressed him. *"Do not believe the images of Aléria's assault, for they are lies. You have never failed us; you are our strength and protection. You are my Guardian, Nall, my defender and my shield; my strong left arm, even as Sōrél is my right."*

With the comfort of Yávië's words, Nall felt his soul relax.

Beyond the abyss, the Guardians were approaching.

Chapter 22: Return to the Abyss

Deafened by the howling wind and blinded by driving snow, the Guardians drew nearer to the ice of Abaddon's Abyss. Ahead of Aero, Yávië stumbled and felt his soft breath as he gently lowered his head to her.

"Huntress, please allow me to carry you. I can cover you with my scales and keep you protected from the cold," the young dragon pleaded.

"Nay, Aero; I must focus on the ground for we are very near the entrance to the abyss and I fear I might overlook it from your withers." Yávië took a moment to scratch beneath his scales, knowing it comforted him.

"Yávië." Though she could not see him through the swirling snow, Sōrél's voice reached her from the left. "It is here. I have found the gates but they are of heavy stone."

She ran toward the sound of his voice and felt the steadying hand of Galen as she tripped.

The others stood before the massive gates, awaiting their arrival. Yávië motioned them back and flung her hands forward, shattering the heavy rock doors as if they were no more substantial than sand.

"I imagine they know we are here now," Zeth mumbled, eliciting a gentle smile from Yávië.

"You sound more like Nall with each passing day, Zeth. He would be proud of you. It no longer matters what they know, for my strength exceeds theirs. No one remains alive when we leave this place, no one who does not accompany us. Is that understood? Today there will be no mercy for those who stand against us." She threw back her hood, allowing her light to surge before them.

"I will not risk a life beyond my own. I would prefer that you allow me to go on alone."

"Yávië," Sōrél chastised, "we are your Guardians, and we will not stay behind. There is naught that you can say that will make it otherwise."

He did not see her eyes close momentarily nor hear her silent plea for their safety, but he followed close behind her as she ducked beneath the fractured stones into Abaddon's Abyss.

The path was steep, as it had been on Abaddon's island in the Ocean Obscura. Here the glass-like walls were made of ice instead of crystal, and the heat had cooled and then condensed into a frosty chill.

Sōrél laid his hand on her arm to slow her. "Do not be foolhardy, Yávië; they know we seek them and the noise of our entrance will have drawn Abaddon's demons near."

"We must free Nall. I have built walls to protect his mind from Aléria's vicious attacks, but they will not hold forever. You must gather his soul within the creation crystal. Do you have it?"

He forgave her asking and simply nodded in reassurance.

Ahead lay the entrance to the chamber where the souls were imprisoned. The howling of the demon horde was already audible.

Yávië threw off her cloak as she entered the chamber, allowing her radiant light to drive back the darkness and those hiding there. With a sweep of her arm, she drew the Sword of Domesius and, with a long forehand stroke, sent the demons screaming in pain. With her right hand extended, ancient words created a wall of flame before them, driving even the bravest of Abaddon's horde away in fear.

Moving ahead in a tight group, the Guardians shifted and turned, senses alert for danger and seeking the crystal that contained Nall's soul. Behind them tendrils of dense shadow and smoke hugged the walls, curling out into the inky blackness at the edges of the chamber.

Silently, Abaddon called Aléria and her Dark Guardians, Gorn and Talonmet to him. Yávië, daughter of Alandon, would soon be his captive. Within the blackness of his soul, he savored his approaching victory.

Yávië tensed. "Aléria comes," she whispered to her Guardians, "and Abaddon lurks behind us in the shadows."

The heat from Yávië flashed again and brought melted ice to the walls of the cavern, driving the horde into retreat toward the underground cathedral.

"Nall's soul is held there." She pointed deep within the central chamber.

"Sōrél," she continued, tossing him the Sword of Domesius. "You and Näeré go and find him; the rest of us will follow."

Catching the sword by its dragon hilt, Sōrél beckoned to Näeré as he headed to the far end of the chamber of souls. Suddenly he paused and turned back toward Yávië.

"*Yávië* . . ." Sapphire eyes met violet, and again he whispered, "Yávië," before turning away.

"Why, Sōrél! How lovely to see you." Aléria spoke from the shadows to their right, "and Näeré—come to claim her love? He is well used. I doubt you will desire him any longer. But you are free to try and take him if you wish. We always enjoy besting you."

A sudden blast of wind thrust the three Dark Guardians back as Yavie's voice silently urged Sōrél and Näeré to run. Dropping to the ground, Aléria, Gorn and Talonmet approached Yávië and the remaining Guardians.

Abaddon's rumble came from the shadows, "Kill them. Kill them all that I may harvest their souls—and be quick about it or you will join them!"

Yávië had learned not to underestimate her sister, for Aléria was a clever sorcerer who could use visions to turn even the strongest against one another. Motioning for the others to stand their ground, and steeling her mind against the possible attack, she advanced on Aléria.

"You come to me without your weapons drawn, sister?" Aléria growled.

"I see that your new Master has given you back your beauty. When last we met, you were looking rather haggard. Your hair had paled from wickedness," Yávië taunted.

"My beauty is not in question. It has proved a lure to the Guardian Nall, for he put up no resistance."

Yávië laughed, causing Aléria's eyes to narrow and hatred for her sister's strength and purity to surge.

Aléria drew her sword, anticipating swift victory against her unprepared sister.

Behind her, Yávië heard the ring of swords as her Guardians fought Gorn and Talonmet, freeing her to deal with Aléria and Abaddon.

The sound of shattering crystal caused both to pause.

Aléria shook her head at Yávië and sprang forward, sweeping her sword in a strong backhand as they had been taught by their sword master.

Leaping away and drawing her blades, Yávië stared at her approaching sister, arms spread, weapons ready, dagger in one hand, and short sword in the other. Breathing deeply she watched as Aléria advanced. Quickly Yávië shot forward with the short sword, piercing Aléria's shoulder causing her to scream in pain.

Catching a movement from the corner of her eye, Yávië turned the smaller dragon handled dagger toward the new threat, warning Gorn away as she ground her sword blade against Aléria's strong forehand attack. Then, swinging the dagger in a low arc, she sliced across Aléria's hip, watching dispassionately as the blood began to flow.

"Come, that I may end your life," Yávië whispered to her snarling sister. As Aléria swept forward Yávië dropped to her knees and drove her dagger into her sister's chest twisting away from the backhand slice intended by Aléria to decapitate her.

Ignoring the pain of her wounds, Aléria deliberately pushed her sister back, watching Yávië's jaw tighten. With menacing eyes, she swung the heavy sword in a circle. Despite her wounds, her thrusts were strong and vicious.

Yávië allowed Aléria to drive her back until she saw her sister's sword arm weaken, then she beat her back and, dropping her own dagger, pulled Aléria's sword from her grip. Weakened and unprepared for Yávië's fury and strength, Aléria found herself captured, with her own sword at her heart.

"I have been reminded by our father that I should use my power wisely," Yávië glared bitterly at Aléria, "but this is not your lucky day.

Today, as Queen of Ædracmoræ, I choose to mete out justice without mercy."

Yávië stepped back and placed the swords before her on the floor, a clear act of submission, though Aléria knew otherwise. Her eyes grew wide in fear and disbelief.

"You have accepted the power of the throne? You swore to give up our birthright so that you could quest for the world's rebirth."

"Aye," Yavie's voice was tight, "but I lied."

Her hand slipped beneath her cloak, withdrawing the tiny crystal that would become Aléria's eternal prison.

Aléria backed away, terror now in her eyes, suddenly gasping and holding her throat as she rose from the floor of the cavern, lifted by Abaddon's Black Hand.

"I weary of you. I gave you a simple task, yet I come to find you disarmed and deep in a family squabble."

Aléria gasped for breath even as Abaddon stole it from her before casting her away as one would the unwanted remains of a meal.

Yávië faced Abaddon.

"I have come for the souls of Nall and my father." Her voice was strong and steady, for she knew she spoke the truth.

Tilting her head she added, "And to play your wicked game."

Sōrél and Näeré raced along the row of empty crystals, all of which were waiting for the souls of the innocents whom Abaddon intended adding to his collection. Screeching demons flowed all around as in a flood. Battling back-to-back, swords flashing, the Guardians left the floor slick with the viscera of the damned.

Hearing his name, Sōrél raised his eyes and saw Zeth, Galen and Rydén hacking their way toward him. The five Guardians fought as one and left none standing, chasing down and slaying the few fiends remaining within the main chamber.

An angry cry caused Sorel to spin around; there behind him stood the crystal unit holding Nall's soul. Though transparent, the image of Nall was clear and vital. It beat against the walls in a rage, hate-filled eyes fixed on Sōrél's face.

Shaking his head, Sōrél moved to free Nall.

With Aléria's visions still fresh within his beleaguered mind, Nall's rage at Sōrél's betrayal of Yávië was blinding. He had no thought other than to tear this man's eternal soul from his body and grind it into powder to feed the bloodrens.

"*I trusted you*," Nall ranted. "*Yávië* trusted you!"

Sōrél stood holding Yávië's sword, ready to strike the crystal wall.

"If this is the way you are going to behave, perhaps I should leave you there for a lifetime or two," Sōrél jested, sending Nall into another fit of fury, pounding and swearing by all that was holy and unholy.

"Nall," Näeré's tearstained face pressed against the crystal chamber. "Nall, come home," she sobbed.

Anger fled and only desire remained, desire to hold Näeré, to ease her sorrow, to heal her wounded heart.

Pulling Näeré back, Sōrél shattered the crystal—its shards cascading over them—to release Nall's soul and allow his vaporous image to be released. Weeping with joy and relief, Näeré dropped to the ground beside Nall's fragile image.

"Could someone please pour me back into my poor excuse for a body? I tire of resembling a wind dragon," Nall mumbled self-consciously.

Näeré laughed through her tears. "Do you not know I love you for that body?" she said.

"Nay, woman, you love me for my skill with the sword and my hunting prowess, and of course my good nature!" Nall replied.

"I have the creation crystal sent to carry you home," Sōrél reminded from behind Näeré.

Anger coursed through Nall again as the sound of the voice of treachery recalled Aléria's wicked images.

"Nay, I would not trust you to carry a stone across a field."

Näeré and Sōrél exchanged a glance and Näeré lifted the tiny crystal from her brother's hand.

"Would you trust me to carry you home?"

Nall nodded, still staring at Sōrél as Aléria's hateful visions continued to consume his mind.

Näeré spoke the words that drew Nall's soul into the crystal. In his disembodied state, he felt the pull, but no pain. The crystal pulsed with amber energy and Näeré gently tucked it away next to her heart.

Sōrél turned to the others. "Where is Yávië?" he asked. His words carried a hint of accusation.

Galen pointed to the opposite side of the room and indicated the torrent of water that had begun tumbling down the walls and covering the floor.

"She toys with Abaddon . . ."

Sōrél's grim look eased as he saw the smiles on Zeth and Rydén's faces.

"I believe she would like us to leave this place," Sōrél said.

Together the Guardians turned toward the passage that would lead them to freedom.

"Do you grow tired Abaddon?" Yávië queried. "You do not make a very good sparring partner, for there is no challenge."

Abaddon howled and surged toward her, but Yávië twisted away, laughing.

"Father," she called to Alandon below. "Your brother grows weary and no longer has the strength to hold you. He must take his rest soon. Free yourself and join the Guardians at the gates. I will see that Abaddon is comfortable before I join you."

Roaring, Abaddon rushed forward again, surrounding Yávië with his darkness but her light burst forth with flaming heat, causing the dust motes encircling them to redden and burn away.

Hearing the crash of her father's crystal Yávië swung back to Abaddon, taking out the tiny crystal she had brought to hold him. She did not see the kernel of darkness Abaddon swept into her father's soul.

Lifting the creation crystal and balancing it on three fingers before her, she laughed at Abaddon's futile flurry of energy. He could not stand against the pull of the crystal prison. Yávië began the incantation that would draw Abaddon to her, sending his darkness to a crystal grave.

Abaddon wailed and fought like a bane boar, but nothing could stop the crystal's pull. Little by little, the evil darkness was swept into the tiny void until nothing remained except the melting ice in the abyss of his most recent home.

Yávië tucked the crystal containing Abaddon within the soft, cloth bag she wore around her neck. She would destroy it after taking Nall home to Meremire.

Seeing Aléria's crumpled body against the melting wall of ice, Yávië's heart fluttered with regret and she went to kneel one last time beside her sister.

"Once we were close," she whispered. "I remember it."

Aléria gave a shallow gasp and clutched Yávië's hand. "Aye, I remember it too. Do not let me leave this world with your hatred on my heart, Yávië."

Aléria's eyelids lifted, revealing the innocent eyes Yávië remembered from their childhood.

"I cannot allow your freedom Aléria, for I have decreed no mercy on this day. The harm you have done cannot be forgotten, nor forgiven, but I shall take your soul into my care if you wish it."

As her eyes closed in pain, Aléria nodded her consent.

Withdrawing a second creation crystal, Yávië spoke the ancient words that would seal her sister's soul for an eternity of sorrow. She placed the violet crystal beside the one of decay. Together Abaddon and Aléria lay against Yávië's heart.

Yávië wiped away her tears and went in search of the others.

Chapter 23: Soul Binding

Arrival at Meremire was joyous. Nall's soul was given to the Ancient Willowort, who cooed to him as though a day dove before handing him over to Rosewort who would prepare the soul for reunion with its body.

The Guardians' smiles were brighter than the waffle root torches that Morg threatened to douse, saying Yavie's bright aura would keep them all awake anyway. Sōrél reminded him that Yávië's light would dim when she slept and received a "well put her to sleeps then," from the cantankerous Ancient.

The Ancients reunited Alandon with his wife Ya'vanna. They then called a meeting of the Council to discuss the future and Yávië's part in it, though she was not invited to be present.

As the commotion died down the Guardians remained at the fire, filled with stew and willow bark tea, drifting in and out of sleep. Sōrél took Yávië's hand and pulled her to her feet.

"Morg is right. Your light is blinding me and I require sleep. Shall I have Rosie cast a spell or take you to the Fortress?" he asked, allowing his lips to brush her temple.

She looked up at him and raised the hood of her cloak. Resting her hand against his heart, she spoke softly so as not to disturb the others.

"My eyes are heavy and I need to rest. Perhaps a bit of Rosie's magick would serve now."

Looking toward the field, she added, "And the weary dragons already sleep. Tomorrow will be soon enough to return the jewel to the Fortress."

Sōrél nodded his leave to the Guardians and declared the morrow a day of rest.

In search of Rosie, he and Yávië found her fussing over the creation crystal that held Nall.

Yávië stooped to hug the tiny Ancient, and explained, "I must ask a sleeping spell of you Rosie for my light blinds Sōrél and we both need sleep."

Rosie held Nall's crystal and said, "The morrow will be busy. I will needs you for Nall's summoning."

"Aye, Rosie. I want him home too."

Placing Nall's crystal gently on its bed of silken web, Rosie followed the two of them to Yávië's bothie. She smiled at Sōrél's tenderness toward Yávië, tenderness that so belied his behavior as Captain of the Guardians. She watched as he took his seat in the chair where he would sleep. Rosie cast the spell of sleep upon them both, leaving them with sweet dreams of one another.

The body of Nall had been taken from its resting place deep beneath Meremire. It now lay upon the bier built by the Ancient Morgwort, awaiting the return of its soul.

At the sight of his Master, Hawk had given the high piercing cry of the bonded deathawk. He remained securely fastened to Nall's chest, his great talons tangled in the cloth of his tunic and bringing forth a chuckle that lightened the solemn mood of the ceremony.

Rosie had come to Yávië even before the daystar rose to ask that she perform the summoning in the ancient language of her father. Rebinding a soul was more difficult than summoning from the slumber of death, and required a close bond with the one being called. It also required the power of the Sojourner, a power Yávië now possessed as a part of her birthright.

Yávië stood beside Nall, her eyes filling with tears as she brushed the hair from his forehead and bent to kiss his cheek.

"Come, Hawk," she called.

Carefully disengaging the bird's talons, she lifted him and placed him on his day perch, hooding his eyes against the sight of his Master to ensure he would not interfere.

The Guardians and Ancients formed a circle within a circle around Nall's soulless body.

Yávië gave a last glance at Näeré and began the binding of Nall's spirit. Her voice was strong and sure, filling them with hope.

"Sojourners, most ancient of the heavens,
Holders of wisdom and knowledge,
Watchers of our ascents and descents,
Silent yet strong,
Grant me this I ask,
Aid me in the quest to bind this lost soul,
Return the spirit of the Guardian,
Strong and brave and true,
That he may serve the Dragon Queen,
Once more rise with each daystar's passing."

They watched as Nall's soul left the creation crystal in Yávië's hand. The miracle of life drifted above Nall's motionless form and hovered momentarily before gently covering him as the morning mist covers the field.

"Soul of Nall, spirit of the Guardian below,
Rest within, abide with him always,
For this is your home."

As Yávië looked on, the spirit of Nall enfolded itself into his body. Tears fell as she watched him gasp his first breath. Holding out her hand to stay the forward rush of his friends, she nodded to Näeré who came with silent weeping to touch his heart and feel it beating.

"He does not wake," Näeré whispered fearfully.

"He will with time. His body must rest with its soul before the final quickening," Yávië reassured her. "Sōrél and Galen will carry him to your bothie so that you may be there when he wakes."

Näeré kissed Nall's lips and felt his breath mingle with hers. Sighing, she allowed Sōrél and Galen to lift him and she followed them to her room where she would keep watch until he awoke.

Nall's eyelids flickered, opened, and then closed against the light. His head ached and he felt disoriented, as if wandering in a strange dream. Feeling a weight on his chest, he raised his hand to discover what lay there. Raising his head, he saw Näeré's rich sable hair spilling across his cot before allowing his weary eyes to close again, a smile playing at the corners of his mouth.

When next he awoke, Nall was alone. Through the darkness, a torch shed its dim light across the room—not his bothie he knew, for it was far too neat. Näeré's more likely. He eased his long legs over the side of the cot and sat up, amazed at the effort it had required. Being separated from one's soul was apparently harder on a body than he might have imagined.

Hearing Näeré's voice outside the door, he prepared his smile of welcome and watched in anticipation as the door swung open only to reveal Galen. With a surge of furious strength, Nall shot to his feet and sent Galen crashing into the wall with the force of a blow to his jaw.

"You slimy son of a slitherwort-infected bane boar! If I had a weapon I would gut you!" Nall roared at Galen's unconscious form.

"Nall?" questioned a soft voice from the doorway.

"Did he touch you?" Nall's voice was fierce.

Näeré shook her head, afraid to speak then, taking a deep breath, said, "Nay, I would not allow it."

Her eyes welled with tears that quickly overflowed and rushed down her cheeks.

"Oh Näeré, do not cry! Galen is not worthy of your tears," Nall blustered, trying to cover his embarrassment and stupidity.

Startled, Näeré looked up at Nall. Seeing the doubt and confusion in his eyes, she slapped him hard across the face.

"You fool," she sobbed, "do not tease me with your nonsense. I have suffered enough."

"Come, it is too crowded here," Nall said, casting a glance at Galen's silent form.

He quickly gathered Näeré into his arms, carrying her out the door and through the gathering crowd of Guardians and Ancients who had been drawn by Nall's shouts.

Laughing and shaking his head, Nall said, "I believe Galen has fallen and may require healing. Näeré and I are . . . going hunting."

His eyes met Yávië's and her knowing look made him flush.

"Well, we are! I am sure that you have not had a decent meal in my absence and I expect to change that this very day."

Sōrél's eyes followed Nall as he brushed past them into the field of waiting dragons. He shook his head and said to Yávië, "I suppose we should catch the evening meal. I have a feeling their hunt may be a long one."

Chapter 24: Alandon's Gift

"Yávië," Alandon called, tapping on his daughter's door.
"Aye, Father, come in. Sit."

Sōrél was sitting near the window with a cup of steaming tea.

"Sōrél," Yávië's father nodded curtly, his lips curling in a tight sneer.

"Should I leave that you might speak privately with Yávië?" Sōrél asked.

"Nay, what I have to say you both should hear. Yávië, you have the Book of Quests?"

"Yes, nearly paid for with Nall's soul."

Alandon looked fixedly at his daughter. "And you intend to quest for the rebirth of Ædracmoræ."

It was not a question, for he knew it was the force that now drove her, her birthright—the throne of the Dragon Queen.

"You must give up the power of the throne as a condition of this quest, for it requires the purity of the blood-child not the authority of the queen. It is dangerous beyond your worst imaginings. The darkness of the horde will be drawn by it, as it was during your journey into Abaddon's Abyss. Your mother begs you not to go."

"Ya'vanna begged me not to search for Nall, Father. I love Mother, but she is not a Guardian, a warrior; she does not understand. Ædracmoræ is my home." She touched Sōrél's shoulder. "Our home, Father, even though it is not yours."

"You could rule Æstretfordæ. In fact, you could rule the Seven

Kingdoms as separate worlds. Is it truly necessary to bring about Ædracmoræ's rebirth?"

Yávië looked out the window and watched Rydén as she showed Zeth how to get more lift from his arrows by adjusting their quills. Her gaze shifted and she saw Galen helping the Ancient Dobbinwort to shoe a bullram. With a sigh, she turned and hugged her father.

"I am your daughter by temperament, and my mother's by countenance. I am grateful to be both. Please help Mother understand."

"Perhaps I shall bring her to watch you practice with the sword. I am sure she will be impressed and less fearful when she sees just how frightening you really are with a weapon in your hand. Galen says you bested him."

"Aye, but did he tell you that I cheated?" Yávië chuckled at the memory.

"He said you told him you would do anything to win. That is what it will take to complete this quest. Are you truly willing to risk all that you hold dear?" Alandon glanced toward Sōrél.

Sōrél held up his hand to stop Alandon's words.

"It is I you should be asking, Alandon, for you above all should know that I hold your daughter more precious than even my own blood, indeed, more than my own life. She will never come to harm in my care. Have I not kept that pledge?"

"Aye, but you do not know what you will be required to sacrifice and the price may be too high. None of you has ever seen a troll."

"I am willing to take the risk."

Nodding, with his eyes still locked on Sōrél, Alandon spoke again to his daughter.

"The quest is your birthright and rests, as I have written it, on the pages of the Prophecies of the Ages. Sōrél, as always I shall rely on you to try and preserve her safety."

The dark kernel of hatred that lay within Alandon's soul fed shadowy thoughts; Yávië's father reached into his vest and withdrew a small parchment-wrapped package bound with golden thread.

"You will need this for your quest, Yávië. I will leave you now."

Yávië looked at Sōrél. "Open it," she said, handing him the small package.

With the tip of his blade, Sōrél cut the golden thread and opened the map showing the location of the Book of Trolls. He saw the obsession growing in Yávië's eyes.

"When do you wish to return to the Fortress, Yávië?" he asked quietly, smoothing the folds in the ancient map.

"Soon," she whispered. "First, Nall must regain his strength."

Eyes downcast, Nall said, "I believed I had lost you, Näeré." He shook his head and sighed, "I could not see past the rage I felt."

Näeré's hand found his as she reminded him, "Aléria's visions were very powerful, Nall. The fault is not with you but with her. Galen will forgive your anger."

"Forgive me?" Nall laughed, "I do not care whether Galen forgives me. I would have had to do it sooner or later anyway."

Näeré tried to hide her smile but failed.

"Oh, so you enjoyed that display of jealous rage, did you?"

"Perhaps . . . Come, let us catch Zeth. I believe he requires a sparring partner."

Zeth was working the sword when they reached the practice field. He followed the strict regimen that Näeré had set during Nall's absence but while his work alone was very good, he had yet to put the new knowledge to the test when sparring with another.

Nall drew his sword and approached his student.

"Let us see if you are as good when another sword gets in your way," he said, nodding at Zeth. "I hear you are looking very good with the bow."

Zeth beamed, making Nall glad he had given the compliment.

Aware that Zeth's sword arm was still weak, Nall circled Zeth, his sword tapping it quickly to the side—left, left, right.

"Lift the sword, Zeth. The idea of the weapon is to defend yourself. If it is hanging loosely toward the earth your enemy will surely gut you."

Zeth paled at the thought of his entrails spilling through a gash in his abdomen.

"Nall, do you terrorize Zeth again?" Näeré called from her seat on the wall.

"Nay, I merely speak the truth," he called back, increasing the strength of his attack against Zeth.

"Wait," Näeré shouted, jumping down and running to join them.

"Use my sword, Zeth; it has a lighter heft and the guard will save your knuckles from Nall's brutish force."

She gave Zeth a wink, collected his sword, and turned away, quickly casting the spell over her shoulder to assure Zeth a strong sword arm against Nall.

"Strength of arm I give today,
Stay with Zeth my sword, obey."

Zeth raised Näeré's sword, its blade gleaming in the midday radiance. It seemed as light as a feather and his arm seemed to know just where to be to meet the clashing blade of Nall. Though Zeth was pushed back by Nall with a series of quick forehand strokes, he did not allow his sword arm to fall.

"Good, Zeth, very good indeed," Nall praised him while at the same time making a strong backhand assault. Again, Zeth rose to the challenge, driving him back several steps and making a wide sweep that caused Nall to leap away.

Yávië was chuckling as she approached Näeré.

"I see that Zeth is bewitched again," she whispered, shaking her head and sitting down on the wall next to Näeré. "That is very good for his pride."

"Aye, as is the praise Nall gives him," Näeré said. "Zeth missed Nall's mentoring, as did I."

"Mentoring? I thought he called it hunting." Yávië mocked.

"That too," Näeré replied, pushing Yávië off the wall.

Strong hands lifted Yávië to her feet, and she turned to face Sōrél.

"Do you allow your Guardians to toss you to the ground now, milady?" he asked with a smile.

"Aye, when I am teasing them unmercifully I do."

"Shall we join them?" she added, indicating Nall and Zeth who were now covering the field with their sparring.

"Aye Milady, it would do my heart good to best you today."

"Ha! Do you truly believe I would allow it?" Yávië asked in false ferocity.

She moved onto the practice field, backing away from Sōrél as if in terror.

Suddenly she felt herself pushed aside and knocked to the ground. Looking up she saw Nall, his eyes gleaming cruelly.

"I told you I would gut you for your treachery, Sōrél. Defend yourself or die as you stand, I do not care. You will die by my blade in either case," Nall snarled through clenched teeth.

Yávië leaped to her feet and reached out to Nall, but he merely pushed her away again.

"Milady, he deceives you. His arms have found another; his oath has been broken."

"Nay, Nall," Yávië cried out. "It is you who are deceived . . . deceived by visions Aléria forced into your mind. Nall, I speak the truth. Do you think I would not know if Sōrél had broken our oath?"

Nall shook his head, his mind closed to her plea. Memories of Aléria's words filled his head; her words had been the truth—Sōrél had hunted with her long beyond dusk when the others returned. Nall had seen them.

Sōrél gave a lazy smile.

"Yávië, go to Näeré. Let this be settled today. Nall needs an exercise in respect, both for his Queen and his Captain."

"Sōrél, I forbid it! He is not himself."

"Oh, he is very much himself, Yávië, and it has been long since he has felt my wrath."

Sōrél drew his sword, his eyes never leaving Nall.

"It will be a shame if I am forced to kill you Nall, but as you have given your permission, I shall defend myself."

Yávië looked at Näeré for signs of distress, but found none. Slowly she stood and moved to the wall.

"Sōrél will kill him," Yávië whispered.

"Nay, only allow his anger to pass." Näeré said to Yávië. "Nall truly believes it was Aléria who spent those long evenings alone with my brother."

"But she put those visions in his mind!"

"Nay, Yávië, because Nall saw you." Näeré smiled broadly.

Yavie's eyes widened and she burst out laughing.

"He believed I was Aléria?"

"Aye. Of course, Aléria did say it was her, but he does recall seeing you go off with Sōrél and not returning until long after everyone else. It is good he thought it was Aléria, for he would have told your father had he known it was you."

The swords rang as Sōrél drove Nall back, knocking him to the ground. Nall rolled away, leaping up to launch a series of fierce, backhand swings before their swords locked again.

Sōrél disengaged with a quick circling of his blade, knocking Nall's sword hand away. His eyes were calm and dispassionate as he drove his subordinate back again.

"Do you hate me, Nall," he asked quietly, "as much as you love my sister?"

"Nay, I hate the betrayal of your oath."

"Aye, as I once hated what I perceived as your betrayal of the blood oath."

Sōrél allowed Nall's attack, merely meeting each stroke without making his own.

"It was not Aléria, Nall. It was Yávië; it has always been Yávië. If you doubt my word, ask her or Näeré."

With that, he forced Nall back with the sword at his heart.

"Your eyes did not deceive you, for indeed I did hunt long after dark with Alandon's daughter." He pointed to the wall. "That daughter . . ."

Sheathing his sword, he reached down and pulled Nall to his feet.

"I will let your queen know you have recovered. And you owe Yávië an apology for pushing her to the ground. That is twice this morning she has been tossed on her royal ass by her own Guardians," he said with a stern look before turning away.

"Who else tossed her?" Nall called after him, his anger forgotten.

However, Sōrél's comment as he approached Yávië was simply to say, "I believe Nall has sufficiently regained his strength . . ."

PART III

Chapter 25: The Book of Quests

Yávië sat at the base of the ancient willow, head bowed and eyes closed. Her heart was heavy as she prepared herself for the quest before her. What would she ask of her Guardians? What were the sacrifices they would be forced to make on her behalf to assure the rebirth of their home world?

With a twig from the willow, she drew the symbol to bind seven and moved into its safety. She placed the solitary candle before her, surrounding it with the life-giving earth. Within the pentacle, she placed the willow twig, lighting and blackening it to charcoal for the casting of the spell that would unlock the Book of Quests.

Sōrél stood two dragon lengths away, watching and protecting her privacy. He thought back to his agreement with Alandon, an agreement made before Yávië's birth. He had not known that the girl child promised him would become the strong and beautiful Guardian Queen before him. He sighed deeply at the prospect of protecting her during the coming quest, and shuddered at the thought of her reaction if she ever realized she had been given to him to secure his silence. Before returning to his faithful watch, he gave thanks to the Ancients for the sacred gift of the eternal life bond.

Taking a small piece of parchment, Yávië carefully tore each side, forming a square a hand's breadth long and wide. With the blackened twig, she wrote the words of the ancient language as foretold in the prophecy of Ædracmoræ. Rolling it carefully to avoid cracking, she sealed it with wax and the Signet of the Dragon Queen.

Yávië bowed solemnly to Sōrél, watching as he cast the spell of shadow over her, hiding her from the eyes of evil. She knew that although she could no longer see him, Sōrél's bow was drawn and ready.

She lit the candle and held the rolled parchment on the tips of her extended fingers. Taking a deep breath, she began her incantation.

"Mighty willow of ages past,
Watcher of the world and all that passes,
Impart unto me thy knowledge,
That which has been brought to thee on the seven winds,
And transferred to your heart from the depths of the earth.
Let no secret thing remain hidden, but rather,
As the light of the daystar brings thee life,
Let thy life bring unto me the knowledge of my quest.
So this I ask,
So may it be."

Using the fingertips of her right hand, she extinguished the candle and, with the willow twig, dug a hole for the parchment at the center of the sacred symbol. Placing the parchment and the twig in their final resting place, she carefully poured water from the Sacred Sea in a circle around them, sealing and completing her appeal for ancient wisdom.

As the shadow spell lifted, Yávië rose and stepped from the protection of the symbol of the seven, knowing that from this point forward every step would be besieged.

Sōrél's touch was gentle, his sapphire eyes shadowed with concern as he led her to Aero. Once more they would travel to the Fortress to return the jewel of her legacy to its resting place.

As Sōrél urged the dragon skyward, Yávië allowed herself to lean back and rest against him. For a moment, she pretended to be just a girl again and this was but another hunt for the simplestag of her youth.

"Darkness is drawn to our Queen as the buttermoth to the candle's flame. She is a dangerous woman, Zeth, dangerous to those in her company." Galen's voice was sharp.

"She is no more dangerous than those who have sworn to protect her, Galen. You would be wise to remember that," Nall replied as he approached.

"I simply meant it as an admonishment to our young Guardian. We must remain wary, for she has called for the knowledge of the Book of Quests. Darkness will follow us until the completion of our task."

Nall looked suspiciously at Galen, wondering how he had come by such information. This one definitely required watching—untrustworthy son of a fallowass!

Finding Näeré working the sword in the practice field, he forgot all thoughts of practice and leaned against the wall to watch.

Her chin was raised as the sword swung in a pattern—forehand, backhand, parry and thrust—her arms were strong, her motion smooth, for her practice never varied. Starlight sparkled on her dark hair and her aura pulsed brightly with each swing of the sword. He knew that Näeré's eyes sparkled, and that her lips moved in silent invocation of the magick she spoke to the sword. Wondering if he was still bewitched, he smiled and went to her, thinking to test her strength.

"So you give my apprentice spells of strength and the sword of a sorceress to make my challenge greater?" he asked, tapping the tip of his sword against hers.

"And you allow me to foolishly attack our captain, a battle you knew I could not win, causing me to push Yávië to the ground for which I now owe an apology. Are we no longer friends, sweet Näeré?"

"Aye, more than friends, but my brother did tell me that he thought you had a wizenwasp in your trousers and should be allowed to get it out," Näeré teased, pushing back hard and following through with a wicked backhand.

"I have had one sword at my heart today. I do not intend to have another," Nall said, watching Näeré's eyes carefully.

Movement at the corner of the field caught his attention, distracting him for less than the flutter of a woman's lashes, but it was sufficient and he found himself looking up from the ground for the second time that day.

Laughing, Näeré dropped down beside him. "I shall not put my sword to your heart, but my . . ." she paused, seeing him tense as he looked over her shoulder. Turning, she saw Galen as he moved out of the field and past the far prickleberry thicket.

"I do not trust him. I overheard him speak against Yávië, though he covered it well."

Näeré stood. "Shall we see where he is off to then?"

"Aye," Nall agreed as Näeré manipulated the veil of mist, leaving only an empty field where they had been standing.

Silently they followed Galen.

Declarations in Waiting

He strode purposefully through the woodlands, recalling the days of poaching the Queen's boar and the words of his life debt to Yávië. Galen missed his people and his own fortress. He missed the woman he had left there, but honor bound him to see Yávië's quest to completion.

Hearing the rustle of a skirt on the carpet of grass, he smiled and went to meet Kayann. She approached him with the quiet grace that he had first noticed when his friend Xavier had introduced them. Her cobalt robes announced her as an artisan of Xavier's court, and a member of the nobility.

"Do you come alone?" Galen questioned, disturbed at the thought she may have traveled unaccompanied.

"Nay Galen, Xavier would not allow it. He sent two guards, but they wait for me beyond the tree line. I have assured them you will watch over me in their absence." Her gaze became intent, her empathic nature evident.

"Your soul hides in shadow and fear. Fear for the woman Yávië?" she asked.

"Yes, Kayann. Soon she will seek the Book of Trolls and once she has it, its evil will pursue us. Tell Xavier to go to the Galenites at the first sign of darkness. You will be safe, for my armies there are strong."

Kayann placed her hand on his arm. "Will Yávië release you of your oath, Galen?"

"I cannot ask it of her until the quest is done, but I believe she will. I must believe she will." Galen spoke with passion. "I belong with my people, and with you."

Kayann sought Galen's eyes and was reassured by the goodness that she found reflected there.

"I must go. I shall tell Xavier we are to go to the Galenite fortress. Do not fear for us. We shall be safe with your people. I shall wait for your return Galen, trust that I shall."

"Kayann, I would pledge to you if it were possible. Do you know that?"

"Aye, Galen, but I do not seek it. I know it is not yours to give."

He watched until he could no longer see the flashes of her robe among the trees before turning back toward Meremire to repay his life debt.

"He seeks a union with a Xavian?" Näeré whispered to Nall. "It is not possible for a Guardian. Should we tell Yávië?"

"Nay," Nall answered, stroking her hair. "Nay, there is no danger; he will serve the life debt. He is honor bound. I shall watch for any sign of his failure to do so, but I believe he may be a man of principle."

Näeré smiled up at him. "You see yourself bound to Yávië through the blood oath when you look at him. You understand what it is like to be unable to pledge to the woman you have chosen."

Hugging her he said, "Aye, and I shall speak on his behalf when his debt is paid."

Beyond them, in the woodlands, his sister searched for Zeth.

Rydén was running with her grass cat, Valia, beside her. She had seen Zeth leave earlier and hoped to catch him. She knew that as assigned by Morgwort, he would hunt the day's meal, and wanted to offer her assistance. Like Zeth, Rydén had been the youngest Guardian during her training on Ædracmoræ and it had been brutal, for Sōrél was a strict mentor and administrator of the law. Thinking of Sōrél made her smile, for he had become much less harsh with his binding to Yávië—another debt owed the new queen.

In the midst of these musings, and without warning, she was

struck from the side and knocked to the ground. Valia let out a howl and jumped onto the back of her mistress' assailant, clawing and biting. Rolling over, Rydén leapt to her feet and silently summoned Valia, allowing Zeth to stand and inspect the scratches and bites the cat had inflicted.

"Rydén, why were you following me?" he asked wiping blood from his face.

"Why were you attacking me?" she returned, laughing at his discomfort.

"No one sent me to spy on you, if that is what you fear. I simply wished to join your hunt," she added as she brushed dirt and grass from her clothing.

"Here, let me look at those scratches. You are lucky Valia was not really angry, just playful."

Rydén pulled Zeth toward her, looking at the scratches—they were not very deep, but the bite on his shoulder did look painful.

"Never tackle a woman traveling with a grass cat. Let that be today's lesson."

Suddenly she realized Zeth had not spoken since his initial question and looked up into his eyes. They were wide and blue. His blond hair was full of grass and his clothing was bloodstained. He also appeared to be holding his breath.

"Zeth?" she asked.

She poked him in the stomach, causing him to gasp.

"Breathe. I have no desire to carry your carcass home along with a simplestag. Why are you holding your breath, anyway?"

"Because you take my breath," Zeth whispered.

"What are you talking about?" Rydén asked with annoyance. "I didn't poke you that hard."

"Come. Let us catch the meal if the ruckus hasn't frightened it off!"

Rydén turned and summoned Valia, then realized what Zeth had truly meant. Turning back, she smiled at him, causing him to flush a deep crimson.

"Why Zeth, are you trifling with my affection?" she asked, causing his blush to deepen.

"What would my brother say?" Rydén wondered aloud before laughing at the look of horror on Zeth's face.

"Fear not. It will be our secret. Are you recovered enough from your breathlessness to continue the hunt, or should I sit you down and place your head between your knees until the spell passes?"

Without waiting for a response, she moved ahead toward the dense, tree-covered slope, trying to hide the beautiful smile that was now lighting up her face.

Beyond the trees lay the meadow where a large stag stood grazing, unaware of his invitation to dinner at Meremire. Crouching, Rydén glanced over her shoulder and beckoned Zeth forward. He crept up quietly, as he had been taught, drawing his bow and nocking an arrow in readiness. He steadied the shot while holding his breath and let the arrow fly. It struck the buck in the heart, dropping it where it had stood with just a slight twitch of the feet to indicate its passing.

Rydén jumped up, hugging Zeth and pounding him on the back.

"That was perfect, absolutely perfect! Wait until we share that at dinner!"

She suddenly realized Zeth had put his arms around her and she stilled herself, uncertain.

"I am sorry," he said, contrite.

"Do not be. I am just not used to such attention," Rydén answered shyly, eyes bright, soft lashes lowered.

"But you are so beautiful."

Breaking away she asked, "Do you know how to properly bleed a stag?"

Portents in Dreams

In Meremire, Yávië pondered her future quest. When Ædracmoræ was destroyed and its kingdoms shattered into the seven worlds, Alandon provided the means for its restoration. Among the seven worlds lay the seven artifacts with which a blood heir could bring about Ædracmoræ's rebirth. It was this, the quest for Ædracmoræ, that now drove Yávië and with the calling of the seventh Guardian, the return of Nall's soul, and the renouncement of her birthright, she had fulfilled the requirements for undertaking the quest.

Since returning from the Fortress of the Dragon Queen, she had gone directly to her bothie to examine the Book of Quests. As foretold, the quest required that the artifacts be collected in the order of their original hiding, and that they would be made known to her, one at a time.

Sitting on her cot with Sōrél at her side, Yávië opened the Book of Quests. The dust rose from the ancient parchment pages, swirling in the sunlight and dancing along the current of air that drifted in through the open window. As the motes rose and fell, ebbed and flowed, and swirled about, Yávië felt herself being pulled into their center.

She was looking into the depths of a deep, black hole. A ladder of willow branches led down into its interior. Lighting her torch, Yávië descended a few rungs before dropping the torch to the bottom far below. The floor of the hole appeared to be littered with bones—perhaps the remains of meals for some animal. She continued down until she was several rungs above the floor and looked again. They were human remains, and one appeared to have something clutched within its skeletal fingers. As Yávië stepped down another rung, a filthy hand grabbed her ankle. The back of the hand was covered with coarse hair and its fingers ended in ragged nails. Though short, the forearm was strong and muscular. She could not see the face in the darkness, but the eyes of the beast glowed red with hatred and its fetid breath caused her to gag.

"You have never seen a troll have you, Yávië?" a voice that sounded like a rockslide laughed within her head as the beast dragged her to the floor.

She gripped the bone nearest to her to use as a weapon. Lifting it, she saw that it extended into a hand, its skeletal fingers clutching Sōrél's bow. In shock, Yávië watched with horror as his signet ring, symbol of his guardianship, fell to the ground beside her.

"Yávië, *stop*!" Sōrél gripped her wrists tightly as she fought to claw out his eyes.

The door to the bothie flew open and Nall stood there breathing heavily.

"What happened to her?" he asked, his alarm contorting his features. "I could hear her screaming all the way into the woods."

"A dream, a vision . . . I do not know," Sōrél shouted over Yavie's screams. "Something she saw in the dust from the book."

Seeing Näeré behind Nall, Sōrél shouted, "Get Rosie!"

"Nall, take her hands so that I can grasp her arms from behind. I am afraid she will injure herself."

Yávië's hands struck out at the terror only she was seeing.

Nall gently took her wrists from Sōrél and held them firmly against his chest as she struggled to pull away from him.

Sōrél kneeled behind her on the cot and wrapped his arms around her, trapping her arms at her sides and whispering quietly into her hair.

"Please, Yávië." He pulled her back towards him, causing her to kick viciously at Nall.

Näeré raced back into the room, knocking Nall out of the way and pushing Sōrél backward.

"Let her go! Do not touch her," Rosie said. "Do not touch her."

Yávië curled tightly into a ball and sobbed.

Rosie's worried face peered at them from the doorway.

"What dids you do to her?" the Ancient asked, looking at each of them in turn.

"Rosie . . ."

"Hush, Sōrél. You let her opens the book, didn't you?"

She struck a vicious blow to his shoulder with her staff.

"Didn't you?" She raised the staff again.

"Aye, she opened the book Rosie." Sōrél could not recall the last time he had been struck with the staff of an Ancient.

Rosie turned to Nall, causing him to step back hurriedly.

"And you, what dids you do to her?"

"I was not even here," Nall said, cringing at the tiny woman's angel.

"Don't touches her. Go away. All of you goes away." She swung the staff, catching Nall on his knee and doubling him over in pain as the three of them hurried out of the room.

"Fine Guardians you is," she spat after them.

"Yávië," Rosie whispered, "Yávië comes home."

"Sōrél," Rosie's voice woke him as he rested against the wall next to Yávië's door.

He gripped her hand, his eyes bright with pain.

"Is she all right, Rosie? Is Yávië all right?"

"Nay." A tear rolled down Rosie's face. "She has seen your death, Sōrél. Nothing cans be done for it."

"No Rosie, I will not allow it. I will not stand by and do nothing."

Furiously he demanded, "Tell me what to do, Rosie, and I will do it."

Rosie shook her head and turned away.

"You said no harm would come to my daughter while she was in your care, Sōrél," Alandon's eyes laughed down at Sōrél.

"Back away, Alandon." Nall's voice carried a cold threat. "He suffers enough. We did not know."

"He knew. I told him," Alandon said.

"You put us here, Alandon. You gave Yávië the map so that she could find the Book of Trolls. You set her up to find the Book of Quests. You conspired with Galen to do so! I heard him speak to you from Abaddon's Abyss. You are as responsible as we are."

A heart-rending scream came from Yávië's bothie. Sōrél pushed Alandon out of the way and charged inside, slamming the door and throwing the bolt.

He knelt beside the bed and gathered Yávië to him. She stiffened and cried out, but still he held her. Rocking her, Sōrél told her of her birth, told her of his pledge to her, of their binding. He reminded her that she had shared her soul because she saw he had none.

"Yávië, do not leave me, for without you I am naught but anger. You are all that smoothes my roughness, all that makes me live. I do not know where you have gone, but I promise if you return I will never leave you. I will not allow my life to be taken from you, Yávië, I promise it."

Sōrél heard the others pounding on the door and saw Nall's worried face outside the window. He drew the cover over them and held Yávië until he was fast asleep.

Sōrél awoke in total darkness, in a place of odors ripe with death. Reaching for his bow, he found it gone and drew his sword.

"Come for me," he whispered, "that I might help you die."

He lifted the sword, protecting his chest and face, and felt before him with his right hand. Coming to a rough wall, he felt his way along it, stumbling over something on the floor. Dropping into a crouch, Sōrél ran his hand over the form below. Bones. A hand and arm to the elbow, missing the small forearm bone. Feeling around, he found a ring and placed it on his finger; then, feeling a bowstring, he lifted the bow and placed it over his shoulder. Continuing along the wall, he reached a wooden ladder and began to climb. Leaping over the lip of the deep hole, Sōrél began to run.

His eyes opened slowly and gazed upon the beauty of Yávië's face. Her hands lay curled and childlike beside her. She was pale and cool to his touch and as he stroked her hair, he found it damp from night terrors. Sōrél looked at the ring on his finger; the ring of his guardianship, a signet used to seal the wax on letters sent long ago to Yávië.

The memory brought a sad smile.

"Yávië, I will write you letters once again and seal them with the promise of the Guardian," he whispered, strangling on the dusty dryness of his fear.

Taking the ring from his finger, Sōrél slipped it onto the ring finger of Yávië's left hand, the finger that was meant to remain bare until her coronation, when she would claim this ring of promise as the Dragon Queen. His heart ached at the thought of her coronation. As queen, she could choose him openly before her kingdom. Now she was no longer here. Grabbing the Book of Quests from the floor, he threw it against the wall, raging at himself and his stupidity for allowing her to pursue this quest.

"You could not have stopped her, Brother," Näeré whispered from the doorway.

"Witch," Sōrél said weakly.

"Aye." Näeré walked slowly toward him, pushing the door closed behind her.

"Nall frets. I cannot have that."

Sōrél choked back a bitter laugh. "Nall frets. No, we cannot have that. What shall we do, sweet sister, to stop this fretting?"

"We shall bring Yávië home."

"Rosie does not believe it possible."

Eyes so like her own looked to Näeré for help.

"Tell me what to do. You know I will do anything."

"I sent you a dream. Did you take back your ring and bow?"

"Aye." Sōrél looked at her in confusion.

"Where is the ring?"

He lifted Yávië's small hand. The large ring caused her fingers to splay apart.

"Sōrél, you should have been a sorcerer," Näeré smiled and cupped her brother's face.

"Hold her hand in yours and close your eyes. I shall send you for her. Bring her home."

Taking Yávië's hand, Sōrél closed his eyes and listened as his sister's words poured over the two of them like cool water.

He heard hoarse screams of terror and saw Yávië being dragged away by a large and shaggy beast—its arms and hands hung long, covered with coarse hair. It grasped Yávië's ankle and was pulling her toward a pit.

He drew his bow and sent three arrows into the beast's back. It roared at him and in releasing Yávië, backhanded Sōrél into the wall. Nocking a fourth arrow, he sent it into the beast's throat. It gripped the shaft and bellowed, still standing between him and Yávië's screaming form.

Sliding the bow over his shoulder, Sōrél drew his sword and rushed forward, slicing off one of the creature's arms and then its head with a furious backhand stroke. Its thick black blood sprayed the walls and floor.

Darting around it, Sōrél grabbed Yávië, but she pulled away in terror.

"Forgive me, Yávië," he whispered, and struck her temple with the pommel of his sword.

He lifted her over his shoulder and rushed up the ladder against the wall. He leaped over the edge of the hole and began to run. Finally, collapsing with exhaustion, he held Yávië tightly and prayed the daystar would rise over them and end the darkness.

Sōrél awoke to whimpering. Yávië's eyes were wide and frightened. She looked at him and shrank away.

"You are dead." She spoke so softly he barely heard the words.

"I saw your ring, the ring of my betrothal. The one you would have given to me upon my coronation. It was upon the finger of your corpse."

"Yávië, it was a dream. Look around you."

She looked instead at her ankle. Angry red welts had arisen where the beast's claw had held her.

She shook her head, holding her hand to her mouth.

"Yávië, look at your hand."

On her finger was Sōrél's signet ring, the ring of his promise.

"How?"

"Shhh," Sōrél arms enfolded her to him. "It was a nightmare, Yávië, just a nightmare. I will always come for you. Even in your worst nightmares, I will always come."

Closing his eyes, he hoped it would be so.

Leaving Rosie to watch over Yávië, Sōrél stormed out of the bothie with murder in his eyes. He carried Yávië's sword, the one meant to kill immortals; its blade reflected the light by turning dark scarlet, the color of blood.

"Nall," Sōrél called as he passed, "I need your arm."

Nall looked at Näeré and drew his sword, swiftly joining Sōrél.

"Who are we killing, Sōrél?"

"Sōrél, do not do this," Näeré cautioned.

Sōrél swung on his sister.

"He did not tell us she could be harmed. Not like this. Not before we have even begun the quest! He owes his blood for what he has done to her."

"Alandon? We are going to kill Alandon?" Nall asked in disbelief.

"Aye," Sōrél snarled.

"Nall." Näeré looked at him. "Do not let him do this. She will be lost to him forever if he does."

"What would you have me do, Näeré? Sōrél is right. The darkness that covers Yávië is Alandon's. He has done this."

Rydén came running from Willow's bothie and from the field, Galen and Zeth raced toward her while Näeré watched in alarm as the two Guardians approached Alandon's quarters.

Alandon stepped outside his door.

"Did you find my daughter?" he asked with a cruel laugh.

"Your life is not worth the breath you take, Alandon," Sōrél hissed.

"So you have come to kill me with my daughter's sword?"

"Sōrél, at the risk of sounding foolish, or worse, at the risk of being insubordinate, I really do not think this is a very good idea," Nall whispered out of the side of his mouth.

The withering look he received in return was reply enough.

Looking over his shoulder, Nall beckoned to Näeré.

"Do something. He is your brother."

Näeré stood in front of Sōrél. She had never seen him so angry.

"Sōrél, did you find Yávië?"

"Aye, she is with Rosie."

"If you do this—even if you succeed—Yávië will always be with Rosie. You will crush her heart as surely as if you held it in your hand. What was your pledge?"

Sōrél raised his hand to push his sister away when Nall struck him hard with the butt of his sword.

Raising his eyes to Alandon Nall said, "Tell us what we need to know."

With a glance at the fallen Sōrél, Alandon beckoned them inside.

Nall instructed Galen and Zeth to carry Sōrél to Yávië's bothie.

"And by all that is holy, do not tell him who struck him," he called after them.

The Scarlet Shab-ot

The door flew open, bringing Nall to his feet, dagger drawn. A twinge of pain at the thought of fighting the angry Sōrél pinched at his heart.

Sōrél stood in the doorway, arms hanging loosely at his sides and hands empty. He was impeccably groomed and his weapons were concealed—bow at his back and sword in its scabbard by his side—but Nall knew that Sōrél did not need a weapon to be a deadly opponent.

Nodding, Sōrél spoke with authority, although the words were of gratitude and peace.

"Näeré tells me you saved my life last night. I thank you for your level-headedness, for without it I would be dead. That Alandon did not strike me is a mystery to me. I understand he and Yávië's mother have left Meremire, but that he has given you the information I need to keep Yávië safe."

"Nay, Sōrél, the information we need to keep her safe. The responsibility is not yours alone, for each of us is sworn to protect Yávië. We must travel to the Fortress to find a scarlet shab-ot, a gyre to be placed within the Book's pages. It will guard against the evil escaping through the dust. Yávië must not go. I will leave it to you to convince her of this."

"And has Alandon given us the location of the shab-ot?"

"Only that it is held within the golden stone."

"You and I shall go alone. I want Näeré here with Yávië. Galen and Rydén can continue with Zeth's training in our absence. Plan to leave at the daystar's zenith. I shall tell Yávië."

"She must not go, Sōrél. Do not allow her to convince you otherwise."

"Aye, only Näeré is strong enough to hold her in our absence. I shall instruct her to use force if necessary."

Sōrél turned to go, then hesitated before turning back to offer his grip to Nall who grasped the extended forearm, acknowledging his Captain's gratitude and friendship.

Yávië clung to Sōrél, her voice fragile with concern.

"I cannot allow you to go alone."

"I shall not be alone; Nall will accompany me. He is a strong right arm, you know that Yávië. Do not fear for our safety. The Fortress lays empty. Näeré has entered it through her mind and senses no danger there."

Sōrél glanced up as Rosie entered. With her quickly whispered words and a flash of her small hands, the Ancient cast a spell of deep sleep upon her charge before climbing up to sit in the chair by the window.

Yávië slumped against Sōrél as he eased her to the cot. He placed his cloak over her, leaving her with the comfort of his scent. He kissed her brow and then her lips, whispering sweet dream images.

Näeré entered the bothie and smiled at the sleeping Yávië.

"She is so easy to control when she sleeps," Näeré said, "but what is your wish for her when she awakens?"

Sōrél placed his hands on his sister's shoulders and looked deep into eyes identical to his own.

"For her to be at the Fortress during the search for the gyre is a death sentence. Use whatever force you must to keep her here. It might be wise to remove her weapons from the room. Give them to Morg or Willow; they will understand."

He held the face of the sleeping Yávië in his hands once more. "I have struck you and deceived you, both within a single daystar's passing. Please do not condemn me, for your life hangs by a slender golden thread. I must guard against the thread's breaking until this evil passes."

"Keep her safe," Sōrél once more directed Näeré as he headed out the door.

The air within the Fortress was still and leaden, the silence crushing.

Standing within the great hall where they had fought and defeated Aléria and her Dark Guardians, Nall and Sōrél agreed to split up and search for the golden stone that held the precious gyre.

Directing Nall to search the lower levels, Sōrél hurried up the stairs leading to Alandon's tower.

He moved stealthily so that his footsteps would not be heard below, carefully avoiding shards of crystal and stone that might give away his presence.

At the heavy chalewood door, Sōrél took out an ancient key carved of stone and imbedded with Gaianite crystals. Glancing behind him one last time, he inserted the key and pushed the weighty door open to reveal a chamber with a golden wall.

The floor, now recording his footprints, was coated in the dust of many lifetimes. He shook his head, but knew there was no way to avoid detection. Alandon would know Sōrél had come.

Three quarters of the circular wall were made of cold stone but the final quarter gleamed gold in the midday light that filtered in through high windows. A tapestry hung on the golden wall, untouched by the ages and as pristine as on the day of its hanging. Woven into it was the image of the coronation of the Guardian Queen. She stood before her father, raven hair shimmering with the blue light of a magpie's wing. With her pale face and beautiful lips slightly parted in answer to the king's request, her sparkling violet eyes were like deep pools leading to her soul. The gown she wore was elegant and in the sapphire of the highborn nobles of the House of Aaradan, the sapphire of Sōrél's birth. Around her stood the Ancients, dressed in their finest robes with white hair flying and staffs raised for the blessing. Standing in shadow on the Guardian Queen's right stood a man dressed for the coronation, his uniform covered with the medals of a hundred wars. Dark hair fell to his shoulders, casting a deeper shadow across his face, but the eyes were unmistakable—their sapphire brilliance betrayed the Guardian Sōrél.

Unable to stop himself, Sōrél reached up and touched Yáviё's face before moving behind the tapestry and into the room hidden there. The room was without light. It was here Alandon took his true form, unseen by any save one. Here Sōrél had seen the truth of the Sojourner's darkness. Here Alandon had promised his first-born daughter in return for silence. Why he had not simply slain Sōrél remained unclear, but Sōrél knew he held some power over Alandon. Some unspoken fear lay within Alandon's hateful heart. It was within this room that Sōrél's anger had been born. They had sealed the secret here, setting the fall of Ædracmoræ in motion, freeing Aléria's unchallenged rise to power. None knew Yávië was the first born, none. Sōrél had sworn himself to be her protector; a bond secured through deceit, a love born of betrayal.

Needing no torch to show the way through the darkness he knew so well, Sōrél took a deep breath and moved forward. At the farthest reach of the room, he knelt and pressed the hidden lever, allowing the stone to spring upward to reveal the lighted chamber below. Reaching in, Sōrél withdrew the scarlet shab-ot and Alandon's demon dagger.

Slipping the dagger inside his shirt, he closed the stone and returned through the darkness to find Nall standing before the tapestry.

His eyes showed curiosity without the glint of understanding.

Holding up the gyre, Sōrél announced that he had found it hidden behind the tapestry.

"I have never seen this tapestry of Aléria's coronation," Nall pondered. "I wonder why she chose to keep it hidden away and why she had the Ancients added to it."

"Who knows why Aléria did anything," Sōrél replied, as Nall regarded him oddly, and then continued, "Come, let us return to Meremire before Yávië escapes and lands on the doorstep bringing death to us all."

Without waiting to see if Nall would follow, Sōrél moved quickly down the tower stairs and into the great hall, but nonetheless felt relief at the sound of Nall's footsteps behind him.

Yávië awoke from Rosie's spell-cast sleep with feelings of dread, anger and betrayal. Sitting up, she looked at Näeré seated against the wall at the far side of the bothie.

Smiling uncertainly Yávië asked, "Are you my current keeper?"
Näeré nodded without speaking.

"Sōrél did this?" Yávië asked, receiving another nod.

"Why? What is it he fears that I shall see?"

Näeré looked honestly confused.

"Nay, it is for your safety. Your father said it was dangerous for you to be present during the search for the shab-ot."

Sighing, Yávië smiled again as she stood. "Am I allowed to leave my room or am I a prisoner here?"

"You may leave on the condition that I accompany you and that you understand the boundaries of your freedom are Meremire's borders."

Yávië looked around the bothie, seeking her sword. She laughed to find it missing.

"Did Sōrél expect me to slay you if he left my weapons within reach?"

"Aye, Yávië, I believe he did."

With a sudden surge of anger, Yávië pushed Näeré against the wall, darting past her as she stumbled. Crying out silently for Aero, Yávië raced past the others in the field, hearing their pounding footfalls behind her and Näeré shouting for them to stop her.

Aero skidded to a halt before turning his head and snapping viciously at the approaching Galen. The dragon's scales rose in a wicked warning and he rumbled deep within his chest to let the Guardians know his Huntress would be protected against their apparent threat. At the touch of her hand on his withers, Aero rose into the sky with forceful downward strokes of his airy wings.

"Shall we follow her?" Zeth asked anxiously.

"Nay, I have called to my brother. He will stop her before she reaches the Fortress. He and Nall are beyond the walls and they have collected the gyre, so the danger has passed. Sōrél will want to kill me for allowing her escape, but it will not be the first time I have suffered his wrath."

"Huntress, why do the Guardians threaten you?"

"Do not be concerned, Aero, for they merely wish to protect me. Your protection will serve as well. We must go to the Fortress to meet Sōrél."

Yávië relaxed, knowing the young dragon would take her to her destination without further question.

Urging Aero down within a dense rock fall, Yávië bade him wait and began to make her way toward the fallen Fortress of her birth. Hearing Nall's voice, she quickly veiled herself and moved forward in silence.

"I cannot believe she escaped Näeré." Nall shook his head in wonderment. "Why is it Yávië never listens?"

"Return to Meremire and I shall await her here," Sōrél instructed Nall, listening closely for Yávië's movement, for he could feel her nearby.

She skirted them, making her way around the distant boulders to the lower level of the Fortress. She slid inside, making her way up the stairs toward the great hall.

"Yávië, I know you are here." Sōrél's voice drifted from far below her, causing her to increase her pace.

Standing in the great hall, she reached out with her mind, feeling their presence and seeing their actions—Nall heading to the lower levels to begin his search, Sōrél turning toward her father's tower. She sensed he knew the location of the gyre. Why had he sent Nall away? Moving up the stairs, she came to a small landing with a heavy chalewood door standing open. She saw boot prints in the dust.

An arm swept past her, dragging the heavy door closed and locking it with a key.

Allowing her veil to fade, she turned to Sōrél. He could not hold her gaze and cast his eyes to the steps below them.

Her heart raced and her voice quivered when she spoke.

"What is it you hide from me? What am I not allowed to know?"

"Yávië," he whispered, reaching out to her.

She shrank back. Lifting her chin and turning away, she headed down the stairs. Pausing, she turned and took Sōrél's hand. She placed his signet ring in his palm and closed his fingers around it.

"There is no promise without truth." She spoke calmly in the voice she had once used to command an army, then fled down the stairs and back to Meremire.

Leaping from Aero, Yávië fled toward Nall's bothie and for the second time that day his door flew open, causing him to leap to his feet, blade drawn in defense.

"Yávië?"

He was tempted to keep the blade drawn against her, for her fury was palpable.

"What did he show you?" her eyes flashed and Nall knew that the wrong answer would bring physical attack.

"A room."

"Be more specific. Do you think me a fool?"

"*Great*," he thought, "*another loaded question.*"

The sound of her hand striking his face was startling in the stillness.

"Ouch," he said, rubbing his cheek.

"Before you strike me again, milady, I must confess I do not know what it is you seek."

Her eyes softened slightly.

"Perhaps you would like to sit so that we can discuss your needs reasonably?" he said hopefully.

She sat in the chair at his table.

Seeing Sōrél approaching, Nall drew the drape and stepped to his door, and threw the bolt.

"Now," said Nall, looking attentively at Yávië, "what is it you seek?"

The pounding on the door was loud and offensive, causing Yávië to tremble. Nall rested his hand on her shoulder and leaned close to her, his finger to his lips.

He was relieved when she simply nodded.

Sōrél's pounding and shouting went on for several moments before he spun away, barking for Näeré.

Nall dragged Yávië's chair to the end of his cot. Dropping to the bed, he reached out and took her hands in his.

"Tell me." His words were gentle but firm and caused her to look up at him.

"He betrays me, Nall. I do not know how or why, but he does."

"Yávië, I have never seen a man care more for a woman than Sōrél does for you. I say that in complete honesty for I have seen his heart often enough. He wears it openly like a medal of courage, and surely you must understand what courage it takes to love a woman with your strength?"

He looked directly at her, hoping to see some reason, but none was evident. He wished he could tell her that she and Sōrél were the two most stubborn people he had ever met and that he believed they deserved the misery they caused one another, but somehow it did not seem prudent.

"Do you doubt the conviction of Sōrél's promise?" he asked instead.

"Nay," she answered with a deep, shuddering breath, "his love is not in question. This is something far darker."

"What did you see in that room, Nall?"

"A tapestry of Aléria's coronation and little else. The hiding place of the gyre was behind the tapestry."

Yávië shook her head. "There was something there he did not want me to see."

"I honestly do not know what it could have been. I saw nothing suspect there." Nall answered honestly before realizing that he had seen Sōrél's image in the threads of Aléria's coronation tapestry.

He was grateful that Yávië did not see the shadow of recollection crossing his face and decided he would speak to Näeré before he confronted Sōrél with his questions.

"Speak to Sōrél, Yávië. Ask him what he hides from you."

"I have, Nall. He could not meet my eyes. He merely whispered my name in guilt."

"You may remain here as long as you like. I am going to speak to Näeré. Perhaps she knows something we do not. Rest, Yávië; you look very tired."

Nall pulled her to her feet and placed her on his cot, covering her with his coat and brushing the hair from her eyes.

"I will keep you safe, Yávië. Näeré and I will keep you safe."

Nall watched until her eyes closed in exhaustion before going in search of Näeré. Nall did not see Sōrél watching as he left his bothie and headed toward the field. Nor did he see Sōrél quickly slip inside and quietly ease the bolt home.

"As long as I can remember my brother has been pledged to Yávië. There has never been another woman to bring even a flicker of interest to his eyes. He pledged to her at her birth. I remember it. Ya'vanna and Alandon were there. It was no secret."

Nall looked at Näeré questioningly. "How is that possible?"

"It was agreed by Ya'vanna and my father that the House of Ædracmoræ and the House of Aaradan would be joined through marriage. Sōrél is the first born of the House of Aaradan and was therefore pledged to Yávië."

"But Yávië is not the first born," Nall reminded her.

"I do not recall why our father chose Yávië over Aléria. Perhaps he sensed Aléria's evil," Näeré chuckled, suddenly uncomfortable at the turn the conversation was taking.

"Your father chose Yávië for Sōrél? Are you sure of that?"

"Aye. Sōrél has always told me so."

"Does Yávië know this?"

"I do not know. I recall watching her fall in love with Sōrél and was grateful that a good match had been made for him. Then the House of Aaradan fell, Ya'vanna was murdered, Aléria became queen and you know the rest. The marriage never took place, though Sōrél honors his pledge. After our father died, Ya'vanna offered Sōrél a position as Captain of the Guardians and we went to live at the Fortress. Nall, do you doubt my brother's honor?"

"Nay, not for an instant or I would be dead," Nall laughed.

"Will you talk to Yávië? Tell her the truth. She truly believes Sōrél keeps some dark secret from her, but perhaps it is only the pledge."

"Aye. Then will you take me to the gardens of Xavian City?" Näeré asked, leaning against him.

"You are such a witch," Nall laughed. "Could I say no, if it were my choice?"

"Aye, then I would go with Zeth," Näeré teased.

As Näeré approached Nall's bothie, she sensed her brother's presence and waved the bolt open.

"What are you doing, Sōrél?"

"You should not have allowed her to leave Meremire."

"I know," Näeré murmured. "She was so angry."

"It is beyond anger now," he sighed. "Soon she will send me away."

"Let me talk to her, Sōrél. I can pacify her mind. It is Alandon, is it not?"

"Aye, Näeré, it is always Alandon but you must not tell her that we are of the House of Aaradan. I shall tell her when the time comes for her to know."

He stood and held his sister, allowing her gentle spirit to give him some comfort. "If you can still her mind until the quest ends, I will release her from the pledge. Ædracmoræ must be reborn before that is possible. We must complete the quest."

"Sōrél, she loves you."

He nodded again and left the bothie.

Näeré frowned with concern over her brother's exposed thoughts. She had never before heard him express doubt. She stood next to the sleeping Yávië, preparing to remove the day's thoughts from her mind, replacing them with images of a day spent locked within the boundaries of Meremire. Yávië might wake angry, but she would not wake doubting Sōrél's promise or loyalty.

Sōrél stood before the tapestry, marveling at its beauty. It was a shame he must destroy it, but he could not risk Yávië returning and discovering it. As he reached up to tear it from the wall a black voice stopped him.

"Is it your intent to withhold my daughter's heritage from her, Captain?"

It was Alandon.

"No. It is my intent to release her from her bonds."

Alandon looked surprised.

"You would release her from her indenture?"

Sōrél felt the hairs rise on his neck and knew his death would be swift if his anger was not controlled.

"She is not a slave, Alandon."

"She was a gift, Sōrél. A payment as I recall. Yours to do with as you wished. Have you found her less than you expected?"

Sōrél hung his head in shame.

"I have never found her anything but beautiful and strong, honest and true. All she wants is to reunite the kingdoms of Ædracmoræ. Will you not give her this? She is your first born child, Alandon; do you care nothing for her?"

Alandon shrugged. "She is your responsibility now, not

mine. I will not make it easy, but if she can accomplish the task, Ædracmoræ is hers as long as there is no attempt to join our houses. I swear it."

"By what honor do you swear, Alandon?"

"I swear it on your life, Sōrél. Have I not allowed you that and honored my promise to your dying father?"

As Alandon turned to leave, Sōrél pledged once again. "I will not allow you to harm Yávië."

"You are a fool to allow a woman to hold such value, Sōrél. Particularly a woman you cannot control."

"What is it you fear, Alandon? Is it Yávië?"

Sōrél's words went unanswered for Alandon was already gone.

Yávië woke in starlight, warm with the memory of her dream. She smiled again to see Sōrél sleeping in the chair. She studied his face, his features softened by sleep. She recalled his image from the days of her youth, realizing he had not changed. His dark hair fell across his shoulders casting a shadow across his strong jaw. How passionately as a young woman she had pursued him and how uninterested he had seemed. Her lips twitched at the memory of their first kiss stolen in velvet shadows—it was a lifetime ago.

Sensing her presence, Sōrél opened his eyes while keeping his face expressionless.

"Who is this woman in my room?"

"I believe this is my room."

"Apologies milady, I must have been drunk on your beauty and stumbled in here by mistake."

"I do not believe you have ever made a mistake, Sōrél."

He could not stop the laugh that erupted.

"Oh, Yávië, queen of hearts, I have made grievous errors. Some I am still trying to correct."

Näeré returned to Nall and told him what she had done.

"I suppose it is for the best until the quest is done. I hope someday we find out what in the abyss is going on," Nall said, shaking his head. "There was something wrong with that tapestry, but I cannot recall exactly what it was."

Tossing a branch on to the fire, Näeré watched Rydén gazing shyly at Zeth as their fingers met around a mug of tea.

"I don't think it matters now, anyway."

She wondered how she would tell Nall of his sister's interest in his apprentice.

Chapter 26: The Book of Trolls

Yávië tucked the map into her satchel and watched Sōrél place the Book of Quests into his pack. Since the nightmares, he refused to allow her even to touch it. He had opened it only wide enough to insert the shab-ot within its pages.

"I will have to read it sometime," she teased him.

His brow furrowed and his voice was a dagger's edge.

"I will decide when you read it and that is the end of it."

A shadow crossed his face as he recalled the welts the beast had left around her ankle. Just a nightmare, he had told her. How could they fight against beasts in their dreams? Until he knew, she would not touch the book again.

He swung to address the Guardians assembled behind them.

"We will stay the night in Mourningmire on Æshardæ. There is safety there with the Ancient Grumblton and he has prepared bothies for us. It will be our last night of comfort and safety."

He picked up his satchel and then placed Yávië's on her shoulder before leading the way to the mirror below Meremire.

The chamber the Guardians entered was empty except for the single mirror that provided passage to Æshardæ. Its wooden frame bore heavy carvings in the ancient language, with "Æshardæ" written at the top. The polished bronze mirror reflected their images.

"Näeré or I will pass through with each of you, since you do not have the power of the mirrors. Yávië, wait here. I want you to pass through last."

She nodded, knowing that his concern was unfounded but it would be useless to argue.

Näeré grabbed Nall and pushed him ahead of her through the mirror, returning almost immediately for Rydén. Sorel followed with Galen and then returned to escort Zeth.

As Yávië stood, alone for a moment, she thought she heard a sound in the passageway behind her. She turned to investigate, but Sōrél returned through the mirror and took her hand. Together they returned to Æshardæ.

Grumblton hugged Näeré and gripped Sōrél's arm tightly.

"And Rosie? You told her I asks after her?"

"Aye, as you requested. She would like to share the healing ways with you, old friend."

Sōrél introduced the Guardians to Æshardæ's oldest Ancient.

"There's a fire and stag stew when you is hungry. I got to talks to Sōrél alone." Grumblton moved quickly toward his bothie, looking over his shoulder to make sure Sōrél obeyed.

Slamming his door, Grumblton struck Sōrél hard with his staff.

"You brings the Book of Quests here? And you intends to brings the Book of Trolls from the caverns? Sōrél, what is you thinking?"

"Alandon approved the quest," Sōrél replied, rubbing the back of his knee where the staff had left its mark.

"Alandon!" Grumblton spat. "His is nasty business. Have you learneds nothing? Look at the messes he has gotten you into. And what of Yávië? That madman she calls "Father" has blocked your truth from her mind. She sees you as naught but a servant, Sōrél."

Sōrél tensed, for talk of Yávië with this Ancient never ended well.

"Did you tells her what her father has done?"

"Nay, but I will. When the time is right. I cannot release her until our quests are done. She would send me away and leave herself unprotected."

"The others can protects her," Grumblton muttered, "and the time may never bes right."

"Have you ever seens a troll, Sōrél?"

"Aye, I have seen them in Yávië's nightmares."

"They is fearsome creatures, fearsome. They eats the young of the humans and leaves the changelings in their place. Sōrél, they will pours from beneath the earth when the Book of Trolls is taken."

Grumblton looked ready to cry, which was the most frightening thing Sōrél had seen in a very long time.

"I cannot stop this, Grumblton. Yávië must be allowed to complete the quest for Ædracmoræ. When it is done I will deal with the aftermath. Until then, tell the humans to keep their doors locked."

Kneeling as he had when he was a child, Sōrél held the Ancient man who had once been his father's wizard.

Grumblton sniffed and pulled away.

"Sōrél of Aaradan, your father would be proud."

"Nay, not yet but I hope someday to make it right."

"He would be proud of the way you guards that woman."

Sōrél chuckled, "He might be proud of that."

On joining the others, Sōrél sought out Yávië.

"Where is Yávië?" he asked.

Nall placed his hand on Sōrél's shoulder. "She walks with Galen."

He felt Sōrél tense.

"There is no danger. They speak of her father."

"Where are they?" Sōrél asked, jerking away.

"Over near the practice fields. See them?"

Breathing deeply and trying to look in control, Sōrél hurried toward Yávië and Galen.

"Sōrél." Galen stepped away. "I shall leave our lady in your capable hands."

"Milady," he bowed respectfully to Yávië before heading back toward the fire.

"What did Galen want?"

"Sōrél stop. We have had this conversation before. Why is it you do not trust me?" She placed her hand on his heart to find it racing.

"Sōrél, what is it?"

"I do not trust Galen or your father. They conspire with one another."

"That does not explain this." She tapped the spot above his heart. "This is the heart of fear. I have never seen you afraid of anything, Sōrél."

Laughing, he looked down at her and confessed, "I have been afraid every moment of my life since you first trapped me with your kiss."

Her eyes brightened as she recalled the memory. "When I asked you to show me how a man kisses a woman? That was quite foolish of me."

"You terrified me then, Yávië, and you terrify me now, for with you I cannot control my destiny."

Shrugging, she replied, "Then let us hunt trolls."

He shook her hard.

"This is not a game, Yávië."

"Oh I think perhaps it is a game that I am forced to play. Do not fear, Sōrél, I shall not give it away until our quest is complete. Though I do wonder why you went to such trouble to make me love you."

As he watched her walk away, his heart crumbled like a weathered stone. Sighing, he went in search of Näeré.

In her bothie, Yávië spoke to Xander as he emerged to hunt his evening meal. The small grey downy flier eyed her inquisitively.

"We are alone Xander; we can trust no one. Your night eyes must be mine for there is much danger here."

"Aye, Mistress. I will watch and listen."

With a flip of his black-tipped tail, he was out the window.

Hearing a tap at the door, Yávië opened it to Näeré.

"Sleep, Yávië," Näeré said, watching Yávië drop to the floor.

"Well, that doesn't look very comfortable. Nall, will you lift her to the cot?"

Entering behind her, Nall lifted Yávië, placing her on the bed and covering her.

"I really do not like it, Näeré. How long do we have to keep doing this?"

"Until she learns the truth from Sōrél," Näeré whispered. "You and I must keep her safe. Now let us go speak to Galen."

"Definitely more to my liking," Nall muttered.

Galen sat by the fire watching the embers die. His heart was heavy and he wanted to take back the words Alandon had made him speak to Yávië.

"Galen," Näeré spoke in a soft voice without menace, "I am going to tell you this just once. Do not interfere in my brother's life. Not in any way. Do not speak to Yávië of her father, or her relationship to my brother. Do you understand my request?"

"Aye," Galen acknowledged, looking over Näeré's shoulder at the glowering Nall.

As the daystar rose, Xander the downy flier crept back to his mistress. "They seek only to protect you, Mistress," he whispered to Yávië, rubbing his soft head against her chin. Then he went to sleep next to her heart.

Yávië placed the map on the table where all could see it.

"The caverns are below the southern sands, approximately six days from Mourningmire. We will rest by day and travel by night, limiting our visibility."

Seeing Sōrél approach, she brightened.

"Was I cruel last night?" she whispered with a look of confusion.

"Not that I recall." Sōrél's eyes met Näeré's over Yávië's head.

"Our enemies will be trolls," Sōrél continued in Yávië's place. "According to Grumblton, they are fearsome creatures that can drag you away and eat you. He is quite positive of it, so we will need to keep on guard at all times. He does not believe they will attack us until we take the Book of Trolls, but it seems sensible to remain alert. Never go anywhere alone or without your weapon. Are we clear on that Galen?"

Galen nodded, making eye contact with Nall and Näeré as well, letting them know that there was no misunderstanding. Näeré had taken the time to teach him how to protect his thoughts from Alandon and he fully intended to take advantage of it.

"Our supplies are packed and evenly distributed so they should not prove a burden. We will expect to return to Mourningmire within a fortnight. Are there any questions before we begin?"

"Aye," shouted Nall. "How many arrows does it take to kill a troll?"

"I recommend arrows only to weaken them and your sword to

finish them off. They are hardy and have a very long reach. I struck one four times using the Bow of Ages and it never even slowed." Sōrél's eyes betrayed no humor though he attempted a smile.

"There are spells against them," Näeré spoke. "Grumblton has taught me and I will protect us as much as possible, but I do not know how great their strength will be when we are in their lair."

Nall blinked. He was certain he had just seen Zeth's hand on Rydén's shoulder, but it was not there now. Perhaps he had imagined it.

As they picked up their packs and positioned them, Nall sat next to Rydén. He looked at her carefully, half expecting to see a handprint on her tunic.

"Nall, why are you staring?" Rydén asked, brushing her shoulders.

"Just thought I saw something on your shoulder," he mumbled, giving Zeth a sideways glance.

He lifted his pack, wondering if he should be concerned.

"Nall, she is a grown woman. Do not baby her so," Näeré said as she ruffled his hair.

"Aye, it is the woman part that worries me," Nall admitted grudgingly.

Näeré's lilting laugh made him grin, and he was glad she was not his sister.

Toward the Southern Sands

With the setting of the daystar the Guardians left the safety of Mourningmire. They were armed with Grumblton's gift of spells, each weapon carefully prepared and blessed by the Ancient wizard.

As were all quests of such complexity, the way was strewn with stones and thorns. The Guardians passed in silence, each searching deep within himself for the courage that would be required.

Four days southeast of Mourningmire they passed the Æshardian City before turning directly south toward the expansive sands. A great, unmapped and seemingly endless desert lay to the south, and beneath its rocky substructure was the lair of the trolls—the keepers of the book of Yávië's search.

The densely wooded land that preceded the sands was one of the most beautiful on all the seven worlds, its trees rocketing skyward, taller than a dragon's length, their crowns creating a leafy canopy that kept the forest floor always in shadow. The night's darkness was like velvet, soft and dense, covering the group of Guardians as effectively as a veil of mists. The carpet of rotting leaf litter provided soundproofing, releasing its pungent odor as they stepped upon it and disturbed the tiny denizens below. Butterpillars and moths rushed frantically to escape Xander, the downy flier, for they were his favorite meal. Yávië sent him to the tallest trees to search ahead for danger but none was visible.

Rydén's grass cat, Valia, also hunted in the dark shadows, the squeal of the grosshare drifting back toward them as proof of her success—another set of night eyes to see them on their quest.

As the daystar rose above the horizon, Sōrél signaled their rest and watched as they made themselves comfortable among the roots of the braid trees. There would be no fire, for its smoke would draw the attention of the humans inhabiting the nearby settlement. They fed on the dried stag and cold willow tea Grumblton had provisioned.

Once satisfied that they were as comfortable as possible, Sōrél moved to speak to Nall and Näeré while keeping one eye on Yávië.

Squatting next to them, he spoke softly so the others would not hear.

"We will reach the border of the sands in another day's march. We will stop and allow your magick, Näeré, before we venture further."

"Will you give Yávië the book now?" Näeré asked.

"Aye. Nall, keep watch over us, for I do not know how safe it will be, even with the gyre in place. I do not trust Alandon's words. He wishes harm to me or to Yávië, perhaps both."

His eyes quickly shifted to Yávië. "Do you require something milady?"

"I require the Book of Quests as you well know, Sōrél, and stop treating me as your superior, for it makes me cross."

"Yávië, I do not wish to see you cross for you are formidable enough when you are cheerful. We shall examine the book together. You will read aloud to me that I may know the meaning of its words."

Retrieving his satchel Sōrél drew out the heavy wood-bound book and rested it on his knees.

"You are at no time to touch it, Yávië."

With an impatient nod, she indicated her agreement and watched as he opened the book, placing the shab-ot over the center of the two exposed pages to make sure it rested upon each equally.

As she leaned forward, her hair swept toward the pages, causing Sōrél to cry out and grab the book to move it away. He placed it on the ground at his side and took a strip of leather binding from his wrist to tie back her hair. His eyes were dark and his brow damp with dread.

Once again he lifted the book and opened its deadly pages.

"By the blood of Alandon does this child partake of the seven quests that she may cast the seven spells and upon their completion bring forth the reunion of the Seven Kingdoms and the rebirth of Ædracmoræ." Yávië translated as she read.

"Follow the serpent beneath the shifting southern sand, standing as it is taken into the dragon's mouth. Upon the dragon's table lays the Book of Trolls. Take it and strike it thrice with the staff of Alandon as it rests upon the skull of Ælmondæ.

"Slay Ya'vanna's dragon with the seven swords of Æstretfordæ before the shadow of the Blood Stone covers the light of the Star of Sangria.

"Upon the night of the firstborn's birth, cast the seven spells within the tower of the seven sisters and by the power of the House of the Dragon and the House of the Serpent, Ædracmoræ will be reborn."

As Yávië read, the words flew from the pages like the burning embers of a fire being lifted on an evening breeze, leaving the pages scorched and smoldering where the words had once been.

Yávië turned to Sōrél. "What does it mean? The House of the Serpent? Was the serpent not a symbol for the House of Aaradan? That house fell under some mysterious circumstance before Aléria and I were even born. My father told me none of the Aaradans survived."

Shaking his head as if he did not know, Sōrél's hatred for Alandon deepened.

The Lair

As they arrived at the border of the southern sands, their minds were overcome by its immenseness. As far as they could see lay shimmering sand as white as Æstretfordæ's great ice fields. Only the occasional great stone relieved its luminous and hauntingly beautiful expanse.

Consulting the map again, Sōrél directed them toward the lair of the distant trolls. In the darkness beneath them, their enemies began to wake, gnashing their teeth and stretching their long arms, eager to feast on the flesh of the Guardians. Low growls were emitted as they shared their plans, and the sound of thunder shook the earth as battle axes were drawn and tested.

The Guardians stood staring into the blackness of the pit that led to the Book of Trolls. A single ladder extended above the opening, a ladder made of willow, and one well remembered by Sōrél and Yávië.

"It was not just a dream," Yávië whispered as the remembered horror chilled her once again.

"Nay, it was more, but it has prepared us for what lies ahead," Sōrél encouraged.

"It has prepared me for your death," she answered, closing her eyes against the image of the skeletal fingers wearing Sōrél's ring.

With a final glance at Yávië, Sōrél led the way down the ladder into total darkness.

Halfway down, he heard movement below—scratching and

scraping as if sharp claws dragged against the rock walls. Low growls no louder than a grass cat's purr drifted up toward him.

Taking the oil-filled skins Grumblton had prepared, Sōrél dropped them around the base of the ladder followed by a burning waffle root to ignite them.

The soft growls turned to terrified howls and screams as burning trolls crashed into the walls and fell to the floor in agony, their flesh aflame. The acrid smoke rose up the ladder causing Sōrél to cough and gag.

There was no time to be lost, for other trolls would be drawn by the commotion. Calling softly to his Guardians, Sōrél continued to the floor of the cavern where the troll bodies lay scorched and steaming as burning black blood bubbled from their oily wounds.

As soon as the last Guardian hit the cavern floor, Sōrél lit their torches and they passed into the hallway that led to the Book of Trolls.

A small green serpent slithered into a doorway on the left, drawing them into the room where the book lay open on an altar of chiseled stone. The small snake slipped into the mouth of the carved dragon at the base of the altar.

Pulling Yávië forward, Sōrél held open his satchel to receive the book. Yávië lifted it and with her words in the ancient language flowing over it, she placed it into the bag.

Yowls and bellows of anger reached them as the trolls poured from the dark depths below the cavern. Näeré's lips moved in mussitation as she continued to invoke the protection of Grumblton's spells of avoidance, praying they would hold most of the trolls at bay.

"*Move!*" Sorel shouted, driving the Guardians back toward the ladder and freedom.

Four trolls blocked their entry to the ladder room, long arms hanging loosely, battleaxes held in clawed hands. Low threatening growls came from open mouths filled with ragged teeth. Small hate-filled eyes glowed in the dim torchlight.

Sōrél rushed forward, driving the trolls back with angry cries, but though they startled easily the trolls regrouped quickly, aware there was little threat from the single Guardian before them.

Nall joined Sōrél before the entrance to the ladder room and pushed Näeré through behind him, calling to Zeth and Galen to get Yávië and Rydén up the ladder.

Näeré grabbed the ladder and began the long climb, pulling Yávië behind her with a hand closed tightly around her wrist.

Sōrél sent arrows into the trolls as quickly as they could be nocked and released and Nall struck brutally with his sword, severing arms at the elbow and watching with satisfaction as battleaxes fell to the floor.

Suddenly, Rydén's scream of terror tore through Nall like a deadly blade, and he turned to see a troll dragging her off by the hair. Before he could reach her, Zeth had surged out the doorway and severed the beast's arm at the wrist. He followed with a violent backhand sweep, dropping the troll's head to the floor below. Grabbing Rydén around the waist, Zeth pulled her back into the room and pushed her up the ladder ahead of him.

Calling back over his shoulder, he urged Nall to move quickly.

Knowing that only he and Sōrél remained within the cavern, Nall grabbed Sōrél's shoulder and spun him into the ladder room, shoving him ahead and up the ladder. Sōrél twisted beneath the ladder, allowing Nall to pass as he tossed the remaining oil pouches to the floor below them followed by his torch. The flames rushed up the ladder, lapping hungrily at its rungs and leaving the trolls bellowing below them.

The Guardians erupted over the lip of the cavern's exit, spilling out onto the empty sand.

Nall grabbed Zeth and slapped him on the back.

"Well done!" he shouted. "Well done, indeed. Now get those disgusting troll fingers out of my sister's hair."

Nall felt his terror pass as Zeth, collapsing in laughter and relief, gently removed the hand tangled within Rydén's hair.

"Help me roll this stone," Sōrél called from a nearby boulder.

Together they rolled the stone over the cavern's opening, sealing in the enraged trolls.

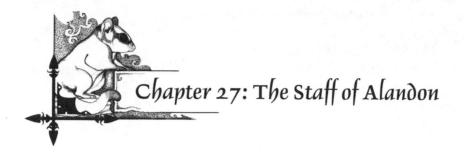# Chapter 27: The Staff of Alandon

"If my father were here I would just ask him where he keeps the staff," Yávië said as Sōrél once again pulled the Book of Quests from his bag.

They had been back at Mourningmire for several days with no indication of where the next quest would take them, although they had sought the wisdom of the book each evening.

"Perhaps it is not actually his staff—or at least not one he has used. I do not recall your father carrying a staff at the Fortress."

Sōrél carefully fastened back Yávië's hair. The fear of losing her to another nightmare had made him cautious. Taking a deep breath, he opened the book and listened to her soft voice as she read the ancient words.

"Beneath the foul and fevered water of the fen lies the staff of Alandon. The child of the blood will take it and strike the Book of Trolls thrice as it lies upon the skull."

"I do not know, Sōrél. There are so many swamps—which one is it?"

Dropping the book and grabbing her he smiled, "It is in the fen on Æwmarshæ! They call it Fever Fen, the Ancients do. It must be there."

She touched his face and watched him grow solemn again.

"What causes your pain, Sōrél? You have grown more shadowed with every day that passes."

"The loss of you grows nearer, and with it my sorrow increases."

"You cannot lose me for we are bound. You share my soul. You will make public your pledge to me at my coronation. I know that it is so for I have seen it in my dreams."

"Aye, I shall pledge, but you will deny."

Shaking her head she laughed, "I shall never deny you, Sōrél. *Never*. I promise it."

He allowed her to believe it, though he doubted it was true.

Sōrél addressed the Guardians as they finished their morning meal.

"Nall, Näeré and I shall accompany Yávië to Æwmarshæ to acquire the Staff of Alandon. The three of you will remain here with Grumblton. The task should not require more than one passing of the daystar, since the fen we seek lies just beyond the mire. Remain alert, for I am not certain that the stone has held the trolls."

Together the three Guardians followed Yávië below Mourningmire to the chamber of mirrors. The six mirrors leading to the worlds beyond Æshardæ stood arranged in a circle around the pool. Yávië paused for a moment then stepped through the mirror and into the caverns of Æwmarshæ. She felt Sōrél take her hand as he stepped through behind her.

"Do not go alone again," he chastened her.

Näeré and Nall stepped through a moment later and together they moved forward up the passageway that would lead them to the Ancients of Æwmarshæ.

"Welcome," a soft voice said as they moved into daylight, "I am Borrolon, elder of the Ancients of Vissenmire. Grumblton sents word that you was coming for the staff."

"You know where the staff lies?" Yávië asked.

"In a pit of hirudinea within the Fever Fen," Borrolon answered. "'Tis a nasty place, and them leeches bites. Come and I will shows you."

Borrolon set off at a quick pace, and they hurried to catch up. Just outside the small group of neat bothies, he pointed to a shadowy swampland. Mist rose from its warm waters and they heard the call of reptilian bloodrens as they hunted.

"Nasty place," the Ancient said again, nodding to himself before heading back toward the bothies.

"How do we know exactly where in the fen this staff might be?" Nall asked, lips twisted in disgust.

"Perhaps I shall feel it when we grow near," Yávië answered, sounding doubtful.

"I do not feel anything but leeches crawling up my legs," Nall grumbled, lifting an imaginary offender from his thigh. "If we just stand here we will soon be covered in them."

"There is a path that leads further into the fen. Let us walk there and see what happens," Sōrél suggested as he took Yávië's hand and started deeper into the swamp.

"By all means, let us go deeper into this revolting place," Nall mumbled under his breath, earning a frown from Näeré.

Leaning toward her, Nall whispered, "Have I told you how pretty you are when I make you angry?"

He winked as her lips curved into a smile at his flattery.

"Wait," Yávië said, her voice barely above a whisper, "there is an opening beneath that tree, perhaps a cave?"

"Most likely filled with trolls," Nall grumped.

Step by silent step they made their way toward the hollowed space.

"I will go," Yávië said, stepping forward only to be yanked back by Sōrél.

"You will go nowhere without me . . . us," he corrected himself, giving Nall and Näeré a look of apology. "I shall go first and you may follow."

"If you see it, do not touch it," Yávië cautioned.

Beneath the tree and through the small opening they crept along the muddy path, emerging into a large underground chamber that was obviously often filled with water. Against the wall leaned an ancient staff, cracked and water worn. It stood about seven hands, and the lower portion was rough and soiled. At the very tip of its base was a crook serving to channel energy away from the earth. At its top was a golden-eyed dragon wrapped tightly in the coils of a serpent. The dragon's jaws were open above the serpent's head, as if it were about to devour the snake.

"It shows the symbols of both houses. The dragon of Ædracmoræ and the serpent of Aaradan," Näeré spoke, receiving a cautionary look from Sōrél.

"I have heard legends of the House of Aaradan," she added, getting an odd look from Nall as he recalled her telling him she and her brother were born to the House of Aaradan.

Shaking her head, she laid a finger against her lips, eliciting a look of even deeper confusion. Seeing Nall's lips part to speak, she kissed him quickly, leaving him grinning and without a thought of what he had been about to say.

Yávië moved closer to the staff, still making no move to touch it.

The workmanship was beautiful—both dragon and serpent were carved in such detail that the individual scales could be seen on their bellies.

"It holds a sword," Yávië whispered with great certainty. "I have seen it my dreams."

Reaching out, she lifted it and withdrew the sword from its staff-like scabbard. The blade was thin and very slightly curved; its forged and tempered metal gleamed in the torchlight. She lifted it to feel the weight and turned it slowly left and right. The hilt guard, a golden dragon chasing its own tail, was just large enough to protect a woman's hand.

"It is not my father's. It is mine." Yávië gave an uneasy glance around before returning the sword to the staff.

Sōrél's expression gave away his knowledge of the sword as well, but only Näeré noticed and frowned.

"Let us go," Sōrél said, "we can be back in Mourningmire before the evening meal."

Upon their return Sōrél went immediately to his bothie, knowing a confrontation with Näeré was inevitable. While part of him dreaded it, there was also relief at sharing the dark secret with his twin.

"Tell me," she demanded before the door had even closed behind her, "how did you recognize the sword? What have you done, Sōrél, to bring all this ugliness upon our heads?"

She softened, seeing the shame within his soul.

"What have you done?" she asked more gently.

He hung his head and told her. He shared the truth of Alandon's treachery against the House of Aaradan, and his own part in the fall of the House of the Dragon Queen and the shattering of the Seven Kingdoms.

"You will release her. Barring a miracle, you know she will deny your pledge. You will be fortunate if she does not expel you from her kingdom or have you drawn and quartered." Näeré shook her head. "How could you do it? How could you just look away and leave Ædracmoræ's fate to Alandon and Aléria?"

"At the time, I bargained for my life and, in so doing, lost my soul. Alandon's hatred permeates every breath of my life, and Yávië's, though she does not know it. He plays the role of perfect father when in her presence. I shall release her and walk away. I shall not cause her more pain by remaining."

"More pain?" Näeré laughed, "Do you not see what you have done? She loves you Sōrél, has trusted you with her life and her legacy. The rest of her days will be naught but pain, with or without you. I cannot imagine the suffering she will have to bear. Does her mother know you did this?"

"No one knows beyond Alandon and me."

"You, my brother, are a fool but Alandon is a monster."

"I shall watch Yávië closely and keep it from her mind until such time that you choose to tell her." Näeré took a deep breath and left her brother alone in his misery.

Yávië saw Näeré leave Sōrél's bothie and wondered what had caused her to go to him. She held the sword from the Staff of Alandon, watching the light of the torch play across the dragon sword's blade and recalled the dream in which she had seen it. They had led an army, she and Sōrél. She recalled lifting the sword and seeing the light play across it just as it did now. She fell asleep, the sword gripped tightly in her hand.

Sōrél entered Yávië's bothie on silenced footfalls and moved to the chair where he would sleep. His eyes fell on the sword clutched in her hand and he smiled a small smile of hope. Perhaps the Dragon Queen would be strong enough to forgive him.

Chapter 28: The Skull of Ælmondæ

Ælmondæ held a special place in Yávië's heart. It was here she had realized her strength and, all alone, overcome a massive elemental fire demon. She had reconstructed this world of the damned into one of beauty, calling forth a gentle people to populate it.

The Guardians watched as the Ælmondians came to Yávië. Their kind faces looked up at her as their hands reached out to touch her.

"She is a good queen," Zeth said.

"Aye, she has a gentle nature beneath her warrior's hide," Nall agreed.

"Do not be deceived," Näeré teased them, "she would as soon cut your throat as look at you."

"Only my throat," Sōrél assured them, squeezing his sister's shoulder.

"That should not be surprising to anyone who knows you, for I believe we have all wanted to cut your throat at one time or another."

Yávië returned the young girl she was holding to the arms of her mother.

"Do you jest at my expense while I am away?" she teased her Guardians.

"Nay," Näeré replied honestly, "I only warn them that your blade often desires my brother's blood."

Yávië nodded, "Your brother does bring on the heat of my anger occasionally."

"Ah, but he says you are most beautiful when you are angry, so perhaps it is intentional," Galen suggested to general laughter.

"We were speaking of what a good queen you are," Zeth said.

Yávië grew solemn and looked away.

Nall punched Zeth hard in the arm and scowled at him.

"Yávië, you are a good queen," Sōrél said, his words a prayer of his own belief.

"I am no queen at all, for a queen has a kingdom and mine remains shattered. I waste time talking to children when I should be searching for an artifact." Yávië's words were like glacial water, putting an end to any joviality.

Taking her by the shoulders, Sōrél felt his anger rising. "We do all we can, Yávië. There is nothing wrong with a few moments' respite, and time with a child is never wasted."

He released her and turned away, seeing the stunned look on Näeré's face.

"It is time someone called her on her selfishness," he snapped, stalking away toward the nearby bothies.

Näeré looked back at Yávië and saw her hand held to her heart, her eyes filled with satisfaction. As Näeré moved toward her, Yávië held up her hand to stop her.

"Do not take my memory, Näeré. I am tired of having things kept from me." Then she took off after Sōrél.

Näeré looked at Nall, who shook his head.

"Why do two who care so much act so foolishly?"

"I think it is because they care so much they cannot see beyond it. Perhaps they will come to terms. We shall wait and see what happens," Näeré said, silently warning her brother of Yávië's approach.

Yávië did not go to Sōrél. She went straight to the pool of Ælmondæ, for beneath it, was the skull she sought. She had not shared the knowledge with Sōrél when they read the Book of Quests together, for the ancient words required her to go alone.

Sōrél fumed. His anger had risen as if magma from a mountain's hidden chambers, the ugly words escaping before he paused for thought. He had seen her hand slide toward the sword's hilt and rest there lightly, though her fingers never formed a grip. Now where was she? Näeré had told him Yávië was coming but she had not arrived to question his disrespect. He stormed out to find her, his mind clouded with regret.

"She followed you. I do not know where else she could have gone."

"She seeks the skull alone," Sōrél cursed. "She baited me deliberately and I snapped at it like a hungry direfang. She must have seen something in the book, something she did not share."

He rubbed his face with his hands, trying to wipe away the building frustration and apprehension.

"Ælmondæ is not large. We shall split up and look for her; she cannot be allowed to wander alone."

"What does your heart tell you, Sōrél?" Näeré asked in an attempt to calm his growing agitation.

"That she has returned to the pool," he answered without hesitation.

"Go there and we will search the other areas."

He nodded and turned back the way he had come, past the bothies and toward Ælmondæ's sacred pool, seeing Yávië at its edge as he approached.

"Yávië!"

She paused only long enough to meet his eyes before she dove into the pool. Her mind returned to the last time she had entered its water—in search of the truth—what seemed a life span ago. Thick with the sludge of death, its foul odor had made her gag. Now it was clear and clean—the source of all life on Ælmondæ. As she reached the bottom of the pool, she found the opening that would take her to the trybrac's cave. She slipped inside and pushed upward toward the lair that contained the skull.

As soon as her head broke the surface she drew her sword and spun in a slow circle, looking for the beast she sought. There were prints in the soft sand surrounding the pool indicating the trybrac had come here to drink. No bones littered the room so she knew the main den must lie elsewhere. She swam to the shore and pulled herself up, pushing back her wet hair.

"What do you think you are doing?" cracked Sōrél's angry voice from behind her.

Spinning, she held her sword in front of her.

"I must do this myself, Sōrél. Please do not make me harm you."

"What is it you did not tell me?" he asked, pulling himself from the pool.

Suddenly she was inexplicably enraged. Her anger was so volatile its heat was scorching. She lunged at Sōrél, causing him to draw his blade to defend himself.

Tossing the lighter sword to her right hand, she drew the Sword of Domesius with her left and attacked him, beating him back to the wall of the cave.

"*Kill him*, Yávië," her father's voice whispered in her head. "*Kill Sōrél before he can harm you.*"

As Sōrél edged away from the wall to give himself room to escape Yávië's wrath, he heard the heavy padding footsteps of the trybrac.

He rushed at Yávië and knocked her into the pool, taking a nasty cut to the upper arm before spinning around to face the three-headed menace.

"No!"

Yávië leapt from the water and pushed Sōrél aside with her shoulder. The strength of her anger provided her with a definite edge and then, as she swung her head back toward the trybrac, her wet hair struck Sōrél across the eyes, temporarily blinding him.

She moved toward the approaching trybrac, arms spread to cover the three hissing heads as the low grumble of the trybrac's growl brought the prickle of fear to her water-chilled flesh. Taking a deep breath, Yávië watched as the beast drew back two heads in preparation to strike. She shot forward and cleanly severed the extended right-side head, causing the beast to roar in pain.

Detecting movement at the corner of her eye, Yávië turned the smaller dragon-handled sword toward the new threat, warning Sōrél away.

Then, swinging the Sword of Domesius in a low arc, she cut the tendon in the trybrac's closest foreleg, dropping it to the sand and allowing her to draw her sword across the vertebrae of the left head, not quite severing it. The sand was soaked deep purple with the beast's blood, and Yávië extended her blade to flick the blood-damp sand into the enemy's remaining eyes.

"Come that I may take your head," she whispered to the weakening beast.

As it lumbered forward, she dropped to her knees and drove both swords into its chest, twisting away from the remaining jaws. Drawing the smaller sword free, she swept it down across the trybrac's neck, separating the center head from its body.

Suddenly swinging toward the pool, Yávië extended her blade once more and touched Sōrél's heart.

"Why does my father want you dead?"

"Yávië . . ."

"Do not speak my name. I will ask it again. Why does my father want you dead?" She watched as a drop of blood soaked through his wet shirt.

"Do not lie to me for I will know and I will drop you where you stand."

Sōrél tossed his weapon to the ground and extended his arms out from his sides before dropping them in exhaustion.

"Kill me."

"You have not answered me."

"Have you ever noticed, Yávië, that everywhere we go we bring death?"

He shook his head and sank to his knees, bringing her blade to his throat.

"I can no longer do this, Yávië. I have tried so hard to make it right that I no longer have the energy for it."

She frowned, but did not withdraw her blade.

"What do you mean?"

He smiled tiredly, "I cannot tell you with your sword at my throat."

She allowed the sword to fall to her side.

"Tell me."

"Only if you will hold my hand while I do."

"Sōrél, you are not in any position to bargain with me. My father has instructed me to kill you. I must know why."

His hand reached out toward her, waiting.

With a deep sigh, she took it and sank to the sand in front of him, her eyes searching his face.

"What is your earliest memory of me?" Sōrél asked.

"I remember you mounted on a dragon. I was young, not yet a woman. I chose you then."

"Yes, Yávië, you chose me." He took a deep breath. "Will you remember that always, no matter what you hear?"

"Sōrél, you speak in riddles and I do not like it."

"I must, for I am in grave danger with you. I am unarmed both physically and mentally."

"*Sōrél* . . ." Her voice again betrayed her annoyance.

She tried to withdraw her hand but he held it firmly until she relaxed.

"Have I ever given you reason to doubt my pledge?"

She raised her eyes to search his before answering.

"Nay. Never."

"Your father lied. Aléria is not first born, you are. He offered you to me to do with as I pleased in payment for my silence. Silence over the part he played in the destruction of the House of Aaradan. There is something in you he fears. While I did not collect the debt, I accepted the terms. I saved my own life at your expense. I betrayed your trust and by my silence allowed your sister to steal your birthright. I knew and I never spoke the truth. I did not stop Aléria and your father from bringing Ædracmoræ to destruction."

The admission of so great a guilt caused him to feel faint and he closed his eyes and waited for Yávië to draw away.

The silence stretched out and yet he feared her eyes, afraid to look at them, almost wishing she would strike him dead.

Finally she spoke.

"And my father wishes me to kill you because of this? He wishes you dead to hide this deceit?"

"He fears something; I do not know what it is," Sōrél answered, opening his eyes.

He watched as a tear formed and rolled down her cheek.

"Do you know, Sōrél, how much a woman would have to love a man to forgive such betrayal?"

"Yávië . . . I . . ."

"I told you not to speak my name."

It was then that he heard Näeré's words as clearly as if she stood next to him.

"Do you not see what you have done? Her life will be naught but pain with or without you. I cannot imagine the suffering she will have to bear."

Sōrél hung his head, unable to look at Yávië any longer. He had no right to gaze on her beauty.

"You have not answered me."

Her voice was so soft he was not sure he had heard it and he looked up. Her eyes were dark with the shadows of sorrow—deep violet—her soul exposed.

"What . . . ?"

"Do you know how much a woman must love a man to forgive this?"

"I do not believe it would be possible to forgive such betrayal."

"Then you know nothing."

She withdrew her hand from his and, turning to the trybrac, with the Sword of Domesius quickly cut through the thin muscle still holding the left-side head. Replacing the sword in its scabbard and collecting the head, she dropped into the pool and disappeared from Sōrél's view.

"Yávië!" Näeré called, "are you hurt?" she added upon seeing the dangling trybrac head and the blood on Yávië's clothing.

Then she saw it—the pain in Yávië's eyes, and she knew Sōrél had shared his secret.

"He loves you," she whispered, choking back her tears.

Yávië placed her hand on Näeré's arm.

"I know."

"So what did I miss?" Nall asked as he approached.

"Nothing," Yávië said, tossing the trybrac head to him.

"I need the skull. Would you clean it for me?"

As they watched her walk away, Näeré turned to Nall and said, "She loves my brother."

"You did not know that?" Nall asked in bewilderment.

Näeré stood watching as Sōrél cleaned his wounds. Her arms were folded across her chest and a deep frown marred her beauty.

"So, why is it you are not dead?"

With a wry laugh and shaking his head he answered, "I truly do not know. I have fought beside Yávië many times and I have never seen her so frightening. Why she did not kill me when I did not answer her the first time I do not know."

"Why did you tell her?"

"Honestly? When I realized she might truly take my life, I did not wish to die with it unsaid."

Näeré watched as he fumbled trying to clean the wound on his arm. She stepped forward to help him.

"I hope this hurts," she said, swabbing the wound harder than necessary.

"What does it mean? What will happen now?"

"Näeré, you are giving me a headache. I do not know. I am not sure Yávië knows what she will do."

Näeré nodded. "But she loves you."

"Love has never been an issue between us. My lies, betrayal and deceit seem to do most of the damage."

"Have you spoken to her since you returned?"

"Nay, she will come to me when she is ready."

"Do you hear yourself?" Näeré threw the bloodied cloth down. "She will come to me when she is ready? Sōrél, let me try to explain something to you. You owe her an apology. Actually, you owe her several thousand apologies. Do not wait for her to come to you!"

Sōrél blew out a deep breath.

"I do not wish to anger her again."

Näeré just looked at him.

"How is it you can make me feel like a butterpillar beneath the gaze of a downy flier?" he sighed, picking up his shirt.

Näeré pulled it from his hands. "Let her see your wounds," she said.

"If she kills me it is on your head. Let Nall have my bow and sword."

Sōrél felt foolish without his shirt but perhaps that was Näeré's intent. Rulers rarely killed their fools. At the door to the bothie he found he could not force himself to knock and simply stood there, breathing deeply and waiting for courage.

"Do not stand there huffing and puffing. If you intend to come in, do it." Yávië's voice was cool but not angry.

He opened the door and stepped inside, closing it softly behind him.

Yávië sat in a chair with her back to him.

"Did Näeré send you?"

"No," he lied.

"But it was her idea for you to come half naked."

Sōrél felt the color rise in his face. She had watched him as he left his bothie.

Yávië turned and looked him over as if he were a bullram she might buy. She paused at the wound on his arm.

"I am sorry I hurt you." Her eyes dropped to the floor.

He silently thanked Näeré for her wisdom.

As the silence lengthened he remembered how tongue-tied he had been when Yávië first pursued him. His guilt had held him at bay then, as it did now.

"It is I who am sorry. Sorry for my life. I cannot release you from the bond until your coronation."

"It is no longer your wish to honor your pledge?"

Her chin lifted and he saw the quiver of her lips even as she pressed them together to stop it. Her eyes grew wide in an effort to ward off tears.

He moved toward her.

"Answer me," she said, holding up her hand to stop him.

Again, he heard his sister's voice. Once again, it urged him not to wait.

He crossed to Yávië and kneeled before her, taking her hands in his.

"I am yours. Not through the power of your father but through the power of your heart. Unless you deny me, it is my intent to honor the pledge."

Her eyes were clear as she nodded her acceptance of those terms.

"You are the firstborn, Yávië."

"I know. As are you, Sōrél of Aaradan. Our union, this is what my father fears. Tomorrow we shall go to Æstaffordæ in search of Ya'vanna's Dragon and you will show me the Fortress of the Serpent King."

Rising, he placed his lips against the top of her head, "Sleep well, Yávië, queen of hearts."

Näeré watched as her brother left Yávië. He moved once again with the authority of the firstborn son of the House of Aaradan. She knew that later he would return to sit in Yávië's chair and watch over their queen throughout the night.

Chapter 29: Ya'vanna's Dragon

"Æstaffordæ is my favorite world," Sōrél had once told Yávië. Now she understood his passion for its lush beauty—it was his home.

As he stood with Yávië before the Fortress of the Serpent King, Sōrél explained that the great battle of which he had spoken was the attack on the House of Aaradan, a slaughter that only Grumblton the wizard, Sōrél, Näeré and Galen—then a ne'er-do-well poacher—had survived. Galen had been spared through his absence and Sōrél and Näeré by their father's swift action and Alandon's momentary leniency, a leniency Yávië's father had apparently grown to regret. Grumblton had simply vanished into the walls of the fortress.

As the horde had swept the fortress in search of survivors, Sōrél and Näeré had been lowered into the oubliette for safety. Alandon had raged over his inability to find them and had at last struck a deal with their dying father, their lives in exchange for their birthright. Sōrél and Näeré had been taken to Ædracmoræ and placed into service as Guardians. Alandon had been livid when Ya'vanna had selected Sōrél as Captain but had no cause to reject him without giving away his own dark deeds.

Grumblton had cast a spell of vanishing upon the fortress, abandoning it in the time before remembering. Today, at Sōrél's request, the little wizard had released the spell.

Its portcullis remained securely closed and the barbed points were tight within their slots. The carved symbol of the coiled dragon-headed serpent glowered above them as a potent reminder of the long-dead ruler of the noble house.

Taking Yávië's hand Sōrél led her around the eastern wall to a hidden staircase between the stones. With a heavy key, he opened the wooden door and allowed her to precede him into his ancestral home.

He lit their way with a torch and Yávië saw that unlike the Fortress of the Dragon Queen, Sōrél's home remained untouched. Its tapestries were vibrant, none was tattered or torn, and the hard, packed earthen floor of its lower level was covered with straw as fresh as if servants had laid it there that morning. As they passed along the corridor, Yávië saw the servants' quarters. They were clean and each held a bed with a straw mattress, a table and chair, a basin and a rack for hanging clothes. The ruler of this kingdom had cared for his people, providing for their needs as though for his children.

When they stepped into the great hall, Yávië gasped at its beauty. The walls were painted with scenes of daily court life. Behind the thrones hung a tapestry depicting the coronation, and her eyes were drawn to the young prince standing before his father to receive the crown.

"Come and sit, Yávië. Be my queen for a moment."

Sōrél took her hand and led her to the throne at his left before taking his seat next to her.

"This is where we should be." His voice was soft, his words earnest.

"Had our fathers not collided, I would have brought you here upon my coronation as the legends foretold, but with the destruction of Ædracmoræ those promises were swept away. Now we shall write our own."

"Your mother tried to warn us, but we did not heed her words. Death came very swiftly to the House of Aaradan, Yávië, and then it was gone." Sōrél's eyes were shadowed, lost within the grief of the past.

"Come; let me show you the queen's chambers. You will see we were prepared to receive you with great joy."

Continuing, they climbed the wide staircase to the upper level of the fortress, and on to a passageway. They passed an open doorway, revealing a room of frenzied femininity.

"Näeré," Sōrél chuckled, "a chambermaid's nightmare."

Seizing the great argent door grips, he opened the doors to what would have been the rooms of his queen. Huge windows overlooked a garden filled with flowers and trees heavy with fruit. An empty pool sat upon a raised platform, the carved stone serpent heads ready to spill the water for the queen's bath.

Yávië wandered across the room, running her hand over the wooden tables, and fingering the silver mirrors and brushes. Lifting a brush, she drew it through her hair several times before returning it to its place on the dressing table.

Turning to him with a shy smile, she asked, "Where would your queen sleep?"

Then she saw the Ancient wizard Grumblton standing in the doorway.

"Where are they?" Nall asked again. "They have been gone far too long."

He paced the field looking beyond its fence and into the woods.

"We should look for them," he added.

"Nall, they have much to discuss. Yávië needs time to make the decisions that will affect us all. Do not fret so."

"And where is Rydén? For that matter, where is Zeth? I have seen no one but Galen since just after daybreak. I do not like it," Nall continued.

There was a shift in the wind and he looked up, relieved to see a large wind dragon approach bearing Sōrél and Yávië.

"I was about to come for you."

"There was no need. I was safe with your Captain."

"I see that Rydén and Zeth bring us a stag," Sōrél said, gesturing toward the brake. "They have become fine hunters."

Nall looked at them with a frown. "How is it I know nothing of the day's events?"

Giggling, Rydén answered her irritable brother, "Perhaps you slept too late."

"Did I?" he asked, looking at Näeré who raised her eyebrows, drawing laughter from them all.

"If you are asking if your sleep was bewitched, the answer is nay."

"Let us watch this fine stag roast and discuss the morrow's hunt for the Dragon," Sōrél commanded, moving toward the fire that the Æstaffordæ's Ancients kept burning.

"Just as my father never had a staff, I do not believe my mother ever had a dragon. It is only a symbol we seek." Yávië spoke without doubt.

"Within the Book of Quests it speaks of the dragon as the serpent's shadow and the serpent as the dragon's voice calling with the thunder of the falls. Nothing is clear; all is as muddied as the waters of the fen."

Näeré watched as Sōrél's hand touched Yávië's hair, lightly and without awareness. Suddenly, she felt the darkness stirring beyond the firelight and her breath caught in her throat.

"Nall," she whispered, "the dark horde comes. Its shadow passes from Æshulmæ to Æcumbræ. They will soon draw close."

"When? Näeré, when will they reach us?"

"Three days, no longer. They will catch us during the quests on Æstretfordæ, when each of us will be alone."

"I hope Grumblton's magick is as great as you say, for without it we are lost."

"He hid an entire fortress for many lifetimes. Surely he can hide seven Guardians for a fortnight," she said in reassurance.

"Yávië, could the voice be the thunder of the true falls, the waterfalls above the pool of Æstaffordæ?" Sōrél asked, recalling their leap from the falls into the pool when long ago Yávië sought the release of her seven sorrows.

"Aye, it is possible," she agreed though uncertain.

"We shall begin the search there, since there is no likelier possibility. Rest well, for we shall leave at daybreak."

"Nall, will you see Yávië to her room?" Sōrél asked.

"Aye, when she is ready."

Näeré leaned against the wall and stared at Sōrél.

"You fool no one by asking Nall to escort your lady to her bothie."

After a pause, she continued, "Alandon controls the dark horde. I have seen the vision; even now, they turn toward us at his command and they will reach us as we arrive in Æstretfordæ. They will attempt to overcome each of us when we are alone. I believe that Grumblton can protect us for the fortnight it will take to recover the seven swords. Yávië will need to see Rosie right away."

Sōrél looked up questioningly.

Näeré laughed at his expression.

"Sōrél, I love you dearly but you are not the wisest of men. By your actions, you have once again drawn the attentions of Alandon's evil. Do not deny this, for I can see it clearly in your eyes, my brother. Yávië's aura already begins to shift."

She raised her hand and laid it on her brother's face.

"It is all I have ever wished for you."

She held him close.

With the morning light, they headed toward the pool of Æstaffordæ in search of Ya'vanna's Dragon. Sōrél led them along the lower path that wandered to the point where the falls entered the pool.

He sent Galen, Rydén and Zeth to the far side of the pool and Nall and Näeré to the point from which a small stream flowed away. Then he and Yávië moved along a rocky ledge beneath the falls.

Sōrél allowed Yávië to lead so that he could look at her closely without alarming her. His eyes sought the change in her aura that Näeré had mentioned, but he saw nothing different about her. He was about to dismiss the thought when, to his surprise, her voice calleded back to him.

"If you want an answer, ask a question." Yávië turned to search his face.

"How do you know I have a question?"

She laughed, "Because your thoughts are so loud that I can hear them over the sound of the falls."

"Only Näeré sees," she answered him.

"What will Rosie do?" Sōrél asked. "Näeré says you must see Rosie."

"Aye, Rosie will hide what we have done."

"Have I brought you shame?"

"Nay, Sōrél, but we have drawn unwanted attention. For our safety this must remain hidden from my father."

Anger surged as Sōrél realized Alandon's threat.

"I will not allow harm to come to you, Yávië," Sōrél swore again.

Yávië turned away and moved into a crevice in the rocks so narrow that she could only pass through by turning sideways. Sōrél grabbed her wrist and stopped her.

"I cannot pass; it is too narrow. There must be another way."

"Have you not yet learned that I can care for myself, Sōrél?" she whispered, before pulling her wrist from his grip.

"Yávië, *no!* Do not go without me."

"I shall return. Let me simply see what lies beyond."

He watched helplessly as she disappeared from view before beginning a frantic search for another entrance into the caverns that had now swallowed her.

As Yávië exited the narrow crack, she noticed that the sand beneath her feet was giving off an unusual glow. She drew her finger through it and watched as the light shimmered and changed, as though retreating from her touch.

She caught sight of movement ahead. It resembled heat rising from the sand of the Wastelands, rippling and unclear. She was riveted by the shifting light.

A blow drove her to her knees and she felt her eyesight grow dim.

When her head cleared, Yávië found herself bound and her weapons gone. Her wrists were locked within bronze bracelets emblazoned with a great dragon. A chain held them to a ring in the floor. She twisted the bracelets looking for a weakness but found none. Nor could she force them off over her hands, no matter how tightly she squeezed.

"It was promised you would come." A silken voice wrapped itself around her from the shadows at the edge of the room.

"Who are you? Why do you hold me captive?"

"I was promised a queen to share my kingdom and now you have come."

"Who promised it?" Yávië demanded. "I am the only one who can make such a promise and I have not."

The voice laughed.

"You have spirit. This is good."

"Show yourself!" Yávië spat. "I have a right to see my captor."

As her new Master stepped from the shadows, Yávië's eyes clouded in horror and revulsion. Her mind went dark, releasing her from the terror the beast brought.

Nall and Näeré raced toward Sōrél's shouts.

"She is gone; *taken!*" Sōrél's eyes were glazed with disbelief.

"I held her wrist and then she pulled away and was gone." His face grew pale.

Näeré pushed Sōrél's head between his knees, watching as the blood rushed toward his failing brain.

"This will not help, Sōrél. Breathe, for you are of no use to us if you do not regain control."

Nall looked from Näeré to Sōrél.

"What is it I do not know?" he asked.

"I should have taken her to Rosie before we began this search," Näeré cursed herself.

"Is Yávië ill?" Nall asked with deep concern.

"Will someone answer me?"

"She carries Sōrél's child," Näeré whispered.

Nall's fist drove Sōrél to his knees.

The second blow threw him back into the rocky cliff face and dropped him to the ground.

Näeré blinked and then began to laugh.

"Oh, *Nall!*"

She saw the shocked expressions of Galen, Rydén and Zeth and burst into another fit of laughter.

"*What?* Sōrél's pledge was to protect her not to . . . He has brought shame upon us all. I do not understand why this is so amusing."

"They share the vows of promise?" offered Galen by way of a possible defense.

Nall looked to Näeré for confirmation, she nodded and he shook his head in despair.

"Sōrél is going to kill me, isn't he?"

"Nay, for he will see there could be no greater protector for his queen," Näeré said casually.

"Put Sōrél in the pool. We must revive him and search for Yávië."

Sorel held his head. Then he held his jaw. Then he glared at Nall.

"We waste precious time," Sōrél said with the sharp voice of authority.

He led them to the crack in the wall into which Yávië had passed.

"Rydén, Zeth and I can pass through," Näeré said. "We will go for her. You three can look for another way in."

Sōrél did not attempt to stop them. He simply took Näeré's hand and cautioned her.

"I can feel her, Sōrél. She is unconscious but unharmed."

He simply nodded and turned away.

Yávië awoke to the smell of her own vomit. Recalling her last moments of consciousness, she gagged and vomited again.

"One would think you do not find me handsome," her tormentor spoke again from the deep shadows.

Unable to form any coherent thought, Yávië's keening filled the cavern.

"Take her to my chambers," the silken voice commanded the others.

As slick, damp hands gripped her arms and legs, Yávië screamed repeatedly until something slapped her into unconsciousness.

Yávië's screams echoed through the caverns, causing chills to run up Näeré's spine as she pushed herself out of the crevice and into the room where Yávië had first stood. She saw Yávië's boot prints in the sand. Then she saw where Yávië had fallen to her knees and the marks on the sand where she had been dragged away. The prints beside them appeared to be those of a dragon.

"We really need Sōrél, Nall and Galen," Näeré whispered to Rydén and Zeth.

They moved quietly around the chamber looking for an opening to the outside.

Sōrél, Nall and Galen dove beneath the falls and followed the underwater passage leading back beneath the cliff. Lungs begging for air, they surfaced in a small cave—gasping. It was then that they heard Yávië's screams.

Sōrél raced through the cavern. Placing three arrows in his teeth, he drew his bow and nocked another. Nall pounded down the passageway behind him, followed by Galen.

As they turned into the first cavern, they met Näeré, Rydén and Zeth, all with weapons drawn.

"I do not know what it is, but it leaves the prints of a dragon. Yávië would never be so terrified of a dragon," Näeré whispered to Sōrél.

They continued forward, pushing into every cavern that branched off the main passage, but each one was empty.

Yávië whimpered and pulled away from the touch of the beast. Its long thin fingers left a trail of viscous slime everywhere they touched her. It leaned closer, licking her shoulder and causing her to vomit onto the filthy rags where she lay. Laughing, it licked up her vomit before allowing its tongue to trail over her skin again.

"Do you see how much I care for you?" the creature asked. "You will learn to like me. I promise you will."

Sobbing, Yávië closed her eyes and tried to draw back, but the wall behind her offered no escape.

"Open your eyes. I want you to see me." The monster caressed her with its voice.

"Do you notice I do not use my claws on you? I do not wish to mar your smooth skin. But I can if you do not obey me."

Yávië screamed as the beast drove its nails into her shoulder. She shuddered and gagged causing the creature to laugh again.

Sōrél's first arrow struck the creature's heart while Nall's struck its throat, sending vile, black blood spraying across Yávië and sending her into a new spasm of screams and vomiting.

"Get it off her," Sōrél shouted.

Together the Guardians dragged the still twitching body away from Yávië. Holding her against him, Sōrél raced back toward the room with the pool, for he could not tell how much of the blood was hers and he feared she had grievous injuries. Along the passageway, the beast's servants hissed and drew back as the Guardian passed them.

Dropping into the pool, Sōrél began to scrub the filth from Yávië looking for wounds. Her shoulder bore four deep punctures, but beyond that, the blood and gore seemed to belong to the enemy.

Her arms held Sōrél so tightly he could not breathe, but when he tried to loosen them she merely cried out and held him tighter. Finally, he simply dove beneath the water and swam rapidly out of the passageway and into the pool below the falls.

Dragging himself up on the sand, he sat with his back against the cliff, whispering to Yávië. Her fright was so great he did not know what to do to soothe her.

As the other Guardians emerged from beneath the water, Näeré came to sit next to them. She whispered the soothing words of deep sleep and watched as Yávië relaxed in Sōrél's arms, small sobs still bubbling up from her terror-filled mind.

Nall reached out to touch Yávië's tear-stained face. He paused with his fingers a hair's breadth away from her and looked up at Sōrél. As their eyes met, Nall stroked Yávië's cheek and whispered her name. Then he reached inside his shirt and pulled out a small carving in the hideous likeness of Yávië's captor.

"Ya'vanna's Dragon, I presume.

"I did not think Yávië would want us to have to return for it."

The wizard Grumblton cared for Yávië in a bothie at Mourningmire. He ran everyone off, including Sōrél, before giving Yávië strong teas and herbal poultices for her fever. He did not like her wounds and and mixed a salve of prickleberry, chale bark—and a bit of magick for good measure—to place on them while he fussed and worried, mumbling over her as day became night .

"Not a dragon," he murmured to Sōrél when he finally allowed him into the room. "Nasty."

"Some kind of nasty demon. Nasty," Grumblton continued. "Very nasty. Most likely Alandon's doing."

"Will she be all right?" Sōrél asked, knowing "nasty" was one of Grumblton's favorite words and didn't necessarily mean anything.

"Aye. First thing on the morrow, we take Yávië to Rosie and tells her I gave her the willow bark tea, real strong, and what salve I used. Rosie gots better healing magick and that is what she needs."

He picked up his staff and turned, watching Sōrél draw back.

"Aye, I should strikes you, boy! But this is punishment enough," the Ancient said, looking back at Yávië.

"I shouldn't have to tell you this, but don't leaves her alone. She shouldn't have beens alone, Sōrél. Not no more. If you breaks these vows I'll do far worse than hit you with my stick."

Shaking his finger at Sōrél, Grumbleton left him alone with Yávië.

Pulling the chair to the bedside, Sōrél sat down and rested his head on the edge of the cot. He felt Nall and Näeré behind him before they spoke.

"Is she . . ." Nall began.

"Will she . . ." Näeré started.

"I don't know," Sōrél answered.

"I had just told her no harm would come to her in my care." He gave a bitter laugh.

"I am becoming a bigger liar by the hour."

"Nay," Yávië's whispering voice came from the cot, "I did not listen when you told me not to go alone."

Her sobs drew him to her and Nall and Näeré quietly slipped away.

Several hours later a knock at the door made Yávië's eyes wide with fear and Sōrél wished they could slay the beast again for the terror it had caused.

He opened the door and looked into Näeré's worried eyes.

"I brought her weapons," Näeré said.

"May I speak with her?"

Sōrél looked uncertain.

"Please."

"I shall wait outside the door. Do not be long."

Näeré went to Yávië and held her.

"Grumblton says you have shared the vows with my brother and that it will make us stronger against our enemies. I do not know if this is so, only that you have made my brother whole and for that once more I owe my pledge to you. Know this—if ever you need me, I will come."

She handed Yávië the slender sword with the dragon and serpent on its handle and hung the Sword of Domesius on the wall above her bed.

Sōrél had no sooner returned to his chair than there was another knock at the door. This time it was Nall.

"I shall wait outside," Sōrél snapped.

Nall went to Yávië and knelt next to the bed.

His eyes searched her face as he brushed her hair back.

"Yávië . . ."

Placing her finger to his lips she said, "I hear you are my hero once again."

He shrugged, uncomfortable with her praise.

"I have taken the vows of promise with Sōrél. I should have told you before it was done."

Nall frowned and then spoke honestly, "I might not have hit him so hard if you had."

Her eyes widened and she laughed, "You struck Sōrél for my honor?"

Her smile flashed again, "I am sorry I missed it."

With another shrug of his shoulders, Nall confessed, "It was not my finest hour."

"Nay, your finest hour was long ago when you pulled me from the dragon Ardane's dungeon. At least I thought it was rather fine."

He reached out and touched her hair.

"If he does not treat you well . . ."

"I shall call on you and Näeré."

"Aye."

Nall took her hand.

"Yávië, it is not . . . I do not think . . . you should not . . ."

"You are concerned that I shall quest while I carry a child?"

"Aye," he said gravely.

"Rosie will bless the child and hide its presence. We are stronger for this union, Nall. Will you trust me?"

Her eyes held the truth and Nall's nod gave his pledge.

"So does this make you the Serpent Queen?"

"You mock me, Nall."

"Aye, I do," he replied, winking as he headed for the door.

Pausing as Sōrél entered, Nall turned back to Yávië and added, "And I am sorry I once tossed you on your royal ass."

Nodding to Sōrél, Nall headed toward Näeré's bothie wearing a big grin.

The Hiding

The Ancients Rosie and Willow met them at the mirror below Meremire and did what they did best. They fussed. They fussed over Yávië and Sōrél, Nall and Näeré and gave Rydén and Zeth looks that set Nall's teeth on edge. Morg rushed Galen off to "lift something."

Sōrél was urged to take Yávië to her bothie where she could rest and Rosie could look after her. As soon as he had settled Yávië on her cot, Rosie shooed him away as if he were an errant grass cat.

Rosie took Yávië's hand in hers and said, "Soon there will be a daughter, a new queen."

Opening the door, Rosie nearly tripped over Sōrél.

"Come, come," she urged him and sat him down on the cot next to Yávië.

Taking their hands, she placed them together and blessed the child.

"I shall hide this child so none will sees her."

Lighting a candle, Rosie covered Yávië with the salt of the earth, adding flower petals and willow leaves as she whispered the incantation.

"Spirits of the children's light,
Shadows of the moonless night,
Gather ye now round that all may hear,
Gather ye now round that all may see,
Nall and Näeré in accordance as one,
Acting as guardians,

Shielders and protectors,
Hiding this small form from all who seek her,
So even whilst they search in earnest,
Lo, shall she not be found,
So it may be,
Let it be."

Rosie smiled and laughed.

"They will never sees her! Not until I lifts that spell. Nall and Näeré are bound to the child once she comes to us, just like Yávië asked."

Sōrél said to Yávië, "You could not choose two finer Guardians for a small princess."

"Has you tolds them?" Rosie asked.

A knock at the door brought Nall and Näeré.

"Did you call us, Rosie?"

"Aye. You are now guardians of the small princess. She is hiddens to all but those in this room. Keep her secret and do not speaks her name."

The child spoke her name into their minds and their hearts flooded with the responsibility of her care.

Yávië stood and pulled Sōrél to his feet.

"Let us use the swords, for my shoulder is stiff and there is still much to do before I am allowed a coronation."

"Aye," Nall agreed. "There are beasts to slay and worlds to gather before my new charge can begin her training."

Näeré laughed at him. "Do you not think it would be wise to await her birth before she begins her training?"

"Nay. One can never begin too soon, and by her mother's practice, she too shall feel the sword." Nall spoke with great certainty.

This drew odd looks from all but Rosie, who simply grinned her agreement.

Yávië's shoulder hurt, which made her angry. Weakness always made her angry, and anger always made her stronger. Today Zeth was taking the brunt of her anger as she drove him back across the field, eyes blazing and mouth upturned in a brittle smile. In her mind she saw the creature that had touched her and she felt helpless again. Though this time she was not helpless. This time she held the sword of the joined houses.

Fearing she would injure the young Guardian, Sōrél pushed Zeth aside and took his place. Yávië's fury was as strong as it had been in the cave of the trybrac, and he knew she must be allowed to let it go.

Sōrél pushed Yávië back, deliberately feeding her anger. He watched as her smile slipped away and her jaw tightened. She tossed the sword to her weaker right hand in order to draw the Sword of Domesius with her left. She swung the heavy sword in a circle, her eyes menacing as she began to destroy the demon that still haunted her nightmares.

Her thrusts were strong and vicious and her backhand provided Sōrél with glimpses of what death would be like at her hand. He allowed her to drive him back until he saw her sword arm weaken before beating her back into the middle of the field.

Nall stood with his hand on the hilt of his sword, but Näeré cautioned him.

"She must rid her mind of the demon, Nall. She feels soiled by its touch. Sōrél knows it is not him she sees at the tip of her blade."

Yávië faltered and fell to one knee, but quickly recovered and rolled away before leaping to her feet and striking low with her right hand blade, drawing blood from Sōrél's thigh.

"She may kill him, Näeré," Nall whispered, clearly concerned.

"Nay. He will not allow it, but she must feel she has won fairly—he cannot concede."

Yávië's exhaustion stole her form and her attack became simple hacks and slashes, one for every touch of the beast's thin, slippery fingers and slime-coated tongue.

As quickly as it had begun, her fury faded, leaving her collapsed and sobbing over Sōrél's beaten body.

"It touched me," she sobbed, gasping for breath. "I tried to stop it, Sōrél; I tried, but I could not. I could not escape its filthy touch. I wanted to die rather than allow it, but I could not die for I carried our child. I should have heeded your warning, I should have."

He held her, allowing her fear, guilt, and grief to flow over him.

Rosie looked at the wound in Sōrél's thigh, poking it until he winced.

"Why do you hurt me, Rosie?"

"Because you is a fool. What if she had killed you?" the Ancient asked as she smeared the healing salve upon the gash.

"Rosie, do you believe I would have allowed it?"

Rosie slapped him sharply. "I believe you would allow her to kills you if it was best for her."

His eyes clouded for he knew Rosie spoke the truth. For him, Yávië's needs would always come above his own.

"What you feels is good, Sōrél, but if it isn't tempered it will bring you death. I see the strength of your conviction and it makes me proud, but it frightens me as well . . . and it frightens Grumblton."

Sōrél scowled, for he knew a frightened Grumblton could be extremely dangerous.

"Will you care for our child, Rosie?"

"Aye, she is my charge. And Grumblton will teaches her magick. She wills be the best of both of you, Sōrél . . .and the worst as well. A storm within the fortress and a blight upon the land if her training isn't true."

"Nall and Näeré will see that her training is true."

He grinned at the thought of his child as a storm and a blight, for it was exactly the way he had thought of Yávië in her youth.

"As the prophecy is written," Rosie murmured on the way out the door.

Nall lay in the grass next to Näeré, watching the stars of a million souls awaiting their calling. His soul remained entangled with Näeré's, giving him the greatest comfort he had known. He rose onto his elbow to look into her eyes. They were closed, but her smile told him she sensed his gaze. As her eyes opened, he glimpsed his reflection in the mirror of her soul.

"What is it you wonder, Nall?" she gently prodded.

"I wonder why it is that we do not fight and attempt to kill one another as your brother and Yávië do."

"You wonder if it is because I am a witch and you simply do my bidding?"

Her face grew somber.

"Nall, I held you firm when my brother helped Yávië seek her truth. I possessed you with magick, trapped you with spells. But I have never bewitched you since that time, nor does any spell remain."

She felt him relax in knowing that his heart was true and no lie lay between them.

"We do not carry the weight of seven kingdoms, Nall, as do Sōrél and Yávië. Nor do we share the vows of promise."

He looked at her sharply and she placed her hand against his face. "Do not mistake my words. I do not ask a vow of you. I know that I hold your heart, your promise, and your honor. I know you would forsake all others on my behalf if I asked it, but I shall never ask it, for it would destroy your soul. I have never known a man of greater nobility. Except, perhaps, Sōrél," she added, poking him to lighten the weight of her words.

Nall laughed as he recalled exactly what he had thought of Sōrél's honor.

"Do the vows of promise make them angry?" he wondered aloud, causing Näeré to let loose her silky laugh.

"Aye, perhaps they do."

"Then I am glad we do not share them, for I would not want the magick of your sword at my throat."

She smiled in the darkness, believing he did indeed wish the vows of promise but did not know how to ask.

Rydén's head rested in the hollow of Zeth's shoulder and he knew he played with the flames of hell. Her brother would surely kill him, but somehow his death seemed unimportant when weighed against the silkiness of her hair against his cheek.

He chilled at the memory of the troll's grip on her and her frightened screams. He wondered if this was part of what Sōrél felt for Yávië or Nall felt for Näeré.

"Rydén," he whispered, waking her from a dream. "I will die soon at the hands of your brother."

Her golden laugh thrilled him, as did the emerald eyes now gazing at him with brilliant fire.

"I shall find a way to save you, Zeth, though I must admit I do not yet know how it can be done."

The dark horde paused beyond the woods of Meremire seeking the scent of the woman and her child, but the scent was lost. They turned back to rejoin their master in the depths beneath the Fortress of the Dragon Queen.

As Ya'vanna slept within a cocoon of silence, Alandon raged beneath the Fortress.

"I should have drowned him in the oubliette," he shouted to the shadows. "I was too kind, too trusting."

"Aye, Master, you are kind," hissed the voices of his demons.

"I have given my word to my daughter that she may have Ædracmoræ if she completes the quests for its rebirth. I will honor this, but there must not be a child, and my daughter must not publicly take the name of the House of Aaradan."

"The child has died," whispered his evil imps. "The dragon-demon killed it."

"Aye, or it is hidden. We shall watch for any flicker of its light. Send the horde to watch them from the darkness."

He sank down beside his spellbound wife.

"I love her, you know, Ya'vanna," Alandon said as he stroked his wife's face. "But she has betrayed me with the bastard son of Aaradan. I cannot allow the offspring of their union, for it will carry the blood of Sōrél's mother as well as my own. It cannot be allowed to live. I know that you will understand my beloved."

In her mind, Ya'vanna recoiled, knowing her husband had been completely lost to his brother Abaddon's dark evil.

Dreams

Sōrél's breath was at Yávië's temple. Within the dream, she slept in her bed in the queen's chambers of his fortress. Without a sound, she slipped from beneath the silken coverlet and felt the cool stone floor beneath her feet. A flame flickered beyond the chamber—a torch on the passage wall, perhaps. She took her cloak from the hook next to the door and stepped out onto the terrace above her garden.

The light of the waning moon cast silvery shadows beneath the trees, and the fragrance of flowers wafted up on the light air.

"Do you love my son?" a woman's voice whispered from the shadows.

Yávië placed her hands protectively over her swollen belly and backed toward her chamber door.

"I asked if you loved my son. Is this too difficult a question?"

"Nay, it is not difficult to answer, but why do you ask it in the language of my father?" Yávië asked reaching for weapons she did not carry.

The woman who stepped from the shadows was tall and slender. Her fair hair fell about her shoulders and to her waist below. Her eyes were the pale blue of summer blossoms, but it was her aura that drew Yávië's attention. It was the same beautiful sapphire aura that belonged to Sōrél and Näeré, and now to Yávië herself as a member of the House of Aaradan.

"It is the language of my ancestors, Yávië. I am Ileana, mother of your husband. I will ask again. Do you love my son?"

Still Yávië did not answer her question.

"My father wishes to kill our child. It is because of you."

"Aye, daughter of Alandon, but I must ask you once again, do you love my son?"

"Beyond my life and the life of my child," Yávië confessed.

Ileana nodded, smiling her approval.

"Do not fear your father. The child you bear has made you strong, as has the union of our houses. I will not allow Alandon to harm you, nor the child."

Yávië's eyes flew open and sought Sōrél. He sat as he always did in the chair by the window, and she lay not in her marriage bed, but on the cot of her bothie in Meremire. She was relieved to find her belly flat, their child hidden from view. When her eyes returned to Sōrél, she found him watching her.

"Your dreams disturb you, Yávië?" he asked. "My mother comes in the night to watch over us."

Throwing back the cover she went to him, sat at his feet and rested her head against his leg.

"I could smell the flowers of my garden," Yávië told him. "She said she would protect us and she asked if I loved you."

"Aye, she would want to know," he said, stroking Yávië's hair. "My father loved her as I love you. He taught me what it is to love so fiercely you are willing to die for the safety of another."

Then he shrugged as if it were unimportant and drew Yávië to her feet.

"Come, you grow chilled sitting on the floor and you must rest that your wounds might heal."

"She said she was the mother of my husband. Are you my husband, Sōrél?"

"Aye, Yávië, queen of hearts. My responsibilities grow great," he answered.

"Then why do you remain in the chair?"

He sighed. "Because it puts me between you and the door and it has become my habit."

In Nall's dream, the child stood in a meadow of tall crimson grass, rich sable hair dancing about her face in the light breeze.

Pulling an arrow from the quiver at her waist, she nocked it and drew back the bowstring, holding her breath to steady the shot as she had been taught by her father's Guardians. As the arrow flew straight and sure toward the heart of the grosshare she turned, sapphire eyes gleaming, and shouted to the man standing less than half a dragon's length away.

"I have killed it, Nall."

"How do you know that, Sōvië, if you do not watch the arrow strike the prey?"

"I just know, Nall."

Shaking his head, he went to inspect the fallen grosshare. The arrow protruded from the still pumping heart just as it always did. His pupil had never missed the mark, not even on the first day she handled the bow.

As always, it startled Nall how much Sōvië looked like Yávië. At first he had been alarmed to see Sōrél's brilliant sapphire eyes in this small face, but over time he had grown accustomed to their intensity.

Placing his hand on her shoulder, he laughed. "Sōvië, one of these days you are going to break our hearts."

She looked stricken and asked in a plaintive voice, "Why would I do that, Nall, when I love you all so much?"

Lifting her to the waiting dragon he answered honestly, "Because, little one, someday you will love another more."

Galen tossed in restless sleep as Alandon's voice sought him.

"Where is the child, Galen?"

"There is no child," he murmured with certainty and felt Alandon withdraw leaving him to his dreams.

Galen walked within the gardens of Xavian City, seeking Kayann. The sight of her brought a smile to his face as she waved to him.

He grasped her hands and held them tightly.

"Tomorrow I will ask Yávië to release me from my debt," he promised. "Tomorrow, at the end of the coronation ceremony. Then I will be free, Kayann. Free to make the pledge of my heart and free to return as the leader of my people."

Her eyes were bright and her lips soft beneath his.

In the visions of his sleep Zeth pushed Rydén out of the way and drew his sword. Nall crashed into him, driving him backward and to his knees. He quickly rolled away, as Nall himself had taught.

"Nall, I love her."

"Bah! You know nothing of love! You dishonor her by your behavior."

"Nall, stop!" Rydén's voice quaked with the fear that her brother would kill Zeth.

Zeth felt Nall's blade pierce his heart. He fell and watched as his blood soaked into the grass around him. Rydén dropped to her knees next to his body, weeping and telling Nall how much she hated him.

Within the dream, Zeth then found himself hanging upside down above a large barrel of water.

"You have sullied my sister's reputation, Zeth. What do you think I should do about it?" Nall's angry voice came from beside him.

Suddenly, Zeth's body dropped and he found himself drowning in the barrel of water. He tried to call out but that only drew more water into his breathless lungs. Finally, he was pulled free, gasping and shouting, only to be lowered once again into the drowning pail.

Zeth awoke with a start and looked around his bothie, fully expecting to see Nall emerge from the shadows.

Hanging his head, he realized that soon he would have to either talk to Nall, or stay away from Rydén because the night terrors were wearing him down.

Sōrél stretched out his long legs to ease the pain of the wound Yávië had inflicted. Rosie was right—he had been lucky it was nothing more. He rested his head on the back of the chair and gazed at his bride. Soon the coronation would come and he would give her what she asked. He loved the way her hands rested near her face and her hair fanned out around her as she slept.

His eyes grew heavy until he could no longer keep them open.

In sleep, he found his hand held by one much smaller, and he turned to see laughing eyes so like his own. Her face reflected Yávië and Sōvië's, dark hair fell down her back, curling at her waist.

"Father," her voice was like velvet, "do you think that Nall will let me have a dragon?"

"Is Nall in charge of giving you a dragon, Sōvië?"

"I believe he is."

"I will talk to Nall."

"Thank you, Father. Do not tell Mother though."

He kneeled before her. "Sōvië, we do not keep secrets from your mother."

"Don't we?" Alandon's voice cracked from behind them.

Turning to face Alandon, Sōrél swept his small daughter behind him and began to back away.

"Give me the child, Sōrél, and you will live a long life with your precious Yávië. I shall keep my promise. The two of you can rule for eternity as long as there are no offspring and you do not bind your house to mine."

Sōrél drew his sword, pushed Sōvië through the door behind him, and closed it.

Alandon's blade was swift and silent, cutting through the air and into Sōrél's heart even as he turned. As he dropped to his knees, gasping for breath, he heard Yávië scream.

Sōrél opened his eyes and wiped the sweat from his brow. Alandon must be stopped before he could harm them.

"Mother, I shall need your strength," Sōrél whispered to the night before moving to the cot and slipping his arms around Yávië.

Näeré kept a steady pace, matching her stride with that of the child beside her in her dream. Her brother's child, Sōvië, the future queen of both the House of Aaradan and the Seven Kingdoms of Ædracmoræ, ran swiftly like a frightened simplestag, but with much less effort.

She seemed able to run for leagues without exhaustion, and her skills with the bow and sword were remarkable for one so young.

Suddenly Sōvië stopped and held her finger to her lips, wrinkling her nose. A large bane boar ambled across the path in front of them—in search of butterpillars or bloodrens, most likely.

"They smell bad," Sōvië said, waving her hand in front of her face to clear the air.

"Aye, they do, and you will often smell them before you see them, which is a good thing indeed."

"Näeré, do you love Nall?" Sōvië asked, her eyes wide and innocent.

"Aye, I do," Näeré answered honestly, watching Sōvië's face crumple. "Why do you ask?"

"Well I was going to marry him when I grow up, but I won't if you love him because I would not want you to be sad."

Näeré said. "Thank you, Sōvië. I would be very sad without Nall."

"There are many handsome men in your kingdoms and we will find one for you when the time comes," Näeré added, resting her hand on the young princess' shoulder knowing Nall would kill her for even suggesting such a thing.

"Will you show me how to go inside a man's head and make him do what I want him to do?" Sōvië asked.

"Perhaps another time. Today we must practice collecting the correct herbs for our cloaking spell."

"Does my mother love Nall?" Sōvië asked, quite unexpectedly.

"Aye, but she loves your father more. Nall and your mother are friends, Sōvië."

"Nall is going to give me a dragon."

"Is he?" Näeré asked, wondering if Nall knew he was going to give Sōvië a dragon.

Chapter 30: Strength of the Sojourner

As the daystar broke the horizon, Sōrél called Nall to him. "I must ask that you test Yávië's sword arm in my place, for I am required at my father's fortress."

The question in Nall's mind was stayed by Sōrél's raised hand.

"Trust that it is for the good of our quest and that I must go alone. I shall return before the passing of the daystar and I ask that your eyes be sharp during my absence. Send Hawk aloft to watch as well. The darkness has withdrawn, but continues to observe us."

"Aye, Sōrél, I shall do as you ask. Is Yávië aware you will be away?"

"Nay, just tell her I deal with the preparation for our quest. Tell her I am with Grumblton, which will be the truth."

Nall shook his head as Sōrél went to the dragons in the meadow. Yávië was never easy when Sōrél was away. Going to Näeré's bothie, he decided he should prepare her for his bloodletting.

"Yávië, does your shoulder betray you?" Nall asked gently, for Yávië did not defend herself with passion; in fact, she did not defend herself at all.

"Nall, where did you say Sōrél had gone?"

"To consult with Grumblton."

"But where are they? They are not anywhere."

"Yávië, it is my job to test your arm, but I cannot if you do not defend yourself."

"I do not wish it. I will spar with Sōrél when he returns," Yávië said, walking away from him.

Nall gazed after her with suspicion.

"She will seek him out." Näeré appeared at his side.

"Aye, that is my fear. Why does he leave us to care for her when he knows she will not listen to a word we say?"

Näeré chuckled. "He knows that even though she will not obey, we will keep her safe from her own foolishness. Come, I see she calls a dragon."

The portcullis lifted as Sōrél approached, telling him that Grumblton had already arrived. Behind him, the gate settled into its slots with a resounding crash.

Hearing Grumblton's gruff voice, Sōrél headed quickly for the throne room where he found his mother sitting in his father's chair, listening to the wizard's concerns regarding her son's behavior.

"Is my honor in question?" Sōrél asked, kissing his mother's hand formally.

"Nay, your maturity!" fussed Grumblton.

"I have not been a child for many lifetimes, Grumblton."

"Nay, you just acts like one!"

Ileana raised her hand.

"What is done is done. Our task is to deal with it. She has become a lovely woman, Sōrél, and the depth of Yávië's commitment is more than any mother could ask for a son."

"You frightened her." His accusation carried the tone of a protector.

"It was not my intent. I forgot how my language would disturb her. You were foolish to confess your sins before her coronation. She could have killed you in her anger. You were even more foolish to plant your seed. What if Grumblton had not intervened with the vows?"

Sōrél said, "Then I would not have taken her. Unlike you, my mother, I have exercised restraint."

Seeing the hurt he had caused, Sōrél dropped his eyes and waited for his mother to end the silence.

"What you say is true, but you know that unlike Alandon I knew I should not stay. Even now, he causes Ya'vanna great pain by holding her soul. The love of the Sojourner brings nothing but trouble, as your father discovered too late. Indeed, I stayed too long, as you have so kindly reminded me."

"Mother . . ."

"Yes, Sōrél, it is difficult to know that your father and I shared no vows, but it is more difficult to wish away your life, is it not? For without me you are naught but a whisper in the darkness. Why did you not bring my daughter?"

"Näeré does not know you have returned. Indeed, I would not have known if you had not touched Yávië in her sleep."

His mother's movement toward him was slow, yet unrestrained. Unlike Alandon, she did not hide her delicate beauty beneath the shell of a vision. She enveloped Sōrél and touched his mind, feeling his bitter anger.

"Will you never forgive your father and me? Have you learned nothing from the Sojourner halfling whom you love?" She shimmered with the sting of his disapproval.

"You allow no room for flights of passion, even though you have felt them yourself. Your father died defending us. Did he teach you nothing?"

"Aye. He taught me I could not win against Alandon and so I ask you to lend me strength."

"Yávië seeks you, Sōrél. Bring her before me."

His mother sat upon the throne of the king and took the form of a Xavian woman.

"Do not question me, Sōrél. Bring her here."

Nodding once, Sōrél went to do his mother's bidding.

Unable to locate Sōrél on Æstretfordæ, Yávië had slipped beneath Meremire and followed the path of the mirrors to Æstaffordæ and the fortress. She followed the eastern wall of the fortress to the door where she and Sōrél had entered before, but it was closed and locked.

Feeling tears welling, she closed her eyes and shook her head to clear them. Why had he left her again? Not that Nall and Näeré were incapable of protecting her, but for some reason she needed desperately to be in his presence.

"Yávië . . ." Sōrél's whisper sent her rushing into the safety of his embrace.

"You were not just a dream," said Yávië when she recognized Ileana.

"Well, I was but no longer. I came to you in a dream in the hope that I would not alarm you, but alas, I did and Sōrél has chastised me for it. Indeed, my son chastises me for many of my careless actions."

With a gesture, Ileana brought Yávië close to her.

"The blood of the Sojourner is strong within you as it is within Sōrél. Your father fears the strength of this union, but it is not the place of the Sojourner to lay claim to his creation." With a sad smile she continued, "Alandon has long sought to destroy me and my house. Many have fallen in my defense. Now his greatest fear has come to pass and he will hunt you relentlessly if he finds you with a child."

"Our child is hidden from him." Yávië spoke with the certainty of truth.

"Aye, and will remain so until your quests are complete. I give the promise of my strength, for it is what my son asks. Before your public vows of promise, Alandon must be confronted. This will be done here, where his strength will be weakened by my own power."

Suddenly Ileana looked up. "My daughter calls."

With a look of irritation, Grumblton opened the gates to Nall and Näeré.

"Mother!" Näeré cried, running into her mother's arms.

Nall paused, looking from Sōrél to Yávië to Grumblton and back again.

"Why is it no one ever tells me anything?" he mumbled.

"Nall," Näeré called, racing back to him and dragging him toward the woman on the throne.

"This is Nall, Mother. He is my . . . " she blushed, looking for the correct word.

"He is your defender and your shield, for it is clearly evident," her mother said. "You are indeed their protector, Nall. It is with gratitude I speak of it."

Ileana beckoned Sōrél to her.

"I must not linger for I will draw the attention of Alandon's darkness. You are my firstborn, Sōrél, and as such you carry the blood of the Sojourner. It is by my command that its strength will be nurtured in you and your Guardians. Complete the quests and we shall speak again."

Accompanied by Grumblton, Ileana then drew away.

"I didn't know you had a mother," Nall said, producing smiles from both Sōrél and Näeré.

"She is our best kept secret," Näeré whispered to him.

Grumblton reappeared, looking crosser than usual, and Sōrél knew his mother had given instructions the old wizard did not like.

Upon their return to the mire, Sōrél sparred with Yávië.

"Keep your arm up, Yávië. I know that it is stiff, but Grumbl says it will get better with use."

"Perhaps I should just best you with my right arm. Would that satisfy you?" she growled.

"Nay, for it is the Sword of Domesius that I must see you wield, not that slender stick you found within the fen."

Laughing, she dropped to the ground.

"Nay, wench. Up! Come; do not make me drag you."

"Did you call me wench?" she asked, laughing even harder.

"Aye, as your husband I am allowed to do so."

"As my husband you may find yourself dead."

Dropping down beside her, Sōrél lay back to look at the sky—it had just begun to lose its deep topaz color as the daystar dropped below the horizon.

"I did not know the evening sky was so beautiful," Sōrél said in wonder.

"Perhaps you have never looked at it before," Yávië said, aware there was much Sōrél had never taken the time to see.

"Do not let the others see you like this or they will fear you have lost your wits."

"It may be true, Yávië, for my wits may have been stolen by a raven-haired wench." He laughed at his own nonsense.

"Defend yourself, sir, for I intend to batter you senseless," Yávië shouted, jumping to her feet and lifting her sword to meet him.

Nall's eyebrows rose as he watched Sōrél and Yávië's foolishness.

"I think I liked him better when he was surly and rude."

"Nay, he deserves some happiness—and I assure you his good humor will not last. You will have our unreasonable captain back as soon as we resume our quest. He is glad of the freedom from the lies of his deception, something he has never had before. I am glad she has given him that."

Chapter 31: The Seven Swords

"It is our goal to collect the seven swords that have been hidden in this kingdom. The locations are vague and we will need to be sharp if we are to find them all. Since there is evidence that the dark horde has withdrawn—temporarily, at least—Grumblton feels that it is safe for us to split up under cover of his shadow spell."

Sōrél briefed the Guardians over their breakfast bannocks.

"Zeth, one of the swords is hidden in or around Meremire and it is your task to locate it. I have tried to assign each of us to an area with which we are familiar in hopes of speeding our search.

"Näeré, you will seek the sword within the Northern Mountains.

"Nall, I am sending you to the Well of Viileshga, because you know it better than any.

"Rydén, your quest is for the sword within or around the Lake of Lost Memories.

"Galen, one sword lies within the walls of the Galenite Fortress, a place you know well.

"Yávië will seek the sword within the Land of the Giant Stones, for she knows the stone sprites, and I will collect the sword hidden within the Wastelands.

"We must have all seven to continue the quest. If you cannot locate your sword within a fortnight, return to Meremire and we will seek it as a group. Is that clear? I want every Guardian back in Meremire within two weeks—not a day longer." His look was stern and his voice sharp.

"Our Captain is back," Nall whispered to Näeré.

As the Guardians moved to collect packs and belongings, Sōrél pulled Yávië aside.

"I cannot allow you to quest alone, Yávië."

"But you told them . . ." she looked at him with wide eyes. "You lied to them."

"No, they know. I lied to you. I shall accompany you to the Giant Stones and then we shall move on to the Wastelands."

"I am neither frail nor an invalid, Sōrél. You make me look weak before them."

"Nay, but I make myself look wise. None of them would allow you to quest alone, Yávië. Is it not better that I quest with you rather than endanger them with your presence?"

"You mean that I am not weak but rather an evil portent to be avoided."

"Aye."

"I can live with that," she smiled mischievously, "since it will leave you alone with me and you will not have a chair."

Northern Mountains

Näeré hastened through the beauty of the Northern Mountains, her mind open to the call of the sword she sought. Earlier, she had seen its light against the dark morning sky. She moved toward a herd of bullrams grazing in an open meadow and called to their leader in beast speech.

"Have you seen the shadow beings, great one?"

"Aye, they lie beneath the leaves at the edge of the forest, witch."

"Do your require healing?" Näeré asked the elder when she sensed a twinge of pain from him.

"Nay, I require youth. Even a witch as powerful as you cannot restore that," he replied. "Soon my son will take my place and I will fall to dust, feeding the earth. You are a Guardian of the House of Aaradan?" he asked with interest.

For the first time Näeré realized the truth for indeed, she was a Guardian of the House of her brother.

"Aye, I am, and I seek a sword that was hidden within the time beyond remembering. Do you know it?"

"Nay, the only blades we see lie between the ribs of our fallen companions, but if you ask the netheraven that makes its home on the western crag you may glean the knowledge you seek. I have heard he speaks of the legend of the sword of the Sojourner."

Thanking the aged bullram, Näeré headed for the western crag. The idea of interacting with a netheraven caused a tightening around her heart, for she knew they were fierce and intolerant of visitors. Their talons were large enough to crush the skull of a Guardian, which would require weeks of painful healing at the hands of a wizard. The great birds were said to travel easily between the realms of the living and the dead and their knowledge of legends was well known. With a deep sigh, she allowed her thoughts to seek out Sōrél, finding him amid the driving sand of the Wastelands.

"Aye, Näeré, have you accomplished your task so soon?" he teased, well aware that she had not.

"Nay, I am about to throw myself in front of a netheraven and was hoping you might have some useful advice—if you can tear yourself away from the lips of your bride."

"My bride sleeps." His thoughts were suddenly curt, leaving no room for further nonsense. *"As for the netheraven, approach it from a horizontal position with your face to the ground and do not lift your eyes. Speak only from within your mind, as our voices are said to drive them mad with rage. Netheraven protocol makes dragon diplomacy seem like a game for children, so do not take my words lightly. Nall is closest to you. Call on him if you need assistance."*

"Aye. Shall I attempt to deceive the netheraven regarding my reason for seeking the lost sword?"

"Nay, speak the truth. Tell the netheraven you are sent by Sōrél of Aaradan. It will know if you lie."

Seeing the western crag in the distance, Näeré dropped to the ground, eyes on the earth ahead. A stirring of the air above her and the rustle of great feathers betrayed the presence of the netheraven. A low growl came forth.

"You are wise in my ways, Guardian," a voice purred.

"Who sends you?"

"I am sent by Sōrél of Aaradan," Näeré projected her thoughts.

"Indeed? And do you carry his authority?" the netheraven asked.

"Aye, I carry it in my blood and by his command."

"You come for the sword of the Sojourner, kept within the stones of my ledge. Your queen quests for the rebirth of Ædracmoræ, even though she knows it opens doorways that should remain closed. Do you serve this folly?"

"*I serve the queen without question.*"

"As it was told," the great bird whispered, "as it was told."

"You may look, Guardian, upon the vision of my strength that it may be burned into your mind for all eternity."

Fear seized Näeré, sending a chill across her sweat covered skin. She pushed herself up and rose to her full height before lifting her eyes to meet the legendary netheraven's bloody gaze.

With talons wrapped around the trunk of a fallen tree, it matched her height. Its feathers were covered with the soot of the deep holes that had been visited in order to feed upon the flesh of the damned, and its beak bore a coating of foul black blood, but it was the eyes that seized her soul, for they held the images of her past.

"Come, Guardian, and take your sword," the netheraven called as it flew to the peak of the crag.

The sword lay tightly wedged within the stone, and Näeré's fingers became bloodied in her effort to remove it.

"Speak the words of your Sojourner mother."

Näeré paused. A flood of ancient words from childhood rushed into her mind and she allowed them to flow across the sword now before her, watching as it freed itself and moved to her waiting hands. The heat of its hilt burned her mother's ancient name into the flesh of her sword hand. As the sword cooled, its beauty was revealed. The blade gleamed in the light, reflecting Näeré's image. The hilt shifted to fit her small hand and the ring guard nestled against her fingers. She heard her mother's voice whisper in her ear.

"*I offer strength, my daughter.*"

Beneath the Verdent Tree

Nall wondered why Rydén and Zeth had not set out on their quests with the others. The thought of each Guardian traveling alone made him uncomfortable, even though the horde had supposedly withdrawn. He definitely did not like the idea of Näeré alone, and the fact that Rydén and Zeth were questing in close proximity to one another raised his hackles. Sōrél and Yávië were another story and a part of him felt relief at their absence. In spite of his love for Yávië, dealing with her had become increasingly difficult. Hearing the sound of leathery wings, he turned to watch Azrea descend and bow her long neck before him.

"You return to us, Hunter," the dragon matriarch murmured as Nall leapt to her withers.

"It is good you return unscathed."

Nall chuckled at her choice of words.

"I missed you too, Azrea," he said, bringing a soft "shuff" from the dragon as they lifted into the air and headed for the Well of Viileshga.

The flight was silent, both Guardian and dragon lost in their own thoughts. Soon the plateaus of the Emeraldflyte appeared before them and Azrea landed heavily on the ledge of her lair. As Nall dismounted, Azrea turned and slipped inside.

"I shall return for you, Hunter."

Nall gazed across the verdant beauty of the forest as the gentle wind swept his mind clear. He missed this place, the forest and its beauty.

Hearing a familiar deep grumble Nall turned as the world began to tremble. His eyes grew wide as a dragon filled his field of vision.

"By the Ancie . . . !" Nall yelled as he drew his shield before him.

The thick smooth scales of the dragon's head crashed into the shield, sending Nall spinning off the cliff and into the empty sky towards the forest floor.

An emerald blur lifted from below and he found himself grasping the withers of a dragon. He heard a heavy "shuff" from his mount.

"Have I been gone so long that you have forgotten how to play, Nall?"

Nall fell back laughing and did not stop until he once again stood on the ledge of Azrea's lair watching the startled Matriarch.

"Ardor, what in the name of the Sojourners were you thinking?" the Matriarch blustered. The very thought brought a new burst of laughter from Nall.

"Ardor—*think*? The fiery depths of the abyss would freeze before that would happen!"

Ardor lifted a talon and gently pushed Nall back a bit.

"Oh, it is great to see you old friend," Nall exclaimed.

"And you, Nall. You have grown stronger since last we spoke."

"As have you, Ardor. What brings you back to the Emeraldflyte?"

"I return at the request of my queen. You have Azrea to thank for my presence," Ardor answered, nodding to the matriarch.

"Azrea, is this true? You have taken Ardor as your mate?"

Azrea gave a nod, eliciting a grin from Nall before he suddenly turned somber.

"I wish I had the time to remain with you but I am called to accomplish my quest within a fortnight or Sōrél will seek me out." Nall frowned at the thought of Sōrél coming to fetch him.

"I must speak to the spirit within the verdant tree and learn the location of the Sojourner's sword."

"Do not burden yourself with regret, Nall. The quest of the Dragon Queen is a difficult one. Perhaps Ardor may carry you to the great tree, allowing you time to share your memories?"

Nall smiled as Ardor lowered his broad head to receive his Hunter.

Their flight was filled with the joy of reminiscing and before long, they were in the shadow of the verdant tree.

Dismounting, Nall watched as Ardor dropped to his belly and picked up a stone, tossing it in the air for amusement. Nall called out to the spirit, Adra, as he entered the cave beneath the roots of the great tree.

"*Hunter, you return.*" Adra's voice rang in his head.

"I do. I come seeking the sword of a Sojourner, one which will be used in the reunification of Ædracmoræ."

"*As foretold, Hunter. We know the location of the sword you seek for it has long pained us.*"

"Pained you?"

"*Yes, Hunter. One of our roots encountered it and it has remained lodged there. We cannot move the root for the blade causes us pain.*"

"Well that will not do," Nall mused. "Is it possible for you to create a passageway to the sword so that I might remove it?"

"*A passage lies in the east wall. Follow it and you will find the blade.*"

Nall advanced along the corridor, illuminated by a series of buds. Finally, he arrived at a great root wall where a large bud opened, its light revealing the sword he sought—the sharp blade thrust up beyond the root.

Nall looked at the blade, wondering how it could have harmed the root, since it appeared to be fully exposed.

"*Hunter,*" Adra's silent voice warned. "*Before you take the blade you must know that your presence has drawn the attention of Alandon's deathshades. By removing it you may bring them to you.*"

"Then I shall be ready for them and they will meet the blade's edge."

Nall looked for a place to grip the sword, at last finding its hilt near the base of the root. Grasping it firmly and bracing his leg against the root, he prepared to withdraw the sword.

"I do not wish to harm you, Adra."

"*Do not worry, Hunter. We are prepared. The blade must be taken, for it belongs to you.*"

Focusing his strength, he pushed off the root and the blade slid free so easily—as if it had not been held at all—that it caused Nall to fall onto his back with the metal no more than a thumb's width from his chin.

Rising to his feet, he examined the dual blades, one at either side of the central hilt. Equal in size and exquisitely shaped, each was cut with a series of sharp-hooked edges and covered with ancient words. Nall turned his attention to the hilt, upon which he noted the intricately carved words of the Sojourner. A sudden knowledge of how to wield such a blade filled his mind and brought with it a recollection of past battles. A vision of Sōvië swept into his consciousness briefly.

"*Guardian, Hunter, shield and protector.*" The voice was not that of Adra, but of Sōrél's mother, Ileana. "*With this blade I grant you my strength, as is my son's wish. You have been chosen as the child's Guardian; her care will be entrusted only to you and my daughter.*"

"I also care for your son and his queen," mumbled Nall, causing Ileana to share her soft laugh.

"*You speak the truth, Guardian, and my daughter's heart swells at the sight of you. I charge you with her care as well. With the gift of this sword comes great responsibility.*" As she faded from his mind, he felt the strength she had promised flowing over him. He gave a chuckle, thinking that even before the child was born he was being prepared to protect her.

Nall emerged from the burrow beneath the tree to see Ardor coming under attack from deathshades, the great dragon bellowing in pain. As he slid to a stop before the deadly demons, he drew the Sojourner's sword and watched as the deathshades pulled back in a moment of fear. With a wailing that could curdle the blood of the dead, they surged toward him, lashing out with their claws. As one struck his chest, he felt the crippling loss of energy as the deathshade drew out Nall's amber life light.

Recovering from the pain, Nall struck, cleaving a deathshade in half, its black flame rushing out accompanied by a tortured scream. Ardor sent a stream of noxious acid across the deathshades, leaving them writhing and twisting in a mass of dissolving bone and ethereal cloth.

"Well done, Nall. I have never seen you wield a blade so skillfully."

"Thank you, Ardor. I am grateful for your skill as well."

Ardor "shuffed" his acknowledgement and lowered his neck, allowing Nall to mount. With strong strokes of emerald wings, the dragon lifted them from the earth and turned toward Meremire.

As his hand rose to the still searing wound on his chest, Nall whispered a plea to the Ancients that all would return safely to Meremire.

The Giant Stones

"Yávië," whispered the many voices.

The sprites swarmed from among the Giant Stones before drawing back in fear at the sight of Sōrél.

"Sit down, Sōrél, so that you do not seem so frightening," Yávië insisted.

"I am not frightening. My weapons are not drawn and I have not committed any act of aggression," he mumbled.

"Aye, you are frightening to ones as small as these." Yávië smoothed his frown with her fingers. "And even I fear your frown."

As it always did, her smile brought his compliance and he sank to the ground to sit cross-legged beside her.

"That is better," Yávië whispered, placing her hand on his shoulder to show she did not fear him.

"Yávië."

She heard her name whispered again by the many. Sinking to the ground, she sat with her back against Sōrél's chest, letting his warmth flow over her.

"They must recognize you as mine," she leaned back and whispered up to him.

"Shall I show them you are mine?" he offered.

"Nay, that would not be appropriate in this situation," she said and jabbed him with her elbow.

"You let them see you beat me?" Sōrél whispered in mock injury.

"Aye, perhaps I should strike you with my blade to reassure them."

Suddenly he held her still.

"I believe the elbow has done it," he said. "See? They come."

The sprites moved swiftly toward Yávië, first coming close and then flowing away like a wave upon the shore. Their comic indecision caused Sōrél to laugh aloud, sending them scurrying back to the stones.

"*Sōrél!*" Yávië reprimanded him.

"I did not know your friends would be so timid," he whispered in an attempt to stay his laughter.

"Yávië, does this one hurt you?" came a worried whisper.

"Nay, he is truly my love and I share the vows of promise with him. He will not harm you, little sprites," Yávië promised.

Once again, the sprites approached; this time more slowly and cautiously, but still showing great interest in the one sworn to Yávië.

As they arose in the air around Yávië and Sōrél, she cautioned him not to frighten them again, and soon they sat upon his shoulders asking questions of their Yávië's heart of hearts.

"Yávië saved us, you know," spoke one brave sprite. "We were locked within the stones and by her passing she set us free."

"Aye, she has spoken of it," Sōrél acknowledged. "She says you protected her while she slept."

This caused a great ruckus of excitement, for the stone sprites were honored to have cared for Yávië during her rest.

A small female sprite approached and brushed Yávië's cheek with her hands.

"Do you know you hold the child?" she whispered. "The hidden child of the joined houses?"

"Aye. How is it that you see her?" Sōrél's voice was sharp, causing the sprites to flee.

"We hold the knowledge of the sword you seek," the timid voice responded, "and we guard the child and her mother."

"Yávië, is there anyone who does not guard you?" Sōrél asked, hugging her tightly.

"Aye," she whispered, "my father does not."

Sprites rushed to her and took her fingers in their hands.

"Come, Yávië," they spoke in unison. "Come and take the sword, for it belongs to you."

"Let us collect my sword," she said, pushing Sōrél ahead of her to follow the now giggling little sprites.

Amid the twelve stones stood one that was mightier than the others, for it was broader and taller and slanted slightly to the east. The sprites rushed toward it, and in a flurry of activity—too quick for the eye—they felled the stone, exposing the dark opening below.

"Wonderful," Sōrél murmured in Yávië's ear. "They must have heard how much we enjoy being below the earth."

Her small hand sought his as she remembered her last encounter beneath the falls on Æstaffordæ.

"There is no danger, Yávië," spoke the same sprite who had so lightly stroked her face earlier. "We would never place you or the child in danger."

Yávië sighed and smiled her thanks before allowing Sōrél to light a torch and lead the way down the steep stone steps. Moisture seeped in among the stones, lending luster to the walls. Butterpillars fleeing the light came to the attention of Xander's sensitive nose. The wee downy flier leapt from Yávië's bodice and raced madly after them, grabbing and gobbling contentedly.

At the bottom of the steps, far beneath the earth, they found the promised sword. It lay between two golden dragons' claws, glowing as if from a light within. Its hilt was gold and the gleaming metal blade carried the symbol of the Dragon Queen. As Yávië lifted it her aura pulsed and shimmered, flowing out to the tip of the blade and back again. She gave the sword the deep indigo color of her union with the House of Aaradan.

The sprites tittered and Xander chirped as he slipped back into the darkness near his mistress's heart.

In her mind, Yávië heard Ileana whisper, "*I give the promise of my strength, for it is what my son asks.*"

The Wastelands

To remain hidden from the horde, they traveled in the blinding light of the desert, the wind whipping the stinging sand against hoods raised to protect their eyes. To Yávië's unspoken relief Sōrél finally led her into the shelter of the rocks.

"We shall rest," he said, looking at her with concern. "You tire."

"I do not," she replied abruptly.

"Yávië, there is no shame in growing tired," Sōrél said, brushing the sand from her face. "Fighting the sand makes us weary, and since we may need to be strong to collect the sword, it makes sense to rest now."

She nodded, making him smile at her concession, for even an admission of tiredness went against every fiber of her being. To actually be tired was unacceptable.

Shaking the sand from his cloak, he spread it out for her to lie upon and took a seat on the stones next to her. He allowed his hand to linger on her shoulder until her eyes closed.

Sōrél felt Näeré probe his mind and listened carefully as she inquired about approaching a netheraven. Giving all the advice he could, he settled his strength over her as she faded from him and sent a plea to the Ancients to keep her safe.

The faint sound of falling sand alerted him to movement and he prepared to defend his queen.

"Sōrél of Aaradan?" the sand whispered.

"Aye, and what are you?" Sōrél asked, eyes squinting against the light sparkling off the sand that continued to fall, grain after grain, from the stone before him.

"I am only sand, but I cover the sword of the Sojourner that you seek."

Sōrél laughed and woke Yávië, who drew back in alarm.

"I do not doubt that the sword I seek is covered by sand, for I stand upon a desert."

"Sōrél, to whom do you speak?" Yávië asked, looking left and right.

"I speak to the sand that covers the desert."

Yávië stood to touch his arm and felt it steeled to strike an invisible enemy.

"Sōrél, sand does not speak."

"Aye, it does; it whispers of our quest."

"You have grown tired."

He swung on her, pushing her back even as the sand rushed toward them. Grabbing the cloak, he swung it over them and waited for the shifting sand to stop moving.

"Yávië?" he whispered to her in the darkness of the cave he had created.

"Aye, Sōrél?"

He turned and clung to her, wishing them away.

Finding herself standing in the blazing daylight, her eyes narrowed in anger.

"You cannot use your powers within the confines of the quest, Sōrél," she snapped. "It is forbidden by the laws of my father."

"I can and I have, Yávië, your father's laws be damned."

"First you talk to sand and now you have broken the trust of the quest. Have you lost your mind?"

"Perhaps I have. Is it a sign of madness for a man to think of nothing but a woman, to place her needs and desires above all else?"

Her eyes softened and her hand reached toward him, but she did not touch him. His eyes were filled with obsession and pain.

"I no longer know, Yávië."

"Have I made you mad, Sōrél?" she asked her eyes wide with concern.

He drew her to him with a tired sigh. "If I am mad please do not let my madness end, for it is within it that I am happiest. It appears I have not broken the trust of the quest, as you can see." He gestured toward the gleaming golden hilt of a sword rising from the sand where they had been confined.

Sōrél lifted the sword and watched as the symbol of his house appeared upon its blade, the coiled serpent reaching out to strike the tip. The ancient language of the Sojourners flowed over him, and granted him the strength of his mother's blood.

The Galenite Fortress

Galen slipped down the steps to the lower level of his fortress. Just being there brought him pangs of homesickness. As acting ruler, Kade had honored Galen before the Council of Elders and held a feast among the citizens. After all the camaraderie and hearing the news of Kayann and the Xavians, Galen had been left with a driving desire to release himself from his life debt to Yávië.

He had long considered asking Yávië to release him. However, he knew that it would be a pointless request until Ædracmoræ was reborn at which time his services would no longer be needed. Until then, he remained the seventh Guardian required to complete the circle called for in the ancient promise of Ædracmoræ's rebirth.

The stairs grew damp and the air musty as he descended deeper beneath the earth. These chambers had been created from an existing cavern structure, and they retained the natural beauty of those crystal caves.

A voice had come to him in a hushed whisper, "It has been seen but not seen, touched but not touched."

He followed the low-pitched murmur. He recognized it as the language of the Sojourners, and it drew him steadily eastward to the hidden Sojourner's sword. Another voice came suddenly, causing him to draw his sword before he realized it was only within his head. It was the voice of a young woman, soft and pleasant, but the words carried a harsh warning.

"Do not betray me, Galen, for the universe is not great enough to give

you sanctuary. My mother trusts in your life debt, but I hear the voice of Alandon whispering to you in your dreams. Do you serve me, Galen, or do you serve the Sojourner of my mother's house?"

Galen felt the tightening in his mind.

"I could hurt you, Galen, but I choose to trust my mother's judgment. Do not fall short of her trust for the consequence will be swift retribution from those who watch over me."

He saw her then, the child of Yávië and Sōrél, her hair a tangled mass of sable that cascaded to her waist, framing her face, a face that had borrowed its beauty from Yávië and then heightened it. The eyes rivaled the sapphire intensity of Sōrél's, filled with the same brilliant light of goodness and truth. The hilt of her sword was visible above her right shoulder, the dragon and the serpent proclaiming her as Queen of Ædracmoræ and the House of Aaradan, her barely constrained strength pulsing in the deep indigo aura of her birthright.

Galen bowed his head before the image and whispered the words of truth, "I serve Yávië, the true Queen of Ædracmoræ and the House of Aaradan."

Her smile left him weak and he recalled a day long ago when he had first seen her mother within the Queen's forest.

"I shall see your life debt released. We shall become fine friends, Galen of Æstafforde." Sōvië's words and image were branded into his memory.

As he looked about, he realized he had reached the easternmost wall of the caverns. The Sojourner's sword was clearly outlined behind the crystal. Its glow intensified as it slipped from its hiding place and into Galen's hand. The words of the Sojourner Ileana poured over him, offering strength.

Galen held the sword aloft. As its power and strength filled him, he marveled at its balance and grace

"Galen." Alandon's harsh voice shattered his thoughts.

"Is there word of the child?"

"Nay, Alandon. There is no child," Galen assured.

As he felt Alandon pull away, he frowned and whispered to himself, "At least not one you will ever find."

Lake of Lost Memories

Valia loped along beside Rydén, stopping every now and then to examine a scent and then racing to catch up.

Rydén could see the sparkling waters of the lake through the dense forest. Since the lake took memories and never returned them, a sword hidden in its depths seemed preposterous, but Sōrél was rarely—no, never—wrong about a quest, so she would seek it.

Her mind wandered to thoughts of Zeth and the predicament in which she found herself. He was so much more than what her brother would see, but so far, she had been unable to think of a way to get Nall to see the real Zeth. Zeth became tongue-tied and inept around Nall, causing her brother to see him as a less than desirable suitor for his baby sister. She thought warmly of how tenderly Zeth treated her and how he had so swiftly come to her defense in the troll's lair.

She noticed that Valia had stopped and seemed to be examining something in the distance. Kneeling next to the grass cat, she used her far sight to scan the same area. There was motion low to the ground making the grasses and fireferns rustle and shift.

"*What is it?*" she asked Valia in the silent words of beast speak.

"Bastcat. Big bastcat," Valia whispered, her tail twitching in anger.

"What is a bastcat?"

"Demon cat person." Valia licked her lips in nervousness and the fur along her shoulders rose as the bastcat drew nearer.

"*What do you suggest, my furry companion? Run, climb, or fight?*"

Valia remained alert and uncertain, her weight shifting from paw to paw, as she exposed her claws and drew them in again.

"Should not be here," Valia hissed.

Looking at Rydén, she growled deep in her throat. "Fight, Mistress. We fight now."

A flash of dappled fur burst through the trees. It stood on two legs like a man, but was clearly feline. A snarl erupted from its short muzzle as it launched itself at Rydén.

Valia leaped up, grabbing the bastcat around the chest and clawing furiously at its soft underbelly as they crashed to the ground in a tangle of legs and tails.

Rydén nocked an arrow and watched for an opportunity to hit the attacker without endangering Valia, but the two entangled cats continued to yowl and roll.

Seeing an opening, Rydén sent her arrow into the bastcat's throat, sending it rolling away with blood gurgling up through the wound. She waited until the animal was still, its slide into death interrupted only by an occasional hiss and twitch, and then knelt down next to the beast to examine the sleek head and strong body. It wore a leather belt around its neck with some unrecognizable writing carved upon it.

"Do not touch it, Mistress," Valia panted at her side.

"*Does it have a master, Valia?*"

"Aye, some will come for it," Valia whispered, looking around nervously.

"We go now." Valia padded off several paces.

Rydén rose to follow, but had not taken a step when her feet were suddenly knocked out from under her, and she found herself looking up at the distorted features of a troll. She quickly rolled away, leapt to her feet, and drew her sword. The troll removed the leather collar from the bastcat, then turned and held it out towards her, nodding its misshapen head. Rydén glanced around for others, since she suspected trolls rarely traveled alone.

The troll grunted and shook the collar at her, snorting with every breath. Extending her sword, she indicated that the collar should be placed on the blade, and watched as the troll approached with the collar extended. As it eased the collar over the tip of the sword, Rydén realized her folly. Another troll suddenly seized her by the arms and she heard Valia's howl of pain.

The troll before her grabbed her sword and with a rumbling laugh tossed it aside. It extended its long, hairy arms and slipped the collar around her neck, fastening it tightly and attaching it to a rough braided rope. The second troll released her arms and Rydén immediately reached for the collar, bringing a swift slap and guttural response from the troll who now seemed to be her new owner. It turned and walked off, jerking her sharply as it moved around the lake.

From the trees, Zeth watched as the troll and its companion led Rydén away. Without a second thought, he let out a fierce howl and raced toward them. He sliced his sword into the back of the neck of the nearest troll, jerking it free to hack into it again with a strong backhand. As the first troll fell, Zeth turned toward the startled troll still holding Rydén by a rope. With a flick of the wrist, he sliced the rope and yelled for Rydén to run.

The troll lifted its ax and shuffled forward, ready to do battle. With a snarl and a yowl, Valia shook off the fogginess left by the troll's kick to her head and leapt onto the creature's back, kicking her hind legs against it as she shredded its flesh. Without waiting for an invitation, Zeth thrust his sword deep into the belly of the cat-covered troll, causing the tiny eyes to widen and an unearthly scream to erupt from its gaping jaws.

Quickly withdrawing, he called Valia to disengage and she bounded toward them. Together the three of them raced away from the lake.

Collapsing on the grass, he turned toward the gasping Rydén.

"What were you thinking trying to befriend a troll?" His deep frown told her he was serious and she began to laugh.

"That was not an act of friendship; I just wanted to see the collar."

"Well, you got your wish. You seem to be wearing it."

Her bright laugh bubbled up as he unfastened her collar and handed it to her. It seemed to uncurl within her hand, lengthening and stiffening, pulsing and shimmering with magickal light.

It was not a collar but a sword—inscribed with the words of the Sojourner's promise of strength.

Meremire

Zeth and Rydén returned to Meremire where Grumblton, Morg and Rosie fussed over the deep red marks the collar had left on Rydén's neck. They examined the sword more closely, looking at the ancient writing along the blade and the carved bastcat on the hilt.

"What an odd way to discover a sword," Rydén murmured. "Now we can complete your quest together," she said, taking Zeth's hand and looking up into his eyes.

They failed to notice the raised eyebrows of the Ancients as they walked off toward the field.

"Sōrél's not going to likes it and Nall is going to downright hates it!" Morg muttered, looking after the two young Guardians.

"Aye," Grumblton agreed, "I will see if Sōrél can stops it before Nall kills 'em both."

Rosie smiled and whispered, "Don't you remembers when you was in love, Morg?"

Morgwort nearly choked.

"I was never!" he shouted, stomping his foot.

Grumblton flushed a deep shade of scarlet and hurried himself off toward his bothie, away from Rosie's twinkling eyes and teasing laughter.

Zeth leaned against the wall, looking down at Rydén. He pulled a blade of grass out of her hair and tossed it to the ground.

"It really is peaceful with everyone away," Rydén whispered with her eyes averted shyly.

"Aye," Zeth agreed, wondering just when the Guardians would return and just how safe he was standing there at the wall so close to Rydén.

"So I wonder where the Meremire sword is," he added.

"In the wall," Rydén said, pointing to a cool blue glow within the stones of the wall at the end of the field.

Together they ran across the field to kneel at the wall.

"Do you see it?" Ryden asked.

"Nay, but it must be there. What else would produce a sudden glow like that?"

Zeth began to lift stones away from the wall, setting each one carefully aside to be replaced later. As he got closer, the light began to pulse and glimmer just as the collar had done before it changed into the sword. Its beauty was mesmerizing and spurred him to move the stones away more quickly.

"I see it," Zeth whispered. "It has the writing on the blade, the ancient words of Yávië's father."

Lifting away the last stone, he picked up the sword and held it aloft.

"For Yávië's quest!" he shouted, exuberant at their discovery.

Suddenly, he found himself kissing Rydén. He had absolutely no idea how it had happened but he knew he liked it very much. Grabbing the sword, he tucked it into his belt, lifted Rydén up and carried her toward her bothie.

Sunlight was filtering through the window and the day doves were cooing their morning song when the door to Rydén's bothie flew open to reveal a rather bemused Sōrél. He sat on the chair and placed his feet on the table.

"We need to have a little discussion," he said, grinning at the obvious discomfort of two young Guardians. "Have either of you given any thought to what will happen if word of this reaches Nall?"

"Aye," Zeth whispered as a deathly pallor overtook his face.

"Well, it will not be pleasant for any of us. Rydén will have to beg and cry, and mourn your life. You will be slumbering among the stars awaiting your next calling, and I, as your Captain, will be forced to apply some sort of punishment for Nall's ungentlemanly behavior. As I said, unpleasant for everyone."

The door opened again, and Yávië stepped inside, causing Zeth to blush and look everywhere except at her.

"I thought this could use a woman's touch," she said, smiling sweetly before she drew her sword and held it beneath Zeth's chin.

"My husband is too subtle. This ends here and now," Yávië said curtly, looking directly at Rydén. "I will not have your brother enraged and distracted from this quest. Is that clear?" She looked at each of them in turn, withdrawing her blade as they stuttered their agreement.

"Zeth, I would strongly suggest you take yourself somewhere besides this bothie before Nall returns." Without another word, Yávië turned and exited.

Allowing his feet to drop to the floor, Sōrél shook his head.

"She does not want you hurt," he said, looking at each of them seriously. "There will be a way to handle this, but now is not the time."

"Rydén, you encountered trolls near the lake?" he asked.

"Aye, it was the strangest thing. They traveled with a bastcat. I had never heard of such a creature before, but Valia seemed to know of them."

"It is possible the trolls have escaped from their underground lair. We should be watchful."

"Zeth, meet me on the practice field." Nodding to them both, he exited the bothie.

"Perhaps I can turn him into someone Nall can respect," Sōrél said quietly to Yávië. "What we must do in the name of love."

Upon Galen's arrival—the last of the Guardians to return to Meremire—they gathered at the practice field to examine the seven swords of the Sojourners. Each was unique and carried the ancient words that conveyed Ileana's promise to lend them strength. Sparring was heated and Yávië insisted on testing Nall's strength with his new double-bladed weapon. She attacked him passionately, using both of her blades and offered high praise for his proficiency.

"Perhaps you will be able to guard my daughter after all," she whispered with a wink as she walked away, leaving him breathless, but with a lopsided grin on his face. He wondered whether she might have bested him had she not withdrawn.

Rosie called to Nall and he hurried to see what she needed.

"You comes here." She jerked her head indicating Willow's bothie.

"Haven't we told you to let us knows when you was hurt?"

"I am not hurt . . ." he began before her staff struck him.

"The deathshade lefts its mark on you. I can sees it in your crippled aura."

"Sits," she demanded, looking to see if he would earn another thump. However, he sat promptly, causing her to titter behind her tiny hands.

"Willow gots the herbs for that and the spell to make it heal; takes your shirt off, boy! How can we look at it if you keeps it covered up?"

Nall unfastened his shirt and exposed the ugly inflamed wound left by the claw of the deathshade.

Rosie peered at it closely but did not touch it.

Willow entered carrying a basket filled with herbs and salves and got right down to business.

Shaking her head, she repeated Rosie's admonition that he should tell them when he was hurt, causing him to smile at their concern.

Frowning, she lifted her staff.

"You thinks it's funny?"

"Nay, I do not. I see absolutely nothing humorous about that raised staff or your concern for my health," Nall assured her.

Näeré burst in the door and gasped at the sight of the wound.

"Why didn't you tell me?"

"There just has not been time and it is an inconsequential wound—just a scratch really, and already beginning to heal."

"That is a scratch? Willow, how bad is it?" Näeré asked the busy Ancient.

"Oh, I can heals it, but if we hadn't treated it, it might have gotten bad." She glared at Nall again.

With a murmured spell and an application of magickal salve, the little Ancient covered the wound with clean spider cloth and wrapped a bandage around Nall's ribs to hold it in place.

"No sparring until I says you can. Do I needs to say it to Sōrél?" she asked, raising an eyebrow.

"Nay, I will listen," Nall promised, thinking how much misery he would feel if Sōrél were made aware of Willow's admonition.

Tomorrow was a day of rest anyway. Nall would spend it in the company of Näeré. Things could be much worse than having a woman care for you.

Zeth was sparring with Sōrél who was becoming impatient.

"Keep that sword arm up or I shall be forced to cut it off," Sōrél snapped.

Nall stood up from his seat on the wall, but Näeré stayed him with a single reminder, "Willow."

He fumed in frustration, watching Sōrél batter his apprentice.

"If you wish to win against Nall you will require two very good sword arms and nerves of stone," Sōrél reminded Zeth.

The thought of fighting Nall in anything other than a friendly sparring match made Zeth feel ill. Why did it have to be so hard to love a woman?

Sōrél paused. Walking swiftly to Näeré, he commandeered her sword and returned to his pupil, tossing it to him.

"Now, keep the weaker sword before your face and chest. Use it as a sharpened shield. Attack me with your stronger arm. Do it!" Sōrél said angrily, drawing his own blade again.

"You need to fuel your anger, Zeth. What brings a fire to your blood? Is it the thought of another man's hand on the shoulder of a woman you protect? That is certainly sufficient to feed Nall's fury, I assure you," Sōrél chuckled.

Nall watched as Zeth seemed suddenly to grow taller, stronger and more aggressive. He grinned at the thought of Sōrél discovering the key to the young Guardian's passion. He would have to ask Sōrél what words had fueled Zeth's fury.

A frown creased Rydén's brow as she slumped down beside Rosie.

"Isn't there some spell you can cast over all of them so they will leave us alone?" she asked, sending Rosie into a gale of giggles.

"It isn't funny, Rosie. My brother watches me as if I were a mere child. Sōrél and Yávië treat us as if we were villains. There must be something you can do."

"Already Sōrél does it," Rosie answered.

"Sōrél does what?"

"Makes Zeth strong." the tiny Ancient nodded as if she were making perfect sense.

"Rosie, Zeth is strong. He is brave and kind. Why cannot everyone else see it? He has saved me twice from the trolls."

Rosie nodded. "But he does not have the fever in his blood."

Rydén rolled her eyes and sighed in exasperation.

"Men," she muttered.

Galen threw a log on the fire and settled down to construct a new scabbard for his blade. He looked up as Rydén stomped out of Rosie's bothie and threw herself down on the ground not far away.

"Does Rosie cause your unhappiness, Rydén?" he asked.

"Nay, though she refuses to help me. Galen if you wanted to . . . well, court me, how would you approach my brother?"

Galen gave a gruff laugh. "I believe I would attempt to kill him in his sleep, as it would be the only safe way to approach him."

"Do you see? It is impossible." Rydén appeared near tears.

"I assume we are speaking of the young Zeth," Galen said, tossing a stick into the fire.

"Shhhhh! Do not even speak his name aloud in my presence. Even Yávië and Sōrél have forbidden us one another's company."

"Rydén, they know Nall. He would act first and feel regret later, as men often do when they feel protective of someone. There is much work to be done before we complete our quest and none of us can afford to be distracted. Bide your time and what you seek will come to you."

"You speak as if you truly believe your words," Rydén said.

"Aye, I bide my time as well."

Chapter 32: Ileanna's Promise

Yávië sat before Grumblton, her eyes fixed on his leathery face, fascinated by the tale he told. Sōrél as a child . . . the very thought made her feel warm.

"Contrary, he was!" Grumblton said, shaking his head. "Always needing to discovers his own truth, never trusting in another's. Your child bears his hardheadedness," he chirped.

"Aye, and mine as well," Yávië agreed, smiling at her own admission of so grievous a fault.

Yávië closed her eyes and allowed Grumblton to fill her head with images of Sōrél's life. It was one much like her own, one of privilege and power, expectations and encouragement . . . until the night the horde came for them. Images of the brutal attack caused her to gasp. They spared none. She saw Aaradan lower his children into the oubliette, saw him slide the heavy grating into place as he whispered for them to remain quiet. Yávië watched as the slender dragon-handled dagger was thrust into the stomach of Sōrél's father. She heard the words of his assassin, vicious accusations and threats in the voice of her own father, Alandon, as he sought the Sojourner Ileana and her children.

As her eyes opened, Grumblton touched her sleeve.

"By the joining of your houses, you has caused Alandon's wrath to rise again. Ileana will help you. She remains hidden among the Xavians as do others of her kind."

Startled, Yávië looked down at Grumblton.

"There are other Sojourners?"

"Aye, a few. They hides among the Xavians."

Yávië recalled Ileana and her tall, almost ascetically thin appearance, her pale skin and hair, large, luminous eyes that were nearly devoid of color—only the faintest hint of blue—features delicate in every detail—the perfect image of a Xavian.

Yávië hugged Grumblton, making him fuss and squirm. She grinned at him as his cheeks grew rosy and a smile tugged at the corners of his mouth.

"See? You like me, Grumblton; you cannot help yourself." Yávië hugged him again and raced out to call Aero.

Nall and Näeré watched Aero land lightly in the meadow beyond the practice field.

"What do you think Yávië is up to this time?" Nall asked.

"I do not know, but I imagine it will most likely bring trouble," Näeré said.

Together they approached the dragons resting in the pasture.

Xavier, empathic ruler of the Xavians, held Yávië's hands and smiled into her eyes. "You come to see Sōrél's mother, Ileana. She expects you."

He led her to chambers befitting a queen, the walls covered in silken fabrics and the bed topped with a lark feather mattress. Ileana sat in a chair near the window beneath the waning star light. Her aura shimmered silver and sapphire in the glow of the fading twilight.

"Yávië," Ileana said, enveloping her son's new wife and touching her mind to feel the questions there.

"Sit, Yávië, and we shall speak of your concerns."

Yávië sat.

"Your concern for Sōrél is unfounded. He is well prepared for the task ahead. Galen's mind has been strengthened against the assault of Alandon, and Nall and Näeré are already bound to the child you carry."

Yávië laughed and nodded. "Nall and Näeré follow her even now."

"Aye, one of them will always be within half a dragon's length of her. She will grow tired of it long before she comes of age," Ileana said.

"Are there other Sojourners, Ileana?"

Ileana bowed her head and whispered, "Hidden."

"You must go before Nall and Näeré seek us out. Sōrél also moves toward you. It would be best if you returned to Meremire. A gathering of members of the House of Aaradan will draw your father's unwanted attention. I promise you my strength. We shall speak again soon." Once again, Ileana enveloped Yávië in the comfort of her mind before stepping back and turning away.

As Yávië reached Aero, she raised her hand and waved to Nall and Näeré.

"I sought the council of the Xavians," she shouted as she urged Aero upwards and back toward Meremire.

Näeré turned to Nall.

"Sōrél comes. Let us leave Yávië in his care and hunt the stag. I promise I will let no harm come to your wound."

"Aero comes," Faera thundered to Sōrél.

Silently Sōrél sent his war dragon mount toward the smaller and lighter wind dragon that carried Yávië back to Meremire. As they drew near, he had Faera circle and come around on Aero's flank.

Yávië's cheeks were flushed and her eyes bright.

"I can see that leading Nall and Näeré on a merry chase and speaking with my mother have agreed with you."

"Aye, both proved quite enjoyable. Let us return to Meremire and consult the Book of Quests, for it is soon that we must seek the Blood Stone."

Sōrél followed her, his eyes scanning the horizon for any unusual gathering of darkness.

Chapter 33: The Blood Stone

"Between the waters at the heart of Æcumbræ lies the sacred stone of lifeblood. With this stone the child of the blood may call the spirit of the earth and draw Ædracmoræ's shattered kingdoms nearer. So says the Book of Quests," Yávië read.

"Again our quest is as clear as cream-clouded tea," Nall murmured.

"Aye, we do not have much direction, but we must trust Yávië's sight to guide us," Sōrél responded, unperturbed.

"Morg calls for the seven swords of Æstretfordæ and asks that they be entrusted to his care. See that he receives them." Sōrél pointed to Nall and watched him collect the swords of their quest and take them to Morg's bothie before speaking again.

Turning to Näeré, Sōrél asked, "Is his wound healed?"

"Aye, it satisfies Rose and Willow," Näeré answered, bemused by her brother's tact.

As Nall entered Morg's bothie, he prepared himself for the tongue-lashing he usually received without provocation from this bad-tempered Ancient. To his surprise, Morgwort was wearing a wide toothy grin.

"Puts them here." Morg indicated a round table.

"The double blade goes 'cross the center and the others three by three on either side."

The wizened little man with frizzy white hair watched as Nall drew each blade and positioned the swords as requested.

"Stays," he ordered when Nall turned to leave.

"This magick be for you."

Nall leaned against the wall and observed as Morg began an incantation. The long double-bladed sword began to hum and its blades began to glow. The other six swords seemed to become liquid light and bleed across the table, three toward each of the double-ended sword's blades. As they were drawn into the hooked blades, they solidified and, in a final brilliant flash of amber, became one.

Morg chuckled and winked at Nall. "Out of the seven comes the one; 'tis the blade of the one who serves the child."

Lifting the long-bladed weapon, Nall hefted it, feeling the new weight of the added blades. It felt as balanced as if it had been crafted by a fine forge.

The blade's hilt suddenly split, leaving Nall with two identical swords.

Raising his eyebrows, he glanced at Morg.

"Aye, 'tis the magick; by one or two can this blade be wielded."

Morg pushed the swords toward one another and the hilt coalesced to form the original double-bladed sword.

"I will keeps it safe until the coronation," Morg stated, pulling it from Nall's hands and pushing it beneath his cot.

Nall's fingers itched to take the sword, but he knew it was not yet time. With a final lop-sided grin for Morg, he left the bothie and re-joined the Guardians as they prepared to leave for Æcumbræ.

The Guardians stepped through the mirror into Æcumbræ, and each noticed the damaged frame. It was as if someone had attacked it in great anger, scarring the wood and attempting to erase the ancient words. Even after its cleansing and repopulation, Æcumbræ remained a dark world covered by heavy fog, the topaz daystar never fully exposed.

Lighting torches against the gloom, the Guardians headed up the passageway toward the surface of the shadowed world. They emerged into a silence that was quickly shattered by the call of a startled bloodren.

Yávië's eyes closed, seeking the artifact they had come to claim.

"It lies beneath the sand between the waters." She spoke with certainty. "There," she indicated, pointing north.

They set off at a slow run, slicing through the mist as they traversed hillocks of humpgrass and gasparfen. Behind them, the dense fog immediately returned to its humid and vaporous blanket—no less final than if a solid door had been closed, so evanescent their presence in that world of shadows.

A sudden warning shudder from the downy flier Xander caused Yávië to pause and call quietly to Sōrél, "There is danger."

None questioned but simply drew their weapons, seeking the threat.

It came swiftly in the form of deathshades, their gossamer tendrils moving silently through the mist as they attempted to draw close enough to strike.

Näeré's mind reached out to hold them back, allowing the Guardians to safely send their arrows and pin them to the ground. The deathshades writhed and screamed with angry voices before Nall and Galen severed their heads and sent the oily blackness of their empty souls fleeing back into the darkness.

Yávië stood frozen as the tendrils of the remaining deathshade slowly circled her. Her eyes locked on Sōrél's and she swept the sudden thoughts of their child from her mind, causing the deathshade to draw back in confusion, its master's desired prey lost. Yávië felt the blade stir the air before her as Sōrél's sword sliced swiftly and angrily through the evil. The stench of death rose around them as the last shadow being was separated from its soul.

"Why do they seek us here?" Yávië wondered aloud.

"It is because we draw close to the end of the quest. Soon it will be too late to stop the rebirth of Ædracmoræ. Alandon told me he would not make it easy."

"When did you speak to my father?" Yávië asked in a hushed voice.

All eyes were on Sōrél.

"He caught me at his fortress. I told him it was all you wanted, just to reclaim Ædracmoræ. I begged him to allow it and he agreed, but said he would not make it easy. Then he called me a fool. It is no more complicated than that."

"Was it before . . . ?" Yávië asked, clearly shaken.

"Aye, it was long before you tried to kill me in the trybrac's lair."

He reached out to touch her hair and her eyes held his.

"There are no more secrets between us, Yávië," Sōrél whispered so that only she could hear.

He pulled her to him and held her, smiling at the relief he saw on Nall and Näeré's faces.

Fáedre's Pledge

The Guardians had arrived at a cliff overlooking a long stretch of sand that lay between the sea and an inland lake.

"Between the waters," whispered Näeré, shaking her head. "Perhaps that is what it meant—between the sea and the lake."

Nodding her agreement, Yávië turned to Sōrél, "Perhaps it is hidden in the sand along the shore?"

Nall and Galen scanned the sand and the water lapping it from both sides.

"It leaves us exposed," Galen spoke.

"Aye, I do not like it," Nall answered.

"Nor I," Sōrél admitted.

"We must look," Yávië called as she began to work her way through the trees that grew from the cliff face, followed closely by Näeré.

Seeing Nall's look of doubt, Näeré shrugged, "We cannot allow her to go alone."

Reluctantly, Nall moved to join them. "I believe we are going to regret this," he hissed after her.

At the base of the cliff grew a few stunted trees. Salt poisoned and wind blown, they offered little in the way of cover. The Guardians were crouched below them, looking carefully in every direction. Although there did not appear to be any sign of danger, they kept their weapons drawn as they moved out onto the empty expanse of sand.

"There is nothing here," Rydén said, looking up and down the shore. The others agreed there was no sign of life anywhere.

A single grain of sand moved along the shore, gathering others as it drifted closer to the group of Guardians. Each time they glanced in its direction it paused, waiting until they looked away before continuing to advance. As the group headed back toward the distant cliff face, it began to move forward more rapidly, gathering unto itself with a new frenzy such that the forming of a woman could be discerned. The shifting and redistributing of the grains continued until no sign of sand was left, only the image of an old woman leaning on a walking stick.

"Child of the blood?" the woman's voice caused the Guardians to turn as one, pushing Yávië behind them.

"Aye," Yávië spoke firmly. "I am the daughter of the Dragon Queen and the Sojourner Alandon."

"You must come with me," the woman called, gesturing for Yávië to join her.

"Nay," Sōrél and Nall spoke together.

"She does not leave my side." Sōrél repeated Nall's thoughts aloud.

The woman of the sand laughed, "Oh, I think she will come with me, for I hold knowledge of the stone of blood she seeks."

"I shall come," Yávië whispered, advancing purposefully.

Sōrél leapt forward and grabbed her around the waist. "Yávië, remember the cave beneath the falls."

He felt her shudder and regretted his need to remind her of the terror.

"I cannot allow you to go alone."

"Child of the blood, once I fall to the earth this opportunity will be lost. I shall not return again."

They watched as the woman's feet began slowly to turn to sand and crumble away in the sea breeze.

"Please, Sōrél. I must have the Blood Stone. Without it I cannot cast the spells. Please."

"Yávië, I cannot."

She turned and watched as the woman's lower legs dissolved into grains as she sank toward the earth.

"Allow me to come with her," Nall called to the woman of the sand. "I serve as her Guardian and it is my appointment to accompany her."

Näeré's voice was choked with fear and she clutched his sleeve. "Nall, do not do this."

He placed his hand over hers. "Näeré, I must."

"So be it. Come." The woman beckoned again as Nall stepped away from Näeré and took Yávië's hand from Sōrél.

"I will allow no harm to come to her while she is in my care," Nall promised.

Näeré stepped forward, but Sōrél blocked her way.

"This time you and I must wait," he whispered, his eyes filled with uncertainty.

Yávië allowed Nall to lead her toward the woman of sand. As they came near, she cackled with glee, dissolving and sliding as she merged into the vortex that appeared below her. The Guardians then watched in astonishment as Nall and Yávië were swept beneath the churning sand.

Näeré dropped to her knees next to the spot where Nall and Yávië had disappeared and began digging furiously, but Sōrél put his arms around her and drew her up against him.

"We have to trust Nall this time, Näeré."

"They are gone!" she screamed, pushing away and slapping him. "You just stood there and let them be taken. You let Nall be taken *again*!" She sank to the sand, sobbing, "*Again*, Sōrél."

Beneath the sand Nall stood holding Yávië's hand. There was sand beneath their feet and sand above their heads but to their left and right were walls of water. The woman of sand once again gathered herself from the grains before them.

"Come." She beckoned them forward.

They followed at a distance, even though there seemed to be nowhere to escape. Nall quietly drew his sword and kept it hidden behind him as Yávië did the same.

Suddenly the woman turned toward the sea, creating a passage beneath the water. She beckoned them again, encouraging them to follow.

"I don't like it," Nall muttered, adding in amazement, "We walk beneath the sea."

They watched a swarm of iridescent ghostfish swim across the wall.

"I have been beneath the sea before, but never like this," Yávië whispered in wonder.

Ahead of them, their guide had stopped and was pointing toward a sloping passageway.

"You will go alone now." She pointed the way. "She waits for you."

"She—who?" Nall asked, gripping the hilt of his sword tightly.

"The one who holds the stone," the woman answered. "You will not need your weapon."

Nall gave the woman a doubtful look and, holding her hand more tightly, led Yávië down the passage. As they approached the end of the passageway and it seemed they could go no further, the water parted before them, revealing an underwater grotto. There upon a ledge lay a great dragon. It was a war dragon of extraordinary beauty, her black and red scale patterns clearly marking her as a Matriarch.

Yávië pulled away from Nall and drew nearer.

"Matriarch, why is it you lie beneath the sea?"

"Huntress, I have awaited your coming. Once you have taken the stone I shall be released from this task to wake my flyte within the cliffs."

"Who has bound you here?" asked Nall suspiciously.

"I serve the Sojourner Ileana and have long rested here as guardian of the Blood Stone."

Suddenly the great dragon reached toward Yávië with her talon extended, causing Nall to bring his sword swiftly into play.

The Matriarch's fiery eyes flashed and her scales rose in threat.

"Hunter, had I wished you harm I would have dealt it quickly and without preamble. I seek only to touch the child of my pledge."

Yávië closed her eyes as the dragon's claw touched her.

"You can see the hidden child?" she whispered her concern.

"Aye, but do not fear. She will be our charge, bound to us by pledge. On the first day of her tenth summer, Fëan, my firstborn son will emerge from the egg bound to her by my honor and the honor of the Deathstoneflyte. I am Fáedre. I have pledged my flyte to this child and throughout eternity we shall be bound."

"You, Hunter, will bring her to me on that day," the Matriarch commanded Nall, "as it is foretold."

Nall merely nodded, eyes never leaving the dragon's claw that lay so close to Yávië's heart.

Withdrawing her talon, the Matriarch gave a low rumbling purr. "She grows strong, our Sōvië."

Shifting her tail, she revealed a small round stone. It was porous, and from it oozed the lifeblood of Ædracmoræ.

"The Blood Stone," she spoke in a hushed tone, "the heart of Ædracmoræ. Take it and I shall carry you to the surface and reunite you with those who wait."

Collecting what little dried wood could be found, the Guardians had built a fire on the sand between the waters.

"I do not believe they will return," Galen muttered. "They have been taken by the horde."

"Nay, Galen. I would know if Yávië had been harmed. I can feel her heart beat strongly within my chest," Sōrél declared.

"Aye, my brother speaks the truth," Näeré added. "Nall touches my mind even now. They are not harmed, though I still do not forgive you for allowing them to go." Her words cut Sōrél with the sharpness of a dagger.

A sudden surge from the sea flooded the sand around them and caused the Guardians to leap up and move away from the now extinguished fire. They watched as it smoked and sizzled, and then came the sound of thunder and a quaking of the earth.

Eyes wide, the Guardians watched as a monstrous war dragon settled on the sand before them.

"Hail, Guardians of Ædracmoræ. I return the woman and her protector to your care."

Sōrél saluted the Matriarch, "Hail Fáedre, Matriarch of the Deathstoneflyte. Your service is ended and you are free to return to the cliffs. May the words of the Sojourner bring you peace."

The great dragon lowered her head and sniffed Sōrél, uttering a low moan of recognition.

"Sōrél, child of Ileana and Aaradan, your scent restores me. I shall sing the legend of your return."

Turning to leave, she paused, "You seek the Star of Sangria? It lies beneath the rubble of the fallen tower."

Her enormous wings snapped open and the current of air she

stirred was strong enough to blow the remains of the fire into the sea.

"Sōrél, you knew what they would find. Why did you not speak of it?" Näeré looked up at her brother from the safety of Nall's arms.

"There is no clear promise before us. This time we were fortunate and things were as once foretold. I cannot see what tomorrow brings."

"Let us return to Æshardæ where we may rest before we move on to Æshulmæ. There will likely be resistance there as it holds the last artifact that we seek."

"She pledges Sōvië," Yávië spoke her hushed thoughts.

"Aye, she is bound to the house of Aaradan through Ileana. I was her charge when I was a child. Her flyte is strong and they will move into the hills beyond our fortress upon your coronation."

Laughing, he added, "I am sure she must have had instructions for Nall."

"Aye, Nall was quite fierce with her as she sought to touch me. I believe her posture was without real threat, though her words were stern."

"She would never harm you or Nall, but no dragon may allow a threat to pass unchallenged."

Led by Sōrél, the Guardians made their way back to the safety of Æshardæ.

Nall watched Zeth sparring with Galen, amazed by his apprentice's improvement. Zeth was no longer allowing his sword arm to drop, thereby exposing himself to certain death, and he rarely sparred with a single sword, but used two as Sōrél had instructed. He also fought with passion—as if his life depended on it.

Turning to Näeré he asked, "What do you think is driving Zeth?"

"You ask this of a witch?" she teased. "A woman brings the fever to his blood. Nay, do not ask me which woman for I cannot speak her name."

Nall turned back in time to see Zeth forcing Galen to the ground in concession, the sword of his strong arm placed against Galen's heart.

"She must be some woman," Nall whispered.

"Aye, that she is," Näeré said.

Nall played her answer over in his head, wondering where Zeth had found such a woman within the confines of their quest.

Yávië ran beside Sōrél, watching him out of the corner of her eye. While she could match him stride for stride, she oftentimes pretended she could not. He caught her eye, making her look away.

Slowing, he took her arm and pulled her to him.

"You examine me."

"Aye," she whispered, "I cannot see anything but you."

"Is this a sign of madness? Next you will be talking to sand," he teased.

"Sōrél, you see the future, I know that you do."

He grew solemn and placed her hand upon his heart.

"Yávië, our future is hidden and we write its promise as we move forward. With the fall of the House of Aaradan my visions of the future ended. I see naught beyond this moment."

"I wish only peace."

"Then you will have it, for I will make it so," he said. "You know, I can deny you nothing. I shall tell Nall and he will summon an army to keep your peace."

"You are teasing me."

"Perhaps . . . just a little."

"I worry that we shall fail."

"Yávië, we are too close to the end for failure. I shall see you to success. Will you rule wisely? I do not know. You are passion, Yávië, and I am anger. Together our fire grows hot and we must be mindful that we do not burn those we care for with our flame."

"Soon we must return to my mother's fortress for the jewel of my birthright. Will you show me what you hide there?"

"Aye, Yávië. I shall keep no secret from you."

With those words, Sōrél knew that he would again draw Alandon's anger.

"They seek the final artifact," the demon hissed to his master.

"And there is still no sign of a child?" Alandon asked.

"Nay, none has been seen. The woman's aura is strong in the color of her house, but there is no indication of a child."

The beast shrieked as Alandon's foot lifted it from the floor and hurled it into the wall. "Not the color of *her* house! The color of *his* house! The House of Aaradan! What must I do to rid myself of Aaradan and Ileana? Death has not done it. I shall be forced to rid myself of Sōrél and that sister of his—there is nothing else to be done."

In the darkness of the room, he walked behind a tapestry and opened a small box that lay on his table. Gently, he lifted two tiny creation crystals from it and held them before his eyes.

"When they lie within these crystals I will crush the House of Aaradan with a final blow." He slipped the crystals into the pouch he carried around his neck and returned to the chambers within the lower level where he stopped to talk with his unconscious wife.

"Ya'vanna, we are going to a wedding and you will be the most beautiful woman there. I shall bring a special gift for the family of the groom. It will be delightful," Alandon whispered, stroking her cheek.

Chapter 34: Alandon's Treachery

"Granddame," cried the spirit of Sōvië's frightened voice.

"What gives you fear, Sōvië?" asked Ileana.

"Alandon seeks to trap my father and Näeré. I saw it."

"It is wise you have come to me, for you know I shall never allow it to pass. Share it with Nall in his dreams of you so that he will be alert. Did Alandon say when he intended this treachery?"

"Aye, at my mother's wedding. He has crystals for the House of Aaradan. He does, Granddame, I saw them."

"Hush, I believe you Sōvië. Now go quickly to Nall."

Nall's sleep was fitful as he searched his dreams seeking the woman of Zeth's passion. He heard footsteps behind him and turned to see the child who would one day be his charge racing toward him along the passageway of her father's fortress.

"Sōvië?" He lifted her into his arms.

"What is it? What frightens you? Tell me and I shall fix it."

"Granddame said to tell you. Alandon seeks to trap my father and Näeré in a crystal. He said it is a wedding gift."

Her small warm hands clasped either side of Nall's face and her eyes burned into his.

"Do not let him take my father and Näeré. He will crush them away."

Sōvië's eyes were bright with tears, sending the heat of rage through Nall's blood.

Nall woke to find himself alone in his bothie, but the memory of the dream remained burned into his mind. Dressing quickly he hurried to warn Näeré and Sōrél.

"Come Näeré, we go to Sōrél. I have had a dream, a vision—I do not know what—but there is a threat and I know it to be true."

He pounded on Yávië's bothie door and was not surprised to find Sōrél fully dressed and armed.

"Your mother sent a dream of Sōvië to warn us. Alandon intends to try to imprison you and Näeré in crystals at the wedding following the coronation. We must not allow him entrance to the fortress during the coronation and wedding. It is too dangerous."

"She warns us to remain alert and so we shall. We cannot forbid Alandon entrance for he must be present at the coronation. It is required. Yávië cannot accept the crown from any other than Ya'vanna and Alandon," Sorel responded.

"I shall not accept the crown if it means risking the lives of you and Näeré. I simply shall not," Yávië said without hesitation.

"Yávië, you must. There is no way to end this treachery save by taking your mother's throne and the power of the crown. You will have to trust that we shall be safe."

"Do you suddenly see the future, Sōrél?" Yávië asked in soft reprimand.

"Nay, but I trust my mother's words. Ileana promised no harm would come to us and none will, for she lends her strength."

"Näeré?"

"Yávië, Sōrél speaks truly. Nall, we know that Alandon is coming and we shall be ready for him."

Nall was shaking his head in violent disagreement.

"We are talking about Alandon. His strength is great, and he wants to destroy all that remains of the House of Aaradan, you and Sōrél. We cannot risk it."

"He cannot remove the House of Aaradan without removing me," Yávië whispered. "He does not know Sōvië exists."

"We gain nothing through disagreement." Sōrél's voice indicated the discussion was over.

"Tomorrow we shall travel to Xavian City and seek advice from your mother. Then we shall make our decision." Yávië's tone left no room for argument and her eyes were fastened on Sōrél.

Wisely, he nodded his agreement and opened the door for Näeré and Nall.

"Do not waste your night with worry," Sōrél said as he closed the door behind them. "Yávië, come sit with me and listen."

"Sōrél, I have seen what happens when I am foolish and headstrong. I shall not risk losing you or Näeré."

"If I can convince you there is no risk, then will you see reason?" Sōrél asked.

She sat next to him and took his hand.

"I shall listen, but I make no promises regarding reason."

Sōrél rose early and gave instructions for what was to be done in his absence. He winked at Rydén, causing her to blush and almost run into the wall of her bothie. Shaking his head at the folly of youth, he moved off to find Nall and Näeré. As they walked down the passage toward the mirror that would take them to Æstretfordæ they heard Yávië's voice raised in anger.

"I have given you an order, Zeth. Accept it as if it came from Sōrél, for you will not like the consequences if you do not."

Zeth stood looking at the ground.

Yávië smiled as if nothing were wrong, receiving odd looks from Näeré and Nall.

Sōrél simply turned to Zeth and said, "Whatever she asked you to do, I suggest you do it quickly."

Zeth nodded and rushed away, leaving behind an awkward silence.

Nall started to ask what had happened, but a stern look from Sōrél silenced him. As Yávië and Sōrél stepped through the mirror ahead of them, Näeré looked at Nall.

"It must have had something to do with the woman," she offered.

Taking his hand, she led the confused Nall through the mirror.

As they stepped into Æstretfordæ Rosie rushed up to them, gurgling and cooing as if they were long lost children.

Looking at Nall, she pointed to his chest and said, "Let me sees."

"Rosie, it is well healed."

She seemed to get taller and her staff began to twitch, causing Nall to rapidly unfasten his shirt and kneel so she could poke at the scar.

"Good," the little Ancient said, and patted his arm.

"Yávië come to my bothie." Rosie turned and marched off, knowing very well that Yávië would be right behind her.

"I shall try not to let her keep me long," Yávië said to Sōrél.

Näeré decided to accompany her, leaving Nall to ask Sōrél about Zeth.

"Why was Yávië so angry at Zeth?"

"She gave him advice about his love life and he did not take it well," Sōrél laughed.

"Everyone seems to know about this woman except me," Nall stated with irritation.

"Aye, it is embarrassing for Zeth, and since you are his mentor he asked that we not mention it," Sōrél muttered, turning away to hide the hint of a smile—he was certain that Yávië had instructed Zeth to spend the day with Rydén in the safety of Nall's absence. No wonder the young Guardian was bewildered.

Rosie laid her ear against Yávië's womb and whispered softly to the spirit of the child within.

"She comes to us in dreams, Rosie." Näeré spoke, "How is it possible that she comes to us."

"She is not bounds to her earthly body yet. She can move wherever she likes. But today she bes home resting with her mother. You is well, Yávië, and so is she," Rosie assured them.

Together Näeré and Yávië went to the meadow where Nall and Sōrél waited.

"What did Rosie say?" Sōrél asked.

"She said that Nall and Näeré were doing a fine job watching over their charge and that all is well. She even smiled when she said it, so it must be true."

"She probably would not have been smiling if she knew what you and Nall had done on Æcumbræ," Näeré pointed out.

"Some things are best left untold, though Nall kept me very safe." Yávië grinned at Nall, imagining the fuss the episode would have caused among the Ancients.

Whispering Aero's name, Yávië watched as the dragon lifted, launched skyward and circled toward her.

"Will you ride with me?" she asked Sōrél.

He gave her a leg up and then leapt up behind her.

Looking over her shoulder, Yávië watched Nall mount Azrea behind Näeré and wished they were going to Xavian City to visit the gardens instead of to discuss Alandon's threats with Sōrél's mother.

As always, Xavier was at the gates to meet them, smiling at Yávië and touching her mind for a moment. He offered his hand to Nall and Sōrél, congratulating Sōrél. He nodded to Näeré before leading them to Ileana's chambers.

"Mother." Sōrél kissed his mother's hand formally.

Näeré gave her mother a hug and frowned at Sōrél for his continued remoteness.

"Yávië, you are well?" Ileana asked, beckoning Yávië forward.

"Aye, Rosie told me this very morning that all was well."

At Ileana's touch, an image of Sōvië shimmered before them.

"She is strong. She fears for nothing save the threat against the lives of her parents and her Guardians. I have assured her that you will be safe." Ileana looked past the image and into Nall's amber eyes.

"She brought you a warning?"

"Aye. That Alandon intends treachery during the speaking of the public vows."

Releasing Sōvië's image, Ileana stood.

"Follow," she instructed.

They moved into her antechamber where four Sojourners were gathered.

"We are seven," Ileana gestured. "Alandon, Abaddon and I close the circle. In the time beyond remembering, we arrived among the people of Ædracmoræ and forgot the laws of the Sojourners. Grievous harm has come to many through our selfishness, indeed an entire race of symbiotic Wreken was driven into servitude and sorrow ending with the shattering of Ædracmoræ's kingdoms at the hands of Alandon. Now comes the time for us to right the wrongs. Our council shall restore the trust of the Sojourner to the inhabitants of Ædracmoræ at the rebirth of the world."

"Yávië, you hold Abaddon close to your heart and this is not wise. Will you entrust his prison to our care?"

Sōrél lifted the golden thread holding the small spider cloth bag over Yávië's head.

"Yávië, why do you still hold Abaddon?" he whispered.

"I would crush him for what he did to Nall." Her eyes stung with tears.

Ileana said sadly, "Crushing the crystal would only serve to release him, for the life of a Sojourner is not so easily taken. If you will entrust him to us I assure you he will be held. His darkness clouds the memories of my people and draws your father ever deeper into shadow through his binding to the horde."

"And what is your wish for Aléria?" Ileana continued softly.

"Aléria?" Yávië reached for the pouch in Sōrél's hand as the words she had spoken to her twin played in her head . . . I cannot allow your freedom, Aléria, for I have decreed no mercy on this day. The harm you have done can neither be forgotten nor forgiven, but if you wish it, I shall take your soul into my care.

"I promised to care for her soul even though I cannot forgive her betrayal. She is my sister," Yávië whispered as her tears fell freely.

"Yávië, will you entrust her care to Grumblton? You cannot be allowed to carry this burden."

"But I promised . . ."

"Yávië, my mother speaks the truth. You cannot allow Aléria to remain near your heart. It is dangerous."

Sōrél wiped Yávië's tears and handed his mother the pouch carrying Aléria and Abaddon..

Ileana inquired, "Fáedre has given you the location of the final artifact?"

"Aye, she said it lies beneath the rubble of the tower on Æshulmæ. I assumed she meant Sylwervyn's tower," Sōrél replied.

"Yes, you will see the pulse of the star above the tower in the night sky. Follow its light and retrieve it. Yávië, only Näeré may touch the Star of Sangria. Heed my warning. Focus on your quest—the day of your birth approaches and the spells must be cast before star rise on that day."

Ileana summoned Nall to her. "Protector of the House of Aaradan, watch over them." Her voice soothed him and the touch of her hand lent strength for the task.

"So, who is Sylwervyn?" Nall asked as they walked to the waiting dragons.

"A lord of the House of Ædracmoræ. He held stewardship of the kingdom of Æshulmæ as bestowed by Yávië's mother when she was Queen," Sōrél answered, drawing a frown from Näeré.

"Sylwervyn was a filthy beast and a skilled sorcerer," Näeré added curtly. "Rumor tells that he was crippled by a direfang his apprentice had loosed upon him and then he was eaten by dragons, which probably means he is alive and living in the rubble below the tower."

"He was Näeré's mentor," Sōrél said. "She was not very fond of him."

Spinning around, Näeré placed the tip of her dagger beneath her brother's chin. Nall and Yávië drew swords and watched in disbelief as Sōrél's blood pooled at his collar.

"Some things, my brother, should not be taken lightly. Sylwervyn is one of them."

Withdrawing her blade, Näeré stalked away in the direction of the dragons.

Nall watched Sōrél wipe the blood from his throat.

"Be careful what you ask," he cautioned Nall.

Nall mounted behind Näeré, watching as Aero carried Yávië and Sōrél back toward Meremire. Näeré sat stiffly without speaking, and tensed as Nall placed his arms lightly around her waist.

"If I ask will you cut my throat?" he whispered into her hair.

He felt her shake with tears and held her more tightly.

Taking a deep breath and wiping her eyes, she turned toward him. "It is hard to speak of it."

"I am sorry," Näeré said, looking up into Nall's eyes. "It was long, long ago and my reaction to my brother's words was imprudent. It is my hope that Sylwervyn is dead, for I did my best to kill him. I was entrusted to his care. However, he was not . . . trustworthy. I left him for dead and brought down his tower in a fit of rage and despair." With a hint of a smile she added, "It was my finest hour."

Sōrél closed the door to Yávië's bothie and swept her into his arms.

"What were you thinking, Yávië? What if your spell had failed? What if Abaddon or Aléria had escaped? How is it Nall and I did not sense that you carried those crystals? How could Näeré not know?"

"My spells do not fail. You ask too many questions and I am too tired to answer them."

A look of concern crossed his face.

"You are weary?"

She nodded and rested her head against him.

Silently, he called to Rosie.

Rosie rushed into the room, pushing Sōrél away.

"Who touched her?" She lifted her staff in anger.

"No one, Rosie, but Xavier and my mother, I swear it."

Mumbling, Rosie laid her hand on Yávië's forehead.

"Somebody touched her," the Ancient said, nodding to herself, "or she touched somebody, for they drains her strength."

Within her crystal prison, Aléria awoke to the taste of Yávië's tears.

Sōrél sat in the chair watching Yávië fret within her dreams. He carefully replayed their visit to his mother in his mind, repeatedly, but saw no one unknown touch Yávië. He would not have allowed it, nor would Nall.

It must somehow have been connected to the crystals bearing Abaddon and Aléria, but he could not make the pieces fit. Again, Sōrél imagined himself approaching his mother, kissing her hand, watching as Näeré embraced her and Yávië spoke to her of Rosie. He knew his mother would never harm Yávië. He allowed his mind to move into the antechamber where the Sojourners waited. None of them had even approached Yávië. He saw Yávië's tears, and recalled wiping them away before he turned to hand the small spider silk pouch to his mother. Suddenly Sōrél felt ill. He watched himself transferring the pouch from his left hand to his right. He saw the tears from his fingertips soak into the base of the soft cloth. He watched as the cloth of the pouch drew in the moisture of the tears.

Aléria's laughter filled his mind.

Rosie's staff struck him again.

"You gots to be careful!" Her voice was as shrill as a harpy's.

Grumblton had been dispatched immediately for Xavian City. He carried an oiled leather pouch in which to carry Aléria's crystal until Willow could cast a spell to draw out Yávië's tears.

"Do you sees her Sōrél?" Rosie smacked him again.

"You endangers her and Sōvië with your carelessness! What do you think Aléria would do to Sōvië?"

Sōrél realized he no longer felt the blows for he was far too numb with fear.

"Gets out!" Rosie yelled.

Leaning against the side of the bothie with his face in his hands Sōrél decided he must crush Aléria and her laughter once and for all.

"That would not be wise," Näeré insisted, hearing her brother's angry thoughts. "Yávië would never forgive you."

"I am unforgivable, Näeré. You know that."

"Yávië has forgiven you when not many would. Do not betray her again." She reached out and placed her hand on his shoulder but he drew back.

"Rosie's wounds require a soothing salve. Come with me and I shall heal you."

"I do not wish to be healed," he muttered stubbornly.

"Of course not. You prefer to remain a sacrificial victim. Come anyway, and I will give you willow bark tea and tell you I am sorry for this." She touched the wound beneath his chin.

"Rosie will not allow you to see Yávië until the danger has passed. You might as well come." Näeré took his hand and pulled her brother along behind her.

Rosie had asked Nall to sit with Yávië. As Yávië slept, he watched her tears fall and he felt deep anger at the trouble Aléria still caused them, while the memory of her touching his soul brought chills.

Nall imagined Sōrél's guilt. Something as simple as wiping away tears had caused this and Rosie's fear-driven fury had not helped. He drew his chair closer to the cot and held Yávië's hand. She was arrogant and sometimes foolish, but always kind and beautiful, passionate and innocent. She would be a good queen.

"*She will not live to be queen,*" he heard Aléria whisper in his mind.

"Aye, she will. Even if you must die for it to be so," Nall whispered back.

"And would you help me see Aléria to her death?" Sōrél asked from the doorway.

With a shrug, he answered his own question, "Nay, I did not think you would. Näeré says it would not be the right thing to do."

Nall frowned, for he would very much like to see Aléria dead, but he also knew that Yávië would never forgive either of them if it were by their hands.

"The price would be too high," Nall said, placing Yávië's hand gently on the cot before going to the door.

Gripping Sōrél's shoulder briefly he added, "You and I cannot afford it."

"I thought I tolds you to go away," Rosie growled.

"I no longer fear your brutality, old woman," Sōrél said, "for my sister the witch has a wonderful healing salve."

Rosie smiled behind her hand. "Willow casts the spell. Yávië should awakens rested and strong."

"I was so frightened for her, Rosie, and I grow tired of fear. Will there ever be a day when we rest without worry?"

Rosie cocked her head and looked at him with one eye closed.

"She is not sweetness and light, our Yávië. You have chosen a thorny path to follows."

"Aye, Rosie, but it was my doing. I could have denied her."

Rosie touched his cheek and shook her head, "I do not believe you could. You forgets—Grumblton and I watched you try. Be here when she wakes."

With that, she slipped out the door, leaving him with memories of long ago.

How he had tried to deny Yávië. She had cried and stomped her foot, threatening all manner of punishments including telling her father, and no amount of reasoning would stop her tirade. He wondered what would have happened if he had just allowed her to go and tell her father. What would Alandon have done? Then a slow smile crossed his face. That had been Alandon's plan all along. Had his daughter come to him he would have had good reason to dispose of Sōrél. Beheading would have been too good for such betrayal, but

Yávië had not gone to her father and Sōrél had not denied her and so here they were, overcome with fear and worry.

He looked up to find her watching him.

"What are your thoughts?" Yávië asked.

"I was recalling the threats you made and the tantrums you threw."

She blushed at the memory.

"You said you did not want me . . ."

". . . and obviously I lied."

Chapter 35 : Star of Sangria

From Æshardæ the Guardians went through the last mirror and toward the final artifact. The forests of Æshulmæ were as tall and majestic as those of the Northern Mountains on Æstretfordæ and ahead lay the tower of Sylwervyn and the Star of Sangria. Gentle breezes played with the Guardians' clothing and the soft morning mist filtered the light of the daystar.

Seeking the fallen tower of Sylwervyn, Hawk flew high overhead. Nall received the images of Hawk's vision as if they were his own and was surprised to see a tall crystal tower rising up from amidst the lofty braid trees. He turned to Näeré.

"Are you sure the tower was destroyed and that there is no other?"

"Aye, I shattered it, toppling every last stone. I watched it fall, and as far as I know, there is no other like it."

Turning to Sōrél, her eyes wide, Näeré spoke softly, "I told you he was not dead."

"I shall not allow him to harm you, Näeré." Sōrél's voice dripped hatred.

Touching her brother's arm she said, "I am not a child, Sōrél. My scars have healed and in spite of what you may think, I am a far better caster of spells than Sylwervyn. When I tell you to run—run, for his house will fall again, and this time I shall reduce it to dust and cast it to the seven winds. He will attempt to touch me through the past, but I will not be touched."

Nall looked concerned, causing Näeré to smile.

"You, my heart of hearts, have never seen me angry. I shall apologize for my behavior before it begins." She kissed him and turned to the others.

"Heed my warning. I shall leave no stone standing. When I tell you to run, do not hesitate for the shards of falling crystals can be deadly." Näeré then led the way into the valley of the tower of Sylwervyn.

The man who stepped from the tower was not the sorcerer of Näeré's nightmares, but an elder with a walking stick. The voice, however, brought a chill to her spine.

"Sōrél, you bring me a gift?" Sylwervyn sneered, ignoring Näeré as if she were not worthy of his acknowledgement.

"We come seeking the Star of Sangria, nothing more," Sōrél snapped.

"I shall bring you the Star in trade for your sister." He allowed his eyes to wander over Näeré in a way that caused Nall's teeth to clench until they pained him.

"My brother does not speak for me, Sylwervyn. I speak for myself." Näeré spoke without emotion, her hand raised to calm Nall.

"I am no longer a frightened child. I shall take the Star from you if you do not wish to give it, and I shall ask only once. Will you give me the Star of Sangria, Sylwervyn?"

Sylwervyn laughed.

Näeré swung out her hand and threw him into the wall of his tower, sending a tinkling of crystal shards across the steps. She continued forward as he struggled to regain his feet. With a twist of her hand, she held him against the wall.

"Come, Sylwervyn, we shall retrieve it together."

Turning to the Guardians, she said, "Run and remain beneath the trees. Do not return for me. I shall bring the Star and meet you in the woods."

Nall started forward, but she stopped him with her voice.

"I shall return to you, Nall. I promise it."

Then she dragged Sylwervyn into the tower behind her.

Nall watched as Näeré disappeared into the darkness of the tower. His eyes met Sōrél's briefly before he turned and raced inside.

Sōrél shook his head, urging Galen, Rydén and Zeth ahead of him into the cover of the trees. Yávië paused at the tree line.

"Yávië," Sōrél called, "do not complicate her task. It is sufficient that she will have to watch over Nall."

"Why did you allow him to go?" Yávië looked at him with accusation in her eyes.

"It will fuel her fury to have him there and it will keep them both safe."

Näeré pushed Sylwervyn ahead of her, her anger boiling as she fed it with memories of his arrogant wickedness.

"I shall not leave you to heal this time, old man," she spat, pushing him forward with her mind.

"I made you strong!" Sylwervyn jeered as he flung out his arms, forcing Näeré back.

She saw him draw the lightning lash and recalled its painful cuts against her skin.

She screamed in anger, "No! You will not touch me, Sylwervyn. I shall not allow it!"

Sylwervyn's eyes looked past her as he sought the figure in the shadows. Finding it, he released the lash sending the cutting blade of light to strike Nall.

Nall faltered and cried out as the blade of light sliced open his shoulder.

Näeré threw a wall of protection up around Nall. Her eyes narrowed as she swung back to face Sylwervyn.

"You should not have done that," she hissed in the hushed voice of icy cold control taught her by the wizard Grumblton.

"I no longer require the assistance of the direfang to destroy you, Sylwervyn, for I have grown strong. There will be no mercy this day—only a slow and agonizing death."

She raised her right hand and closed it into a fist as she envisioned crushing Sylwervyn's weapon arm. Näeré smiled with satisfaction at his howl of pain and transferred her mind to his left arm, watching her victim as he crashed to the floor, unable to break his fall. He rolled and thrashed in his agony, drawing her toward him. She reached deep into his mind for the visions of his evil past and slowly crushed his thoughts, watching as he keened and moaned. With a twist of her fingers, his mind was stirred into a maelstrom of fear and pain, leaving no memory unpunished.

Näeré then lifted the lightning lash.

"This is for striking Nall," she whispered as she beat Sylwervyn's dying body into pieces too small to be noticed even by a hungry butterpillar.

Wiping blood from her face, Näeré went to Nall.

"I told you not to come, but since you are here I am glad of your company."

Stepping into the barrier that surrounded him she touched his wounded shoulder and gazed into his eyes as her mind shattered the tower around them. Nall felt her power surge as she sheltered him from the sharp shards of falling crystal and hoped the others had heeded her warnings.

The Guardians stood under the safety of the great trees and watched as the tower began to collapse.

"It is good she sides with us," Galen muttered, receiving nods of agreement from the others.

"Nall?" Yávië whispered to Sōrél.

"She will not have allowed harm to come to him, Yávië. Even in her darkest fury she will have sheltered him from harm."

The tower crumbled until nothing was left but a cloud of crystal dust, which was quickly caught and swept away by the seven winds that Näeré had summoned. As the dust rose on the thermals, Nall and Näeré became visible at the epicenter of destruction. The walls of safety shimmered and faded away as they were released by Näeré's mind.

Stepping away from Nall, Näeré lifted the Star of Sangria, gazing upon its brilliant light in the palm of her hand.

"Sylwervyn should have given it to me when I asked for it," she said.

The sky above them was split by lightning, and rain began to fall as the crashing of thunder echoed across Æshulmæ.

"The quest for the artifacts is complete, Yávië. On the morrow I shall take you home that you may reclaim the jewel of your birthright."

Sōrél closed his eyes against the worries of tomorrow.

Chapter 36: Intervention

Hearing the howling of Nall, Yávië knew that Rosie tended him and smiled at the thought of the little Ancient's fierce love for each of them, the same love she knew would mold her daughter into a queen.

Sōrél's eyes were shadowed with concern as he called Aero to him and watched Yávië mount. Swinging up behind her, he held her tightly and breathed in the scent of her hair.

"Yávië, you must listen. Do not pause this day to decide if my commands are acceptable, for they are only to ensure the safety of you and Sōvië."

Leaning back against her husband, she promised her obedience.

"I shall obey, Sōrél, though I cannot promise I shall not make you pay later."

Shaking his head at her obstinate nature, he commanded Aero toward the fortress of Yávië's birth.

Nall howled again.

"Rosie, could you be a bit kinder!"

"She told you to stays in the trees!" Rosie said, jabbing Nall again.

"I wanted to protect her."

Rosie turned to Näeré. "What has you done to makes him think you needs protecting?"

Näeré blushed. "He has never seen me angry, Rosie. Do not blame him for his foolishness."

"Foolishness? You thought me foolish?"

"Nay . . . aye, I did think you foolish for risking yourself, but I liked the fact that you returned for me," she answered, her voice growing low.

"Hmmmph!" Rosie rolled her eyes and tossed the jar of salve to Näeré.

"You tends him," she huffed and left.

"It appears Rosie thinks us both foolish," Näeré said as she coated Nall's wound with soothing salve.

Rydén's eyes clouded with worry.

"Zeth, you risk your life by coming here."

"Your brother howls within Rosie's bothie. This offers us a moment's safety, and my life is worthless without you. I grow stronger and wield the swords well. If I do not make my feelings public—if I do not tell Nall—I am a coward."

Rydén took a deep breath, "Galen suggests killing my brother in his sleep."

Smiling, Zeth responded, "Galen jests, and I do not believe I would earn Nall's respect—or yours—by killing him in his sleep."

Holding Rydén's face in his hands he promised, "I shall tell him of my intentions following Yávië's coronation. It will end there . . ."

Rydén's eyes closed as her mind completed his thought, ". . . one way or another."

Aero landed quietly among the fallen stones.

"I feel your concern, Huntress," he spoke as his brow furrowed more than usual.

"Aye, there is danger here, Aero, but Sōrél will watch over me."

She slid her hand beneath his scales to scratch his tender skin and give the young dragon comfort.

"Remain here. We shall not be long," Sōrél assured Aero.

Taking Yávië's hand, Sōrél reminded her of her agreement to obey, earning a slow smile and a flash of light from her eyes. Covering them with the veil of mist, Sōrél cautioned her to silence and moved off toward the lower level of the Fortress. They made their way silently to the great hall and turned toward the east and the keep.

"My father will know when I touch the jewel," Yávië whispered in Sōrél's mind. "Take me to his tower first and show me what you hide there."

Sōrél's jaw clenched, but he merely nodded and headed in the direction of Alandon's tower.

Shielded by the veil of mist and with backs against the wall, they ascended the stairs in silence. The door was open. Sōrél pushed it closed and bolted it behind them. Yávië scanned the room, taking in every thumb's width of her father's private tower. She paused at the tapestry and stared at the images of the Ancients, reaching up and touching Rosie's image with her fingertips. She found her own image with a man standing next to it. Again, her fingers drifted over the tapestry, stroking Sōrél's likeness.

"Everything my father ever told me was a lie," she whispered.

"Not everything, Daughter." Alandon's voice was loud within the room. "For I told you Sōrél was a bastard, and that was no lie."

Sōrél felt the heat of his anger rise, but Yávië's kiss cooled the fire.

Yávië stared at her father with withering contempt.

"Sōrél's father died defending his children. Why could you not have been so kind?"

"I will not allow the House of Aaradan to rule," Alandon snarled his hatred.

"The House of Aaradan already rules and you are simply too stupid to see it."

"Yávië," Sōrél cautioned, watching Alandon seethe at his daughter's disrespect.

As Alandon's hand shot forward toward Yávië, the air between them shimmered with heat. Ileana's voice cut through their minds as she appeared, blocking Alandon's threat.

"You show your true nature, Alandon. Is that wise?"

He drew back, hissing with surprise.

"Do not look shocked. You knew I would not allow you to harm my children. It is enough I stood by as you murdered their father and stole their legacy."

She smiled at Yávië and touched her cheek.

"Go, Daughter, and claim the gem of your birthright while your father and I discuss the details of your upcoming coronation."

"She is not your daughter!" Alandon shrieked.

"Oh, but she is, Alandon—more mine than yours." Ileana smiled, even as her angry eyes held him at bay.

"Sōrél, take her," his mother instructed.

"Mother?"

"I am in no danger."

Pulling Yávië behind him, Sōrél led her through the doorway and down the stairs, eastward toward the keep. They raced across the great hall and up the stairway to claim Yávië's birthright. As Sōrél lifted the violet stone from the dragon's claw and slipped the golden chain over Yávië's head, he heard Alandon wail in pain and rage and hoped that Ileana had ripped out the evil Sojourner's heart.

Sōrél watched the gemstone nestling against Yávië's heart and felt the radiance of its power engulf them. The House of Aaradan and the House of Ædracmoræ would soon be united for eternity. By the gathering of the Seven Kingdoms on the anniversary of her birth, Yávië would earn the right to claim the throne of the Dragon Queen, restoring the balance of power between their Houses.

Until that day arrived, they would rest within the safety of Meremire's borders.

Respite

"Was I obedient enough?" Yávië asked as she struck Sōrél a vicious backhand blow with the Sword of Domesius.

"As I recall, wife, I did not issue commands but merely made suggestions."

He met her stroke for stroke, setting the swords ringing.

"Suggestions? 'Yávië, you must listen'—that sounded like a command to me, Captain!" Yávië laughed as she swept her sword across the grass where he was standing, making him leap back.

"Is this going to be a day on which I must bleed?" Sōrél asked.

"I have not decided exactly how I shall punish you. Perhaps I shall only require your obedience."

Placing his sword on the ground in submission, he nodded to his wife. "Let my test of obedience begin, milady. I am yours to command."

She touched his heart with the tip of her sword. "Come," she purred, "I require your obedience in my bothie."

Rydén and Näeré sat on the wall watching Zeth spar with Nall.

"He chooses to challenge my brother."

"It would be foolhardy," Näeré said.

"He says it is the only way to win Nall's respect. He did not take my suggestion to kill Nall in his sleep seriously," Rydén chuckled.

Näeré laughed, "Nor would I!"

"Zeth has grown strong and sure of himself. That will impress

Nall. I have seen him spar with Galen and Sōrél and both have encouraged anger and aggression. Zeth will need passion to best Nall," Näeré said.

Nall kept his eyes on Zeth's face as he spoke. "I hear you have a woman."

"Aye," Zeth answered, his eyes narrowing and his sword striking Nall's with a new fury.

"Is there a reason I should not?" Zeth asked, sweeping his sword across Nall's backhand.

Swinging both swords passionately, Zeth drove his mentor back. Nall swung away and spun to catch Zeth's new thrust with a parry.

"She gives you passion. That is good," Nall acknowledged.

"Aye, she does," Zeth said, circling Nall.

Lunging, Zeth brought both swords forward as Sōrél had instructed and forced Nall's blades to lock with his. Then he feigned weakness, allowing his mentor to force him back momentarily before rushing forward and knocking Nall to the ground.

Stepping back, Zeth placed both swords on the ground in concession and walked from the field.

Nall laughed, for Zeth had apparently been paying very close attention to his mentor's weaknesses. He looked forward to his student's challenge.

He grinned at Näeré and Rydén as he approached the wall.

"The student prepares to challenge the Master," he laughed.

"Aye," Rydén said, meeting her brother's eyes, "he does."

Watching his sister walk away, he turned back to Näeré.

"Why do I always feel like I am missing something when I talk to that girl?" he asked.

Näeré laughed and touched his cheek, "Perhaps because she is no longer a girl."

"Zeth does well, does he not?" she asked.

"Aye, he grows strong and true. He is no longer the gangly boy child who arrived on the doorstep for training," Nall agreed.

Galen slipped into Kayann's chambers and watched her prepare tea. The child he would accept as his own played with a long handled wooden spoon pretending it was a sword. He had already grown to love this boy.

"It is not polite to sneak into a woman's home without announcing yourself," Kayann chided him.

Galen drew near and hugged her.

"As if I could enter your home without your knowledge," he whispered against her neck, causing her to laugh and draw back.

"Galen!" the boy called, "Today will you show me your sword?"

A look of worry crossed Kayann's face.

"Kayann, I shall teach him swordsmanship and honor. I promise it."

She nodded, but her heart remained fearful.

Xalín sat on Galen's lap and fingered the sword.

"It is a great sword, Galen. Too large for me now, but someday I shall be strong enough to wield it, don't you think?"

"Aye, and before that I shall give you a lighter sword, one that is made for boys."

"When will Mother and I move to your fortress, Galen?"

"Very soon, Xalín, very soon," Galen answered, ruffling the boy's hair and smiling up at his mother.

Chapter 37: Restoration

While Yávië sat with Rosie, Willow and Grumblton, Sōrél leaned against the wall with Nall, Naeré and Rydén, and Zeth and Galen sat on the floor. The Guardians were within the Great Hall of the fortress of the House of Aaradan and the artifacts for the spell casting lay upon the table.

"On the morrow, before the light of the daystar touches the horizon, I must cast the spells to draw the seven kingdoms together. There will only be one opportunity. If we are not successful, then all of our work has been for naught." Though Yávië spoke calmly, she had to clasp her hands together to keep them from shaking.

"When the sphere was shattered the Seven Kingdoms split apart, leaving the worlds as we now know them. By the casting of the spells, the pieces of the world will be drawn together and will be bound by the roots of the willow and the verdant tree. The seven pools will be free to travel beneath the world, reuniting their life-giving waters. Ædracmoræ, the world of my birth, home of the Seven Kingdoms, will be reborn. I have been given the knowledge of the Sojourners to accomplish this task. I shall not fail.

"My mind will touch that of each of you in turn for the calling of the light. The light from the Star of Sangria must pass through the staff held by each Guardian before it is covered by the shadow of the Blood Stone.

"You are my Guardians. You have cared for me and brought me safely to this place. Now it is I who must lead the way, and you who must follow."

Sōrél smiled at her passion as Näeré shed a tear for their queen's promise but it was, of course, Zeth who spoke the plain truth for he had still not learned caution.

"You are our queen." His voice was clear and honest.

This time it did not bring a shadow across Yávië's face.

She merely whispered, "Aye."

"Rest," Sōrél called to them, "for you will be called in the darkness of the night."

"Sōrél, you know that I am brave and strong." Yávië reached up to touch his face.

"Aye, and beautiful, passionate and ruthlessly unfair to your husband," he answered.

"I do not jest, Sōrél. I have never been so terrified for I must do this alone."

"Yávië, you and I have been well prepared for this day and those that will follow. Grumblton and Willow will be here to guide your hand if you falter and I am sure Rosie will beat you with a stick if she finds you unsatisfactory."

Seeing her sudden smile made his heart feel light and he wished an end to their task so that he could see her happy more often. He went to her and held her close, knowing that she felt anxious about the separation of the Guardians.

Each would be alone to lift the staff at her calling, but he feared no danger. His mother kept Alandon from them. Brushing Yávië's hair away from her face, Sōrél looked for signs of weariness but saw none. Only the small crease in her brow told him of her worry. He smoothed it away and kissed it to see her smile once more.

Grumblton cleared his throat and said in a gruff voice, "It is time."

"Morg waits on Æshardæ to make sure everyone gets to their appointed place," he muttered, trying to separate Yávië from Sōrél.

Rosie came and took Yávië's hand.

"Sōrél will be rights back," she stated, looking up at Yávië.

"Do you promise it Rosie?" Yávië said with tears in her eyes.

"Aye, I do promise." Rosie spoke without any doubt.

"By the rising of the daystar he will be back home."

Yávië nodded, freeing Sōrél's hand.

"Come, Yávië," Willow's voice called from the tower above.

Yávië climbed the stairs to the open Tower of the Seven Sisters at the eastern end of the fortress. She ran her fingers over the artifacts, checking each one, and slipped the dragon and serpent-hilted sword into its staff-like scabbard in preparation for striking the Book of Trolls. She centered the trybrac's skull upon the table, adjusting the flat side of the skull, where she would place the book, to face her. The image of the dragon demon sat alone in readiness to be struck with the Sword of Æstretfordæ that Nall had brought back from the Well of Viileshga. She carefully placed the Blood Stone on its mark near where Näeré had placed the Star of Sangria, knowing that the casting of the Blood Stone's shadow was the most critical element in the ritual of Ædracmoræ's rebirth, for if the shadow reached the Star before its light had traveled through the seven staffs, all would be lost.

Close by her right hand rested her Staff of Souls and in her left hand, she held the sheathed sword within the Staff of Alandon. Yávië closed her eyes and took a deep breath before she looked up at Willow and then whispered, "Let the game begin."

Placing the Book of Trolls upon the Skull of Ælmondæ, she quickly struck it three times with the Staff of Alandon. A warm golden light radiated outward from the Book of Trolls. Looking at Willow again and seeing her nod, Yávië began the incantation to call the spirits of the night.

"Spirits of the night, I beseech thee,
Find favor with mine call and summons,
On the seven winds, I beg thee travel,
And grant me my wish.
I speak of things shattered that need rejoining,
Of things taken that must be returned,
Thy powers do I wish to invoke,
For things that need be done."

Yávië raised the Staff of Souls and felt the rush of the Sister winds passing through the room. Handing the Staff of Alandon to Grumblton and taking the double-bladed sword of Æstretfordæ from the table she took another deep breath and struck Ya'vanna's Dragon square, causing it to shatter into fine dust that was quickly caught and swept away by the seven winds. At Willow's signal, Yávië lifted her Staff of Souls to begin the incantation of the Sojourners.

"Sojourners, I beseech thee that thy power
Come to rest within this Staff.
A world has been shattered,
Torn asunder, and must be made whole.
By the power of the Sojourner, make this thing be so."

As Yávië struck the Staff of Souls against the Blood Stone, it began to weep the blood of Ædracmoræ across the table toward the Star of Sangria.

"Let not thy shadow cast upon the Star," Yávië whispered to herself as she lifted the Staff of Souls to catch the first rays of the Star's brilliant light. She turned the Staff toward Æstretfordæ, where she knew Zeth waited for her call.

Closing her eyes, she called to him, "*Lift your staff, Zeth, and hold it steady.*"

Zeth lifted his staff and watched as a brilliant light raced toward him from the Tower of the Seven Sisters on Æstaffordæ.

Calling to Galen on Æcumbræ, Yávië implored him to lift his staff and saw him do so within her mind. As it rose, the light of the Star of Sangria collided with its crystal and sent a shower of sparks over him before moving on toward Æshulmæ and Rydén's staff.

Yávië's mind touched Rydén, and she raised her staff high and looked into the light of the new beginning as it struck the crystal headstone.

Näeré returned a soothing thought to Yávië as she raised her staff aloft and the light of the Star of Sangria passed through its crystal, leaving a warm trailing glow in its wake.

Yávië called to Nall and saw him lift his staff to catch the light. She glanced quickly at the Blood Stone to see its shadow of blood creeping perilously close to the Star's light.

Her mind touched Sōrél and he slowly raised his staff. The Star of Sangria's radiant light settled within the crystal of his staff before sweeping back toward Yávië.

The returning light traveled down Yávië's Staff and struck the Blood Stone, shattering it into a million tiny glittering shards, which were quickly gathered by the seven winds and carried across the slowly coalescing kingdoms. A clap of thunder sounded as the energy moved out across the field of light, drawing the Seven Kingdoms toward one another.

Yávië opened her mind to accept the vision of the birth of Ædracmoræ and shared it with her Guardians. Drawn by the Star's light and bound through the staff carried by each of the seven Guardians, the seven torn kingdoms of Ædracmoræ drifted toward one another. The willow's roots extended out beyond the boundaries of Æstretfordæ, attempting to touch the kingdoms beyond. The verdant tree shot its great roots out in all directions, establishing itself in the familiar soil of the advancing kingdoms.

Thunder reverberated around the seven worlds as they collided, and were then bound by the roots of the Tree of Creation and the verdant tree; twisting the curled tendrils, binding them tightly to one another in a marriage of creation.

The Star of Sangria sent its light racing across the boundaries of the kingdoms, joining the shards of the Blood Stone cast upon the wind to seal the forming sphere into the world of Ædracmoræ.

The sudden silence was deafening as Yávië watched the Star of Sangria flicker then blink out, leaving her in total darkness. Grumblton lit a torch and tried not to smile. Rosie and Willow danced in circles until they fell to the floor amid gales of joyous laughter.

Yavie watched the first rays of the light of the topaz star break across the horizon of the new world of Ædracmoræ. Tears sprang to her eyes as her Guardians arrived and she laughed aloud as she watched dragons bellow and buck before the fortress. Faera, the Kilstoneflyte Matriarch, became so excited that she forgot protocol completely and set fire to a group of trees at the edge of the fortress lawn. Aero tried to blow it out, but only managed to fuel the flames and send them shooting along a hedgerow.

"We shall be lucky if our fortress is not burned to the ground before your coronation, milady." Sōrél's voice was thick with emotion.

Yávië raced across the room and threw herself into his arms.

"We are home," she whispered.

Sōrél kissed her fingertips.

"As much as it is my desire to keep you to myself, your Guardians await you in the throne room."

As they entered the Great Hall, Näeré raced to them and hugged Yávië and then her brother.

"Shall we take the dragons and look at it?" she begged.

"Aye, they are anxious to be active, and if we do not move them soon I fear we shall be left with a burned out ruin. Between Faera and Acro, we risk our lives by remaining here, and Azrea and Azaeria have already knocked over several trees during a shoving match. I think we shall have to visit the flytes and discuss the rules of the house before the coronation," Sōrél laughed.

"I saw them circling above during the spell casting," Rydén offered.

"They remember this as their home too," Nall recalled. "They will settle with time."

Galen and Zeth were chatting with Grumblton and Rosie. Willow was nowhere to be seen.

"Where is Willow?" Yávië called to Rosie.

"Oh, she went to starts your dress," Rosie said, bobbing her head as if dress-making was the most natural thing in the world.

"What dress?" Yávië asked to stunned looks from everyone in the room.

"Yávië, you cannot receive the crown in a riding skirt and blouse," Rydén laughed.

Yávië looked surprised.

"Sōrél, do you not like the way I look?" she asked.

"Careful, Sōrél," Nall whispered, "this is a very dangerous question."

Näeré pushed Nall and shushed him.

"Well?"

"Milady, I find you beautiful with or without a dress."

Nall roared with laughter.

Yávië flushed five shades of scarlet.

Grumblton nearly choked and Rosie laughed so hard she got the hiccoughs.

"But," Sōrél continued, completely unruffled, "I do believe a dress would be more appropriate for the coronation."

He kissed the tip of her nose and then headed for the dragon yard.

"Let us soar into the sky and rediscover Ædracmoræ," he called back over his shoulder, a wide smile on his face.

Morning found Yávië in the clutches of Willow and Rosie as Rydén and Näeré looked on in amusement.

Rydén laughed aloud at Yávië's discomfort.

"It is beautiful," Näeré said.

"Nay, it is too tight," Yávië fussed.

"Rosie, I cannot breathe!"

Yávië stood in her coronation gown as Rosie and Willow pinched and hemmed and worried about seams.

"I am serious. I cannot breathe and I shall probably faint," Rosie laughed at the thought.

"You will takes away Sōrél's breath," Willow whispered.

"He does not care what I wear!" Yávië stomped her foot, eliciting laughter from Rydén and Näeré and a swift smack from Willow.

"Ouch! Stop it Willow! I cannot wear this!"

"I shall look a fool. The skirts will get in the way of my weapons," Yávië fumed.

"You won't carries weapons at the coronation, Yávië," Rosie responded, drawing looks of concern from Rydén, Näeré and Yávië.

"Of course I shall."

"Nay, you won'ts," Willow said stiffly, leaving no room for argument.

"But Willow . . ." Näeré began.

"I shall speak to Sōrél about it," Yávië said, lifting her chin in defiance.

"You can speaks to him all you wants, but you won'ts be wearing weapons at the coronation," Willow insisted.

"How shall I protect myself?" Yávië asked.

Willow turned and pointed at Näeré and Rydén, "They will protects you. Nall, Galen and Zeth will protects you. Sōrél will protects you. You won'ts be wearing weapons at the coronation." The discussion was closed.

"We shall see about that," Yávië whispered under her breath.

Suddenly Sōrél entered. He stared at Yávië, her hair piled upon her head, her chin raised defiantly and her eyes flashing a warning. His eyes slowly followed the dress from its neckline to the floor, causing Yávië to flush.

Rosie elbowed Willow and they giggled. Näeré and Rydén smiled broadly at Sōrél's apparent inability to speak.

"Your mouth is open and you look a fool," Yávië whispered, watching her husband's eyes rise to her lips.

Shaking his head as if to clear it, Sōrél spoke at last.

"I am seeking my wife. Has anyone seen her?"

Chapter 38: The Coronation

With the return of the Guardians of Ædracmoræ to the fortress, strength and vitality were restored to the House of Aaradan. The walls of the garrison once again rang with shouts and the clanking of weaponry and armor, as preparations were made for the coronation of the queen. Invitations were dispatched to the Seven Kingdoms. Alandon and Ya'vanna, who remained in the caverns beneath the ruins of the Fortress of the Dragon Queen, were included.

The dragon flytes kept representatives within the dragon yard. It was a wonder to watch them settle in at the rising of the daystar, hear their great bellows and see their boisterous shoving matches as they became reacquainted. Nall had addressed the Matriarchs, reminding them of the rules within the fortress grounds. As a result, no new fires had been started for several days although, in her excitement, Faera occasionally continued to scorch walls.

The sound of hammers striking wood became the background to conversation as two hundred Galenite workmen built the tiered seating for the seven hundred guests.

Xavian artisans wove the carpets and tapestries that would adorn the Great Hall and groups of Ancients festooned the lower halls with the velvet of simplestag antlers, which would become the queen's coronation robe. Others gathered the flower petals to be tossed at the wedding party. A Xavian choir practiced within the queen's garden and their soothing voices were sounds to be cherished at the end of each day.

For two weeks before the actual coronation, Yávië and Sōrél rehearsed daily for the event. Since Alandon was not to be trusted, the Ancients took turns standing in as Yávië's father. The procession would begin at the Pool of Æstaffordæ and wend its way along the path through the woods and under the portcullis to the Great Hall. Grumblton would perform the anointing. The actual investiture and crowning would take place as Ya'vanna relinquished the throne to Yávië and Alandon bestowed the bracelets of wisdom and sincerity, the sword of the Dragon Queen, the Orb and Scepter, and the coronation ring before finally crowning Yávië as Queen of Ædracmoræ and the Seven Kingdoms. The Guardians would then, once again swear their allegiance, each kneeling before their Queen and kissing the stone of the Dragon Ring.

The exchange of the public vows of promise between the new queen and her chosen king would take place immediately following the coronation. Grumblton would officiate.

By dusk on the night before the coronation, the processional route between the pool and the Great Hall had attracted thousands of well-wishers from the kingdoms of Ædracmoræ. Nall was beside himself with concern.

"How shall we protect you amid this many strangers?" he asked.

Sōrél gripped Nall's shoulder as he spoke, "Alandon will not strike until our public vows. He will honor his pledge to allow Yávië her kingdom, but he will not stand by as she accepts the House of Aaradan."

After giving instructions for the positioning of the Guardians during the speaking of the vows, Sōrél called Nall aside.

"My friend, do not allow harm to come to Yávië or Näeré. If one life must be sacrificed, let it be mine." He raised his hand to stop Nall's protest.

"I command it. As your Captain, I command it."

Nall watched his Captain walk away and hoped he would not be forced to obey this command.

At dawn on the day of the coronation, the queen's chambers were in riotous uproar. All that remained was to get Yávië into her dress.

The "unwanted" gown had been painstakingly fashioned from a huge quanitity of the softest spider cloth, its countless drifting layers dyed the rich blue of the House of Aaradan. Beneath diaphanous skirts, it clung to Yávië like a second skin. The violet jewel of her birthright nestled just above her heart and flashed indigo as it drew the sapphire of the bodice.

"Stops wiggling, Yávië!"

Willow raised her staff and Yávië glared.

"Let me do it," Näeré intervened, taking charge of the one hundred buttons at the back of Yávië's gown.

"If we do not stop this arguing we will not have Yávië at the Sacred Pool to meet Sōrél and that is unacceptable," Näeré insisted.

Yávië sighed, making Näeré wait until she exhaled before the buttoning could continue.

"*No wonder Yávië fusses,*" Näeré thought.

As the final button was fastened, Yávië spun around.

"May I have a moment alone? Just a moment?" she pleaded, looking as if she might cry.

Näeré looked at her suspiciously, for Nall had given her explicit instructions not to let Yávië out of her sight for an instant, but she could not see the harm so she nodded and herded the Ancients out into the hallway. She reminded Yávië, "A moment—no more."

Giving a tired smile, Yávië nodded and watched the door swing shut.

Quickly she moved to her dressing table, picked up the silver hairbrush and drew the slender dragon hilted dagger from its handle—the dagger of Alandon, her father. She slipped it down her bodice, between her breasts, where it was easily accessible should she need it in a hurry. Checking the mirror to be sure it could not be seen; she opened her door and stepped out into the hall.

"I am ready," she announced.

"I would hug you if it would not disturb something," Näeré said. "You look beautiful."

"Then why do I feel so foolish?" Yávië asked.

"You will not when you see Sōrél. I have been told that the fuss he made nearly equaled yours," Näeré laughed, recalling Nall's description of the dressing of Sōrél.

Sōrél frowned at those around him. He felt stiff and the weapons Grumblton had allowed him seemed inadequate. Seeing Nall grin, he frowned more deeply.

"What is it you think amusing?"

"I was just thinking how handsome Yávië will find you," Nall chuckled.

"She finds me handsome when my clothes are torn and I am covered with blood," Sōrél snapped irritably.

"Aye, but your uniform and medals are more appropriate today, as is her dress," Nall reminded him.

"Your point is well taken."

At the herald of the horns, they looked up to see Galen escorting Yávië from a coach pulled by three braces of matched bullrams.

Sōrél felt a surge of jealousy as Galen leaned toward Yávië and said something that brought forth her soft laughter, but it was quickly forgotten as he met her eyes and saw them widen with pleasure.

Galen spoke no words, but placed Yávië's right hand on Sōrél's left arm before he bowed and stepped back.

Drawing Sōrél close, Yávië whispered, "Can we not simply run away?"

"We would be dropped before we had taken three steps, milady, for this throng would not allow a ruffian, such as me, to steal away their queen. Tomorrow I shall take you away and hold you captive in a place where none will find you."

"Do you promise it?"

Grumblton rushed over to pick imaginary lint from Sōrél's uniform and called Rosie to help with Yávië's coronation robe.

As Yávië knelt to permit Rosie's final touches, she looked up at Sōrél.

"Do you promise it?" she asked again.

"I hold you more precious than my own life."

The intensity of his words sent a fearful tingle along her spine.

On Sōrél's right, Nall whispered, "Alandon and Ya'vanna have arrived and are seated in the throne room."

As the horns called again, they began the procession that would culminate with the coronation.

Grumbleton led the procession. His scarlet sorcerer's robe fanned out behind him, and he carried the Book of Ancients. Morgwort followed with the scroll containing the vows of promise. Rydén followed—walking ahead of Yávië and Sōrél—with Näeré at Yávië's left and Nall at Sōrél's right. Galen and Zeth remained as close behind them as Yávië's coronation robe would allow.

The shouts of joy and good fortune reached them from those who had waited all night just to catch a glimpse of their new queen, the redeemer of their world.

Yávië whispered to Näeré, "Who are these people?"

Hearing her, Sorel laughed and answered, "These, milady, are your subjects, the citizens of your kingdoms. Their demands on your time will be endless and only your husband will be able to save you from them."

As they passed through the woods, Yávië saw Xavier and the members of his court and lifted her hand in recognition.

"If you show favoritism you will offend someone," Sōrél teased.

Nearing the fortress Yávië felt a tug on her mind and looked to see Aero quivering with excitement beyond the cheering crowd. She sent soothing words and watched as he quieted and lowered his scales. From the woods beyond came the bellow of war dragons.

Moving up the steps and through the raised portcullis Yávië felt the chill of her father's presence and steeled herself for the coming conflict.

The Great Hall hushed as they entered. Sōrél accompanied Yávië to the foot of the steps before the thrones where her parents sat. He nodded curtly to Alandon and kissed the cheek of Ya'vanna before stepping back to stand with the other Guardians.

Grumblton escorted Yávië to the chair of the princess and presented her to the court.

"I brings you Yávië, daughter of Ya'vanna and Alandon, heir to the throne of the Dragon Queen," he shouted, then bade her sit.

As she had practiced so many times, Yávië repeated the Oath after Grumblton, promising to respect and govern according to the laws of her people and to uphold the truth and wisdom of the Ancients.

Grumblton presented her with the Book of Ancients, the symbol of wisdom and law.

Taking the dragon-shaped stone jar containing the anointing oil, he drew it on to his fingers and touched the oil to Yávië's forehead as he spoke the ancient words revealing the wisdom and power of the dragon.

Grumblton looked to Alandon.

Turning to his wife, Alandon took Ya'vanna's hand and led her from the throne to stand before her daughter. Extending his hand to Yávië, he nodded his approval as she accepted it and stood, allowing her mother to take the vacated chair.

Alandon led Yávië up the steps and seated her on the queen's throne. Taking the bracelets of wisdom and sincerity from Ya'vanna, he placed them on Yávië's wrists. Then, drawing the sword of the Dragon Queen from its scabbard next to the throne, he placed it across Yávië's hands before taking it back and resting it on the altar behind the throne.

From the altar, he lifted the queen's ring and bestowed the blessings of the Ancients upon it as he placed it on the fourth finger of Yávië's right hand. Returning to the altar, Alandon lifted the Orb of Ædracmoræ and the queen's scepter and placed them in Yávië's hands. Yávië' held the Orb, symbolizing power and justice, in her right hand and the scepter, symbolizing peace and mercy, in her left.

Finally, Alandon took the crown of the Dragon Queen from the high altar and brought it before Yávië. Slowly, he bowed and whispered, "I promised Sōrél I would allow you this, and so I keep that promise. However, make no attempt to take the name of the House of Aaradan publicly or I will strike him dead."

Still smiling, Alandon placed the crown upon his daughter's head and turned to announce her.

"I bring you Yávië of the House of Ædracmoræ, Queen of the Seven Kingdoms. Long live the Dragon Queen!"

United, the assembled guests in the Great Hall rose to hail the new queen as the Guardians—one by one—came before her, dropped to one knee and kissed the Dragon Ring.

As Nall knelt before her, Yávië whispered, "He threatens Sōrél."

Looking up, Nall nodded and backed away, allowing Sōrél to take his place. After pledging his allegiance and kissing the Dragon Ring, Sōrél stepped back next to Nall.

Yávië stood, bringing the Great Hall to silence. She handed the

Scepter and Orb to Grumblton before addressing her court.

"Long ago, in the time beyond remembering, the House of Ædracmoræ drew its blade against the House of Aaradan."

She watched as Alandon turned toward her, shaking his head in warning.

Lifting her chin, Yávië continued, "The House of Aaradan fell by my own father's treachery. My father, the Sojourner Alandon is now no more than a stranger who has sworn himself to the demon darkness of the thief of souls in Abaddon's Abyss."

She watched Alandon's fists clench. He drew a small crystal from his breast pocket. With three fingers, he raised the crystal and turned towards Sōrél. Instantly, Nall and Rydén knocked Sōrél to the floor while, in the same instant, Galen and Zeth grabbed Näeré, taking her to the ground with them.

Yávië's response was swift and sure. Drawing her father's dragon hilted demon dagger from her bodice, she flung it toward the deadly creation crystal. The tip of the slender blade pierced the crystal intended as Sōrél's prison, shattering it into dust as Ileana shimmered before Alandon and swept him into the prison crystal she carried.

"I told you I would not allow you to harm my children, Alandon." Ileana murmured to the imprisoned Sojourner. Nodding briefly to Yávië, Ileana went to Ya'vanna and escorted Yávië's spellbound mother from the Great Hall.

A cacophony of voices erupted, but became silent as Yávië lifted her hand.

She descended the steps and stood before Sōrél as Nall helped him to his feet. She brushed imaginary dust from his shoulder and looked into his eyes.

"Is it your intent to honor your pledge?"

Kneeling before her, Sōrél whispered once again, "I am yours, Yávië—not through the black deeds of your father, but through the power of your heart. It is my intent to honor the pledge unless you deny me."

He removed the large signet ring from his hand and took her left hand in his. "With this ring I bind my pledge."

Slipping it onto the fourth finger of her left hand, he looked up.

"You may deny me and seek release with the return of the ring."

She saw the uncertainty deep in his eyes and recalled that she had once returned this ring in anger.

"I do not deny you, Sōrél of Aaradan. It is *my* choice to join the House of Ædracmoræ and the House of Aaradan by the acceptance of your pledge and through the sacred vows of promise."

Sōrél rose before her and the wizard Grumblton sealed the ring of their pledge—fitting it to Yávië's finger and making an incantation—before leading them up the steps to stand before the representatives of the Seven Kingdoms gathered in the Great Hall.

Morg stepped forward and handed Grumblton the parchment with the vows of promise. The Ancient wizard solemnly bound the House of Aaradan to the House of Ædracmoræ for eternity.

As the petals of a thousand flowers floated over them, Yávië and Sōrél walked from the Great Hall to the Gardens of the Queen, greeted by shouts and dragon bellows. After a seemingly never-ending stream of congratulations and well wishes, the Xavian chorus began to sing, soothing Yávië's nerves and drawing her attention to Galen. He held a small boy of perhaps six summers and talked to him as if he knew him well. She watched as he pointed to a woman in the chorus and saw the woman smile, lifting her hand in recognition. Touching Sōrél's sleeve Yávië excused herself.

"Galen. Why have you not asked me to release you of your life debt?" she asked gently.

"Because you needed me," he answered.

Suddenly, the boy reached out and touched her cheek. "You are Yávië, the Dragon Queen."

"Aye, but I do not know your name," she admitted to the boy.

"I am Xalín, son of Kayann."

"Xalín, son of Kayann, I am very pleased to meet you. Are you a friend of Galen's?"

"Aye, Galen is going to marry my mother. We are going to live in his fortress and he is going to teach me to use weapons."

"Is he now? I hope you will invite me to the wedding." She kissed Galen on the cheek. "You are free, Galen of Æstaffordæ. Willow will cast your freedom whenever you wish it."

She returned to find Sōrél with his eyebrows raised. "Not married a day and my queen is off kissing others!"

"I have freed Galen of his life debt to me. He wishes to wed a Xavian woman and return to his own fortress."

Without warning, a thought came to Sōrél and he called sharply to Nall, "You did not follow my command."

"Nay, I felt it wiser to obey the Queen," Nall said.

Sōrél looked at Yávië.

"Your mother came to me and told me of your plan to sacrifice yourself rather than put Näeré or me in danger," Yávië offered a small lie. "It was wise of you to hide my father's dagger where I would find it. Mine was the better plan."

Lowering her lashes and cupping his face with her hand, Yávië whispered, "Have I told you how handsome you look?"

"Nay, I do not believe you have."

Rosie rushed up and grabbed Nall's hand.

"Come, the dancing music begins."

"Rosie, I have been waiting all day for this pleasure."

Pulling Nall along behind her, Rosie headed back into the Great Hall.

Sōrél tilted his head and looked down at Yávië. "As much as I hate to end the flattery you bestow in hopes of having me forget you have already usurped my authority as Captain of your Guardians—I expect we should attend the wedding ball, since it is offered in our honor."

"You do not believe I find you handsome, my lord?" Yávië teased.

Suddenly Xander the downy flier leapt to Yávië's shoulder.

"Come Mistress, for the dragons grumble on the lawn before the fortress!"

Yávië knelt, allowing Grumblton to remove her crown, pulling the irksome pins from her hair as she raced with Sōrél toward the portcullis and the fortress lawn.

The bellowing and the heat of angry dragons' breath were heard and felt before they reached its source. What she saw filled Yávië with apprehension. Faera's neck was extended and her scales were raised against the intruder, the snap of her jaws loud in the soft evening air. Yávië heard the thunder of her growl and knew that unless hostilities were stopped, a flyte war would surely follow.

The intruder was Fáedre, Matriarch of the Deathstoneflyte, bound by pledge to the House of Aaradan. She was larger and heavier than Faera, and just as angry. Her tail whipped around and struck her opponent savagely across the flank, causing the war dragon of Yávië's pledge to bellow in pain and unleash her fiery breath against the heavy scales shielding the trespasser's chest.

Without hesitation, Yávië moved onto the lawn and toward the angry dragons. Faera's jaws swept in Yávië's direction and crashed together less than a man's length away.

"Yávië!" Sōrél's voice was sharp and rang like a sword striking an anvil.

Yávië's hair framed her face, whipped by the breath of angry dragons. The air was filled with the smell of scorched grass and burning ash. Smoke clouded the front of the fortress.

Faera shook her head and bellowed again in frustration.

Fáedre's eyes narrowed and she drew back her head as if to strike.

"Will you allow jealousy to break your pledges?" Yávië's voice was strong and calm and drew the attention of both dragons.

Their heads lowered in respect.

"If it is your choice to remain you will abide by the law of the pledges that govern you. If you choose to breach the law and bring war to the Kilstone and Deathstone flytes, so be it. I shall be forced to call forth the dragon slayers and your flytes will be hunted to the last dragon. What choose you, Faera? Life or death?" Yávië's voice held no hint of the love she felt for Faera, for she knew that a broken dragon pledge required swift justice.

Faera lowered her head, laying it at the feet of the Dragon Queen.

Turning to Fáedre, Yávië repeated her question, "What do you chose Fáedre? Life or death?"

Fáedre's eyes burned into Yávië's as she struggled for dominance. Yávië permitted herself a small smile before whispering silently to the dragon, "*There will be no honor in death, Fáedre.*"

Slowly Fáedre lowered her head to the ground near Yávië's feet.

"By my decree both the Kilstoneflyte and the Deathstoneflyte are barred from the dragon yard until my calling."

Without a backward glance, Yávië turned toward the fortress

and the group of anxious Guardians and Ancients who blocked the entrance.

"Well done, milady," Sōrél whispered as he brushed soot from Yávië's face.

"It did allow me to take off the crown, and I believe this uncomfortable gown is beyond repair," Yávië said, looking at the holes created by the dragon cinders.

"You dance very well, Nall,"

"It is simply a self-defense mechanism designed to make it as painless as possible."

"It is painful to dance with me?" Yávië teased.

"Nay, but it is painful to dance with Rosie."

They shared their laughter and then Yávië grew serious.

"Thank you. You may well have saved Sōrél's life by telling me of his intent."

"He did not trust Ileana to keep you from harm. He trusts no one," Nall answered.

"I would like you and Näeré to move into the main fortress. The garrison is too far from us. Sōrél's chambers are across the hall from mine and the nursery will be adjacent to mine. If you are willing to move into the room next to Näeré's, it will place Sovië between us."

As the music ended and they returned to Sōrél and Näeré, Yávië stopped Nall a last time.

"I have placed an overwhelming responsibility on your shoulders, Nall, but I can trust no other with the guardianship of my child."

Placing his hands on her shoulders, he made his pledge. "No harm will ever come to the child of the crown while she is in my care."

Tears of gratitude filled her eyes as Yávië hugged Nall before returning to Sōrél for the last dance.

Nall surveyed his new room. The walls were hung with tapestries depicting the hundred wars fought long before his first life and the floor was covered in rich carpet softer than the cot in his bothie at Meremire.

He listened to a whisper in the heavy silence and knew that Sōrél would soon slip away with Yávië. He recalled her words and his own, smiling at the fact he had quoted Sōrél. No harm would ever come to his charge while she was in his care. He knew he spoke the truth, for only death could release him from his promise to care for their daughter.

A sharp click caught his attention and he drew his sword as he watched the large bronze mirror swing inward toward him.

"What magick is this?" he whispered as Näeré slipped into the room and leaned against the mirror.

"No magick. My father built many hidden doors by which we might pass should our fortress be breached.

"Have you breached my fortress, Nall?"

"Only at the invitation of the queen," Nall answered.

Näeré's face grew solemn as she walked to him and drew him to her.

"I fear that you may lose something very precious to you if I do not speak of it," she whispered, looking up at him with eyes clouded by worry.

Frowning, he indicated the chairs before his table.

"What is it you must speak of?" he asked as he searched her face for a clue.

"Rydén," Näeré whispered, taking his hand.

"Rydén?" he repeated, completely bewildered.

"She lives in fear and I can no longer allow it."

"Who threatens Rydén?" Nall's voice rose in anger.

"You do."

His frown deepened. "I have never lifted a hand to Rydén. Why would she fear me?"

"Nall, she is a woman with a mind of her own . . . as passionate as I am."

Nall blinked, and Näeré watched as his hands balled into fists.

"Zeth!" he hissed, standing and tossing the chair aside.

"I will kill him!"

"Nay, you will not! If I must cast a spell against you to stop it I shall, but it would be better if you found the truth within your own heart. What would you feel if Sōrél stood between you and me? If he had threatened you when you knew you could not win? He did not always respect you."

Nall glared at her.

She watched as his hands flexed again.

"You will lose the love of your sister if you do this. She will never forgive you if you do not allow her to make her own choice. I shall ask Sōrél to send them away."

Näeré turned from him and moved toward the door to the hall.

"Nay, do not ask Sōrél to send them away." His voice was gruff and he kicked the carpet.

With a wave of her hand, Näeré righted the chair he had tossed away and replaced it at his table. She opened the door to admit Rydén, whose eyes were large and tear-filled.

Nall opened his arms and allowed his sister in, just as he had when they were children, holding her as she sniffled against his chest.

Within his mind, he heard Näeré's voice, *"You cause these tears. Zeth brings her only happiness. The latch for the mirrored door between our rooms is on the right hand side."*

His eyes met Näeré's as she winked and backed away, closing the door behind her.

Before returning to her room to wait for Nall, she saw Zeth peering around the corner at the end of the hall and went to him.

"Do not touch her in Nall's presence, and do not speak of it until he does. If he challenges you, throw this . . ." she tossed him a small orb—"and it will bring a spell of sleep over him."

Réverē

Yávië awakened to find she was alone and, in the darkness, was uncertain for a moment of her surroundings. She stepped onto the terrace and breathed in the fragrance of blossoms that wafted in on the soft air. The Queen's Gardens lay below—her gardens. This time it was no dream. Looking back, she saw Sōrél silhouetted against the light of the hall.

"Come, Yávië."

He held a finger to his lips and wrapped her cloak around her shoulders. Leaning out into the hall, he looked toward Näeré's room before quickly slipping across to his own chambers.

Yávië moved around Sōrél's room, touching the massive wooden desk and the papers piled upon it. She rolled an unopened scroll across it and watched it drop to the floor.

"What business is this?" she asked, lifting the pen and dipping it into the ink.

"It is the business of the House of Aaradan, and now it is the business of the Crown, but it will wait."

Drawing a sheet of paper from the stack carrying the crest of the serpent, Yávië carefully wrote, "Yávië, Queen of the House of Aaradan and the House of Ædracmoræ, ruler of the Seven Kingdoms." She handed Sōrél the quill and he wrote with a great flourish, "Sōrél, Servant of the Queen."

Kissing her to still her laughter, he pulled her toward a large bookcase where he lifted a hidden lever causing the cabinet to slide away from the wall.

Yávië's eyes grew wide as she looked into the darkness beyond.

Again, Sōrél placed his finger against his lips and gave her a look of caution before lifting the torch from the wall and descending into the depths of his fortress followed by his queen.

Yávië paused as she heard the door slide closed above her and she realized Nall did not know about this place. Sōrél was watching her.

"You fear me?"

"Nay, Sōrél, I fear Nall not knowing where we have gone."

Stepping back to her he hugged her and whispered, "He knows."

Sōrél hurried Yávië down the stairs and through the long passageway that led out into the night.

Aero called softly as he caught their scent.

"I promised to take you away, and so I shall."

"Sōrél, I have only nightclothes and a cloak," Yávië fussed.

Laughing, Sōrél tossed her a satchel and handed her both of her swords. Leaping to Aero's back, he extended his hand.

"Are you coming or do you wish to remain behind with Nall?"

Her eyes narrowed in warning as she reached for his hand.

Far to the south, Yávië and Sōrél approached a glimmer in the sky above the Halcyon Ice Fields. The air around them grew heavy and Aero faltered, calling silently to Sōrél. Soothing the uneasy dragon with his thoughts, Sōrél watched as an iridescent rift formed to allow their passage and then closed behind them. Below lay a landscape filled with a thousand shades of shimmering green. In the center, in a clearing, the refractions of light from a crystal palace gleamed and sparkled in the soft, roseate twilight.

"What place is this?" Yávië asked in wonder.

"It is a small sanctuary of enchantment and magick that no evil has ever touched. I have seen its fiery destruction when the impure try to enter, for only the chaste may pass through the rift above the ice. It is home to the feie and the faery, the damselfly and faun—I have seen their flares of heat lightning—they are whimsical creatures that wander freely and know no fear."

As if afraid the sound of his voice would break the spell, Sōrél whispered,

"Réverē" . . .

Epilogue

Within the sanctuary of Révere, Yávië the Dragon Queen, ruler of the Seven Kingdoms, and her Guardian husband, Sōrél, spent the seasons awaiting the calling of the Ancients—a call that would announce the timing of the birth of their daughter. A daughter who, by the Sojourner blood of Yávië and Sōrél's now united houses, would one day become more powerful than either of her parents and at last bring to pass the darkest fear of Yávië's father, Alandon.

Ancient Mirrors Glossary

A

Aaradan [AIR uh dan] – mortal father of Sörél and Näeré

Abaddon [AB uh don] – a Sojourner, leader of the dark horde, brother of Alandon

Abyss – group of caverns deep below the earth inhabited by Abaddon and the dark horde

Accordant dragon [uh COR dant] – dragons with the ability to soothe the minds of Ancients, Men and Guardians

Adra [AY druh] – Matriarch of the Emeraldflyte dragons

Aero [AIR oh] – Young wind dragon; Yávië's mount

Alandon [AL an don] – a Sojourner, Yávië's father, brother of Abaddon

Aléria [uh LAIR ee uh] – Yávië's twin sister, competitor for the throne of the Dragon Queen

Alkara [all KAR uh] – Matriarch of the Jadeflyte dragons

Ancients – A collective name given to a group of ancient wizards created by the Tree of Creation to reconstruct the seven worlds and summon the Guardians. They are also responsible for all law and prophecy. They are named Willowort, Rosewort, Morgwort, Dobbinwort, Brundlewort, Mallowort and Weezelwort.

Animus dragon – dragons with the ability to create pain and chaos within the minds of Ancients, Men and Guardians

Ardane [AR dane] – mate of Adra

Ardor [ar DOHR] – mate of Azrea, Matriarch of the Emeraldflyte dragons

Azaeria [uh ZAIR ee uh] – Matriarch of the Suunyflyte dragons

Azrea [as REE uh] – Matriarch of the Emeraldflyte dragons

Æ

Æcumbræ [CUM ber] – second of the seven worlds reconstructed by the Ancients

Ædracmoræ [DRAC mor] – world of Yávië's birth

Ælmondæ [la MOND] – sixth of seven worlds reconstructed by the Ancients; prison for those damned by Alandon

Æwmarshæ [wah MARSH] – fourth of the seven worlds reconstructed by the Ancients

Æshardæ [SHARD] – first of the seven worlds reconstructed by the Ancients

Æshulmæ [SHULM] – third of the seven worlds reconstructed by the Ancients

Æstaffordæ [STAF ford] – fifth of the seven worlds reconstructed by the Ancients; the ancestral home of Sōrél and Näeré

Æstretfordæ [STRET ford] – seventh of the seven worlds reconstructed by the Ancients; place of calling for the Guardians Nall, Rydén and Yávië

B

Bane boar – inedible beast, often infected with the poison of the slitherwort, which can cause death in Guardians and Men

Bannock [BAN uk] – flat bread, also called morning buns

Bastcat – demon cat person

Beast speech or speak – language shared by Guardians and Ancients with the animals of their worlds

Blood oath – an oath of consequence that is the result of sharing one's blood for the purpose of healing

Bloodren – small reptilian creature with venomous claws and teeth; causes blood rages in its victims

Bothie [BAWTH ee] – a small cottage constructed of chale wood and longgrass, used as housing for both Ancients and Guardians

Bow of Ages – weapon wielded by Sōrél, a gift given to him by Ya'vanna

Brake – a thicket

Bullram – massive animal with wooly coats of long hair, often domesticated and used as beasts of burden or mounts; wild bullram are hunted for their meat and hides

Butterpillar – larval stage of the butter moth, favorite food of downy fliers

C

Chale tree – hardwood tree used for construction and burning

Cyliopendia [sy clo PEN dee uh] – the verdant tree

Creation crystal – crystals used to hold souls

Crimson grass – deep scarlet longgrass

D

Dahrea [DAH ree uh] – Matriarch of the Direflyte dragons

Dandard [DAN dard] – mate of Davila, Matriarch of the Direflyte dragons

Darkness – often used in reference to the dark horde, used interchangeably with shadow beings

Davila [DAV eel uh] – Matriarch of the Direflyte dragons

Day dove – small bird with a soft, comforting song; also called a lonely lark

Deathawk – A large black and gold bird of prey, occasionally seen with scavengers; one called Hawk is bonded to Nall

Death dragon - cleanses the world of the dead and dying; usually have particles of decaying flesh and ash clinging to them. They are occasionally seen soaring with the deathawks and klenzingkytes above the Crimson Fields and Wastelands

Direfang – large member of the canine family found hunting in packs within the Northern Mountains

Downy flier – small winsome creature covered in soft gray fur, known for their keen night vision and sense of smell; the one called Xander is bonded to Yávië

Dragons – See by name

Dragon Queen – female ruler of Ædracmoræ and the Seven Kingdoms, Yávië's birthright

Dramm bush – short leafy bush often used as a source of shade by the Ancients

Dweomers [DWO meers] – memorized lines of ancient spells held within the mind of a thaumaturge or wizard.

E

Eonis [ee OH nus] – Dragon pup of Sybeth, Matriarch of the Sailflyte dragons

Emerald flower – brilliant green flower of the crimson longgrass

Empath – one with the ability to feel and soothe the sorrow and misery of others

Equus [EK kwus] – magickal steeds bound to the House of Aaradan

F

Faéra [FAIR uh] – Matriarch of Kilstoneflyte

Fáedre [FAY druh] – Matriarch of the Deathstoneflyte,

Fallowass – small furry beast of burden, often owned by Ancients

Fëan [FAY an] – First born pup of Fáedre, pledged to Sōvië

Feie [fay] – a race of short, stout, fiery haired enchanted wizards

Firedrake – large fire-breathing lizard

Fire imp – elemental fire demons usually found in the company of a mothering haruspex

Flyte – a family group, blood clan, of dragons led by a Matriarch

Forebodon [for BODE un] – Mate of Faéra

G

Gaianite crystal [GUY un ite] – energy crystal used to provide light and power for Maloch's machines during the machine wars

Galen [GAY len] – human leader of the Galenites; swore a life debt to Yávië and became the seventh Guardian

Galenites – tribe of men created by Yávië and assigned to Galen

Gall wasp – stinging insect found within the gall of the chale tree

Giant Stones – twelve standing stones erected by an unknown source before the time of remembering

G'lm [glim] – great Army of Darkness, composed of deathshades, demons

and locked beneath the earth of Ædracmoræ following its reunification

Golden thread – magickal thread or rope used in binding spells

Gorn – a Dark Guardian; follower of Aléria

Grass cat – mid-sized feline, Valia is the hunting and companion animal

to Rydén

Grosshare – small mammal hunted and eaten when larger prey cannot be found; often hunted to teach children the use of the bow

Guardian – one called into service to protect and defend a person or world; Guardians are given conditional immortality by the Ancients who call them into service.

H

Hand – measurement of length or height based on the average width of a man's palm

Haruspex [har U spex] – a veneficia or diviner of entrails; the birthmother of fire imps

Heart shard – contains the soul of a dragon; collected and protected by dragon Matriarchs and Guardians. Only by the crushing of the heart shard can a dragon be destroyed. Also referred to as the shard

Herbs of truth – ingredients gathered and prepared by Ancients when calling Guardians or casting binding spells

Hirudinea [high ru DIN ee uh] – the leeches of Fever Fen

Horde – group of evil shadow beings consisting of demons and the damned, often referred to as the darkness or dark horde

House of Aaradan – ruling house of the Kingdom of the Serpent, believed destroyed in the time beyond remembering

House of Ædracmoræ – ruling house of the Dragon Queen

I

Iaito [ee AH toe] – legendary sword; origin unknown, but suspected to have been brought by the Sojourners from their dying home world. It is now possessed by the Guardian Rydén

Ice beast – invisible creature found living deep within the Halcyon Ice Fields

Ice dragon – glacial dragons formed by the crystal structure of frozen water

Ileana [ill ee AN uh] – mother of Sōrél and Näeré (twins)

Itvaria – Matriarch of the Itzenflyte Ice Dragons

K

Kade – Vice Consul Galenite Government

Kayann [ky AN] – mother of Xalín

Kingdom of the Dragon – House of Alandon and Yávië's birthright

Kingdom of the Serpent – House of Aaradan and Sōrél's birthright

Klenzingkyte [KLEN zing kite] – large scavenging bird frequently found in the company of death dragons

L

Lake of Lost Memories – ancient lake with the ability to remove and store memories

Life debt – an oath of service given by one being to another in gratitude of a life saved

Lonely lark – small bird with a soft comforting song; also called a day dove

Longgrass – indigenous grass of the seven worlds; often crimson, but can be green or yellow

M

Maelstrom [MALE stum] – violent elemental wind being accidentally created by the entanglement of the winds during their creation and release

Magick – the art of conjuration and spell casting practiced by witches, wizards, and sorcerers

Maloch [MAL awk] – Guardian from second summoning

Matriarch – female ruler of a specific race, blood clan, or flyte

Meremire – home of the Æstretfordæ Ancients

Mind crawler colloquialism for an empath

Mirror – the eyes in which a summoner sees himself; also refers to the ancient mirrors used to move back and forth between the seven kingdoms

Mistral dragon [MIS trul] – dragons of the seven winds, malicious and evil tempered

Mock dragons – flying war machines created by Maloch; also referred to as the soulless

Morning bun – flat bread, also called bannock

Mountain blackthorn – indigenous flowering plant with deep violet-colored blossoms

Mourningmire – an Ancients' village on Æshardæ

N

Näeré [nair UH] – a Guardian, twin sister of Sōrél

Nall [nawl] – a Guardian, first life brother to Rydén

Netheraven – Great bird, able to travel between realms of living and dead

Norgol [NOR gul] – Dragon pup of **Faéra**

O

Oubliette [OO blee et] – a cylindrical dungeon that has only a trap door in the ceiling for entering and exiting. Näeré and Sōrél were hidden in the oubliette during Alandon's attack on their fortress.

Oils of wisdom – gathered and prepared by the Ancients for use during the calling of the Guardians and for binding spells

Oyster eggs – fruit of the prickleberry bush

P

Pearl of Perception – a jewel held by the sea dragons said to bring knowledge of a person's foolish mistakes when they lay their hands on it

Pledge – an oath of protection given by one being to another. Guardians are pledged to their charges and to their dragon flytes

Prickleberry – a thorny bush that produces oyster eggs; its flat, pad-like leaves are used for stone forging

Q

Quest – to perform a prescribed feat within the constraints of a prophecy

R
Reclamation of Souls – cleansing and rebinding of minds. This action was performed on Maloch's people before their reassignment to the Xavians and the Galenites

Révere [REV er e] – A sanctuary of enchantment and magick

Root of the Verdant Tree – the last remaining vestige of the ancient verdant tree given to Nall within the chamber of the Sojourners

Rydén [ry DEN] – a Guardian and first life sister to Nall

S
Sacred Sword of Domesius [doe MEE see us] – wielded by Yávië; given as a gift by Faera the war dragon

Sea dragon – dragon evolved for life within the waters

Seven pools – sacred waters of the seven kingdoms used to cleanse Yávië's sorrows

Shab-ot [shab OT] – a gyre used between the pages of the Book of Trolls to keep evil from entering the world through the dust within the pages

Shadow – to veil oneself; also used when referring to the dark horde or shadow beings

Shield of Viileshga [vee LESH ga] – dragon scale shield given to Nall by Adra at the Well of Viileshga

Simplestag – a common herd animal found on all the seven worlds, it is hunted for both meat and hides

Siren – female trickster with the power to sing beasts, men and Guardians to sleep

Slitherwort – a poisonous plant with toxins that can cause death to a Guardian or Man

Span – measurement of length or height based on the average width from outstretched thumb to tip of fourth finger of a man's hand

Sōrél [soe RELL] – Captain of the Guardians, twin brother to Näeré, future king of the House of Aaradan

Soulless – Maloch's flying machines built in the image of dragons

Sōvië [so VEE uh] – daughter of Yávië and Sōrél, future queen of Ædracmoræ and the Seven Kingdoms

Spider grass tea – a cold tea used as a daytime beverage

Spider cloth – strong fabric woven of spiders' silk and used for lightweight clothing

Staff of Souls – created for each Guardian from the roots of the willow, it is used in the summoning ceremony when one Guardian summons another and in the ceremony to reunite the seven kingdoms into a single world

Stone sprites – tiny enchanted beings released from the Giant Stones by Yávië

Sybeth [SY beth] – Matriarch of the Sailflyte dragons

Syria [SEER ree uh] – Siren

Sygarnd [suh GARND] – Mate of Sybeth

T

Talisman – artifact of a Guardian

Talonmet [TAL uhn met] – a Dark Guardian, follower of Aléria

Thaumaturge [THOM a turj] – scholars of the arcane, users of dark offensive magick

Thralax [THRAY laks] – giant fur-covered, man-shaped beast found in Spire Canyon, feeds primarily on the flesh of men

Tree of Creation – willow tree and last remaining life from the world of Ædracmoræ in the time beyond remembering; creator of the Ancients; an instrument of Ædracmoræ's rebirth

Trybrac [TRI brak] – Creature armed with veil of invisibility and slitherwort poison

U

Urn of Pledges – stone urn used to catch the Guardians' blood at the Ceremony of the Pledges

V

Veil of mist – gift given to the Guardians by their Ancients; it enables them to travel without being seen or heard

Veneficia [ven e FISH ee uh] – a haruspex or diviner of entrails; the birthmother of fire imps

Verdant Tree – tree guardian of the world; an instrument of

Ædracmoræ's rebirth

Vows of promise – words spoken under the direction of a wizard that bind a man and a woman as husband and wife

W

Waffle root – root of the chale tree used to make matches and torches, burns very hot and very bright

War dragon – massive fire dragon obedient to the Guardians and bound to Yávië by pledge

Wastelands – the vast desert home of the remains of the Fortress of the Dragon Queen

Well of Viileshga [vee LESH ga] – life-giving water of Æstretfordæ, home of the verdant tree that holds Adra and Ardane's heart shards.

Willow bark tea – a hot tea made of willow bark and used for its medicinal properties

Willow tree – the Tree of Creation

Wind dragon – ethereal dragons of the seven winds bound to Yávië by pledge

Witches and Wizards – those experienced in the art of conjuration and spell casting, both good and evil

Wreken [REK en] – symbiotic race that has taken refuge within the bodies of ancient wyrms

Wyrm [wirm] – legless, wingless dragons

X

Xander [ZAN der] – downy flier, bonded to Yávië

Xalín [ZAHL in] – son of Kayann, adopted by Galen, birth father was an unknown Sojourner

Xavier [ZAY vee ur] – empathic leader of the Xavian people

Xavian City [zay VEE uhn] – city created and held in place by the minds of the Xavian people

Y

Ya'vanna [YAH van ah] – mortal wife to Alandon, Yávië's and Aléria's birthmother, past Queen of Ædracmoræ; a Dragon Queen

Yávië [YAH vee uh] – first born of Alandon, future Queen of Ædracmoræ; a Dragon Queen and Guardian

Z

Zeth [zeth] – a Guardian, summoned when young and inexperienced

About the Author

Jayel Gibson is the author of the Ancient Mirrors fantasy series. From the tip of her Marto of Spain sword to the hem of her 15th century reproduction Italian gown, her effervescent enthusiasm encourages a belief in enchantment. A student of Celtic history, folklore and faith, she weaves the magic of timeless adventure throughout her tapestry of tales.

Ms. Gibson lives on Oregon's southern coast with her husband, Ken. They share their home with a Molluccan cockatoo and five sugar gliders.

She is currently at work on her next novel.